Charles O'Beirne was born in Co. Leitrim and he describes his schooling as having been 'educationally catastrophic'. None the less, he read widely, from Dickens to Orwell and Chekhov, and he also developed a taste for drama which got more scope when he emigrated to England in the mid-1950s, and began to frequent the West End theatres. 'Out of sheer perversity' he taught himself Irish and says it was the best thing he ever did. He lives in Cambridgeshire where he works for a finance company. *The Good People* is his first book.

THE GOOD PEOPLE

Charles O'Beirne

THE
BLACKSTAFF
PRESS

34602.

First published in 1985
by The Blackstaff Press
3 Galway Park, Dundonald, BT16 0AN
with the assistance of
The Arts Council of Northern Ireland

© Charles O'Beirne, 1985

Printed in Northern Ireland by
The Universities Press Limited

British Library Cataloguing in Publication Data
O'Beirne, Charles
The good people
I. Title
823.914F   PR6065.B/

ISBN 0 85640 315 6

To my
father and mother

1

The flitting

It was Uncle James who built the house just at the turn of the century. It was a plain, stone-walled, one-storeyed thatched house, with a door and three windows at the front. The walls, both inside and outside, were whitewashed. The doors and the woodwork of the windows were painted red.

Uncle James said that he chose this site for the house because it was a dry bank. By this he meant that it was drier than any other part of his little, thin-soiled farm. The site had a narrow lane on the west side. This lane went up to Micky Gaffney's, two hundred yards away. On the other side of the dry bank was a stream of wine-dark water, which was known locally as the mearing drain. It ran swiftly northwards, deep between steep banks. The lane and the stream almost came together at a small bridge of dressed limestone which carried a sandy and undulating road that ran east to west. This road connected Aughabeg crossroads, half a mile away, with the ancient village of Ballydoon, nestling comfortably two miles in the opposite direction.

Uncle James's new house was in the townland of Drumlahan, and he always claimed that it was a storey and a half high. This was because it had a loft, and a window on the east gable. But there were some people who said that the dry bank was not the real reason for Uncle James's choice of a building site. They hinted that it was all a deep plot of his to get out of the parish of Clonmoher, a wild and rural territory, and to establish himself in the parish of Ballinwing, which included the town. A man could become a district councillor, or get on the Board of Guardians, in this way. Uncle James was no tricks when it came to matters that required involved thinking and cool calculations.

Terry Jack built the house for Uncle James, and it was common

1

knowledge that Terry was of unsound mind. It was only the speed with which he could build walls and raise roof-trees that stopped people from committing him to the mental hospital at Sligo. What a waste it would have been to have a man like Terry locked up, idle and living on the rate-payers' money, when there was so much work waiting to be done. There was always the danger, of course, that he might suddenly cut his own throat, or someone else's for that matter; but it was a risk well worth taking. The peelers frequently dropped around to wherever he happened to be building, and viewed him critically from a distance for manifestations of insanity. They then invariably enquired from the neighbours how he was behaving. 'Is it Terry ye mane? Ah, sure he's bully these days, God bless him. Divel a loss 'id be on poor Terry, if some people would lave him alone.' Even the most thick-skinned peeler could take a hint, sometimes, and observe that he wasn't welcome and go away.

And so the houses went up, fast and furiously. Terry often forgot to ask for his wages. It was rumoured that it could be dangerous to life and limb to remind him of this important fact.

Scraws that had been left to dry in the bog for a few of the summer months were placed on the new rafters, and a deep coat of fresh straw thatch was placed on them and pinned down firmly with sally scollops. The house was then ready for occupation. So one morning Uncle James, his wife Nan-nan, his sister AB and his schoolchild niece Veronica left the old house (or the ould house, as they called it) on the Aughabeg side of the mearing drain and trooped into the new dwelling across the water in the townland of Drumlahan. The women wore the heavy, dark-brown shawls used for going on short trips.

They brought with them a few crickets in a jam jar for luck, a dresser, two beds, four chairs, two stools, a metal kettle, a pot, mugs and plates, porringers and noggins and an iron gridiron for baking oaten bread that had been in the family for generations. Also there was a black, carved crucifix in bog oak with the date 1723 cut into the back of it. It too had been in the family for generations and it was said to have been used in Penal Days for the celebration of Mass out on the hills. It was fourteen inches high.

Finally, they took with them a live glowing coal from the last fire on the hearth of the ould house. This was carried in a tin can by AB to start the fire in the new house. It would have been unthinkable to let the family fire go out, even briefly. It had been burning continuously for centuries.

There were snags, of course. Uncle James and Micky Gaffney didn't speak for years afterwards. Micky was outraged that his view of the road and all who used it was now obstructed by the new house that James McCartin had built. James could see everything now, couldn't he? While Micky and his wife Mary could see nothing. They were blinded, exiled. But they were utterly bewildered also when, in a few months, Uncle James came home from the market with a load of young deal trees in the ass-cart and proceeded to plant them between his own house and the busy road. This meant that in the fulness of time Uncle James himself would be unable to see the road or the traffic. What madness, thought everyone. For to have a clear view of the road was regarded as an education and a luxury and a vital source of news. The following year he bought six young apple trees and carefully planted them in the grassy space between the deals and the house. The dry bank was now utterly changed.

A further snag emerged when the building of the ould house was converted into a place for cattle and pigs and other stock. To feed the pigs or the calves it was necessary to prepare the buckets of animal food at the new house and then to carry them down the lane, across the bridge and up the road to the gate at the ould house. Soon everyone was cursing and complaining because of the long walk with the heavy buckets going over, or the full gallons of milk coming back. Moreover, there was always a crowd of young fellows gathered at the bridge in the evenings chatting, playing skittles and looking for news. Every mother's son of them took the full of their inquisitive eyes out of the buckets of food or the gallons of milk. This meant that the whole country would soon know the amount and the quality of the feeding stuff that Uncle James gave to his animals, as well as the amount of milk that his animals gave to him.

Uncle James always considered himself to be an open-minded

man. However, there were some matters that he did not want his neighbours to know, and what went on between him and his animals was one of these things. It was no-one's business what sort of food he gave to his pigs, or how much milk his cows gave to him. Strangely enough, Uncle James hadn't foreseen this contingency. So one day when Nan-nan had become unusually violent, even for her, and had complained of how mortified she felt to have the *stucauns* at the bridge gaping into her buckets, he resolved to settle the problem once and for all. He immediately cut down two alder trees and made a foot-bridge or a plank, as he called it, across the mearing drain, just at the end of the house. It may have been that Uncle James's bridge-building skills were in some way deficient, for whenever one ventured across the water, the alder planks bent steeply at every step. This was all very necessary, he said. Otherwise the timber would snap in years to come. All bridges swayed a little, he claimed; even those made of steel and of dressed stone. It seemed incredible; but there was no-one about who could argue with him.

However, when one tried to get across the stream carrying two heavy buckets, whilst the plank went up and down with every step, one's situation could become critical indeed. And with a jostling crowd of rumbustious pigs and pleading calves threatening to advance from the other side to meet one halfway across, even the bravest could feel jeopardised. Uncle James was content to threaten the animals with hellfire. Nan-nan would release a flood of heated and dire warnings to the crowding livestock: 'If you don't go back, I'll stiffen ye; I will indeed! I'll pull me fist red out of your belly, ye brute ye! May you burst wide open! To perdition with ye, for a savage! Such tories!'

The calves and the pigs were unimpressed and would not be intimidated by such language. They continued to jostle; and it often meant man and beast, and sometimes both in one go, being tumbled headlong into the icy waters of the mearing drain, buckets of feeding and all.

Thus it continued for a generation or more after Uncle James built the new house. People and animals were constantly falling into the stream. And the family ended up with all of them having a

4

headful of cuts and scars. Only the niece, Veronica, never seemed to have had the unique experience of seeing the world upside down for those memorable seconds which elapsed whilst a body lost footing on the alder plank and travelled to the stones and the sand and the icy water. But when she grew up to womanhood and married, her children were quick to take on the family tradition, and to add even a degree of spirit and dash to it during the passage of youth.

In time, of course, an art for getting across the plank safe and sound was developed. You had to prepare the feeding well in advance, long before the animals had an inkling of what was afoot. Then you grabbed the buckets and made a dash for it.

Falling from the alder bank and into the water remained a dark family secret. It was the lesser of two evils. No-one wanted the *stucauns* at the bridge, who would go into your pocket for news, to be gaping into one's buckets of feeding or milk. It was far better to risk the plank and the water than that.

Resting on the window-sash of the new house was a heavy Waltham pocket watch. It was bought by Uncle James when he began to work at the making of the Leitrim and Cavan narrow-gauge railway in 1885. He was a young man then, with two sisters, one of whom was AB. He had a small morsel of poor land, about nine acres in all. The railway job gave him a little financial leverage; and when the work was finished and the trains running, he began doing small contracts for the Board of Guardians. This consisted in making paved culverts, a skill he had picked up on the railway.

He was on good terms with the local landlord, the Hon. James W. Borroughs, whose family came to the Tully district from the Bass in lowland Scotland in 1610. He regarded Burroughs as a decent enough man in himself. Yet he took an active and secret part in whatever anti-landlord activities went on, because he abhorred the landlord system. He believed that the people should own their own land and that it should be in their possession alone. He regarded the landlords in general as robbers and the descendants of robbers. They got what they had by confiscation.

In common with other young men of his age and stamp, he went to work in England occasionally; and St Helens in Lancashire became familiar territory for him. So, when work started on the Manchester Ship Canal, he pocketed his heavy Waltham and made a bee-line for the nearest excavation. He had no trouble in obtaining lucrative work. He also became involved in a controversy in a local Manchester newspaper concerning cremation. He wrote many letters under a pen-name, and he was very proud of this particular effort for the remaining years of his life. It may have convinced him that he would rise glorious and immortal, and in his Sunday best, on Judgment Day, instead of in a puff of smoke and ashes, as so many of the heathens and free-thinkers around Manchester seemed to wish for themselves at that time.

When the canal was completed years later he returned permanently to Aughabeg. He had enough money saved to give the fortune of a hundred pounds to each of his two sisters on their wedding day. No girl could get a husband without this fortune or dowry; and the boy who inherited the home and the farm usually waited till his sisters were married and the house cleared before rushing to take unto himself a wife. However, Uncle James surprised everyone by being the first to marry. He didn't wait to clear the house. He just went eight miles up the mountain wooing and came back with Nan-nan.

The family never recovered from the shock. Nan-nan was a sturdy, vigorous punch of a woman who rushed around the house and the haggard singing the strangest songs as she worked. She could unleash an unheard-of volley of verbal abuse at anyone or at anything that came in her way. The two sisters gaped in amazement. They were horrified that their brother James could have married such a coarse woman. But she had her hundred-pounds fortune, and much more besides. The mountain farmers were far quicker at getting fortunes for their daughters and at marrying them off advantageously than were many of the low-land men. Nearly every second lowland household had an unmarried sister, the spinster and the last of a big family, solely because neither her brother nor her father could gather the necessary

6

hundred pounds when it was needed and the chance there. This could never happen on the mountain; and their girls went out and mothered half the population of the seven parishes with spirit, industry and verve. Among the goods and chattles that Nan-nan took with her to Aughabeg as a bride was an attractive patchwork quilt.

Uncle James was something of a spell-binder as well as a man of action. He convinced the two girls that they should postpone marriage, just for the time being. There were no men in sight who were good enough for them, in any case. In the meantime he would use the money he had saved up for their fortune to stock the land with the new high-yielding, shorthorn breed of cows that were just coming out. Mr Burroughs, the landlord, had told him about them: they were great value. It would also enable him to buy old Tim Redican's five fields, if indeed Tim wanted to sell. Both himself and the whole family would have a very fine farm then. And well stocked too. The money for their fortunes would be safe and sound and ready whenever it was needed. Confidentially, he was sick and tired of listening to Nan-nan criticising the cows that he had then. Greyhounds with goats' heads, she called them, that wouldn't give enough milk to colour one's tay. The two girls giggled knowingly. It seemed a great idea. Uncle James had visions of wealth for all and a better class of husband for his sisters.

So the cows were bought and the land was bought. And soon all the money was gone. The cows never paid. Two of them passed away early on, although every cow-doctor for miles around tried to save them. Even Mr Burroughs took an interest when he heard that one home-cure had brought about what then appeared to be a hopeful convalescence. From then on he kept in daily touch with all the patients as the end approached. And the end was always inevitable. They all died save one that Uncle James took in haste to the fair of Carrigallen and sold cheap. When they died they were duly skinned before burial as was the custom, and something made of iron bought with the few pence the skin was sold for. This was supposed to bring luck. Meanwhile the dogs of the neighbourhood grew fat on a surfeit of carrion and the two sisters remained unmarried.

7

The younger and the more handsome of the sisters, Maria, solved her problem in spectacular fashion by eloping with George O'Rourke. There was no need to elope, really; but it seemed a daring and a romantic thing to do. And she and George were in love, God help them. He had a small but thrifty farm, and he also had a job, sometimes, repairing the roads. They settled down happily two miles beyond Aughabeg crossroads in a little house at the foot of a hill and facing east in the townland of Drumdarnet. They had eleven children, four of whom died in infancy. There was a little window in one of the bedrooms in the ould house and it was known as Maria's window. It was through this window that she was supposed to have made her escape on the night that she eloped. People marvelled for years that any girl, even one of Maria's slender proportions, could have got through that window and lived.

As the years went by Uncle James took out more contracts for culverts and paved drains. He also got deeper into the activities of the Land League and was regarded as a steadfast, resourceful and daring man when there was a difficult job to be done. Unexpectedly, he had a row with the landlord about the mineral rights of the land, which he claimed should be vested in the tenant rather than in the landlord. This led to a protracted series of lawsuits with his good friend and neighbour Phelie Keaveney. Ostensibly the lawsuits were about fifty yards of scraw-covered drain that ran between the McCartin and the Keaveney farms. But under the scraw it was a trial of strength between James McCartin of Aughabeg and the Hon. James W. Burroughs late of the Bass, Scotland. The landlord backed Phelie Keaveney to the hilt. And Uncle James saw the struggle in terms of the people against the tyrants; of right against wrong; of Ireland against England. James McCartin saw himself as a symbol of the changing times and of the ending of an age and an era.

Bridget, or AB as she was called, waited patiently for the hundred pounds that would enable her to marry. The years marched by. Then one evening she secretly put a few small belongings in a parcel and, a little later, walked out into the darkness of a November night, unknown to Nan-nan or Uncle

James. She did confide in the niece Veronica before she went. She said she had to go and that the niece would not understand; she made her promise never to tell anyone. She was missing for three years. The niece kept her secret without fail. 'No one ever keeps a secret like a child.'

What drove her away? Despair? Shame? Escape from unrequited love? Pride? Rage? Adventure? In any case it seemed to be no more than a mad gesture; for nothing came of it. Why didn't she go to America, as many girls like her in the neighbourhood did? Had she no friends? Was she afraid? Why didn't she go to some of the towns and find work as a servant? All she did, it emerged, was to tramp along the roads to the town of Enniskillen, sleeping in hay-ricks and out-houses at night. She received no charity from anyone. She asked for a mug of water: she was told that there was a spring well about a quarter of a mile further along the road. She never afterwards felt any warmth for the Northern people; but for the rest of her life she respected them.

Eventually she returned to Aughabeg, shamefaced, defeated, enigmatic, and settled down to the dreary life of a spinster sister, which would be her lot until God called her. In time she became very religious. Her rosary was seldom out of her hands; and during the hours of darkness the clicking of the stone beads came to be part of the quiet sounds of the night for almost half a century.

Nan-nan threw herself whole-heartedly into the lawsuits that Uncle James had going at full steam ahead. They were ruining him, it was plain for all to see; but he and 'Torney Kiernan saw eye to eye on what a man should do and how the nation should be shaped. They worked hand in hand in the Cause.

But after a time Nan-nan had geese and ducks and hens in plenty. Pigs abounded. There was milk and butter for all now. Despite the incessant lawsuits they had recovered at last from the loss of the shorthorn cows that had replaced the goaty greyhounds and then died. She went out in the fields and worked side by side with Uncle James. She was active with him in the meadows making the hay and in the bog cutting the turf.

Every Tuesday, which was the market day in Ballinwing, she took her basket of eggs and her pat of butter and went tripping breathlessly from sleeper to sleeper along the railway line, which was a short-cut to the town. She had no fear of the trains: she feared only the Permanent Way Inspector, who could suddenly come around a bend at any time pedalling on his trolley and looking at the condition of the rails and the sleepers. He was always particularly active on a market day, for he knew there would be many trespassers. He could make Nan-nan get off the railway and climb over the fence into a field, because the Law said so. But he could not stop her calling a torrent of abuse on his head, and invoking the wrath of God and the intercession of His Blessed Mother and His own holy angels and saints. It was her hope that the celestial powers on high would chastise this heartless brat of a peeler's son and stop him tyrannising over decent, hardworking people on their way to the market.

Now and then she set out for the mountains, to Tullylaken-more, to visit her old home and her delicate brother, Odey. There were twelve brothers and sisters in the family. The sisters set out to marry, or to work at first as milliners, dressmakers or shopgirls, in places like Belfast, Clones or Cavan. They all looked after Odey, who had asthma. They sent him to visit Dr Kniepe in Germany, who used cold-water baths as a cure for many ailments. Odey took the treatment conscientiously. He retained his asthma, unfortunately; but over the years, he somehow acquired a taste for good red whiskey. He never married. Yet he found a way of running profitably his large mountain farm, with the aid of two good sheepdogs and a generous measure of diplomacy.

2

A child in the house

Veronica, Uncle James's niece, was astonished when her three sisters, who lived at Drumdarnet, went off to become nuns, one after the other. She had secretly been toying with the same idea herself. But when the three others upped and renounced the world with all its works and pomps she thought to herself, enough is enough. Thereupon she married Tommy Flynn, who lived with his brother in Lisagirwin, a mile away. He brought with him a farm of hilly limestone land, and he and Veronica set up house under the same roof with Uncle James, Nan-nan and AB. Everyone thought that the young couple were mad to do such a thing.

After their first child, Seamus, was born there occurred great domestic turmoil in the Flynn household. Who was going to stand for him at his christening? That indeed was the question. Nan-nan was determined that she should be the woman. Nevertheless, AB, the poor old spinster, coughing, wheezing and religious, was just as determined that she would 'stan' for the *aurcaun*', as she called the infant. Nan-nan was childless; but AB considered that she had first claim to be the godmother. Wasn't the child of her own flesh and blood? What was Nan-nan but a total stranger – a wild woman from the top of the mountain – when all was said and done?

Uncle James did not interfere. It would have been dangerous for anyone, even a man of his bravery, to attempt to mediate or to advise in a case of such complexity.

'Let the two ould bitches stand for him together, if they want to,' said Tommy, the child's father, under his breath.

'Tommy, are you going soft in the head, or what?' enquired Veronica when she got him alone soon afterwards. 'Two women,

11

or two men either, can't stand for a child at a christening! Don't yeh know that? Or have yeh any religion left in yeh at all? No priest would allow such a carry on'.

'And why not?'

'Tommy, in case yeh don't know it, this is a christening. It is your child! Can't yeh talk sense for a change! Just for once!'

'Sense be damned! With all the quibbling and codology I've a good mind not to have him christened at all. Just call him any name that fits, like a horse or a dog. It'll do good enough. And forget about your christening.'

Later on, when a tearful Veronica confided to AB the gist of her conversation with Tommy, the old lady immediately withdrew her candidature. She did it for peace sake, and in the interests of Christianity, she said.

But then it emerged that Jim Gaffney, Micky Gaffney's reprobate son, for reasons best known to himself, expected that he should be asked to stand for the infant. When Veronica heard this she took fright. Anyone but Jim Gaffney! He wasn't a fit person to stand for anything, never mind a child. And wasn't it a well-known fact that children frequently took after those who stood for them at their christening to a greater extent than they took after their real and flesh-and-blood parents. Having Nan-nan for a godmother was bad enough indeed: but to have Jim Gaffney for a godfather as well would be a total calamity for any child. In desperation, she nearly asked AB to come back again, but quickly dismissed the idea that she knew the priest would reject. Yet, Jim had to be stopped at all costs.

A blood relation and a neighbour usually acted as godparents. Veronica had an unexpected brainwave.

With a devilish glint in her eye she explained to Jim Gaffney that Nan-nan was not really a blood relation. But of course she could not be denied the privilege of standing for the *aurcaun*, all the same. Thereupon, Jim assented and gallantly withdrew his candidature also. A triumphant Veronica promptly hurried Tommy off to Ballinwing to grab one of the town cousins for the post of godfather while the going was good. It was a near-run thing and no mistake.

In this manner Seamus came to approach the heavy limestone baptismal fount at St Patrick's chapel in Ballinwing on a cold and blustery morning in March. He had only just made it. It was touch and go. It might never have happened at all. Nan-nan insisted that he should be called James, after her husband and the child's great-uncle. And so, James, it had to be. However, in view of the extremely patriotic climate of the age in which they lived then, Nan-nan raised no objections when AB insisted in turn on translating the name to Seamus. And Seamus indeed it was.

The whole episode was a tricky and a trying business. Everyone was relieved when the parish register was signed and the ink dried. They then wrapped the *aurcaun* tightly in a shawl, climbed into the waiting horse-trap and trotted merrily back to Drumlahan.

From infancy AB took Seamus for long walks, almost daily if the weather was dry. At first she pushed him in the pram; later on she held him by the hand as they strolled along the roads or up and down Lisagirwin lane. When he became dimly aware of what was going on, he realised that she was either singing hymns in a very low voice or telling stories about many things, but mostly about heaven, the angels and saints, and Ould Nick, the devil himself, his imps and his legions.

The hymns were about a happy land that was a very long distance away. When she began to talk, instead of singing, it seemed from what she said that you could meet a saint or an angel, or God himself, anywhere, even walking along the road, dressed like a beggar or a tramp, or a man or woman driving a few head of cattle or doing other ordinary chores. You could never know who would come around the next turn of the road. The old boy himself, Ould Nick, was the same: you could meet him anywhere, looking like an ordinary man going about his business. There was just one thing that gave him away: he had a cloven hoof, like a cow or a bull, and he could neither hide nor change that into a human foot. That's the way you could always spot him: the cloven hoof. Ould Nick could never be easy! He was forever rushing around looking for people to take away with him. Needless to say he was always on the lookout for disobedient little boys who would not eat their stirabout. No names mentioned, of course.

She often spoke of a place called St Helena. The weather was so hot there, according to what she was told, that when the sun was rising up in the morning you could hear it crackling.

Another terrible place was the Burning Mountains. This seemed to have been an outcrop of hell; for many people just walked steadily towards the flames and nothing could make them turn back. There was a priest once who saw the Burning Mountains in the distance. He gazed at them for a few minutes; and then he began to walk towards them. People called and called at him to come back. But he never heeded them. He walked and walked, despite their calls and pleas, and quietly disappeared into the flames of the Burning Mountains. He was never heard of again.

She showed him the thin new moon, scarcely visible in a pale, western sky; and she made him say a prayer for the Dead with her. She claimed that one should always stop whatever one was doing and say a prayer for the souls in purgatory whenever one saw the new moon for the first time.

She talked often about the Battle of Ballinamuck, when the army of Napoleon came to help the Irish fight for freedom. The French army passed through Ballydoon, along with the crowds of Irishmen who joined it. Next day they were all slaughtered at Ballinamuck by the English. The fields around Ballinamuck were soaked with blood. The English killed every priest they could lay their hands on: ripped them in the stomach with their swords.

'There were crowds of priests running around wild, with their puddins hanging out!' said AB.

She talked also about a very holy man called St Colmcille. He went to heaven when he died, of course. But, would you believe it? He went to heaven blindfolded.

The walk that she and Seamus liked especially was up the long, sheltered Lisagirwin lane that ran south from the dressed stone bridge along the foot of the hill and which led to Uncle Peter's house.

Opposite a bank where they occasionally sat was a swing-barred gap. Sometimes she took him to the gap and then they gazed across the meadows and into the distance where a number

14

of white stone buildings with red roofs could be seen. Did she tell him so, or did he come to the conclusion of his own accord? In any case he came to believe that that cluster of red-roofed buildings was indeed heaven itself. He had no clear idea of what heaven was for, or why it was over there across the fields and meadows on that rising ground, with the trains going up and down past it several times a day. Yet, there it was.

He didn't think much of it; but it was interesting to know where it was. That was where so many people were going to, or wanting to go to. He wasn't impressed at all. He would have been far more interested in the Burning Mountains, if someone would show them to him. He would like to see St Colmcille going to heaven, blindfolded, and maybe bumping into things on the way. He thought a lot about Ballinamuck; but he wasn't sure if he would like to have been there. He thought of the swords and what they could do to anyone, priest or person.

AB was a frail, pale, drooping little woman, shy but with an impish glint in her hooded, pale-blue eyes. There was sometimes a faint pucker of amusement at the corner of her mouth; but she seemed to want to hide that side of her nature.

When her sister, the eloping Maria, died she kept house for some years for her brother-in-law, George O'Rourke of Drumdarnet and for his two sons. The youngest boy ran away and joined the Connaught Rangers. He later deserted, but got into the 1914–18 war and died at Salonika in Greece. The other boy farmed quietly until he joined the Volunteers. He was to fight the Black-and-Tans, live through the Civil War and become an officer in the army of the new independent Irish state.

AB had a bad chest and she was often coughing and wheezing and complaining about the east wind. Life would be better for her if the wind would only keep out of the east and not bother the poor old chest. At any hour of the night the click of her dark stone-and-wire rosary beads could be heard coming faintly from her bedroom. The heavy, dark, steel-and-wood crucifix attached to the rosary beads she sometimes kissed resoundingly.

She took a great interest in the house interior and was always dusting, arranging and shining anything that could be made to

15

shine, from knives and forks to Uncle James's heavy Waltham pocket watch, resting idly on the window-sash. She kept the little lamp with the red globe burning constantly on the bracket that hung under the gaudy picture of the Sacred Heart. And she frequently touched and straightened the three other pictures that hung in the house: one of Uncle James seated on a pony; one showing the coat-of-arms of the family her sister Maria eloped into; and one document-like picture in the upper room dedicating the whole family to the Apostleship of Prayer with the names written in the Irish language.

In a drawer she kept the carved bog-oak Mass cross that was made in 1723; and also a Lough Neagh hone, once used by Uncle James to sharpen knives and razors. She went to great pains to explain to Seamus that if a piece of wood from a holly tree was left long enough under the waters of Lough Neagh, the biggest lake in Ireland, it would turn into stone. It could then be used as a hone, just like this one that belonged to Uncle James.

She would like to have been able to wind the big eight-day clock on the wall that chimed every half hour, but she hadn't the muscular strength to turn the heavy key. She looked wistfully at the aneroid barometer, scrounged by Tommy from some unknown place, and wished that it would tell her when the hay-weather was coming or when the wind would change from the east. The instrument never worked.

AB saw to it that every child in the house had an *agnus dei* or a miraculous medal hung around the neck, next to the skin and inside the clothing. To go outside without this form of protection was just tempting every evil going, from Ould Nick himself to the evil eye or just plain bad luck.

She liked to feed the dogs, Foreman and Sammy, and she took a keen interest in the hens. She was forever picking up a surprised bird and 'trying' it, as she called it. By this she meant trying to find out if it was laying, on the point of laying, or just hopeless. She loved floating hatching eggs in warm water to see if birds were inside; and when eventually the chicken pecked its way out of the shell, she hastened to remove the small, shell-like particle attached to the point of the nib.

16

She had great respect for the local Protestant farming people. She seemed to attribute virtues to them that would have surprised them had they only heard about them. She admired their thrift, their honesty, their good taste. She said they were 'good doers'. By this she meant that they were skilful in their work and in their dealings. In some obscure way the spirit of the old Irish people seemed to live on in her: the dignity, the courteousness, the capacity to absorb suffering and disappointment, and yet to retain one's self-respect and rightful pride. They were all there in her personality, if indeed in a quiet and muted form.

3

The visitor

By summer 1933, Mr de Valera had won his second general election; and far-reaching and unexpected changes had come over the locality and over the house that Uncle James had built in Drumlahan so many years earlier.

A square, squat, ugly concrete porch had been built onto the door at the front of the house. At the back there was now a lean-to kitchen with one door and two windows. Nan-nan and AB had been getting the old-age pension of ten shillings a week each for some years by then. Veronica had three children – the boy, Seamus, and two girls, Maria and Nell.

Uncle James was dead. He passed away suddenly on a November Sunday morning while chasing a goat that was thieving into Micky Gaffney's cabbage garden. The goat was acquired to provide milk for the young Seamus, who was considered to be delicate and in need of great care and attention. The animal may have saved Seamus's life; but it also helped to kill Uncle James. Yet, all his aims were by then achieved and he must have died happily, if suddenly. He won all his lawsuits in the end; he saw the downfall of the landlord system and he witnessed the departure, bag and baggage, of the landlord Burroughs, after more than three hundred years in Tully; he saw Ireland unexpectedly free after seven hundred years. And although he had no children himself, his own seed and breed, in the form of Seamus, was toddling at his feet, even if precariously sustained by sips of goat's milk. And of course he died where he wanted to die: on the right side of the mearing drain, in the parish of Ballinwing and on the dry bank he chose as a building-site so many years before. He never made the Board of Guardians; but he did become an active and a well-known district councillor.

18

It is a fine summer evening and beginning to get dark. Tommy and the three children are sitting in the porch – an unusual occurrence – with an eighteen-year-old visitor from Glasgow, whose mother was a first cousin of Veronica's and who was known in the family as Scotch Bridgie. It was his life's ambition to come to Ireland for his summer holidays; and now his wish was fulfilled. The light of a bonfire and the sound of cheering, as well as the music of fifes and drums, came from the fork in the road on the side of the hill, a little above the railway station and about half a mile away.

'Oh, they're celebrating de Valera's victory in the general election,' said Tommy ruefully, in answer to a question put to him by the young Scot. This was one household where Mr Eamon de Valera and his Fianna Fáil party were not very popular. Many of Tommy's friends and neighbours would be at the bonfire that evening. There would be no ill-feeling or unfriendliness between him and them about the election result, just polite and forthright disagreement. When there was a pause in the fifing and drumming there ocurred an outbreak of cheering.

'Up Dev! Up the Republic! Up Mary McSwiney! Good girl Mary, give it to the shoneens!'

Matthew McGoohan was the Scotsman's name. He was an apprentice shoemaker; and for years afterwards his annual arrival at Drumlahan railway station in the middle of July was an event that everyone, even the neighbours, looked forward to. He was city-bred and from the Gorbals area; but his strange and attractive accent, his good humour and his curiosity about country life fascinated the local people. He tried his hand at milking cows; he fixed sharp rings in the quivering snout of a screaming pig, and afterwards looked as satisfied and fulfilled as if he were a great surgeon who had just performed a daring operation.

'He'll be a toppin' pig ringer – if he's well fed and minded,' remarked Tommy when the operation was over and the patient was energetically burying his snout in the clean, fresh straw thrown into the sty for the occasion.

He tried eating stirabout, the porridge made from homegrown oats, and he could put away plates of it, either with milk in a mug,

19

or on a plate with a nob of butter melting in the centre. Fresh buttermilk delighted him; churning with a dash he regarded as a miracle; and a cow calving was a mind-expanding experience. He could not believe that cows could drink just so much water out of a tub on a hot summer day; it astonished him how and why cows could pass so much dung.

He loved to jump across drains and gripes. And he became uproariously popular with all the children in the area by misjudging the distances and landing in the watery and muddy centre, with his lower parts deep in ooze and gently sinking. This would be the signal for cheers and yells of delight; and the children were always prepared for the event and would throw him a rope and proceed to haul him back onto dry land. They had seen their fathers and the neighbours use tethers to haul out a cow or a bullock from a drain many a time. This was their opportunity to play grown-ups.

Frogs amused him, especially if they turned russet at the approach of rain; horses and donkeys he admired. It took him some time to commit to memory correctly that a mule had an ass for a father and a mare for a mother; while a jennet had a horse for a father and a she-ass for a mother. But he loved nothing better than to sit in the lane under the beech trees in the darkness of a July night listening to the corncrakes. The countryside seemed to be alive with them; and their song came all through the night: from near and far, from up in the bottom meadows as far as Lisagirwin to down in the valley and along the canal.

He was very unsteady at first when he tried to learn how to ride Tommy's bicycle. There were many falls; and when the front wheel seemed to be stuck crossways, he thought he had wrecked beyond repair Tommy's favourite mode of transportation. He looked over his shoulder one day on the road when he heard a noise, and saw Mulligan's bread-van coming after him at full speed and in a cloud of dust. He dashed up Lisagirwin lane to get quickly out of its path. But when he glimpsed across his shoulder to reassure himself that he was safe, he saw that the bread-van was coming after him again in a most malicious manner. The van was merely going to turn at the foot of the lane; but how was the cyclist to know? It seemed determined to get him. He saw an open gap into a field, and he pedalled swiftly through it with terror in his heart. He missed a cow, grazed a calf; and before he could begin to think clearly, he surged towards the mearing drain. New to this sort of situation, he thought he could make the bicycle jump the drain, something he had seen motor cyclists do on the back pages of the *Glasgow Herald*. Alas, he did not make it. He hit the far bank and landed flat on his back in the wine-dark waters of the mearing drain, with the bicycle resting across his prostrate body. The front wheel was spinning merrily.

There were no children with ropes and tethers to assist him to dry land now; and he had an uneasy feeling, when his mind cleared and the front wheel stopped spinning, that he was going to sink slowly and forever into a slimy, muddy and weed-choked underworld. By this time cows and calves, as well as a horse and a dog, had assembled on the bank. All of them were breathing heavily and twiddling their ears. They were joined by a donkey.

What was he to do? If he climbed out he might be attacked and eaten live. If he remained still and did not breath, as he once heard one should do when confronted by snakes or wild animals, he was convinced he would slowly sink into the deep forever.

Finally he made his decision: he would risk being eaten alive. With great difficulty he got to his knees. He became entangled in the bicycle, but managed to free himself and to move on his knees towards the bank. As he reached it a cow snorted; whereupon all the others turned on their heels and tore away up the field. The cows raised their heads and their tails; the horse pranced and snorted; the donkey threw back his ears, lowered his head and raced away as if trying to keep in the laughter. The dog had vanished.

Next morning he came back to the drain with an angry Tommy to recover the bicycle he had clean forgotten about. When the man of the house wanted to hurry off to the town to buy a feather-edged file to sharpen the blades of the mowing machine, he found that his bicycle was not available. No one could remember where it was last seen. However, under close questioning the mind of Glasgow Matthew began to clear; and as the sequence of the previous evening's events came back to him, he hinted that if they

21

were to walk up Lisagirwin lane and to enter a certain gap, and then proceed to a certain spot along the mearing drain, the staple form of transport could be found. And so it was.

At night he knelt like everyone else and joined in the family rosary. Nan-nan and AB were watching and listening closely. They were convinced that many of the Irish quickly lose their religion when they go abroad, or just give it up. Coming from a place like Glasgow this fellow might well be an outright heathen for all they knew. However, he surprised them by pulling a fine, carved horn rosary from his hip pocket and then by going on to answer the decades in a good, strong, clear voice. No mumbling! No drowsy muttering either! His widowed mother and the Franciscan fathers had done their work well.

AB always led the rosary. The young Scot was rather surprised and a little impatient when he discovered that this Drumlahan rosary was taking longer than he had anticipated and that it did not end exactly where he had expected it to end. It was a new experience to him: he had never heard of the trimmings that followed every rosary in Drumlahan. The Glasgow rosary was a stark affair by comparison.

AB continued unperturbed. There was an Our Father and three Hail Marys for the poor holy souls; three Hail Marys for the good hay-weather; an Our Father and three Hail Marys for Tom Scollan who died that day and who was a decent sort of a man; then there was one Our Father, one Hail Mary and one Gloria for the foreign missions; and just three Hail Marys for those in temptation or in danger of death. Finally there was an Our Father and three Hail Marys for the conversion of Mary McSwiney, that God would put some sense into her head and stop her from leading the youth of the country astray. And then it all ended with just three Hail Marys and one Gloria that God in his infinite wisdom would make de Valera see the evil of his ways and that he would stop ruining the farmers, before it was too late.

Everyone got up from their knees then and the two old ladies congratulated Matthew on how well he could say his rosary.

'You're a credit to Bridgie. God knows then but you are! The way you gave out that third joyful decade was splendid, splendid, I tell ye. You're a credit to your mother. Troth then you are. She

22

didn't let you run wild around Scotland and neglect your prayers.' Nan-nan nodded knowingly as she poured her rosary beads from one cupped hand to the other. Her face was crinkled in smiles.

'He's a topper at the rosary,' said Tommy, 'a real king whizzer, and no mistake about that.'

'It takes a little longer here than it does in Glasgow,' remarked Matthew with a questioning tone in his voice. Then he blushed and tried to change the conversation by enquiring who was this Mary McSwiney girl and what was she doing to the young people.

'She's a holy terror. If only her poor brother Terence, who died on hunger strike in England, could see the way she's behaving now. He was Lord Mayor of Cork so . . .'

'All that will have to wait till tomorrow AB,' interrupted Tommy. 'It's time all decent people were going to bed.'

Tommy had a meadow to mow next day and he expected to be ready to start cutting with the horse and the single mowing machine well before six o'clock and before the heat of the day set in.

Matthew learned that night that the rosary had more uses than he had ever imagined.

When his two-week holiday was over he said goodbye all around: he waved to the cows in the field; he rubbed the horse's nose, he scratched the sow's back and he patted the two dogs, Foreman and Sammy, on the head. Then he picked up his suitcase and the entire household walked with him to the foot of the lane where they all shook hands. He walked up to the railway station with Tommy and Seamus to catch the three o'clock train that would take him to Belturbet, Clones, Portadown and Belfast. He would be in Glasgow early next morning. It was to be like that every year for a long time to come. His departure always left an emptiness and a silence in the house.

4

Tommy

Tommy Flynn, the man of the house, had neither the energy nor the spiritual fire of his father, Charles, who died when the family was young and when Tommy himself was eight years old. Charles grew up on a small farm in Ballydoon parish and then served his time as a shop-boy in Ballinwing. He soon had his own grocery shop with an attached public house and also a small bakery. It was commonplace then for the townspeople and the shopkeepers to support the farmers to the hilt in their struggle against the landlords. Charles Flynn was no exception in this respect and he was arrested four times for his activities and received two short jail sentences. The Royal Irish Constabulary was both officious and brutal. On what was to be his last arrest he was offered the choice of going to jail or of signing an agreement not to indulge again in any work for the Land League. His fine business was going down, despite all his wife, Rosie, could do to keep it going; his young family was being neglected. Yet he refused to sign the agreement. For him it would be unthinkable.

He was immediately sent to Galway jail and put on the treadmill. This was the cruellest and the worst form of punishment one could receive. It consisted of keeping a machine for spinning wool working efficiently by treading on the steps of an endless staircase. The pressure of the prisoner's foot moved the wheel that drove the belt to the machinery as he trod from every step to the next at a brisk pace. A strong, slight but vigorous man, Charles Flynn served his sentence to the full; but he came home a physical wreck to his ruined business, his harassed wife and his family of five boys and one little girl, Kate, who was the youngest.

In bed one night, a month after his release, he began to cough loudly. His wife lit a candle. The bedspread was splashed with blood. He seemed to be choking as he coughed up more blood. The little girl, sleeping in a cot beside her parents' bed, saw the blood and went berserk. By morning Charles Flynn was dead. In a week his daughter Kate followed him in a small, homemade coffin to the family burial ground, near his old home in the parish of Ballydoon. That was one family where the police, the landlords and the agents and toadies who kept them in power were viewed with a hatred that was implacable and undying.

Rosie tried to run the business on her own. For a while she succeeded. As the boys grew up fatherless, they grew beyond her control and began to run wild. They were thoughtless and no help whatever to an overworked and grieving woman. Eventually Rosie took to drink and the business failed completely. The boys were taken here and there by cousins and relations. The eldest, Eddie, had his fare paid to New York, and he went through his first winter in death-defying fashion without an overcoat, before he became a 'Yankee'. Tommy was sent to serve his time in a shop in Newry, County Down. A year later Rosie died suddenly. It was the end of a home and of a family.

Tommy spent three penurious years in the Black North, but he talked about it nostalgically for all the remaining days of his life. He learned to sing many of the Protestant and Orange Order songs such as 'The Sash My Father Wore', 'Kick the Pope', 'The Orange Lily' and 'Dolly's Brae' and he sang them with irony and with gusto. The songs were very popular in Drumlahan, but only in so far as they gave a look into the Orange mind. People laughed, and shook their heads in wonder at the ignorance and backwardness of the Northern Protestants who could sing songs like that and, worse still, believe in them. Local Protestants around Ballinwing would be too sedate and too good-mannered to sing songs of this sort:

> Up came a man with a shovel
> In his hand,
> And, sez he, 'Boys go no farther'.
> He tightened up his rope,
> And he made them curse the Pope.
> And, sez he, 'Boys go no farther'.

He often talked about the festive arches erected by the Orangemen around every twelfth of July when they celebrated the victory of a Dutch king over his English father-in-law at the Boyne in 1690. Catholics and Nationalists regarded it as a humiliation to have to walk or drive under these arches. He learned to play hurling in Newry. Hurling and Gaelic football were played for enjoyment, of course; but they were also played to show the Protestants and the English that Catholic Ireland had its own national culture and its own national games and that both were older and grander than what the invaders could produce. Tommy Flynn learned that you made sure you attended the matches; that you cycled or marched in formation, with your hurling stick in your free hand. You took special care to see that the team was properly and correctly turned out: jerseys washed and clean, togs ironed. You attended the meetings without fail. You went to early Mass on the Sunday morning and you made the rest of the day active and full and manly and a credit to the youth of your class. Protestants frowned on Sabbath pastimes, and their youth had little to do on a Sunday afternoon. They seemed bored.

'They just lounged around lusting after the girls,' said Tommy.

He learned Irish dancing, something he knew nothing about before, and he began to learn the Irish language from the books edited by the County Meath priest Fr O'Growney. As a consequence he was later on forever telling Seamus that if he had the money to spare he would send him to a place in County Waterford to learn Irish. 'They'd make a fluent Irish speaker out of you in six months.'

He talked of Drumalane, where John Mitchel lived, and of the 'old Rostrevor' mentioned in his *Jail Journal*. He was a great admirer of Joe Biggar, the old Belfast MP who used obstruction tactics in the London House of Commons in order to make the British give time and attention to Home Rule matters in the days of Parnell. 'We are too long rubbing the English down and asking kindly for Home Rule. We should try to rub them up, instead,' said Mr Biggar. He was as good as his word.

But the darling of Tommy's life was Ernest Blythe, the Protestant from County Antrim who worked as a farm labourer in County Kerry so as to learn the Irish language, before he tramped the country organising for Sinn Féin, when no Catholic wanted to listen to him. 'Great min! Great Irishmin!' was Tommy's opinion. 'And all of them Protestants too.'

And he never forgot the gesture of the quiet, insignificant little Catholic man in Newry, who although he was too old and too unlettered to learn the Irish language himself, or to attend its classes, refused to buy or smoke his favourite tobacco again because the manufacturers, Carrolls of Dundalk, did not subscribe to a Gaelic League collection that year, or so it was said.

He recalled having once seen Sir Shane Leslie, a convert to both Nationalism and Catholicism and a first cousin of Ireland's arch-enemy, Winston Churchill, striding up the road in a kilt and muttering in Irish grumpily to himself. An Irish wolfhound, that looked both hungry and sleepy, trotted obediently at his heel. Such was life for Tommy Flynn in the Black North.

When his time in the shop was nearly served he seriously considered accepting a job in the north of England peddling Ulster linen. It was at that juncture that he received a wire from his Uncle Dennis asking him to come back quickly to help him run the farm at Lisagirwin. So he returned to County Leitrim, as thin as a rake, and with nothing but the clothes he stood up in, apart from a patched and splintered hurling stick.

He never tried to wear a kilt, when times became better for him and more patriotic for the people. He didn't try to acquire an Irish wolfhound either. Instead, he fell under the spell and the influence of Old John Hollohan of lower Drumlahan, and got himself a noisy tongue-hound pup. He called him Rambler. He tried, without success, to interest the youth of Ballinwing in hurling from time to time. 'It's the fastest stick game in the world! And it's more than four thousand years old,' he told them, with a worried look on his face.

The youth of Ballinwing was not impressed.

5

The railway

The narrow-gauge railway passed within five hundred yards of the house that Uncle James built. It connected the wide-gauge Great Western that ran from Dublin to Sligo with the wide-gauge Great Northern that ran from Cavan to Belfast. It had a spur of about fifteen miles that went to the coal mines in County Roscommon. When it was completed towards the end of the last century it linked the south of the county commercially with the rest of Ireland.

'An old man told me,' said Tommy, 'that when the railway was made, he saw hundreds of people leaving that railway station there above for Australia. And not one of them was ever heard of again. Not a single word! I often heard that if they went to America they always wrote, sometime or other. Very seldom did a letter ever come back from Australia. Much less a letter with . money in it.'

The halt, or railway station, as it was called, could be seen up the road about a quarter of a mile from Flynn's on the side of the hill. It was a stone-walled, slated, two-storeyed cottage, white-washed and with an adjoining wooden waiting-room painted in dark green. There was a platform of forty yards. Further up the line was a points system with a spur of two hundred yards, where wagons with coal, Indian meal or artificial manure could be shunted aside for the local country shopkeepers' use. It was called a lie-by. Two large heavy wooden gates, painted white, swung over the road or the railway as was appropriate. In this cottage lived Ned Martin with his wife Julia and a houseful of jolly, high-spirited, brown-eyed children, the eldest of whom was a schoolboy named Jack.

Ned was a milesman. He had two gundogs: Grouse, an Irish

setter, and Shot, a cocker spaniel. His double-barrel shotgun, 'the Barker', gleamed on a rest over the kitchen fire. A trout-rod and a net were hanging in the hallway. There was a carpenter's workshop behind the house, with all the carpenter's tools there, together with banks of fragrant wood shavings. An overflowing vegetable garden stretched along the railway on one side, and a crowded flower garden rested on the other side of the rails and opposite the cottage door. White Leghorn hens picked along the rails and between the sleepers for grains of Indian corn fallen from the passing wagons. On the side of the road five ugly-faced Muscovy ducks dozed. Down along the railway embankment, and almost out of view, two goats tugged among the lush grass, contentiously and in opposite directions.

The railway and the trains were of tremendous interest to the children. In winter darkness there were the showers of sparks shooting from the funnel; in summer there were the fires along the railway slopes and embankments and the sweet distinctive smell of the smoke.

Just like all the other young ones, Seamus never lost an opportunity to run to the gates and to the fences and look at the trains as they passed. He knew all the vehicles and the rolling stock. He knew all the engines with their numbers and brass plates with names on their sides – Isabel, Kathleen, Violet, Edith and the others. They were the names of the daughters of the men who started the railway. He also knew the great 'King' Edward, which was used only on the days of the big cattle-fairs. He knew the carriages, first, second and third class, with the guard's vans, goods vans, horse boxes, coal wagons, cattle wagons, goods wagons and long wagons with spikes in them for the transport of rails. And he never failed to glance at the cow-catcher on the front of the engine hoping secretly for signs of blood, skin, hair or bits of broken bones.

How exciting it was whenever a train broke down and the fog signals were heard exploding in the night! It sounded like heavy gunfire. And how ghostly it was to listen to the railway telegraph poles humming sometimes all though the day! Jack Martin said that the humming meant that messages were being sent in the wires to Dublin or Belfast. Tommy said that it wasn't true, that it was simply a sign of rain. But Seamus preferred to believe that it was true; and he would sit there along the hedge with his ear to the telegraph pole listening to the distant, weird and fascinating sound.

Frequently Mrs Martin had the red flag in her hand. This caused the train to stop. The engine drew to a halt then just between the gates; and one would be almost up against it as it stood there, hissing deafeningly, with its clouds of steam and smoke and its wonderful smells and noises. The greatest event of all was to get talking to the engine driver or the fireman, or to see them shovelling coal into the fire-box. What a marvel it all was!

He collected curiously shaped cinders along the railway that came from the engine. There were bolts and nuts and small bits of tools and implements, as well as spent fog-signals; and he buried them like treasure, in the dark mould beside the turf shed.

Like everyone else, he soon learned to tell the time of the day by what went on on the railway. The buzzard clock at the railway station in Ballinwing sounded at half past seven in the morning, and at set times throughout the day, for the guidance of the men in the workshops. The trains went up and down punctually, except for cattle specials and coal specials. The life of the little farms was guided by this measurement of time. One could also tell the sort of weather to expect by the clarity or vagueness of the sound of the buzzard and the whistle of the train in the distance. The intensity of the noise of the trains could indicate a change of weather to the trained ear. The way the smoke coming from the funnel lingered or disappeared could tell much about the weather to the experienced eye.

Everyone used the railway as a short-cut to the town, even the children going to school; and on fair days or market days pedestrian traffic could be heavy. Amateur drunkards, ashamed to be seen on the road, frequently used the supposed privacy of the railway as they staggered home. Some of the more adventurous dogs around Drumlahan were known to sneak off in the darkness to pay a surreptitious visit to the Ballinwing slaughter houses. They too went by the railway. Occasionally, their mangled bodies could be seen along the slopes and embankments whence the cow-catcher had propelled them. The young and the able walked to Mass on Sundays, stepping from sleeper to sleeper along the railway line. It was only then that one came to know of the long distances that cats can travel at night. And it was evident that they also made use of the railway. On Sunday mornings the dew on the surface of the rails was undisturbed by trains; and the tracks of the cats' paws could be seen for miles on the polished steel.

As the years passed, many of the old people were reluctantly obliged to find other means of going to Mass and to town; and it became a sad sign of the passage of the years when one felt that the railway was too much for one. There were many who stubbornly refused to call it a day, and who could be seen stumbling and slithering along breathlessly between the rails on a Sunday morning. Veronica regarded it as of the utmost importance to get Nan-nan and AB off the rails. And it was no mean feat of diplomacy on Tommy's part that he succeeded in having the two old ladies agree to let him drive them to Mass every Sunday in the horse-and-trap.

Consequently, the entire household clambered into the trap at a quarter past ten on Sunday mornings. Billy, the heavy quarter-breed Clydesdale, clopped over the road towards Aughabeg crossroads on the way to Mass in Ballinwing. He never trotted smartly, as other horses did: he achieved a sort of jog-trot that got slower and slower as the journey progressed. This obliged Tommy to make faces and thumbs at the drivers of traps and side-cars that were crowding up behind him and Billy. He was urging them not to be ashamed to pass him out and to surge on to Mass at the spanking speed that their animals were capable of. It would have been bad manners to pass out without being signalled to do so by the slow one. All the horses appeared to enjoy going to Mass on Sundays, with their polished, glittering harness and the light, carefully painted vehicles behind them. Not so Billy! Of course he could show them what was what when it came to pulling a plough, or a mowing machine, or a cart of hay on a bad pass. Yet, going to Mass was something that seemed to infuse him with a killing lethargy. He was a different sort of horse. He was said to have come from County Galway and to have been bought at the Ballinasloe horse fair by a local dealer.

Going to Mass on Sundays Tommy would be puffing clouds of smoke from a pipe of Murrays smouldering tobacco. Veronica, all tensed up and looking ever so holy, was buttoned into a tight overcoat and crowned by a tighter hat. Her prayer book was the *Treasury of the Sacred Heart* and she gripped it and her rosary as if for dear life. The kids, scrubbed and rigged out in their Sunday best, were quiet and obedient. They looked forward, not to the Bread of Eternal Life that would be dispensed during Mass by the priest, but to the bull's eyes and the slab toffee that they could expect when Mass was over, and dispensed by Timmy Greehan or Judy Travers.

Nan-nan dressed always in her half-length black skirt, her black cape and her bonnet, with two black ostrich feathers shivering over her head. Periodically, she painted the bonnet with gum to make it gleam and glisten. A thick, dark veil half-covered her face.

AB wore a long, dark coat that hung to her black-stockinged ankles. A tall, dark churn of a hat, wrapped in black satin ribbons, ascended from her small head and made her pale, long face seem still longer. She also wore a heavy, dark veil with little black knots on it. As she neared the crossroads and the Sunday traffic, she pulled it down to cover her entire face.

The roads and the walls of Aughabeg were heavily painted with political slogans to catch the attention of the worshippers on their way to chapel. By the following Sunday those signs would be painted out and new and more topical ones inscribed in their places. In the darkness of Saturday nights much painting and daubing took place, indeed.

'What's that painted on the bridge, Daddy?'

Tommy read the yellow lettering slowly as he screwed up his eyes and exposed his teeth. The pipe smouldered aromatically in his left hand; the reins were in his right hand. UP O'DUFFY! UP THE BLUESHIRTS! TO HELL WITH THE SPANIARD!

Nan-nan and AB were delighted. Each put a hand to the mouth to stifle the spluttering laughter. Nan-nan lifted her veil with her free hand to read the news better. AB was too sedate to go that far

32

on her way to Holy Mass. Nan-nan thought of herself, dropped the veil, composed herself and resumed a more ladylike stance.

'Daddy, what's the Spaniard?'

'De Valera, I suppose. And will yeh keep yer voice down, yeh little *aurcaun* yeh. Everyone can hear you with that squeaky voice of yours.'

'Yes indeed! Everyone can hear you asking silly, impertinent questions and you on your way to Holy Mass.' That was AB: all serious and forbidding again.

There were many young fellows and men walking along the road on their way to the chapel, all of them in blue serge suits with the hands deep in the trouser pockets. The trouser legs were wide, almost bell-bottomed, and every man seemed to get an additional flick into his step in order to show off the fashionable trouser legs. They walked briskly, in step and in file. They broke file to let the crowding traps and side-cars pass.

There were many bicycles; all new. This was an increasingly common sight and it caused Nan-nan great wonder. The bicycles were to continue to increase; and soon there would be no files of blue-clad young men walking steadily and talkatively to Mass on Sunday mornings. The Mass mattered of course; but it was just as important to be out and about with your fellow-men and to be as good as the next in your blue serge suit, with its bum-freezer jacket, its double-breasted waistcoat and its flickable, wide-legged trousers. And across the meadows could be seen the distant figures of people going to Mass along the railway and over the metal bridge that spanned the canal.

More signs on the road.

RELEASE THE PRISONERS!

THE BULLOCK FOR THE ROAD AND THE LAND FOR THE PEOPLE!

UP DEV!

DOWN DEV!

STAND BY O'DUFFY, BY THE ACA, AND BY IRELAND!

Nearing the town the paintwork increased. Nan-nan and AB almost twisted their necks trying to read the painted slogans. AB put on her glasses to extend her vision. She did it slyly and ladylike beneath her veil when she thought no-one was noticing.

33

SMASH PARTITION!

'What's Partition?' asked Nan-nan with irritation.

'The dismemberment of our ancient Irish nation,' replied AB with lofty superiority.

'Troth, then it's not! I bet it's something else!' rejoined Nan-nan. The word 'partition' was a new one to her. She confused it with perdition, which was a favourite curse she often used.

They passed by a five-barred gate. A sandy-haired young man was sitting on it smoking drowsily. He wore black trousers, a blue uniform-like shirt with buttoned pockets and epaulettes. On his head was a heavy black beret. His bicycle rested on the grass. He was a Blueshirt.

'Where's the meeting the day?' asked Tommy jovially.

'Longford,' answered the young man, as he took another deep draw on his cigarette. He was from Clonmoher parish, where the Blueshirt cause was very strong.

Horses were beginning to shy and to take fright at the paint-work on the crown of the road and on the walls. Tommy was getting tense. He gripped the leather reins tighter. His dead pipe was still in his mouth and held firmly between his teeth. He knew well that Billy would not budge no matter what appeared on the road. Other horses were beginning to look dangerous, with twiddling ears, lathers of sweat, prancing madly and tossing of the head. Nan-nan and AB were now in loud argument about Partition, and were appealing to Tommy for judgment. In a way he was glad the horses were uneasy: it absolved him from having to settle the problems of the ancient Irish nation. Seamus was getting afraid. Berney McGovern's horse stopped dead. He was gazing with raised head and erect ears at a large sign before him on the road: SUPPORT DEV AND IRISH INDUSTRY, IRELAND FREE AND ONE!

John Stretton's horse began to dance and back the trap. He was hoising, rearing faintly. There was a bold bit of painting in his path. UP ACA! UP CROININ! UP UIP.

The Strettons all disembarked quickly. John rubbed his hand along the animal's back and shoulders and on to the neck. He gripped the reins just below the bits.

'Atta boy now! Atta boy! Buzzh – calm down now. Well might

34

you frighten at that clauber. Quiet now, boy!'

'Bloody yahoos!' exploded Tommy, in sympathy with the Strettons. 'Out painting the roads at night, when they ought to be in their damn beds! There'll be someone killed yet if a horse runs away, or something, on this very road! Should bloody well be ashamed of themselves!'

As expected, Billy didn't budge or flick an ear. He jogged on in his own sweet way over all sorts of painting and political philosophy and he passed out the other animals that were now being calmed and pacified. A few minutes earlier they had passed him by, at a spanking pace and full of confidence. Now they seemed to be reduced to nervous wrecks: confused, in lathers of sweat and in need of cold drinks.

Soon they were near the town with the Mass bell ringing urgently and people hastening towards the chapel. They crossed the railway. Seamus had regained his colour; the two old ladies had ceased to argue; Veronica seemed lost in pious thoughts. Tommy pulled the hat well down over his eyes and gripped the dead pipe still tighter as Billy clopped onward and deposited the household safe and sound outside the chapel gate.

All during the Mass Seamus wondered why Billy did not take fright at the painting on the roads when other horses did so. Also, why was it that he wouldn't trot faster on Sundays, just as other horses did. In the end he concluded that it must have been because he came from Ballinasloe, in the County Galway. AB interrupted his thoughts with a sharp nudge and she pointed to his prayer book and then towards the altar where Fr McFee was saying Mass in a loud, sharp, cranky voice.

Getting back quickly to Billy and the other horses, he decided that he'd like to go to Ballinasloe one day, just to see where Billy came from. Maybe, Billy's father and mother and sisters and brothers and cousins would be there. Ball-in-a-sloe! It sounded a nice name. How would you go there? Up the Cloone Road? Or over to Ballydoon? He'd have to find out soon.

'Ugh!'

He received another nudge from AB. This time it was very sharp and it startled him. There was no peace.

35

After the dinner was over the whistle of a train could be heard coming very slowly from Ballinwing. Trains didn't run on Sundays, except for special occasions. This time it was the Blueshirt rally and meeting in Longford. Seamus had a good vantage point, half way up a spindly ash tree at the back of the house. Soon the train came out of the cutting on the tail of the hill and advanced slowly along the high embankment towards the railway station. Mrs Martin could be seen beyond the gates with the red flag in her hand.

'By jingo! There are two engines pulling the carriages instead of one.'

He began to count the carriages – three, four, five, six: still more coming; nine, ten. And all full. They were packed with men and women with black berets, blue shirts, black ties and black trousers or skirts. Heads were sticking out of every window and there were many standing out at the end of every exposed carriage platform.

When the train finally halted at Drumlahan station, where Mrs Martin stood with her red flag, Seamus had a chance to count the carriages. There were thirteen in all; some were old and grey and weatherbeaten and were seldom in use.

No-one bothered to come out of the Flynn house to see the spectacle. Nothing like it had ever been seen before. He had the view all to himself. Two engines and thirteen carriages, all full of uniformed people, cheering and calling and waving their flag – the old blue flag of Ireland with the Cross of St Patrick. The two engines started up and the train slowly moved up the hill and out of view. He was never to see anything like it again. He had just seen a part of history. The sound of the train soon died away as it hurried onwards on its narrow-gauge rails among the drumlin hills and into history and silence.

6

Ceiliers

All the men, and many of the women, went ceiliing at night. This simply meant visiting a neighbours's house when the day's work was done and having a chat or an exchange of gossip. A ceili could last anything up to two to four hours. There were early ceiliers, who went home at a reasonable time. And of course there were late ceiliers, who could stay on till midnight or later. They were not too popular; but people managed to sound welcoming all the same.

The Flynn children delighted in listening to the ceiliers. They were such good talkers and had such interesting things to say. Uncle Peter had been in America and he seemed to have enjoyed his life there so much. Danny Mulvey never left Clonmoher in his life, but hunting with the tongue-hounds gave him a deep and detailed knowledge of the countryside and the people. He was a bachelor; he was wall-eyed, red-faced and he wore puttees. A crooked pipe was permanently in his mouth. Berney McGovern lived in Aughabeg. The oldest of the ceiliers, he had a round friendly face, a clipped moustache and a big family of likeable children. He was a strong supporter of de Valera and his party. Jim Gaffney's reputation as a womaniser had travelled far. He too was a regular ceilier, when he wasn't out on the prowl. He was tall and slim; he had a neat appearance; he was a good listener. The other ceilier was Jim Murray, a little Englishman from an orphanage in Rochdale. He never lost his strong Lancashire accent. He was a sports fanatic; a proud and loyal Briton with great belief in the value of the British army and deep confidence in the wisdom of British statesmen. He was an avid reader of the books of Edgar Wallace and Charles Dickens. Another regular ceilier was Ned Martin from the railway station.

Uncle Peter in his young days had been a great handballer, a melodious whistler and an entertaining singer of ribald songs. His family had fallen on hard times when his father died and there were only two courses open to him if he wanted to make a living for himself: he could emigrate, or he could join the police, the Royal Irish Constabulary, locally known as the RIC. To join the police would have been unthinkable in that family: they were hated and despised. So when the fare could be scraped together he set out for America and he sailed from Moville in County Donegal on a ship of the Allen Line. He landed in New York and took the first job that came his way. He did nothing spectacular in the New World; but when he returned he took with him a wealth of tales and memories of his rare experiences.

In New York he worked as a bar-tender, a taxi-driver and as a waiter at different times. His elder brother, Eddie, was in New York years before him, and it was evident to all then that he was never going to set the Manhattan River ablaze either. He gained a degree of notoriety by going through his first winter in New York without an overcoat. It was generally accepted, however, that a good tough Irishman could just risk doing this during his first winter in the New World. After that he would be a Yankee, and used to the soft life of Yankeeland. Eddie picked up an asthmatic condition that remained with him all his life as a result of that first terrible winter. He was a great fiddler as a young man: he was also a great fowler. After New York he neither fiddled nor fowled again. When he eventually returned to Ballinwing he was nick-named 'the Yankee' within the family circle and when he was out of earshot.

Uncle Peter claimed to have been on talking terms with the great coloured boxer, Joe Jerome. He would often stand up and give demonstrations how the great Joe had told him to stand and how to hold his fists for defensive boxing. Evidently, even Joe was quick to spot that Uncle Peter was not by nature an aggressive man, and that he could get by on defensive measures alone.

Like all local people who went to America he seemed to have established instant rapport with the German immigrants, whom he and all his friends admired and regarded as being the same sort of people as themselves. It was a rapport which cut through language and religion. For all the Germans that Uncle Peter met were Lutherans and Freemasons – qualities not very acceptable to Irish Roman Catholics, or so one would think. He especially admired their womenfolk as being great cooks.

'I declare to God Almighty, them women could prepare a feed out of nothing that you'd eat till you'd burst!'

He told stories of people from Ballinwing and the surrounding districts who had made good in New York. One of them came from very far up on the side of the mountain, and he owned a high-class restaurant; another had a flourishing florist's business; someone else had a number of saloons; one had a big delicatessen place. A few did well in the building trade. One man became fabulously rich from nothing really, with an undertaker's business. A few had stores of various sorts.

But there were others who did not do so well. Some could just not settle down to life in the big city and they would give or do anything to be back in Ireland again. They would gladly live on potatoes and salt for the rest of their lives if they could but escape from the New York hell. There were men working on the underground railways who knew they were ruining their health. Other jobs were available; but they could not get time off, at the right time, to go for an interview. They died like flies of TB, asthma, bronchitis or pneumonia. There were those who could not stand the jobs they had, but who did not know how to change nor how to adjust. There were those who eagerly and ostentatiously threw up their religion as soon as they went over. 'We're far too busy for that old game now,' they'd boast. 'That stuff is OK in the old country; but not over here.'

There were the poor, old, lonely men, sad and in tears, who would never see Ireland again, and who pined for the chance of spending just one day in the homeland that they had left so full of hope in their youth. They lived with the lowdown and the broken in flop houses. Their drink, when they could afford it, was moonshine for the most part.

Uncle Peter seemed to find great interest in New York and its life and its people. There were very many Irish who saw nothing in it to wonder at, and who were pleased to regard it as a place for making money as fast as possible, and then getting out of it speedily. The Irish helped one another to a very large extent, and would do everything they could to get a new immigrant started in a job. In some Irish businesses it was common practice to sack someone on the staff who was not Irish if a new arrival from the old country came to the door, especially if he had a recommendation from someone influential in the Irish community. A young Greek was among an Irishman's employees when a man just off the Moville boat arrived with a recommendation. There were no vacancies. But the solution was simple: 'Sack the hure of a Greek!' And in that instant another young exile of Erin had found a foothold in Yankeeland.

When Veronica, Nan-nan and AB threw up their hands in horror at the treatment meeted out to the hure of a Greek, the men present laughed at them. Uncle Peter explained that the Irish had to do that kind of thing. It was a rough, tough world and not at all like Drumlahan or Tullylakenmore. The other nationalities in New York did the very same thing.

He did not like the Jews. 'Many's the poor divel of an Irishman they flung out of a job and a badly needed job at that.'

He was wary of the native Americans, or narrow-backs as they called them. 'Very straight people in a way. But if you let them down once, or if they thought you let them down, they were finished with you for good.'

He met a few English and he liked them. One of them was a musician, and he often used Uncle Peter as an audience while he tried out some short classical pieces on his violin. He was very delighted that Uncle Peter listened to him when no-one else would. He was convinced that the Englishman had talent, having heard plenty of good violinists with the travelling shows that came to the Market House in Ballinwing when he was growing up. He soon lost trace of his New York Englishman; but he often threw his eye over the names on concert programmes for Carnegie Hall in case he'd see his old friend's name there.

In the basement of a hotel where he worked he came upon an Armenian sound asleep, dead to the world and snoring viciously.

It was the noise that attracted his attention at first. The man should have been working instead of sleeping, and Uncle Peter was dumbfounded when the man told him where he came from. Never having heard of Armenia before, he thought the man had said that he came from Ardmeenan, which was a hilly townland two miles south-east of Ballinwing. He knew that no-one from Ardmeenan would ever lie down, much less go to sleep, if there was work to be done.

The Armenian lost no time in telling him of all the terrible suffering his people had endured at the hands of the Turks. The Irishman listened respectfully for twenty minutes. He was beginning to tire a little of all the blood-letting, and he hoped secretly that it would all end soon. After half an hour it was still going on, and there was no end in sight. So, at a loss to bring the atrocities to an end and to get the work started, he just mentioned, casually, that the Irish also had endured much; but at the hands of the English, of course.

This stopped the Armenian dead. He was dumbfounded: he would not believe that the English would harm a fly, never mind the Irish. Moreover, who did Uncle Peter thing he was to dare to compare the so-called sufferings of his miserable Irish Micks with the horrors endured by the heroic sons of Armenia?

Uncle Peter saw that action must be taken. He tried to draw the Armenian's attention to the horrors of the Famine, not to mention the aftermath of the Battle of Vinegar Hill. This only made his adversary more incensed, and he decided to bring out the big guns: The Flight of the Earls, The Confiscations and Father Murphy from old Kilcormack.

None of these had any effect on the Asian; so he threw in Luke Wadding, Cromwell at Drogheda, The Manchester Martyrs, Robert Emmet and the poisoning of Eoin Roe O'Neil. He was about to mention the sad death of Brian Boru and the massacre of Mullaghmast, but the Armenian cut him short and recounted a list of atrocities that made the Irishman admit to himself that if they were as bad in fact as they were in sound, they could have resulted in nothing less than an orgy of racial extermination and the disappearance of old Armenia for good. Was this poor fellow,

41

in the basement of a New York hotel, similar to the last of the Mohicans? Or was it just the after-effects of heavy sleep on a stomachful of strange food? In any case he was rolling up his shirt sleeves and spitting on his palms; and Uncle Peter was trying hard to remember the defensive measures that the great Joe Jerome had taught him. He was convinced that they would be applicable to a situation of this sort. Reluctantly, he began to unbutton his jacket. Then before the two antagonists could prepare themselves further and round one get underway, a bell jangled loudly somewhere in the building.

'Knocking off time.'

'Aye – knocking off time!'

The two grabbed their discarded garments and rushed to the lift together like old friends. It was all right to fight and to settle ancient wrongs and avenge aspersions on national pride in the bosses' time. But there were more useful things to do during a working man's own time.

The people who incensed Uncle Peter and his compatriots most were the Italians.

'People that no respectable person could associate with,' was how he described them. 'They all came from the heel of the boot. That's a district in the south of Italy. You couldn't make any sense of them. They were all dead against the Pope. "Cateramangi? Cateramangi? God damn Pope no good!" That's what they'd say. They were always at that.'

That was bad enough, and it sufficed to make Irish blood boil. But worse was to come.

'The Italians had a bit of a song,' continued Uncle Peter, 'and whenever they happened to see an Irishman in the street alone, they'd start to sing it at the top of their voices.

> Giravi shovel and giravi pick.
> And giravi job for the Irisha Mick.
> Sa-cra-*mento!*
> Sa-cra-*mento!*

'I knew a man in New York be the name of Prior. He came from below the town. A daycent man. An' sez he to me wan day,

42

"Peter!" sez he, "tell me is it true that the Pope is an Eyetallion?" Well, I didn't know what to say; but I couldn't tell the poor fella a lie, especially about the Pope. "Well, Tom Prior," sez I, "I'm afraid it is true. The Pope is an Eyetallion all right." "Glory be to God, Peter, how can that be?" sez he. "How could the Pope be an Eyetallion? I can't believe that the Holy Father himself could be wan iv them. God between us an' all harm."'

Uncle Peter saw a tramp asleep on a park bench one day. He passed by; but thinking that there was something vaguely familiar about the discoloured unshaven face, he retraced his steps and had a closer look at the sleeper. He immediately prodded him awake. It was an old friend from Ardnaboe or the hilly end of Ballinwing. They were in the same class together at school; they received First Communion and Confirmation together. The sleeper was overjoyed to see Peter. His nose was purple; he was on moonshine; he was hungry and cold and dirty and louse-ridden. His name was Larry Dougherty.

'I came down from Canada four months ago, I had a bad time up there.'

'What in the name of God ever tempted you to go to Canada?' enquired Uncle Peter in amazement.

'Isn't that where all the Protestants go? Any Protestant who ever left Ballinwing. went to Canada. They'd never go to Yankeeland or to New York. They go where the money is. And look how well they do.'

'May God give you sense, Larry! You're stone mad. Protestants go to Canada because they go to their own kind. They look after their own. And the Freemasons see to it that none of them ever go to the wall. But you should know that Canada is no place for the likes of you or me.'

'It was only a gamble. I had no-one that I could go to in New York. I thought Canada could be a good place to go,' said Larry ruefully. 'I nearly died of hunger up there. I'm here in New York now for the past four months and I can't stand it. I just can't stand it, Peter.'

'But you'll have to stand it, man.'

'It's just like hell to me. I'm finished.'

'Aw, very apt,' said Uncle Peter consolingly. 'I'll get a bed for you. Only a flop house in the Lower Bronx; but it's better than the open air. And then I'll introduce you to a fellow I know from Glann to see about a job. But you'll have to get shaved and washed and cleaned up a bit first. I'll show you a place where you can do that. Don't ever tell anyone about going to Canada. They'd die laughing at you for that, Larry.'

'But I hate this place. I hate New York.'

'Hate be damned! If you don't pull yourself together you'll starve and you won't last till Christmas. Clean yourself up. Have a bite to ate. Have a good sleep. And then I'll take you to the fella from Glann. Will you do that now? And for Christ's sake don't mention Canada.'

'All right!'

'And you know you could have a fine time in this town. Keep off the booze. Go to the music halls or the dances or the museums. You could spend a great time in the museum or the picture gallery. There's plenty of things there that used to be in the old sixth school book. And there's Ringling's Circus. Aye, why don't you go to the circus. You must pull yourself together!'

Larry did pull himself together. He was nick-named 'Canada' Dougherty even after when he made enough money to return to Ballinwing and to set up in grocery business in Ardnaboe, with tea, wine and spirits as additional lines to his commercial activities. Moreover, his shop became known as 'Canada', first to the wags; and then to everyone; even to the parish priest.

Uncle Peter claimed that New York could at times be a dangerous place. This depended on the person concerned of course. It did not apply to him for instance, because he was able to look after himself, having received instruction from Joe Jerome. As a consequence of this he wandered all over the city just to satisfy his own curiosity. He even crossed the river and explored part of New Jersey where the laws relating to firearms differed so much from the laws of New York. Gangsters? No! He never came face to face with a gangster. But there were hobos who would try to snatch your wallet or your watch and chain. And if you had a ring on your finger, they wouldn't bother pulling it off. They just cut off

44

the finger, for speed. They had a big thing like a pincers that they carried in the inside jacket pocket specially for that purpose. It was very handy for getting a ring. It wasted no time at all.

7

Tullylakenmore

Nan-nan was very popular with the children, and indeed with everyone else also, whenever she began to tell yarns about the events that occurred and the people she knew when she was a young girl in Tullylakenmore. There was a neighbour who lived only a field away and further up the lane, named John Keaney. He was known to everyone as the ould Doctor, because of his skills and his abilities in acting as a link between the people and the fairies. As Seamus grew up, he began to perceive that his father and his mother, and indeed all the neighbours, were just as impressed as the children were by what Nan-nan had to say about ould Doctor Keaney and the things he did for the people of his neighbourhood. She could bring to a halt any discussion that was going on among the ceiliers whether it was of politics, scandal or the price of cattle, by just mentioning John Keaney and the remarkable powers he could exercise when called upon to do so.

It seemed that once darkness fell in the locality where she was born, 'the others' simply took over the countryside and proceeded to disport themselves till dawn came over the Cuilceach Mountains and crept slowly down the heather from Skeheroo. It was accepted generally that anyone who ventured out of doors at night ran something of a risk. He could get a fright (or a fret, as it was called) and never be the same man again. He might even disappear for a time, or forever.

There were some people favoured, or over-looked, by the fairies, and they could go anywhere they liked at night. And there were brave men, who just did not care a damn for the fairies, for their tricks or for their threats. A man of that stamp would put a live coal from the fire into his pipe, tuck his ash plant under his oxter and go off up the mountain for miles in the darkness to ceili, to play cards, to look at a beast he was thinking of buying, to woo, to matchmake, or the devil only knew what else. Such a man knew, and everyone knew, that he was taking a risk; but there were always people who liked to live dangerously. Nan-nan could tell tales of men, even the brave ones and the favoured ones, who got a fret when they were out at night, and who were at death's door for long and long, until restored to health through the good offices and the ministrations of ould Doctor Keaney.

People could become ill, or sickly, or out of sorts and pine away for years, when in reality it was the fairies who were at work. People could seem to die and be buried and be thus lost forever. That was where the ould Doctor came in: he could usually persuade the fairies to think again; to have a heart; and the man, or even the animal, as was often the case, usually recovered or was returned or restored.

Two young fellows from Meenahill had their suspicions about the sudden illness and subsequent death of their only sister. Their grief was intense. On the second night after the burial they stole away with shovels and spades, dug up her grave and opened the coffin in the deserted chapel yard. It was empty, save for a heather besom neatly tied with a blue ribbon, her favourite colour. They quickly filled the grave and made it neat and tidy, so as not to attract attention or start rumours. At dawn they reached the ould Doctor's house and knocked on his door. He almost collapsed when he saw the heather besom with its blue ribbon. He turned pale; he trembled; they had no need to tell him what it was; they had no need to tell him what they wanted.

'Lads, yez should not have done this. But I'll do all I can for yez. Yez should have come to me before she died.'

He took them into the house. He bolted and barricaded the door. He hung sacks over the small windows to keep out the daylight. He built a huge fire on the hearth. He placed the besom on the nearby table. He began to look from the besom to the fire. He was muttering. He looked agitated and nervous. He began to talk to the fire, to urge it to get bigger, to burn, burn. He waved his hands upwards as if to encourage the flames. Frequently, he could be heard to mutter, 'I'll do what I can for yez.'

This continued for some time. But when the heat was so intense that they were all drenched in sweat, he suddenly made a dash for the table, grabbed the besom and rammed it into the dancing flames. There was immediately a blinding flash, followed by an ear-splitting shriek; and the room filled with a dense, dark smoke that obscured the firelight, but which quickly vanished again.

When they came to their senses the door was open, the hens were clucking on the flagstone, the autumn sun was slanting through the window panes. The fire was burning sweetly on the hearth. The ould Doctor was seated on a chair, slumped and looking sad.

'It was too late, lads! I'm sorry. It was too late lads. There was nothing I could do.' The girl's name was Julia Cafferty.

He paused.

'Go home now, like the good young men that yez are. But, whisper! Never do the like of that again. Promise me that now? And don't ever let anyone else do it either.'

They went home; they had a good sleep; their grief very quickly went away; they lived happy ever after. And in some strange way they began to find it difficult to remember their sister in later years, or the events of the night in which they dug up her grave and opened her narrow, homemade coffin in the dark and deserted chapel yard. It seemed like a vague dream that the mind could not get hold of properly. It came to be something that they felt to be of no importance to them at all. Eventually they forgot all about it.

Nan-nan and her sister-in-law, AB, held sharply differing views about the fairies. Nan-nan's fairies were robust in character. They had immense power and influence. And whenever they were actually seen it was as dour, tall-hatted horsemen in black coats white breeches and black shiny riding boots as they went careering across the countryside at night on the backs of matchless steeds. They were masterful, tyrannical and daring. A man could be going on his ceili at night and walking quietly along, minding his own business. Quite suddenly, and without warning, the fields on either side of him could become crowded with those silent, determined horsemen, fully rigged out in their tall dark hats, their black coats and their white riding breeches.

48

The best plan, if caught in a situation of this nature, was to lie down flat at the butt of the nearest hedge or ditch. With luck, one would not be detected; and the horsemen would suddenly whirl around and tear away as quickly as they had come. Such were the fairies of Tullylakenmore.

AB believed in the existence of the fairies, of course. They were to be found around many of the old forts that looked like circular mounds of earth and which were usually covered with bushes and briars. There was an abundance of these forts in the Drumlahan and Aughabeg area; and it was noted that every fort was sited so as to have a clear view of its neighbouring fort in the distance or on the side of a nearby hill. AB's fairies were never seen; but their presence was always felt. She believed that some-times they could be heard fiddling and dancing at night; and that, occasionally, lights could be seen moving slowly from one fort to another when the countryside was quiet and everyone was asleep in bed. She believed that they had immense power and that they were capable of perpetrating much evil. They rarely did that, simply because God and his Holy Catholic Church kept them in bounds.

Yet, you always referred to them as the Good People. You were never disrespectful nor mocking when you spoke of them; and you lowered your voice fittingly when you mentioned them. Also you added 'God speed them': 'The Good People, God speed them.' You referred to them as fairies only when talking to the ignorant or the insensitive.

The fairies of Drumlahan and Aughabeg kept very much to themselves. There was something that was close to a tacit arrangement between them and the local people. They were not above snatching the occasional infant at birth, and fooling the distraught parents that it was a case of infant mortality, as was well known. But many a man was called at night by a tap on the window pane, or by an unfamiliar voice, if a cow or a horse was in danger. And there were drunkards who, having fallen asleep in the hard frost outdoors at night, were shaken by the shoulder and restored to wakefulness and their lives thus saved. But there were the peals of laughter that echoed from an adjacent fort, in broad daylight, when a spiteful, land-grabbing, husband-beating woman was killed by a kick from a horse. And there was the flute player who could never forgive the Good People for the way they laughed, after he had spent two hours searching in the darkness for the instrument he let slip from his fingers as he crossed a stile, only to find it in his overcoat pocket later.

AB's fairies never took the butter from the milk or had the victims churning for days or years, as Nan-nan's fairies were wont to do. Neither did AB's fairies cause people or cattle to pine or die or disappear. These were activities that they shunned. But the humans, who practised witchcraft or who were in league with the devil, seized the opportunity in Drumlahan to snatch from their neighbours the things that the Good People did not want and would not touch. The evil eye, also, could cause far more damage than anything the Good People would ever do.

There was, of course, just one of the Good People who was sometimes seen around Drumlahan and Aughabeg. That was the leprechaun. But he was an exception and an eccentric; a show-off and a loner. He was just looking for attention, with his shoemaking and his supposed wealth. Some would see him as a teaser, or as a purse-proud little runt. There was a degree of sympathy and understanding for the Good People themselves on account of this silly little creature. Every family has its black sheep. AB, like everyone else, respected the Good People, but she had little time for the leprechaun.

The contrast between the lifestyle of the Drumlahan fairies and those of Tullylakenmore was a bone of contention between the two women. Each despised the other's fairies. Each could manage the sarcastic laugh or the 'would you believe it' shake of the head on hearing of some event in the other camp. They argued fiercely and loudly about everything. However, neither would dare to raise her voice in anger or in contempt about the fairies. For you never knew who was listening.

AB knew that God and His Holy Church could keep the fairies in their place and in hand. Nan-nan knew that if it came to a showdown between God and the fairies then the Almighty had better watch his step, or think again.

AB and her neighbours firmly believed in ghosts, especially in haunting ghosts. It went without saying of course, that there were plenty of ghosts going around quietly that were never seen by anyone in Drumlahan or elsewhere. But there were also the haunting ghosts who, from time to time, appeared in certain places at night. Every ghost kept to his or her own pitch, because they had died there, or had something significant or painful happen to them at that spot during life. It did not always follow that ghosts appeared because of having lived a bad life, or because of having died in deep sin. Sometimes a ghost appeared to draw attention to something, because of an injustice suffered or perpetrated, or even as a plea for help. It could happen that they were just the souls of people who could not be accepted into heaven by God, until they had expiated their sins and their transgressions. They haunted and wandered as a penance. A kind neighbour, or perhaps the person who saw the apparition, could help by having a Mass said for the unfortunate and restless spirit. Yet, it would be no mean task to have enough Masses said to relieve all the ghosts that were known to be around the locality and, in this way, to render the townland unhaunted and ghostless.

There was a ghost at the white gates, half a mile up the road on the way to Ballydoon. No-one knew whose ghost it was; but it was suspected by some, and concluded by others, that it could only be the ghost of Skelper Burroughs, a reprobate member of the ruling landlord family, who had died in the distant past. He was the sort of man who would of necessity have to do a considerable amount of haunting. It was just routine and normal for him. There was a ghost at the crossroads, where the bonfire blazed to celebrate de Valera's election victory. And late at night, an unknown man could be seen sitting beside the kitchen fire in the railway gatehouse where Ned Martin lived. The ghost just sat there looking quietly into the ashes. Those of the household who came in late always went discreetly up the stairs, so as not to disturb him. A woman was seen at the well stick, the stile that led to the springwell.

At Berney McGovern's brae a black dog could frequently be noticed late at night running in terror along at the butt of the hedge towards Aughabeg crossroads. There was something seen at Stretton's gate. No-one knew what; but everyone was convinced that something was seen there. A tall dark man was occasionally observed leaning again Berney's gate on moonlit nights. He was a complete stranger. Weird and unearthly noises were heard in the hazel thickets that flourished along the road near the crossroads.

Worst of all were two dark-clad women who sometimes moved in rapid walk, with flowing robes and flailing arms along the stretch of road from Aughabeg to Ballydoon. Who they were, or what they meant, no-one knew. A half-drunk man challenged them once and demanded who they were and where they were going. He dared to ask openly what everyone else was asking secretly.

They had passed him by before he had finished his sentence, so rapid was their stride. Abruptly, they spun around and grabbed him, one on each side. Silently they began to frogmarch him towards Ballydoon with its crowded graveyard. For a minute or two he was powerless and utterly surprised in their vice-like grip. Then he began to struggle. A powerful man, he halted them and a terrible fight ensued. 'He downed them; and they downed him,' was how AB described it.

For hours he fought them up and down the road in the darkness. There were times when his strength ebbed and he felt he could not continue; but the revulsion for the two that grew in him as time wore on spurred him to dogged resistance. It was a long night, but with the tail of his eye he noticed a faint brightening on the horizon. He did not know that it was the dawn. Suddenly they left him and hurried away, with flowing robes and flailing arms. He heard a cock crow in the distance. Then he lost consciousness. In the morning he was found by a poacher in an exhausted and bruised condition. He did not recover fully for almost three months; and he gave up drink for the rest of his life. When it was all long past, and he thought it over, he remembered that he did not experience fear during the struggle. He felt only that driving and consuming revulsion. And he remembered also, that long as the struggle lasted, he never once saw either of their faces.

Nan-nan and her family and neighbours in Tullylakenmore had little belief in haunting ghosts. To them it was the fairies who counted, and the manner in which they manifested themselves as daring horsemen, and as beings who could exert a tyrannical power behind the scenes. Ould Doctor Keaney was indeed a godsend to a sometimes harassed and frightened people.

Yet AB was adamant that the Good People, the ghosts and those who exercised the evil eye or practiced the devil's work by taking their neighbours' butter or by turning themselves into hares were all of them curbed by prayers that the priests had commenced to say after Mass. Nan-nan reluctantly admitted later that she shared AB's opinion in this. Towards the end of the nineteenth century these prayers began to be recited by the priests at the foot of the altar after the Mass had ended with the *Ite missa est*. Among other things, they asked the deity to 'restrain the devil and all the other evil spirits that wander through the world for the ruin of souls.'

Matters were never the same again. It did not mean, of course, the end of the fairies or of their power. They still survived, an omnipresent population, hearing, listening and, sometimes still, doing. Yet, it was possible now to get on without the services of the ould Doctor: and when he died he had no successor, and no-one stepped into his shoes. The prayers after Mass, in an underhand way, supported those who had always wanted to defy the fairies, but who dared not. They were a face-saver for those who wanted to commit the sin of kicking over the fairy traces and then going on to outright apostasy. And eventually the prayers after Mass set a band-wagon in motion that so many wanted to jump on. It was soon as fashionable to blaspheme the fairies, the ghosts and the evil eyes, as it had once been to respect and to fear them. None the less, when people were on their way to the fair or the market or even to Mass itself in Ballinwing, and when they casually looked up and saw that fort on the side of the hill, with its clear ring of sturdy whitethorns, they secretly knew well that the fairies did exist, no matter what others might say. Yes; they were still there, and they always would be there.

8

The loy

It could be truly said that the old order, and the old way of life, finally came to an end in Drumlahan in 1935. For once the loy ceased to be regarded as a credible agricultural implement, life in that district was never the same again.

The scythe had fallen to the single-horse, twelve-fingered Pierce or Bamford mowing machine a generation earlier. It was an easy victory. Most of the farmers had at least a quarter of their land under meadow. This was usually the most fertile fields they owned. There was always a fierce struggle to save the hay quickly in the damp and unreliable climate. Often the whole crop was practically lost, or was saved in very poor condition and was, consequently, of very poor quality and nearly worthless as a feeding-stuff for cattle. The loss of stock during the winter following a wet summer was sometimes heavy through malnutrition or disease. Milk production fell; calves were born weak; and cows became dangerously thin, to say the least. The hay looked bad, smelt bad and was sometimes extremely dusty.

It soon became apparent that if a man could afford a mowing machine, he could save his hay quickly, and have good hay also, by snatching at the few good sunny days that always came even in the wettest of years. And there were many wet years and dark summers in Drumlahan in those days. To be sure there was still enough manpower in the country to mow the meadows with the scythe; but the weather was now the deciding factor. With the drop in tillage and the increase in the numbers and the value of cattle, the heavy rainfall and the mowing machine made decisions that no-one in Drumlahan could resist.

Of course it was firmly believed by many wise people that meadows would never be the same again once they had been shaved by the blades and the fingers of that Pierce single-horse mowing machine. The grass would grow slower and a nasty tough moss would creep over the sole, it was said. Thistles and scoutguns would flourish; and the soil would harden and become like a brick or a wall.

Worse still, the hustle of the mowing machine would put paid to the age-old ritual involved in hay-making. There would have to be less turning and tedding; lapping would have to go and handshakings to be cut to the minimum. There would be no time for tramped cocks with the shanks neatly trimmed; there would be no time for the twisting hayropes that were a delight to the eye; never again would every massive cock of hay be topped by a cap of scythe-cut, green grass. The rick-making, with all the neighbours involved, would be threatened by the new invention; not to mention the jollification that always followed, with dancing and singing and the drinking of porter. All that and more was in time to vanish and die as the clickety-click of the mowing machines advanced across the meadows. But it did mean more and better hay for the cattle and less strenuous work for the farmers and for their families.

The loy, however, was a different matter: it was more stubborn than the scythe and it held out bravely for much longer. It was a heavy, wooden, homemade implement, generally of ash and about four foot six inches long. It had a heavy blade made of iron that slipped easily onto the base when the blacksmith had made it red hot.

The loy had many things going for it. Firstly, there was no time problem and no weather problem involved. A man could stroll out to his chosen field, even in early February if he liked, and although drowsy after his annual hibernation, he could proceed to have all his oats-ground and his potato-ground ready by mid-April. It did not matter to him what sort the weather was during that spring period. In fact the loy could have a decided advantage on land that would be too wet for the horses and plough, perhaps until mid-April itself.

When Ned and Danny and Berney or Uncle Peter gathered in Flynns' on their ceili at night, there would be much argument about whether the plough or the loy gave the heaviest crop. Ned Martin and Berney were strong loy men: the loy made it easier for the potato bud to come up through the soil; the ploughed sod was too deep and too glazed, like a plastered wall. Tommy and Danny argued that a root or a bud would push their way through anything, even concrete. Look at how the roots of a tree will push their way down through a rock and through stones in a wall or in a quarry.

'A prata and a tree differs,' countered Ned.

It was all very difficult, very worrying. Some people tried to compromise by ploughing one sod of the potato ridge with the plough and by digging the other side with the loy. It wasn't just diplomacy: it was fear of the unknown: it was a cautious testing of the waters.

Furious arguments flared up everywhere. Strong men went about their daily work uneasy and afraid and with weights on their minds. For a time it looked as if the matter could be far more divisive in Drumlahan than the Anglo-Irish Treaty had been or the Civil War that followed it. It was thrown in the faces of the loy-men that they were unprogressive; that they were the same sort of people as those who had resisted knapsack spraying machines, creameries, mowing-machines, artificial manure and the castration of cattle by Burdizzo instead of by the blunt knife.

The arguments of the loy-men were subtle and sometimes almost theological in quality. The loy meant that the work could be spread over a longer period of time. All the tillage was done, well done and done in time. The sod was exposed to the air and to the weather longer before planting and sowing. Easier growth and better crops resulted. Horses and ploughs tramped the soil into a horrible putty or tramped it down so that it baked hard in the sun later on. Neither did the loy-dug field suffer from drought as easily or as badly as the ploughed field. Ploughing also resulted in bad and untidy farming, with large areas at the head and the foot of the field going to waste and remaining untilled.

The loy-men caused fury when they taunted the plough-men with being bone lazy, shiftless and with just going soft – they did nothing during winter and they were trying to corner another two months for moping about when they could be out digging in God's fresh air. The most stinging taunt of the loy-men was that the use of their implement was a more patriotic activity than following the plough. After all, weren't their fathers and grand-fathers, and even their long-dead Irish ancestors, faithful to the loy through famine and brutality? And wasn't there a priest not far away who had started a back-to-the-loy movement? In no time the Church would come out in favour of the loy, you'd see. Soon the heavy wooden iron-shod implement became, to some, a symbol of manliness and of uprightness, of decency and of stability.

Of course, there was the usual changing of sides. Some weakened and went over to the plough. A few came scurrying back, shamefacedly, spat viciously on their palms, muttered 'never again!' and grabbed the nearest loy. Some others there were who found excuses for going over to the plough and deserting the loy. The most common excuse was pains (rheu-matics, to the locals), which was closely followed by getting old, family growing up and going away, and, of course 'herself'. This last excuse meant that the wife was kicking up stink in the domestic field.

None the less, it soon became clear to the young men, the farmers' sons and the labourers, who had to do most of the actual digging, that there was little or no difference between loy-work and plough-work when it came to crop yield and the harvest. They were very concerned about results – which meant more money in the pocket and in the bank – and they came to believe that yield depended on factors other than the plough or the loy. Yield depended more on the weather, the quality of the seed, the length of the growing season, temperature and correct and ample manuring, lime content, type of soil or, when necessary, thoroughness of spraying.

The controversy raged unabated for some years; but the crunch came in Drumlahan when Micky Callaghan, a man who had blithely gone over to the plough earlier on, suddenly turned his coat and came back to the loy.

It happened one January evening when he came back half-shot

57

from the fair of Arva where he had sold an in-calf heifer for what was considered to have been a very good price. He sat down at the upper end of the table and announced to his wife and to his two bewildered sons that, henceforth, all the ground for the potatoes and the oats, as well as the bit for rye down in the bottom, would have to be dug with the loy. A very knowledgeable man from Gortnagullion that he met in Heeran's pub had convinced him, he said, that it was a great error of judgment for him to have gone over to the plough. He knew a man who wanted a cheap plough. He'd see him after second Mass in Ballydoon on Sunday and sell it to him. The quicker they got the infernal thing away from about the house, the better for everyone. He expanded then on the virtues and on the manliness of digging with the loy. It was great exercise, especially for the youth. His announcement was greeted with dead silence and utter amazement.

Micky then took possession of an armchair on the other side of the kitchen and quickly dropped into an alcoholic snooze. He had a hissing snore that was almost indistinguishable from the sound coming from the pot of potatoes that was boiling furiously on the fire beside him. The mother and the two sons rushed around the yard, feeding pigs, foddering cattle, milking cows and closing doors and gates for the night.

When the last job was done, Tim, the eldest and the quietest of the family, washed his hands at the pump. He was next seen to run across the yard and into the house. He grabbed his slumbering parent roughly by the shoulder and shook him. 'Waken up! Waken up! You silly ould *amadáun* yeh!' he shouted.

The father's knees shot up towards his chin and he awoke with a snarling snore and a resounding grunt. He sat up straight in the armchair; rubbed his popping eyes and then drew the back of his hand across his soaking moustache. He had never seen Tim in a rage before. 'Tim, the dummy' he called him always.

'You can forget about that bloody loy!'

'What loy?' exclaimed the father. He had forgotten about his speech of half an hour earlier. But his mind quickly cleared.

'Look! You and that eejit from Gortnagullion can get out and take you own flaming exercise with the loy, if yez want to. I'm not doing any more loy-work and that's final.'

'You'll do what I say, my boy! You'll do what is best for this house and for your family. And don't let me hear you saying things like that about the Gortnagullion people. Don't forget either that your grandmother – and my own mother, God rest her – came to this house from Gortnagullion long before you were born.'

'I don't care a damn if she came from the back streets of Carrick or from hell, either!'

'Such impertinence from a young pup! Is he possessed by the devil this evening, or what?'

'Look! If that oats-ground and the ground for the spuds is going to be dug, then I'm not digging. D'ye hear?'

'You'll dig it, my boy, and no arguments.'

'I'll not! Divel a loy I'll ever sink in them fields again. I'll be beyant in Derbyshire! I'll be in Buxton be St Patrick's Day.'

And so he was.

Whether this was the reaction of a progressive young man to the out-of-date; or whether it was the little push, the hidden excuse that a hesitating Irish emigrant needed to get him on his way, we can never know. He left behind him his inheritance – fifty acres of fine land and a decent sum in the bank – and he worked hard as a labourer for some years at the lime kilns in Buxton.

From the fateful day that his father met the man from Gortnagullion in Heeran's bar until he took the train for England at Drumlahan station, Tim talked volubly to all and sundry about the old man's crazy plan to revert to the loy. He was incensed. He cursed his father for being so daft and for refusing to see reason. Rather than accept that state of affairs he would emigrate and leave behind him all that was rightfully his. Rather than lose face, the father was just as stubborn and was prepared to lose his son. A quiet, diffident young man, the very devil seemed to have got into him.

This family row and especially its implications were a topic for hectic debate all over the parish. In a way, Tim Callaghan became a moral leader of the young people and of the anti-loy people, although he was never to realise it. Parents took the hint: they did not want their sons setting out for Buxton in a similar mood or in similar circumstances. No disrespect to Buxton, of course — there was good money to be earned there. But circumstances do alter cases.

Quite soon all the debate and controversy died down; and from then on all the tillage was performed by the horses and the swing plough. The one-wheeled plough began to roll in almost immediately. The loy became a thing of the past. Soon it was being used only for planting cabbage in ley ground; or for digging graves, in the claggy soil of the new graveyards.

It was just a family tiff that took place in Callaghans' on that January evening after the fair of Arva. But because of the two antagonists it grew into something that finally ruined the family; but which in its repercussions was felt far and wide by many people, both young and old. It ended much argument and recrimination. It hastened the end of a way of life that was age-old. It was indeed the end of an era.

Tim and his family lost contact with each other soon after his departure for Buxton. Afterwards he worked with a building contractor and he moved all over the United Kingdom. As his mother lay dying she called his name all through a day and a night. He could not be found. An SOS was broadcast on the radio, but it was in vain. He fought later in the war and he was in uniform from the very beginning to the very end — just like his Uncle Joe in 1914–18.

Forty years after his flight from the loy, he returned to Drumlahan railway station. He was staying in a hotel in Ballinwing; but he returned just to see the old home, now sold three times over. He went as far as the garden gate and paused. He went no further: he turned and slowly walked away. He could not see the fields now where once he had wielded that controversial implement. The untrimmed hedges had grown so high. There was no tillage in evidence now. All the fields were under rough, wild grass. The days of tidy farming were gone. It was a complete reversal of the old challenging slogans that were once so frequently painted on the roads when Tim was a young man going to Mass on Sunday. In contrast they could now have read: THE LAND FOR THE BULLOCK AND THE ROAD FOR THE PEOPLE.

9

The egg trees

Some time after Tommy and Veronica married they acquired a gramophone. It had a large horn, which Seamus later used for playing soldiers by putting it on his head. It had a small crank for winding it up, and there was a large collection of records of every sort: Irish traditional dance music, jazz from the Savoy Hotel in London, two Gilbert and Sullivan records with *HMS Pinafore* on each side, and also many records with traditional ballads, all of them sung by a man named Shaun O'Nolan. John McCormack was represented; there was something from *The Maid of the Mountains*; and one faint, scratchy side had Sandy MacPherson playing an organ. Comedy or crude farce was represented by a number of 'Casey' records, in which the versatile Michael Casey went to the dentist, fought and lost a thumping match with little Owney Geghegan and later proposed marriage to a reluctant but rich widow. There was 'The Laughing Policeman', and a yellow-coloured record from America with 'Alexander's Ragtime Band' on one side and the story of a philandering bigamist, named Dapper Dan, on the other side. There was also a record with, on one side, a fellow who claimed to be 'a gay cabellero, coming from Rio Janeiro', while on the second side an individual with an oily voice asserted that he wanted 'to be alone with Mary Brown'.

Over the years many more records were acquired in dribs and drabs, from here and there. Many records were dropped also, never to sing again. This would lead to much recrimination and lamentation. Records were always being borrowed for weddings and parties, or when Yankees returned from New York or other American cities. They were meticulously returned. Gramophones were borrowed and loaned gladly for such special occasions.

Many of the more staid women quietly visited one another on

Sunday evenings. There would be much secret talk and exchanging of confidences. If there was a gramophone around they closed themselves in a room and listened avidly to every available record, while the men went elsewhere. Men learned to keep away from sessions of that kind.

Another acquisition some time after the marriage was a large crystal ball. It rested mysteriously in a glass bowl with wavy edges at the back of a drawer. It was said that if you went into a quiet room, placed the crystal ball on a black cushion and gazed steadily into it until you had forgotten about everything else, you could see many of the events the future held for you.

Veronica was very careful of the crystal ball. Seamus went suddenly into his parents' room one hot afternoon in summer. She was sitting at the beside with her head resting in her hands, which also covered her ears. She was gazing intently at the crystal ball which was resting on a black cushion on the counterpane. He retreated silently.

Whenever Tommy was away, Jimmy Gaffney sometimes came in, mostly on a Sunday evening. Nothing was ever said about the crystal ball, but Veronica knew what he wanted. Quietly she produced the black cushion and the ball and, closing the kitchen door, she went out, leaving him to his explorations and his fortune telling. Afterwards, he would swear that he could see the most surprising things in that ball. He invariably went away with an abstracted look on his face.

Tommy was ever on the scrounge. He could disappear now and then without anyone noticing his absence. He would have gone to the town, two miles away. The disappearances took place at night, after the cows were milked and all the work finished. He would return in the dark and come into the kitchen looking cold and pale and quiet as he began to pull things out of his pockets or from an old patchwork shopping bag made of cloth.

'I went into the town for a bit of tobacco,' he'd say in a matter of fact tone. No-one believed him.

He then proceeded to display, rather diffidently, old newspapers of every sort: American comics, copies of *Picture Post* and *Social Justice*, an American magazine edited by Fr Coughlan, old cowboy paperbacks, *Dublin Opinion*s in abundance, dozens of *Agriculture Ireland*s, the *Garda Review*, the *Catholic Standard*, collections of ghost and murder stories, *Pearson's Weekly*, the *Smallholder*, the *Irish Digest* and a few old copies of the *Far East*, a Catholic missionary magazine, and some very old editions of *Our Boys*. Everyone could find something he could browse through. Ned Martin and Jimmy Gaffney, when they came in, always picked up plenty from the supply. Tommy seemed proud of this and of his ability to cater for their reading requirements. Jim Murray, the Rochdale man, was in his element on such occasions. He cornered plenty and stuffed his pockets.

Tommy was frequently on the lookout for gramophone records; and from time to time he returned home on dark nights, after slithering his way out the railway line from sleeper to sleeper, with many interesting items of plunder. Some of the records were in top-class condition; some were cracked and requiring that the needle be lifted over the injured spot. Others were so old and hoarse that the performer was scarcely audible.

He didn't like many of the records sold in McLoughlin's in the Main Street. He liked reels and jigs and the fiddle-playing in general. He could not stand patriotic ballads. In fact he disliked Irish songs, apart from Moore's melodies.

He was a proud man when he came home one night from the tobacco run with two particular records: one had 'The Blue Danube Waltz' on one side and a waltz called 'Over the Waves' on the other side. The second record had Heddle Nash singing two songs from *Maritana*, one of which was 'There is a Flower that Bloometh'. '*Maritana*, the best Irish opera. Yeh might say the only Irish opera there ever was. An' all by Bill Wallace from Waterford.'

He wound up the gramophone and had both records going for hours. He called Heddle Nash, 'Hedd-ley Nash'. This was the kind of music he had learned to enjoy when the travelling light-opera companies came regularly to Ballinwing, when he was running wild as a turbulent youth without parental control, after his father's jailing and death. He also heard some light opera in Newry, in the Black North, when they were having him taught drapery. He liked jazz; he loved Percy French and could sing many of his comic songs; and he delighted in Jimmy O'Dea doing the old Dublin woman.

It was quite by chance that Seamus discovered the egg trees. They were growing in a large clump on the edge of the mearing drain, and not too far away from the plank across the stream. He was attracted first by the little white eggs which grew on the branches. They were smaller than marbles and they exploded with a little shot when pressed between the finger and the thumb.

Later on, when the bushes were covered with foliage, he got down on his hands and knees and crawled beneath the dense undergrowth. He found to his surprise that the ground was heaped with broken glass and crockery of every sort. There were mugs, dishes, cups, saucers, plates, bottles, jars, crocks and teapots. He was delighted. Some were washed clean by the rain and sparkled in the sunlight. Some were covered in a dark green moss. They were of all shapes and strange sizes. It was the debris of the kitchens of four generations of McCartins.

He did not tell anyone about what he had found. How could he explain this treasure? He would be called a *glincín*, as usual, and admonished for being 'so giddy'. But the egg trees became a refuge for him. And whenever he wanted to escape domestic displeasure or to think, or to muse, he slipped into the clump of egg trees beside the mearing drain.

The first time he found the egg trees useful was some days after his father happened to say to him that the bones of all animals are soft immediately after birth. He added that the same went for humans. In fact the skull of every baby is soft at the crown just after birth. This surprised Seamus greatly. He fingered his own small skull and found it to be quite solid. But he decided to investigate further. He remembered that the new baby at Martins' would be in the pram at the railway gates. He walked quietly up the road and advanced to the pram. He touched the baby gently with his fingers on the top of the head. He pulled back his hand quickly and ran for his life. The skull was soft and hot and something seemed to move inside it. By the time he reached home he was feeling ill and weak. He could not risk telling anyone about the experience. He took refuge in the secrecy of the egg trees. It was a long time before he regained his composure and crawled out on his hands and knees to face the world again.

Nan-nan said that everyone must die. In the egg trees he thought it over and came to the conclusion that he himself would never die. He could not imagine what it would be like to die. But it could never happen to him. He would live for ever.

All the local men smoked – Woodbines, Players or Murray's and Clark's tobacco. Some of them chewed tobacco. Tommy said that, by all the gods in heaven, he would kill Seamus if he ever attempted to smoke. Up to then he had never thought of it. But a great longing to smoke seized him and he did not know what to do. Then he hit on peeling a leaf off his father's plug of Murray's tobacco and having a quiet chew alone in the egg trees. The taste was awful; but the excitement was great.

It was in the egg trees that he began to hear certain sounds of the countryside for the first time. He could hear the bells of six chapels ringing the Angelus at different times, depending on the direction of the wind. He could hear the water cascading at lock four and lock five on the canal. People said that when lock five could be heard there would be frost. When lock four could be heard the weather would be dry and warm.

He could hear the swans calling out on frosty nights now as they swam frantically to and fro on Clonmoher lake in an attempt to stop the ice from forming. He first heard them from the egg trees.

And sometimes in the evenings was heard the distant puff-puff of the engine at the sawmill in Ballinwing that drove the dynamo to produce electric light for the town from dusk to midnight.

He attempted to entice the two dogs into his haven. Neither would come in. Foreman, the tongue-hound, would not come near the egg trees. Sammy, the sheepdog, would come in for a piece of bread, and would immediately run out again. But when poor Sammy died of distemper, Seamus began to train the terrier pup, Snap, that came in his place, to enter the egg-tree haven. He was fully successful in this.

And as he sat there among the broken pottery and crockery chewing tobacco, he pondered the problems of his life. How could he persuade Jack Martin to take him along whenever he went to dare that bull at a gate beyond Aughabeg bridge. How could he get Jack to show him how to make explosions with a canister and carbide. He'd love to be able to do that. He could frighten the life out of Nan-nan and AB. It would be great fun.

He first heard the Ballydoon Fife and Drum Band out practising when he was sitting in the egg trees. And how often did he sit there listening to the noise of the train as it started up at the station in Ballinwing, came out to Martins' at Drumlahan, and then slowly puffed its way over the hill and past two other stations before its sound eventually died away in the distance.

His great worry of course was stirabout. Nan-nan and AB insisted that he devour a mug of it morning and evening. To him it was as poison. How he hated it! It was something which was just too distasteful to ponder on in the egg trees, where there was peace and quiet and where the birds came so close to you that you could almost touch them.

10

Dealing men

The cattle fair of Ballinwing was held on the first market day of
the month. Nan-nan and AB had business in town, and they
decided to take Seamus with them. They walked briskly up the
road, boarded the train at Drumlahan station, and soon they were
in Ballinwing. It was Seamus's first day at the fair.

The railway station was situated at the upper end of the town,
in Ardnaboe. The two old ladies had an extremely low opinion of
Ardnaboe and of all those who lived there. They placed Seamus
between them; each gripped one of his hands; they stopped
talking; and they set out from the station walking very quickly.
They seemed to expect that they could be attacked, or that
someone would attempt to snatch the *aurcaun* who was toddling
between them, and then sell him to the tinkers, or worse.

AB kept her head well down and her free hand was held firmly
across her mouth and nose on the outside of her veil. There were
sights she did not want to see; there was air she did not want to
breathe. Nan-nan, in sharp contrast, held her head defiantly high,
with her nose in the air and her brown eyes surveying the scene
with menace. Her right hand, which was free except for an empty
shopping bag that hung from the elbow, was gathered into a tight
fist. It moved slowly up and down, and it was ready to defend, or
to attack, as need might be. The two soon began to converse in
fitful undertones over Seamus's head.

'Did you see that, Bee? The tory! The blackguard!'

'Tch! Tch! Tch! Indeed I saw it, Anne!'

'Let us walk as quick as we can and get down to the Main Street.
This place is a danger to both God and man.'

'Aye indeed! Watch your bag, Anne! They'd whip it.'

'Troth then I will, Bee! Nothing is safe nor sacred here.'

The danger they were encountering seemed to make them more civil and confidential to each other than they usually were. A great change for the better.

It was true that in some quarters Ardnaboe had a very bad name indeed. To say you had any truck or relationship with anyone who lived there branded you immediately as not being up to very much.

'Aw, Ardnaboe, is it? What would you expect? Whin yeh lie with the dog, yeh get up with the flays! Ardnaboe is it? The home of every foul-mouthed corner-boy that ever God created!'

If you were accused of using Ardnaboe language, it could mean that either your soul or your grammar needed attention. If you came from Ardnaboe itself, you were thought to be lazy, probably dishonest, and of weak moral fibre. And every epidemic that plagued the parish, whether it was flu, measles, diphtheria, mumps, the common cold or any other obscure ailment, was thought to have originated somewhere in Ardnaboe.

It scandalised the two women who conducted Seamus through this moral and medical slough, that Tommy Flynn, the boy's father, was on very close terms of friendship with many of the Ardnaboe people. He had cronies in Ardnaboe, no less. He confided in them and they confided in him. He even attended their wakes and their funerals when they died. His brother, Peter, was on the closest terms with some of them in New York, whither so many had emigrated that there was one whole street in the Bronx called, unofficially, 'Ardnaboe'. Neither Tommy nor his brother would ever let one bad word be said against the people who lived in the little thatched houses by the narrow streets that crept up the hill high above the railway station at Ballinwing. The people of Ardnaboe had not the pride of ancestry nor of blood that characterised Nan-nan, AB and the late Uncle James. Neither were they cast in the same heroic mould.

'They're decent; but unfortunate,' Tommy and Peter often would say.

Ardnaboe people knew all about dogs, cats, ferrets, bantam fowl and fighting game-cocks. Many of them could make motor-cars start when no-one else could. And, once started, they could make anything on four wheels perform like a racer. They were good with gramophones, clocks, broken-down radios or cat's whisker jobs. A few of them were first-class tinsmiths. They produced many musicians, who were certainly not traditional, but who performed in an interesting mixture of styles and who could entertain and compel attention. You could always recognise the peculiar sound of an Ardnaboe man playing an instrument or singing a song.

They picked blackberries and wild fruit seriously. They knew every trick of the angler and of the poacher, from making your own flies to putting hot lime in trout streams. Many of them joined the British army, and names of exotic places like Mesopotamia, Antigua, Bombay, the Khyber Pass, Singapore or Fiji were constantly rolling off their tongues in a quiet and matter-of-fact way. They did not indulge in crime or in law-breaking, except for the occasional petty theft. Their family rows and quarrels were no more frequent than anyone else's. But perhaps, in their social innocence, they were much more loud and much more indiscreet and public in their domestic disputes and differences.

Few of them had a solid trade. Many worked as casual farm labourers at such times as the setting and the digging of the potatoes and at the reaping of the oats. But they would have had no taste and, one sensed, less ability, to run a small farm success-fully or to endure the usual drudgery that it entailed. They had no property and no urge or ability to acquire it. They were far better travelled, both locally and in the world, than any other section of the community. They were religious and prayerful; and yet were not thought to be so. They were good at football; but better still at handball and card-playing. They were considered to be late to bed and late to rise. Their children were poor attenders at school.

The only way out of Ardnaboe was the British army, or Yankeeland when the fare could be scraped together. But in the New York Bronx they lived almost the same simple, innocent life that they did at home; and they quickly established another Ardnaboe there to suit their tastes and their cast of mind. A few of them had close links with the travelling tinkers; and periodically they went on the road themselves, for a year or two, only to return

69

eventually and set up house in the old homeground again. Tommy, Seamus's father, was often lamenting one of their girls, a beauty, who married a tinker and went on the road with him, and never came back.

'Kathleen Skinnion. As fine a girl as you ever left eyes on! Married that wastrel and went on the road with him for the rest of her life. A tragedy. A crying shame, if ever there was one!'

And how did Ardnaboe come to be there in the first place, one might well enquire. One of its poorest families, in a way, partly explained it. Originally, they were extremely small, poor farmers and were living out Clonmoher way. They were reduced to selling their only cow to pay unavoidable bills. But they had two young heifers still left. The evening the husband sold the cow at the fair, he came home in the heavy rain and hid the money in a safe place in the rafters, high over the narrow half-loft in the cabin. He went out then to help a neighbour who was in difficulties. As darkness fell, two men with blackened faces came in and demanded the money from the woman. She refused them. They punched her; they twisted her arm; they ignored the two toddlers screaming in terror. They gave her one more chance. She refused it. They ripped off all her clothes. Stark naked they held her sitting over the flames of the kitchen fire. She soon told them where the money was hidden.

That family was ruined. All was lost. They were lucky to find a little shack in Ardnaboe. It was the children and the grandchildren of people like that woman, as well as the children of the weak and the effete, that Nan-nan and AB held in such fear as they hurried down from the train to the Main Street. There was indeed much truth in what Tommy and his brother said about the people of Ardnaboe. 'They are decent; but unfortunate.'

Nan-nan and AB advanced down the town with the poor little *aurcaun* trotting between them. They were soon among the cows and the calves, the bullocks and the horses, the heifers and the carts full of pink, sucking pigs. There were the shrewd-looking men mooching around in search of a bargain. There were smugglers galore, trench-coated and with sharp, uncomfortable Northern accents. There was loud bargain-making with plenty of banter and abuse. There were the show-offs putting prices on cattle and chinning horses that they hadn't the means nor the intention of buying. They fooled no-one; not even themselves. There were people with delft and household goods spread out in squares along the street, roaring themselves hoarse. There were several cantmen with their covered standens, selling clothes for humans and harness for horses. AB hurried Seamus past the cantmen.

'We don't want the child to pick up any of that coarse, vulgar language. You can't be too careful with childer. They hear everything; they take in everything.'

'Troth, Bee, there's great value he's selling now. Not half the price you'd pay for it in a draper's shop.'

Nan-nan was hanging back covetously. The *aurcaun* had a woman pulling on both of his arms and was writhing in pain. AB won the goat-pulling contest and led the two moralistically further down the street.

They came to the Market House. There was a large clock high in its stone-cut wall. It had a blue face and golden hands that hung limply downwards. AB said that the clock didn't strike because the man forgot to wind it up. They could see through the heavy wrought-iron gates that the market yard was full of carts loaded with bags of potatoes and oats. There were loads of hay and several carts of turnips.

The three turned and went back up the street again. Unexpectedly they met Tommy and Jim Gaffney strolling nonchalantly towards them with dung-covered boots, open overcoats, hats on the back of their heads and each with an ashplant under the right arm.

'Did yez sell?' roared Nan-nan, evidently glad to see them.

'Aye, we did,' said Tommy.

'Was it a good fair?'

'Divel a good! If it wasn't for the smugglers there wouldn't be a hoof bought the day.'

Tommy and Jim both had something to sell that day. They drove their cattle to the fair together. They were lucky to sell so early in the day as well. The farming community was in the grips of the economic war with England. Some would say that Tommy and Jim were soft sellers: they always sold when they went out. Many went to several fairs before selling.

'We have some business to do,' said Nan-nan, after they were talking for a while with the two men. She and AB moved away.

'All right,' said Tommy. 'We'll take Seamus.'

He walked along with them. They bought chocolate toffees for him and they lingered with him before the cantmen. He could learn all the coarse language he liked now, so far as they were concerned. The two of them walked on further and they helped to make a bargain at the sale of a cow, and later at the sale of a pair of sucking pigs. There was much spitting on palms, slapping of hands and loud talk about 'splitting the difference' and giving 'a good luck penny'. Tommy left Jim gazing into a cart of sun-bathing sucking pigs and, dragging Seamus by the hand, nipped into the public library to borrow a book. He wanted it to be a secret and that no-one should see him.

'Did you get what you wanted?' asked Jim when they returned from the library with two books instead of one.

'Aye, Aye! The Bulldog and wan of Zane's.'

By this he meant Bulldog Drummond and Zane Grey. He stuck a book furtively into each of his overcoat pockets.

'We'll show Seamus the pluckers,' exclaimed Jim.

'The very thing – aye, we'll show him the pluckers.'

They walked down the noisy, bustling, dirty street that was crowded with man and beast, the bookworm and the womaniser, with posterity trotting between them, in short trousers and a nap coat with silver buttons. A cap, many sizes too big for it, was wobbling on its light little head.

They cut up Church Street, which was just as crowded as the Main Street. Tommy knocked on a door in a high wooden shed. A man from Ardnaboe opened to them. He had a great welcome for them both.

'We wanted to show this young man what happens to the hens, the turkeys and the geese when we sell them.'

Two men sat grinning at the far side of the shed, plucking and in a bank of feathers. A young fellow, not much bigger than Seamus, was packing the feathers into bags. He was covered with down.

He was like a young snowman come to life and eager to earn a living for himself away from the winter and the cold. Afterwards, the two pluckers scarcely lifted their eyes from their work; the man from Ardnaboe and the two men from Drumlahan never stopped talking; the boy who was bagging the feathers and the boy Seamus never stopped looking at each other intently and questioningly.

When, at length, they left and the door of the plucking house closed behind them, a loud, sharp noise caused Seamus to start.

'Did he ever see the sawmill working?' asked Jim.

'How the divel could he? Wan iv his age!'

Without another word, they entered the sawmill, which was next door to the plucking house. There was heat and power in the air. The huge wheel spun menacingly. The engine exploded slowly and steadily. The long belt drove the saw that screamed when the workmen pushed in the tree trunks, as they half-closed their eyes and turned their faces aside to avoid the shooting sawdust. There were heaps of the fragrant dust everywhere. The noise was oppressive. Tommy took great pains to point out the town's dynamo to Seamus. It was driven at night by the same engine that was now driving the saw. He remembered that he could hear it from the egg trees. But he wanted to get away from it quickly now.

It seemed so quiet afterwards as they went down Church Street where a crowd of the townschildren were skipping and playing with scooters and yo-yos. It was great to be out in the fresh air and away from that wheel and that awful circular saw. The crowds seemed to have thickened in Main Street. Someone was playing a melodeon.

He could now see it was a medium-sized man, a little lame, with black, wavy hair and tanned skin. He had a slow, friendly face. He had been in the Great War, with the Inniskillings, he said. Got a bit of shrapnel. Came back to the girl he left behind him. 'She was still there; waiting for her soldier boy, as she called him. There was no more to be said. This song tells the story better than I could:

Farewell Enniskillen, farewell for a while,
And all around the borders of Erin's green isle.
When the war is over we'll return in full bloom,
And they'll all welcome home the Enniskillen Dragoon.'

The crowd cheered with delight. They pitched in the coppers and they made him sing it again. Most of them, especially the young ones, had never heard the song before. They were delighted with it and with the lame man's rendering of it. He suddenly limped towards a public house to slake his thirst, his instrument hanging carelessly on his chest. He was a most likeable little man.

'Don't be long!' someone shouted. 'And don't get boozed! We want more iv that stuff. It's a sight better nor jazz!'

'Is it "The Enniskillen Dragoon"?' Tommy asked a rhetorical question. 'I heard me brother, Eddie, singing that song years and years ago. Many a man from around here joined the Inniskillings in the ould days. Any of the Ardnaboe lads that joined the British army nearly always went into the Inniskillings, or into the Connaught Rangers. But you know, the Rangers were outright devils, even when they were sober, never mind when they were blithero. The "Devil's Own" they used to call them. You had British regiments called the King's Own this, or the Queen's Own that. The Connaught Rangers were called the "Devil's Own".'

The three strolled up the town again and soon they met Nannan and AB, who were coming towards them, laden down with parcels and talking energetically to two other women of their own stamp and age, also heavily laden. There were effusive greetings all round.

'It's not such a bad fair at all, I hear.'

'Yeh may thank the smugglers for that.'

'Had yez anything out?'

'Two suck-calves. He got eighteen shillings for them.'

'It's better nor cutting their throats and selling the skins for seven and sixpence apiece!'

'Terrible times we're living in. Bad luck to de Valera! But isn't the music great?'

'It's grand music. It would lift your heart, God knows.'

The little Inniskilling Dragoon had started up again. The music could be heard above the tumult of the fair.

'Aw, Tommy, is this young *gossin* here a son of yours? I didn't notice him there. Isn't he the grand lump of a lad, God bless him, and quiet too! He's wan iv yours Tommy, isn't he?'

One of the talkative women who had arrived with the two grandaunts was suddenly full of curiosity about Seamus.

'That little *aurcaun* there, is it?' said Tommy, nodding his head towards Seamus enquiringly.

'Aye indeed. He's a fine *gossin*. He has his mother's eyes; but he's like you in the face, somehow, Tommy.'

'Aw, he has his mother's eyes, no doubt. But he's not my son. He's a son of Danny Mulvey's. Yeh know Danny that hunts with the tongue-hounds?'

There was stunned silence; but only for a few seconds. The two talkative women and Jim Gaffney burst out in peals of laughter. Nan-nan and AB looked at each other in disgust. They shook their heads in shamed disapproval.

'Never mind him, Julia,' said Nan-nan. 'That's going a bit too far. Some of the younger generation have no manners these days. Fancy such talk before a young and innocent *gossin*!'

'Come on, sonny,' ordered AB, gripping Seamus's hand. 'We'll catch the train and get home at wanced. There's far too much bad language in this place for children's ears.'

'Troth, then, you could say that again Bee!' agreed Nan-nan.

'But look here, Julia,' said Tommy. 'Before you go now, would you look at that head? Now, did you ever see the like of that in your born life before?'

He had gently pushed Seamus towards Julia and her companion. He parted the hair on Seamus's scalp tenderly to show the *ares* of the cuts and the wounds sustained from time to time by falling off the alder plank and into the waters of the mearing drain in Drumlahan. Tommy seemed to be proud of them.

'In the name of God, where did he get all the cuts and *ares*. It's a wonder he's not dead! How did he get them at all?'

'Falling into the river.'

'God bless us! He'll kill himself.'

'Divel a kill! There's great bone in that child. The Mulveys were all a tough, rough breed. And whisper, Julia. Seamus isn't the only one that walked the plank and took the plunge into the mearing drain, head over heels.'

'Come on, Seamus. Goodbye, Julia,' said AB.

Tommy continued: 'If some people would take off their feathery bonnets and their tall, black caubeens, there'd be more cut and battered heads about than you would ever expect.'

Just then the melodeon music started up again nearby and when the musician swung into 'The Enniskillen Dragoon' there followed an outburst of clapping. Many who were at a loose end were moving towards the melodeon player. Those who could not move and who were minding cattle or pigs, were humming or whistling the tune to themselves. All were listening to it, even when looking at a pig in a cart, when restraining a frustrated bullock, or when making a bargain. Some hissed it through their teeth.

Nan-nan and AB had grabbed Seamus in haste and went up the town in silence. As they entered the Ardnaboe district, they began to talk about Tommy and his bad language, especially in front of children. No names mentioned of course.

When coming to the fair they had walked through Ardnaboe in comparative silence and in deep apprehension. On their return they seemed to have forgotten about their earlier fears. Instead, they talked with vehemence about what Tommy had said, 'out before the whole town', as they stood talking in Main Street. He was long-tongued and no mistake.

'Danny Mulvey, indeed! Tch! Tch! Tch!' mused AB.

'And falling off the plank into the drain. I don't know where Tommy's decency is gone to,' lamented Nan-nan.

Seamus thought that it was all great fun. His father could tell great jokes indeed. And he could make Nan-nan and AB vexed. He liked that. He liked listening to grown-ups talking. They sometimes said so many things that weren't true. It would be strange to have Danny Mulvey for a father. He didn't think he'd like it at all. But then perhaps a *gossin* could have two fathers. He'd have to ask Jim Gaffney the next time he gave him a ride on the ass's back. Jim was good at explaining things.

11

Buffmen

Party political feeling was running high, and all the household was united in condemning de Valera for the terrible things he was doing to Ireland. Cattle, whenever they could be sold, fetched the lowest prices in living memory. Calves were being slaughtered: the carcases were thrown out and the skins sold for seven shillings and sixpence each.

'Cromwell! That's what he is! Cromwell! He's even worse than Cromwell ever was,' Tommy asserted, truculently.

Eggs were being produced in abundance. There was an unlimited demand for them at fourpence a dozen.

'Christ!' said Tommy with indignation. 'You have to sell fifteen dozen eggs to pay the dog-licence.'

There was a demand for pigs; but so many of them were being produced that gluts were a frequent occurrence. Bookings had to be made nearly two months in advance by the farmers with the buyer or his agents to avert having the animals left on their hands. They were fattened in twos, threes and sometimes fours, on potatoes, skim-milk, crushed oats and Indian meal. They were slaughtered at home, disembowelled amid scenes of hectic activity, and hung by the hind legs in a barn or outhouse under lock and key. Later they were taken in a horse-cart, or an ass-cart, stiff, white and naked, to the pork market in Ballinwing.

The best buyers were usually from across the border, Portadown or Belfast, until they were threatened and warned off by men who did not live by bread alone. One of their buyers was the chubby, jovial Mr Tummon from Clones, with his dark clerical suits and his bowler hats. He was a great favourite among the farming community as he strutted up and down the town.

The new Irish bacon factories at Cavan and Claremorris were

unable to organise purchases in a smooth manner. Neither were their prices very good. A small firm, Shesgrean from Ballybofey, County Donegal, rescued the farmers of the district many a time. They were reliable buyers and they gave a fair price. Their rescue-operation came to be highly appreciated by everyone; and although the pigs they purchased eventually went over the border, the Shesgreans were never threatened or interfered with in any way.

'The cattle trade is gone, thank God! The British market is gone also, thank God!' Mr de Valera was reputed to have said. 'Now Ireland can be self-sufficient and free.'

Nan-nan and AB never stopped cursing him. The economic war was at its height. De Valera, after his election, refused to pay the land annuities to London. But before doing so he asked the lawyers for their opinion on the matter. Fully aware of what his inclinations were, they informed him that he had no moral obligation to pay. Sometime in the late twenties Mr Cosgrave, who was Mr de Valera's predecessor, had also asked the same lawyers for their opinion on the payment of the annuities. Fully aware of what his inclinations were, they had told him the annuities had to be paid to the very last penny.

These land annuities consisted of the money which was due to London to recompense it for the funds given to the landlords to purchase the land for the Irish farmers at the time of the various land acts at the beginning of the century.

De Valera halved the annuities. The farmers paid only half of what was paid by them formerly: but they paid that half to Dublin, and to Mr de Valera's government. Tommy said that this was a good thing in itself; the landlords were robbers and the descendants of robbers, in his view. Nan-nan, AB and Veronica did not agree with him at all. They argued that a bargain was a bargain, even if made with the English or the landlords. Nan-nan was strongly supported by AB when she loudly proclaimed the great and far-reaching benefits that the land acts brought to the hard-pressed people of her generation. A bargain should be kept, and she would consider herself in honour bound to stick to the letter of an agreement; and never mind de Valera, with his

78

crooked arguments and his high notions. He was a disgrace to Ireland, she asserted.

One form of retaliation used by the British government to offset the loss of the land annuities was to put a tariff on Irish cattle going into British ports or across the border.

It was this measure which caused the price of cattle to drop to levels that would have been laughable but for the despair and the demoralisation they engendered in the farming community. A farmer could go from fair to fair with his cattle without ever being asked where he was going. The arrival of the smugglers from across the border on a fair day lifted the heart of every man on the fair-green who had cattle to sell.

The smugglers were always thin, shifty-looking men, with smoking Woodbines glowing in the cup of the left hand as they eyed a beast critically. In the right hand would be an ashplant or a heavy cane, which they used to poke and measure the animal. They had sharp, nagging Northern accents, of course; but they never had very much to say. A battered hat pulled well down over the eyes and a dirty, loose-fitting trench-coat covered their slim bodies. Their popularity also stemmed from their evident skill at besting and giving the slip to the despised and anti-Catholic Royal Ulster Constabulary. For reasons that were understandable, they could buy cattle only in small numbers; but their purchases were highly valued by the farmers. Meanwhile AB added another Hail Mary to the trimmings of the rosary every night, so that God in His infinite mercy would deliver the nation from the hands of Eamon de Valera.

Mr de Valera's campaign to grow wheat at home, instead of importing it, and thus to make Ireland still more self-sufficient, and to create more employment, was regarded by very many as an impracticable dream. Among other problems encountered, the flour produced was very difficult to bake. Almost every cake of soda bread had a dark, glue-like seam at the bottom; and many cakes collapsed and the crust sagged in spots or over the entire surface after baking. It took much domestic experimentation, and a wealth of inter-family consultation, before this defect could finally be overcome. Ireland may indeed have become self-supporting in many respects; but the same could not have been said of Irish soda bread in the early stages. And soda bread was always the pride and joy of every household in those days.

None of the family regarded de Valera as being engaged in trying to do the patriotic thing, trying to make the freedom of the country full and complete, using the Treaty as it was meant to be used. To them he was a troublemaker, an unscrupulous, scheming politician with the cheek of the devil himself. They said that he was prepared to ruin the country and the farmers in order to get power, and then to keep it. Yet, when Frank McDermot – 'the Prince of Coolavin' as Veronica called him, and a member of the opposition – praised de Valera for a certain measure he had introduced, Tommy said that it was a good thing to have men like McDermot around who would speak out with honesty when needed.

None the less, the last straw for Nan-nan and AB came when word went out that Dev was going to stop the importation of tea because it was a product of the British Empire. People would soon get used to the light Spanish wine he had in mind for them instead.

'May the devil choke him and his wine!' Nan-nan's rage was awful to behold. Anyone who would dare to tamper with her mug of tay must be in league with Ould Nick himself, or have a cloven hoof at least. AB looked silently and wistfully into the fire on the hearth when she heard the news. Ned Martin was just as indignant as Nan-nan was.

'I can take care of as many pints of porter as any white man in the county of Leitrim the day. But if that eejit tampers with the tay, he deserves a volley from the Barker – two barrels at that – up in the arse!'

The Barker was the pet-name he had for the double-barrel shotgun that he used for fowling.

Berney McGovern laughed quietly. With a straight face he said that the country was never in its right mind since the tea became common. It rotted people's insides, on the quiet. The native drinks couldn't be beaten: buttermilk, whey, home ale, not to mention poteen. He wasn't in favour of light Spanish wine, but he had a glass of claret once, and it wasn't bad stuff at all. No good for a man digging with the loy or cutting turf, of course. But not bad stuff at all. Maybe Dev was right.

Berney was still a staunch supporter of de Valera, and he always sought to defend him. Yet, in deference to him, heated arguments were avoided and the conversation often changed. There were always dozens of other topics for passing the time of night.

Whenever someone went to town or to the village of Ballydoon, a newspaper was bought and the Dáil debates read out in a loud, strong voice by Tommy or Nan-nan. Reading a bit out of the paper, so that those who were working could hear it, was regarded as good manners and making for good company. Reading the newspaper silently excited the envy and the curiosity of others: they felt they were being deprived of news. And news was so dreadfully important, local or national.

Veronica seldom read the newspapers, but she did know what was going on. She avidly scanned the advertisements: day-old chickens, cabbage plants and the mail-order advertisements of Clery's and Guiney's of Dublin: she was always getting boots and shoes through the post for all in the house. The children's clothes she made herself on her Singer sewing machine. Her real reading consisted of the detective stories and the love stories she got from the library in Ballinwing.

AB read the Dáil debates quietly to herself again after the hubbub of the first reading had subsided. She indulged in much head-shaking and tch-tching at the doings of Mr de Valera, but especially at the doings of his Minister for Agriculture, Dr Ryan.

The unfortunate doctor was so despised in the Flynn household that one of the calves, a ghostly half-Jersey that could not be fattened and that could seldom be found in the evenings, was nick-named 'Dr Ryan' by all. The Minister for Agriculture was a genial, tubby, well-fed citizen with a fine national record. The weird and odd problem-calf which was called after him was just skin and bones; he had dirty blond hair that stood on end like the spines of a hedgehog; and his eyes bulged in what looked like a state of chronic terror.

Yes, Dev was a schemer, all were agreed. Yes, he caused the Civil War, all were agreed. Yes, indeed, he was right to stand up to the English now and not let them wipe their shoes in the country. Yet, he was ruining the farming community in the process. His language also was too extreme for one who put up to be a statesman. Less would do him. He criticised Cosgrave for wearing a top hat on state occasions: he himself wouldn't wear a top hat, because it looked too English and too undemocratic, he said. Yet, when he went abroad, and when he thought no-one was looking, he pulled the old top hat out of his valise and stuck it on. You couldn't be up to him! And the Flynns always said that when there had been real fighting to be done and the Black-and-Tans howling around the roads, Dev's strongest supporters now had been under the bed then, and he himself had been safe and sound in America and out of harm's way.

They believed that in Paddy Hogan, who was Minister for Agriculture in the Cosgrave administration which preceded de Valera's electoral victory in 1932, the farming community had a powerful and an understanding ally.

One more cow, one more sow,
And one more acre under the plough.

That was his non-partisan slogan, and it was known to everyone in the country. In Drumlahan they agreed around the turf fire that farmers lost heart under de Valera. Previously they had spent the winter months cutting and repairing hedges and fences, carting out top-dressing to the meadows, thatching, opening drains and sinking shores, putting new handles on implements and making loys and swingle trees. With the change of government, all that stopped, and the minimum was done to produce a crop and to try to save it.

The plough killed the tillage!
The barbed wire killed the fencing!
And the dole fucked the whole country!

Worse still, the farming community, who were once so proud and independent, began to look down on themselves as a class. Ned Martin, or anyone like him with regular hours and regular pay, was the object of not a little envy. He was considered to be very fortunate indeed. They frequently referred to themselves as 'buffmen'. The term originated in Ardnaboe and was used halfderogatively to describe anyone from the country as distinct from those of the town. But the farmers took it over themselves, something their former pride would never have let them do, and they lashed themselves with it as a term of abuse.

He's dirty, oily and greasy,
When he goes to the fair he can't sell,
And when he comes home it's like hell.
Answer: The buffman.

Berney McGovern, Uncle Peter and Jim Gaffney could often be heard saying that, or citing it from time to time as the mood took them. And hadn't Jim Gaffney himself a rollicking song that he sang to his admiring girls:

I'd rather marry a man, Ho!
With an apple in his hand, Ho!
Than marry a whiskery buffman, Ho!
With a thousand acres of land, Ho! Ho!

Everyone clapped; even those who did not hear him sing. Jim was an awful card, and no mistake; but his song found a ready response. Everyone knew what he meant. And they agreed with him: something their fathers' and mothers' generation would never have stooped to do.

Yet, all was not sunshine and tumbling in the hay in the days of Paddy Hogan. The terrible weather of the year 1924 caused catastrophic losses in cattle. Many in the west were ruined: no hay, because of incessant rain, followed by a cruel winter. Everyone expected that the new, native Irish government would find a way to help them. Alas, not a finger was raised to assist those who felt it was their due after standing up to the Black-and-Tans and quelling the disastrous Civil War that followed. They had an ultra-conservative government in power.

'What the Black '47 did to the people in Famine times, the Black '24 did to the cattle in our times,' was how Tommy described it.

The trains continued to go on Sundays with cheering crowds to the meetings and rallies of both sides. A few ultra-republicans disdained to join the raucous throngs and went to Bodenstown instead, where, at the correct time of year, shots were fired over the grave of Theobald Wolfe Tone, the Protestant father of Irish republicanism. Crowds came cycling from Clonmoher parish to board the train when it halted at Drumlahan station. Both political persuasions always pushed their bicycles up the lane and left them in Flynn's turf-shed for safety. They would never ask permission to do this, of course. Tommy might regard the followers of de Valera and the IRA as 'political yahoos'; but they knew they were free and welcome to leave their bicycles in his turf-shed. They would be safe and sound there until the train returned in the evening from honouring Dev or Duffy or the 'Prince of Coolavin'.

In Ballydoon one Sunday evening, Ned Martin, when half drunk, had a heated argument with a few members of the opposition on their way home from a heady rally. It ended in a fight in which many took part. Jim Murray, from Lancashire, went into the melee to assist Ned Martin. Ned was black and blue and unable to go to work next day: the first time he had ever been away from a job in his life. Jim Murray did better: he was out working, bright and early next morning. But he was urinating blood for nearly a week afterwards.

12

Bank robbers

It was a devil of a day. Tommy, Jim Gaffney and Uncle Peter had a terrible time rounding up all their young cattle and injecting them for blackleg. By the time they were finished with that job the braes of the roads were black with people going to the funeral of Michael Fox. It was a sad and cruel death, for Michael was a mild man, who lived with his married brother and his wife. He went to the bog to thatch a rick of turf that the wind had ruffled. By ten o'clock that night he had not returned, and the brother went to look for him. He had said that he would come home early to go to Ballinwing for groceries. It was an overcast evening and it began to rain. Sarah, Michael's sister-in-law, heard one of the cows in the byre lowing and went out to see what could be the matter. A gap came in the clouds and she saw that the full moon was rising behind the nearby pinewood. Its slanting light caught something dark hanging from the cross-beams of the hayshed. She thought that this was strange, and she approached curiously to have a closer look. It was a man's body. It was swaying ever so gently in the slight breeze which had come with the long shower of rain. Michael had not gone to the bog that morning to thatch the rick of turf. He had grabbed a rope and hanged himself in the hayshed instead, when he was sure that there was no-one looking.

Tommy was on his way home from the funeral when he heard that during the night the biggest of Ballinwing's four banks had been robbed. The sad death of Michael Fox and the immense proportions of his funeral would have been the normal topic of conversation for some time. There would have been much speculation, many theories and some fault-finding. But the robbing of the bank pushed all that aside, and Michael Fox was quickly forgotten in the excitement that followed.

Ned Martin knew all along who the robbers were, or so he said. No-one would ever have expected that particular bank, of all banks, to be robbed, for it was situated next door to the police barracks. And there were three hefty, eager policemen inside that night. They swore that they didn't hear even one unusual sound. Full of suspicion, no-one believed them. Yet, the three policemen were telling the truth, the whole truth, and nothing but the truth. They were sound asleep throughout the exploit.

And even if they had not been sleeping they could never have heard anything out of the ordinary. For the perpetrators of the crime had invited the bank manager earlier in the night to a friendly game of cards in a quiet room at the back of a pub at the lower end of Main Street. He was a master card-player, and he soon cleaned them of every penny that they had in their pockets. There were no hard feelings, of course. Moreover, it so happened that there were two bottles of whiskey which just had to be consumed before cock-crow. The bank manager was also better at drinking good red whiskey than were the green young men whom he had just beaten at cards. He had the right type of kidneys and intestines, they guessed. But they knew that, in his heart of hearts, he was much prouder of his skills as a card-player and his fame as a drinker than he was of his skills in banking and finance.

As the night wore on, the older man became drowsy and his words became slurred. Respectfully, the green young men carried him home. It just would not be the thing for the police to find a decent man like the manager of the Ulster Bank staggering home along the deserted streets of Ballinwing at one o'clock on a cold winter's night. They silently opened his hall door; got him up the stairs; and, taking off his shoes and his jacket, placed him comfortably between his sheets. Then they hurried homewards to their own warm beds, they said later on.

At 2.30 a.m. a flashlight shone on the bank manager's placid face. He could hear someone asking him for his keys. He was annoyed by the intrusion. But of course it must be that drip of a cashier, Armstrong. Impatient to get back into his sleep again, he indicated that the keys were in the left-hand drawer of his dressing table. So indeed they were. The rest of the operation was easy.

The town quickly filled up with police and detectives and there were many newspaper reporters mooching around also. People were questioned severely and interviewed diplomatically. Houses were searched and back gardens gazed upon. Fr McFee, the jumpy and bad-tempered curate with the red face, had hard things to say from the altar on the following Sunday. The old parish priest was in a state of distress, for he considered that his parish was going to the dogs. Too old and feeble to do regular parish work or to read Sunday Mass, he never failed to appear on Christmas morning and to celebrate last Mass at one of the side altars. Secretly he blamed the curate, Fr McFee, for the low moral tone now so evident in the parish and the town, let alone in Ardnaboe and the surrounding districts.

He decided he'd have to have a mission; and his housekeeper, Mrs Tubman, took down, in her very best hand, what he dictated. He signed it; he sealed it; he sent it to the Redemptorists. The news went around the town like wildfire. Fr McFee was the very last to hear of it. When the news did eventually reach his ears, he knew that his goose was cooked and that he could expect to find himself removed to some backwater away, far away, from Ballinwing and its excitements. In a way, he wasn't sorry. For him, Ballinwing meant three things: too much work, impossible people and not a spare minute for fishing.

'Never a minute to wet a line!' he often grumbled.

The parish priest thought that two Redemptorists preaching every morning and every evening for a fortnight could possibly stop the rot and halt the slide downhill. Maybe the Redemptorists could be instrumental in finding the plunder or in prompting the robbers to repent and to give themselves up. The ways of the Lord were not the ways of man.

St Mogue's Street, where the chapel was situated, soon began to fill up with stalls and standens full of, among other things, all sorts of statuary representing the saints and the blessed. There were crucifixes, holy water fonts, rosaries, medals, scapulars, *agnus dei*s, prayer books, Sacred Heart lamps and holy pictures in abundance. The stall-holders did a roaring trade as the mission drew near.

87

The two Redemptorists arrived one afternoon on the train. They were two young, tall, hungry-looking men in long black habits that reached to the ankles. They must have been starving themselves doing penance for the sins of the world. The local men thought, with glee, that two young fellows like that would never have the experience or the insight to handle the variety and the volume of sin that Ballinwing and the neighbouring districts were capable of producing. The women pitied the two starved holy creatures and wished that they could cook a few good meals for them. It was a shame to have the poor things going around like scarecrows. A bit of good cabbage and bacon would soon bring colour to their ghostly cheeks.

For their part, the Redemptorists were delighted to be in a famous town like Ballinwing, which had just had such a spectacular robbery. They were intrigued by the police activity, and they had to be shown where the robbers got in, and where the robbers got out. They wanted to speak to and shake the hand of everyone who was affected by the event. They seemed to be more inclined to play the role of the detective than the role of the priest. They were always on the lookout for clues, and they secretly advanced some incredible theories as to who the robbers could be and where the money was hidden. One of them seemed to have read more Sherlock Holmes than was good for him; the other frequently pulled from his pocket a huge magnifying glass which he fingered in a very curious fashion.

The mission went off without incident. The two Redemptorists preached every morning and again every evening to overflowing congregations. A few drunkards took 'the pledge' to keep away from drink, as they had often done before. They broke the same pledge after a few weeks, as they had often done before also. The people quickly got to like the Redemptorists: there was no harm in them, as Ned Martin said piously, no harm at all. They were interesting, because they were strangers and because they spoke about an area of one's being that the people understood and which interested them. A highlight of every mission was the night on which the priests preached on the Sixth Commandment and on its mutations and ramifications: company-keeping, courtship, fornication and all the sins of the flesh. These two young Redemptorists went easy on all that. Perhaps their own innate niceness and simplicity did more good than two weeks of thunder and brimstone from the altar would ever have done. They were soon gone and forgotten. In this they were just like Fr McFee, who went away quietly to an obscure, hilly little parish behind the mountains, where he had plenty of time to fish for fish, rather than for men and their immortal souls. But there were two people who could never forget Fr McFee. Nan-nan and AB could never forgive him because, when he came out to Uncle James after he had collapsed in Micky Gaffney's cabbage garden, he refused to anoint the prostrate man. The two women said that Uncle James was dying and could still be anointed. Fr McFee said that he was already long dead. He walked away, withholding Extreme Unction. This was not forgotten. Neither was it ever forgiven.

The months dragged by and the great crime remained uncracked. Neither the police, armed with the law of man, nor the Church, armed with the law of God, were of any use in this case.

Yet, in an unexpected way the seal of the confessional was playing its role. One young man had second thoughts about the exploit. Basically, he wanted adventure; not other people's money. Like the young Redemptorist priest, he may have read too many of the wrong sort of books. He began to feel, as time went on, that he would like to have a heart-to-heart talk concerning the whole matter with someone who was absolutely trustworthy. He decided to go to Lough Derg. He knew that there he would soon find a priest, independent, disinterested and experienced in handling all sorts of sin. Another feature of Lough Derg was its privacy and its air of confidentiality. There would be the dark confession box, in a corner of the basilica, on a small island, in the middle of a lake, in an out-of-the-way sort of place like County Donegal. Nothing could be more private than that.

The priest was polite, friendly, very understanding, and he told the sinner exactly what Fr McFee, or anyone else who sits in a confession box, would have told him: all the money would have to be returned or paid back, even if done secretly. There must be restitution. Then he could seek God's forgiveness.

'Was anyone hurt in this . . . happening?' asked the priest.

'No, Father.'

'Thank God for that!'

It occurred to the penitent that this priest mustn't have read his newspapers lately. Yet, how could it be otherwise, living on an island, in a place like Donegal? But he let that pass; and a long, long whispered conversation followed in which every aspect of the problem was examined.

It was a tiresome trip home from Lough Derg, but he felt very relieved. He knew well that, but for Lough Derg, he would never have spoken to anyone about it. He had not discussed it with his confederates in crime. In fact he had seen them only at a distance since the night of the event itself. It was good to get it off one's chest, though. He felt much better; his mind was clearer: he could definitely plan and think better now. So he bought six hundred pounds' worth of tickets in the Irish Hospitals' Sweepstake with some of the bank money. He was bound to win. All would be paid back in God's good time, every red penny of it, now that he had made a good confession, had done penance in Lough Derg and had walked around in his bare feet on the island.

Afterwards, years afterwards, he regretted that he hadn't spent still more of the money on sweepstake tickets. He should have spent at least a thousand. And he should have asked the others to join him. A syndicate could have been formed if he had known about it at the time. For the six hundred pounds that he had spent on the sweep tickets gained him nothing. He never won a rex. That was the most cruel blow of all; especially as his mind was so full of good intentions after that long talk in Lough Derg. He began to drink more than was good for him, more than he could handle. And he had neither the intestines nor the kidneys of the bank manager. The large measures of good red whiskey that he began to imbibe were much more than any green young man could ever cope with in times of stress. The ways of the Lord were certainly not the ways of man.

Old Willie Redican spent many years in the British army. He knew the Khyber Pass and the Sudan and Egypt. He was in South Africa and in Mesopotamia. And he saw Queen Victoria pass by, nodding vigorously to the lines of soldiers and to the cheering crowds. She always sat on a very springy cushion in her carriage to help her nod with greater ease. Willie could conduct himself well when under fire; but, poor and all as he was, he could never organise the robbing of a bank. And that was because he was an Ardnaboe man, with all the weaknesses of his people. He was a good man to thatch a house or a stack of oats or hay. That was why Francie Harkin asked him to do what he could with a rick of hay that he had standing in his back meadow unthatched for months and going to loss. Willie was a neat worker. He was also a grumbler.

'The state of that rick!' he muttered to himself peevishly as he began to work. 'The best force grass hay in the parish going to loss – rotten, rotten! Should have been thatched three months ago! The carelessness of people these days is hard to believe. It'll take me two solid hours to clean it down, never mind thatching it. There's a full day's work there. Instead of the three hours he talked about. People id drive yeh mad sometimes.'

He came better speed than he thought he would; and by the time the Angelus bell rang he had it all cleaned down and ready for thatching. He took off his cap, said the usual short prayers, teased a bit of tobacco, lit his pipe and was soon ready to start. Looking up at the side of the rick, he noticed that it was bulging a bit. He climbed up the ladder and began to trim the bulge. With that movement he uncovered a treasure. Bundles of bank notes of all shapes and sizes, both Irish and British. He had found the money robbed from the bank.

Willie was, perhaps, the poorest man in the parish. He had a wife and six young children to feed. He had few manual skills except thatching, digging potatoes and plucking hens. He didn't think twice of what he should do with the money. He could have bought sweep tickets, or have attempted to make a discreet escape, for he was a travelled man. Instead, he went straight to the police barracks. He knocked at the door and told them to come out and take possession of the plunder. It was in the ass-cart that he had parked at the kerbside.

The school inspector spent all of the following day counting the

91

money in the dayroom of the barracks and under the strictest police surveillance. There was no-one else to count it: the local banks were under a cloud. Willie received a hard grilling from the detectives, who were strangers. The local officers were also under a cloud. The four culprits were soon apprehended: they almost gave themselves up, led by the man who went to Lough Derg. For the truth was that they had no idea how to use the money when they got hold of it. They got it into the rick of hay, but they didn't know how to get it out. They did not want to leave Ballinwing and sail into a prosperous and lonely exile. They received a short sentence and were soon free. No-one thought less of them or held their exploit against them. Soon it was all over and forgotten. And no-one thought a whit more of Willie Redican for what he did: nor for what he did not do. He was, in the long run, no better off than the robbers were in the degree of respect that people had for him. Perhaps he was much less so.

The old parish priest was very pleased indeed and he was convinced also that the good name of his parish and his flock had been restored. His large old brown eyes recovered their kindly twinkle and he slept easier on his feather bed at night. Yet, his tranquillity was ill-founded, had he only known it. Four of his parishioners had robbed a bank, more or less as something of an experiment. Now three more of his flock were planning a murder. They were seething with revenge and determination. They meant business. They wanted blood.

13

Rabies

As time passed, Seamus found that the egg trees hideaway was playing an increasing part in his life. He had dug up the strangely shaped cylinders and bolts which he had found on the railway and had taken them into the egg trees. He had also acquired six horns that his Uncle Peter had sawn off the heads of bullocks. They also found a place in the egg trees. He often thought of the pain that the bullocks must have suffered, securely tied up with ropes, during the operation. It was frightening to see the blood spurting from the animals' heads as Uncle Peter sawed away at the horns.

Sometimes he simply sat in the egg trees, hidden and chewing tobacco and thinking over what he heard people saying. His father was now saying that Henry Gallagher, the big fat man with the handlebar moustache who lived near the Strettons, was his father. Was this in addition to Danny Mulvey? How could a *gossin* have so many fathers? Now it was three. He'd have to discuss the whole thing with Jim Gaffney, as soon as possible.

His mother was talking a lot lately about having some of his teeth 'drew'. She said that she didn't like the way they were growing. He resolved to keep his mouth firmly shut henceforth when in her presence.

Nan-nan often said that Uncle James's Waltham watch could easily be got to work after all these years, if it were taken to a watchmaker. But there were so many jewels in it that she was afraid to do this. The watchmaker would only pick the jewels and leave the watch useless. Curiosity caused the watch to be taken to the egg trees where it was opened. No jewels were to be seen. The watch was quickly taken to Jack Martin. He had no trouble in pointing out the jewels and making them sparkle in the sun. It was later noted that whilst it was easy to steal the watch from the window-sash, it was extremely difficult to get it back there undetected.

It was with great joy that the Lough Neagh hone was stolen from its drawer and taken to the egg trees also. How marvellous to think that it was once part of a holly tree. However, AB noticed that it was missing just two days later.

She searched the house for it from top to bottom. She questioned everyone carefully and severely. She was in a state of great agitation. Seamus hoped she would forget about it. She didn't. She began a novena to St Anthony, the patron of things lost or mislaid. No-one could join her in her prayers: they were all too busy. So she roped Seamus in to answer her solemn Hail Marys. It went on for two days. Suddenly on the third morning she opened the drawer and there before her very eyes was the Lough Neagh hone! An undoubted miracle! No-one could beat St Anthony when matters became grave. No more prayers, thought Seamus. But great was his indignation when she informed him that she would continue the novena for the remaining seven days – just herself and himself. It would be in thanksgiving to the great man from Padua for restoring to her the Lough Neagh hone that was lost. A grim seven days followed for a certain young collector of bric-a-brac.

He liked to take Snap to the egg trees and to place his ear against the terrier's stomach and listen to the strange sounds that came from inside. It was almost as interesting as listening to the humming of the telegraph poles.

But it was quite by accident that he made a discovery of great importance. He came to observe that if Snap was chained in the turf-shed and denied food for a day, he would drink an inordinate amount of skimmed creamery milk when released in the evening. Afterwards he would lie down in the turf-shed and fall into a heavy sleep which lasted about an hour. As soon as he awoke he would thereupon have a violent attack of fits.

Whenever Snap had fits he seemed charged with a truly demonic energy He ran madly around the house barking and yelping. Hens and turkeys flew for their lives. The ducks remained quietly in the mearing drain; the geese waddled silently away looking over their shoulders; Foreman curled up in the turf-shed and pretended to be asleep. Nan-nan, AB and Veronica barricaded themselves behind closed doors and prayed. Seamus took refuge high up in the branches of an apple-tree so as to have an unobstructed view of the events as they unfolded.

It took some experimentation of course, but soon Seamus was having events of this sort by order. He simply starved Snap. Then, when the skim milk came, he poured it from the creamery can into the tub. He let the dog drink his fill; saw him safely asleep and waited an hour for the action to start.

Snap sometimes flung himself dementedly against the kitchen door with a tremendous thud. Occasionally he sprang upwards as if to grab the knocker. The two terrified old women peered out through the window. Seamus, high in the fork of an apple-tree, made faces at them and waved defiantly.

They had a suspicion that Snap had rabies, or 'rabbys' as they called it. They feared that if the dog bit Seamus then he too would begin to tear around the house screaming, throwing himself against the doors and frothing at the mouth. If events came to that, he would have to be tied with ropes and taken in the horse-trap to Glann, where a man named McGovern could attempt to cure him.

14

'God bless the cows'

The small outlying farm of limestone land at Lisagirwin that Tommy brought with him when he married Veronica carried sheep as well as cattle. He had inherited it from his Uncle Dennis, who had called him home from Newry and who was said to be aristocratic in bearing, lazy, highly respected, useless, trustworthy and a fine judge of a horse. Uncle Peter, on his return from New York, inherited the home portion of the farm.

The ould house was now the centre of the Drumlahan holding. There were situated the byre, the stable, two pig-sties, two wooden houses for calves, the hayshed and a draughty house for the horse-trap, the harness and the one-wheeled plough.

There were five or six cows; the same number of calves; a few young cattle and a sow with two or three fattening pigs. A goat ran along with the cows. This was supposed to be lucky and to keep away certain diseases of farm-stock. The horse, Billy, and an ass completed the farm animals. The sheep remained in Lisagirwin winter and summer, but there was much driving of cattle up and down between the two holdings.

Except at ploughing time the stable door was left open so that Billy could go in and out as he pleased. Horses were said to know when rain was approaching; and if Billy was seen to return to the stable at nightfall, a wet night could be expected.

'For weeks and weeks before the earthquake in San Francisco in 1906 the horses couldn't be kept quiet. Stamping their hooves and swishing their tails and shaking their heads like the devil, so they were. They knew well what was coming, when no human being knew it.' Berney McGovern often told that story.

Billy had a period of violently stamping his hooves in the stable at Aughabeg also, but his trouble was greasy heels rather than the approach of an earthquake. At times like that, horses bite at the itchy heels and inadvertently swallow wisps of hair from the fetlock and hoof. This hair is generally passed out in the dung in the form of a small, dark-coloured object about the size of a golf-ball.

Tommy seemed to boast, almost, that greasy heels were caused by bad management and neglect of the horse. Who should know better? There would follow the usual request to Ned Martin for a jamjar of wagon grease from the railway works at Ballinwing. He then proceeded to rub the ointment, mixed with a mysterious powder hidden in the eight-day clock in the kitchen, into the horse's inflamed heels – a hazardous occupation indeed. However, he was richly rewarded when he was cleaning out the stable one morning and he spotted a hair-ball in the dung. A more practical man might not have noticed it.

He placed it on a ledge in the stable; and when it was hard and dry a few days later, he picked it up; felt it; smelt it, and with a triumphant smile, dropped it into his jacket pocket. From then onwards whenever he met anyone, he held up the hairball to them between his thumb and finger and asked the puzzled onlooker to guess what it was.

He was in his element then. Few could guess correctly and he felt himself to be in possession of superior knowledge. He took pleasure in explaining the grim details to every woman he met. This incurred their disgust as well as their disbelief. They crinkled their faces; turned up their noses and walked away.

But matters were evened up now on the domestic and family scene. Veronica had her crystal ball; Tommy had his hair-ball; while Seamus had his fragments of ancient crockery and his shelter in the egg trees.

All the fields of the farm had names: the point field, the little bog, the lea, the pound field, the red hill and the well field. AB, for reasons best known to herself, insisted on naming the gap at the end of the ould house, St Anthony's Gap, in honour of the patron of things lost or mislaid. She demanded that everyone should say a short prayer when going through the gap, especially the children. The parents didn't object. The children were showing distinct signs of heathenism as matters stood. If a prayer to the patron saint of things lost or mislaid could help, well and good.

Veronica was very keen on poultry, and the hen population was always high around the house and the haggard. She had a small incubator which entailed getting up many times in the night to see that the temperature was right. Sittings of eggs reached her from Richard Rodwell, 'just outside Manchester', and there was a flock of gobbling turkeys to which she offered tasty food on the tips of her fingers. They had to be coaxed to eat.

When there were no foxes on the hills, a gander and his two geese made nests on the double ditch at the back of the hayshed and hatched out flocks of sleepy green goslings. Every morning a drake and his nine ducks disappeared into the nutritious waters of the mearing drain. If they swam downstream towards the canal their eggs were blue and firm, if they swam upstream towards the bog their eggs were a deep, rich, red colour in the yolk. But in going downstream they could be snatched by otters: in going upstream they could be killed by foxes from the limestone rocks at Lisagirwin.

There was a hive of bees at the back of the house, facing south and sheltered by Scotch pines. All the children had fits of sitting near the hive and watching the incoming bees alight with little balls of pollen fastened on their hind legs, and then walk slowly into the hive. When coming out, they paused on the landing board. Then they suddenly flew upwards over the pine-trees and away from the fields to gather more pollen and nectar for the hive.

Every morning a great rush and bustle developed to get the milk into the creamery can and on the roadside so that it could be collected by Tom Carey and his large and hurrying cart. In the evening the can was returned with its pale skimmed milk, which was fed to the pigs and the hens. It was never fed to calves: it could cause them to be pot-bellied.

Sufficient milk was kept back always. It was later ripened in large earthenware crocks so that butter for the house could be produced. This operation took place about once a week when the entire family gathered around the dash and dabbler churn and laboured diligently until the butter appeared.

It was something of a social occasion. Nan-nan and Tommy seemed to form a new sort of relationship at the churnside. They appeared to take refuge from the work in conversation that skipped and hopped from person to person and from place to place.

Veronica and AB joined in also, but were more interested in the progress of the work than in anything else. The history of local families, as well as some of those in Tullylakenmore, was retailed, as Nan-nan and Tommy raised their voices in animation, high above the noise of the churning. Who did so-and-so marry? Didn't they go to America? Didn't they come back and buy Gukeen's land in Dunarawh? That's the man that ran for the County Council about ten years ago, is it? How many childer had they? No! John never married. I saw him the fair day before the last one. Getting very stiff. The brother was as decent a man as you could meet, poor fellow! Aw, she was a right trollop. She had it in her face. That's the man that was killed with a kick from a horse? They had a son a priest and he went to Australia. A great footballer. They were all strong Parnellites in the old days, I often heard Uncle Dennis saying. Asthma! He'd have gone to Germany with Odey, if he had the fare. Two of his childer died with the fever in Bawn workhouse. The two that died were left the whole night, till late next morning, in the same bed as the living childer! That house was built the year after the Black-and-Tans! Usen't he to do a bit of match-making one time? Where do they bury the Keegans of Altakeeran? After he was ordained he was sent to the Philippines. He was a curate in Ballinaglera. He died in Templeport, I think. That jennet was the best animal I ever saw ploughing. He started from nothing. He could buy out Ballinwing the day, never mind Ballydoon. They were a very nice family; and they used to have great crops of oats and potatoes. No, he's still alive: he doesn't be out much. Except for Mass.

It was at other times that politics and the price of cattle, pigs, eggs and potatoes were discussed and debated. This could never happen during churning time. No-one would ever dream of whistling or singing while churning was in progress either. Among children, the first sign of growing up was to be allowed to stand on a stool, grab the dash and take a few brashes.

The dash was handed from person to person. Nan-nan and Tommy churned vigorously with rolled-up sleeves, as they talked. Veronica churned slowly, as if in meditation. AB churned fast, with her head to one side and the dash aslant. She seemed to be a different person when churning, full of energy.

The kettle of hot water, or of soft water, was added from time to time as it was required.

'It's broke!' someone would exclaim, after more than half an hour.

The dash was then pulled up high and scrutinised. Little pale globules of butter could be seen on the shaft. There was general agreement that the milk was indeed 'broke' and this meant that the churning would soon be over. AB would ejaculate:

'God bless the cows!'

Everyone else assented, either audibly or in a whisper, 'God bless the cows!'

As the churning continued, now at a slower pace, the globules became larger and larger. The talk died down; soon the globules coalesced and began to assume the colour of butter.

More water was added: hot or cold, according to what was judged to be necessary. Finally, the churning was considered to be completed when no more butter was seen to be adhering to the shaft. The lid was then knocked open with the dash and the good yellow butter viewed critically by all the participants as it floated on the white, sweet-smelling buttermilk below.

If a neighbour or a caller happened to arrive during churning, he or she would immediately walk over and, taking hold of the dash, have a few brashes and say, 'God bless the cows.' They were free to come and go then as they pleased. It would have been considered rude not to take the customary brash and nonchalantly call on God to bless the cows. The custom came down from the days when a visitor who came during the course of churning could steal the butter through the power of witchcraft. By taking a brash and invoking the deity this evil power was thwarted. By the time of the economic war no-one really believed the butter could be stolen; but the observance of the custom showed politeness and goodwill for the churners and the household.

Tommy liked to make beestings cake whenever a cow calved. This was achieved by taking milk from a newly calved cow, which was always considered highly unsuitable for domestic use, and pouring it into a frying pan or into the heavy circular metal oven used for baking bread. When a little gentle heat was applied, the liquid would begin to bubble. After about fifteen minutes it would have reached a stage when it resembled a yellow sponge-cake in appearance. Tommy then up-ended the cake onto a large plate or dish. It had an attractive smell. He quickly cut it into wedges and sprinkled it with salt. Then he armed himself with a mug of strong tea and began to devour the beestings cake with a relish that was truly gluttonous. Strangely, this always took place at night or on a Sunday.

Nan-nan and AB went around the kitchen exchanging knowing glances and nodding their heads in an 'I told you so' manner. It was one of the very few matters on which they were in full agreement: for drinking beestings, or worse still, converting it into a cake, they considered to be uncivilised, low and almost anti-Christ.

As the fury of Tommy's ingestion moderated somewhat, he would soon have the *Irish Independent* or a Bulldog Drummond book flat on the table beside him as he shovelled beestings cake into his champing mouth while reading. Occasionally, he burped resoundingly, which was quickly followed by an absent-minded 'Pardon me, Ma'am.' He horrified the two women once by trying to get Seamus to partake of the beestings cake. When the boy refused it he seemed hurt and let down in front of the two women.

'It would put hair on your chest, *gossin*,' he advised.

'What a thing to say to a six-year-old child!' exclaimed AB looking towards heaven for solace.

'That's right,' asserted the man-of-the-house. 'Beestings cake would put hair on a man's chest – and sand in a woman's gizzard.'

The two looked at each other in disbelief. What was the world coming to at all? Times and people were going to the dogs, and no mistake.

After his feast, he always had to wash the plate and the other utensils he had used. Neither of the two women would touch anything used in the preparation and the disposal of beestings cake. At times like that, after a good meal, he was wont to break into a snatch of an old food-song that he knew so well:

Sure, they cut my hair with a knife and fork,
And they rolled it up like a cabbage stalk,
And I got so thin I couldn't walk,
When I joined the hungry army.

Up came the sergeant with a big tin can,
And he gave a spoonful to every man,
And I got so fat I couldn't stan',
When I joined the hungry army.

When all was washed and tidied up he usually took down the pack of cards and began to play patience. The annoyance of the two old ladies knew no bounds. Beestings cake; dreeling for hours into them silly books from the library; trying to lead the child astray; playing cards on his own — it was the younger generation, the crudeness of modern youth. But wasn't there a touch of Ardnaboe about it all too? 'Wan can't lie with the dog but wan'll get up with the flays,' went the old proverb.

15

The healers

Before her mother died Nan-nan received from her the power to make three cures: the cure of the sty in the eye, the cure of the burn and the cure of the strain. She seldom had occasion to make the first two cures; but her cure of the strain was in wide demand and was said to be of great efficacy. Consequently, when someone knocked at the door one night, and a small, thin, woebegone man entered with a Clarendo meal sack over his shoulders Nan-nan knew at once what he wanted. His name was Dan Murphy. He had been attacked by a bull and he asked her if she would make a cure for him.

'Iv coorse, Dan, iv coorse, Dan. You are very welcome indeed. Sit down, *a ghrá,* and I'll make it for you the minute I have this cake in the oven.'

Dan seated himself and soon she handed him a mug of hot tea and a thick slice of soda bread, with butter and rhubarb jam, on a plate. She kept up an unceasing flow of friendly conversation with the patient until her work was finished.

Then she took off his sack and his overcoat and bared his swollen and bruised blue limb. She asked him to move his fingers. This he did to her satisfaction.

She made the sign of the cross; the patient did likewise; and she began to pray and to rub the arm with long strokes. She covered it from the shoulder to the tips of the fingers. This continued slowly and regularly for about three minutes. Then she suddenly made the sign of the cross on the arm and blessed herself also.

'God bless you now, Dan. You'll be toppin' in a day or two. If it is slow in getting better, be sure and come back again to me.'

She helped to draw down his shirt sleeve and to put on his coat. He seemed so relieved. He thanked her and sat down, apparently a new man although his arm was still stiff and sore.

Many diseases and conditions of both man and beast were treated by cures. A cure was the power handed down from one person to another through the ages for the purpose of healing. Usually an old person who had the cure would hand it over to a younger person as the end of life drew near. A cure usually consisted in touching, saying the prescribed prayers, as in the case of Nan-nan's cure of the strain, or in taking medicine prepared by the person who had the cure. Prayers were usually recited by the curer and the patient in the case of medicines also. Every cure had a set formula of prayers and touchings and a strict recipe for the medicine, when this was involved. Both were secret, of course. Either men or women could have the cure.

Cures could be made for animals; and Nan-nan was hurried into a horse-cart one day to go three miles to make the cure of the strain for a bull with an inflamed knee and lameness. She dressed up just as if she was going to Mass: cape, bonnet and black shoes and stockings. If she was going to the shop at Aughabeg, or to collect her old-age pension, she would wear her heavy dark-brown shawl. Her Sunday best was necessary on this special occasion. AB sprinkled her generously with holy water, in case she'd be gored by the brute. Then, as Nan-nan went out the door, AB threw the iron tongs after her, as was customary to bring luck. Perched high on the cart, no doctor hastening to a dying patient ever looked more important. Afterwards, the owner of the beast declared that she had not only effected a cure: she had also performed a miracle.

Mary Gaffney, Micky's wife and the mother of Jim the great womaniser, who lived farther up the lane, had many cures, including the cure of the strain. She seldom used it, however. Her strong point was the cure of the jaundice. This cure required certain herbs, which had to be gathered after sunset. They were boiled and mixed in exact proportions and to the accompaniment of prayers known only to Mary. A bottle of bitter-tasting liquid was then given to the patient; it had to be taken at certain times, whilst prayers were said. As with Nan-nan, and her cure of the strain, people came from all over for her assistance for the cure of

104

jaundice and many other ailments also, including infestation by worms.

There was the cure of the cow's foot, or scald, the cure of the toothache, the cure of the heart, the cure of the worms in children, a cure for headaches, a cure for deafness. There was a reed-bound lake at Kesh where the water cured erysipelas if you filled the bottle under the surface of the lake and between sunset and sunrise.

And wasn't there a man who lived over at Drumcool, named McKeon, who cured pains in the back by treading with his hobnailed boots, and his full weight, on the naked flesh of the patient. He was a great favourite with the women, and his ministrations were renowned for the alleviation of aches, pains and displacements in the female corpus. At one time there seemed to be an epidemic of bad backs; and an unseemly number of staid and apparently serious-minded women, went frequently to Drumcool to be walked on in their nakedness and in strict confidence by the healing hobnails of the redoubtable McKeon.

Mary Gaffney was getting old, and people wondered what she would do with her many and very useful cures. Others of her age would have by then passed them on safely to a member of the younger generation so as not to have them lost to posterity. It would be a terrible careless thing to take them to the grave with one.

Jim, her son, always boasted that he would take the cures and carry on the tradition when his mother passed on. After all he was a responsible citizen, wasn't he? No-one believed him; and Mary seemed reluctant to give up the reins. She was afraid he might poison someone, rather than cure them. But in actual fact he didn't want the cures; he scarcely believed in them. He only promised to take them over so as to humour her and to keep her quiet. Yet it came to pass that, after a particularly violent row, he rashly promised again to take over the cures. Suddenly, she there and then bequeathed him the whole lot of them. He turned pale: he knew he would have to practise them now till she died, which might be years; the weight seemed to crush his soul and also his body. He was round-shouldered for a week.

105

Mary went around all smiles. The apple of her eye could now make all the cures. Wasn't it great?

When Nan-nan heard this she shook her head in disbelief and disapproval. When AB heard it she made the sign of the cross and looked heavenwards. 'God between us and all harm!' exclaimed Nan-nan. 'Fancy a reprobate like that getting all them cures! How could God allow such sacrilege?'

Nan-nan was of the opinion that one should be pure of heart to make a cure. No, it was not like the priest going to say Mass; but one should be decent and good-living all the same. No, you hadn't to be in the state of grace, just decent. AB nodded her head in pious agreement with this viewpoint. So where did that put Jim?

People considered that Jim Gaffney was indeed a hard man for the girls. Fathers and mothers were inclined to hide their daughters when he was around. Some, it was claimed, paid the annual licence on their shotguns and took the weapons out and cleaned them before the public gaze only because Jim Gaffney was on the prowl. But it was noteworthy that whenever Jim was working in the fields, girls going past on bicycles dismounted and went to his side in high heels and across ploughed sods for a chat. The girls were always crowding around him. He was irresistible.

'I wouldn't trust him with a black cat going through a skylight,' coughed Ned Martin, through clouds of cigarette smoke. He was saying this as a veiled warning to his own daughters. And now Mary Gaffney was going around, as proud as punch, despite her misgivings, and boasting that Jimmy would soon have all the cures at the top of his tongue and the tips of his fingers.

Everyone, especially Nan-nan, knew about and remembered clearly what he did to young Teddy Muldoon years before. They were playing cards in the forge on a snowy night. Teddy was a young gawk of a fellow who wanted to play cards with the men. The trouble was that he would fall asleep in the middle of a game. Jimmy Gaffney was playing and losing; he lost his temper with young Muldoon and lifted him up and carried him over and threw him onto a bag of hay. He scarcely awoke, and soon he was asleep again and snoring at full blast, with his mouth wide open. Jimmy was still losing and was furious with the sleeper. In a sudden outburst of temper he did something next that Nan-nan would never forgive him for, but which many others thought very funny.

'Up he jumps; over he goes to Teddy; and he suddenly starts to pee right into his open mouth. He filled his mouth with hot piss. It's a wonder to God he didn't choke him!'

The sleeper suddenly came to his senses. He jumped to his feet coughing and spluttering; he ran around the forge two or three times as if in a daze. Then he vanished through the doorway in a cloud of vaporised urine. That was just one more reason why Nan-nan did not consider Jim Gaffney to be a fit person to receive the power to cure and to heal, as his mother had done before him.

'Ah, divel a bit harm it'll do,' said Tommy Flynn, always the easy-going liberal. 'Sure the best doctors you ever heard of are often drunkards. The best priests are often worse. Divel a bit harm it'll do for Jim to have the cures. Maybe, he'll be twice as good as the mother. It's the song, and not the singer, that counts.'

Just after this Nan-nan and AB, following much conference, decided that Seamus must have worms. They thereupon sent an urgent message to their cousin, Mary Haley, who lived in Dernaheiltyahmore O'Donnell. They could not ask Mary Gaffney to make the cure, now that she had just relinquished her powers to Jim. And it would be unthinkable that a reprobate like him should be trusted with making a cure for Seamus. It was an emergency, and it had to be Mary Haley. She arrived suddenly one morning in a long black coat that reached her ankles and a big, high-crowned hat, tightly wrapped in black satin. It had a very wide rim, which had the effect of making her look further away than she really was. She had heavy brown eyes, tanned skin and a most serious and profound expression. She talked through her nose, a surprisingly deep and sonorous note. She gazed at Seamus for some time in silence, and then nodded her head ominously again and again.

Suddenly Mary Haley snatched a bread knife from the table. She and AB immediately grabbed Seamus, one by each arm. In grim silence they dragged the worm-infested youngster out

107

through the door and frog-marched him towards the darkness of the deal trees. He tried desperately to resist, first by jamming his heels into the ground, then by attempting to kick Mary Haley on the ankle and on the foot. It was at this stage that he bit AB. He had her thumb between his back teeth and he was chewing on it with all his dental strength. She yelled.

'Me thumb! The savage! The savage *aurcaun*! He has me thumb gone! God help us, this night and this day!'

Abruptly, terrified by the news that he had indeed bitten off the thumb, he released his grip. He spat out fiercely in case he might swallow it. They got him to the trees and they made him kneel down. Mary Haley produced the knife. She raised her eyes to heaven and began to pray in an intense whisper that was audible to everyone.

She cut a small sod from the grassy soil with the knife and held it on the point of the blade under the nose of the patient, praying to God to clear out the worms that were infesting the entrails of this unfortunate child. Meanwhile, AB was whimpering over the injuries sustained by her thumb.

Three times did Mary Haley cut a little green sod and hold it under his nose, praying fervently. Three times did she return the sods to the place she cut them from. She levelled each down and glazed it over with the knife, cutting the sign of the cross into the soil every time. Then the two women said the Hail Mary loudly together. They nudged the patient so that he would join in. He remained rebelliously silent. The task over, they began to walk in leisurely fashion towards the house.

'He should be transported,' said AB in great pain.

'You're an imp of the devil, young man,' said Mary Haley, looking down at him. Her brown eyes seemed to be of a great weight. 'There's more than worms in you, I'm afraid.'

'He should be fed on bread and water, the little *aurcaun*. The cat-o-nine-tails is too good for him.' AB always lapsed into convict and prison-ship language at times of stress or youthful waywardness.

When the news broke that AB had nearly lost a thumb, it was all that Nan-nan could do to save Seamus, her godson, from getting the whaling of his life. She wasn't too keen, privately, on the same Mary Haley, when all was said and done, cousin and all as she was.

'The unholy ingratitude of the little *glincín*,' complained Veronica. 'To bite poor AB's thumb, just like a savage in the field. And she after getting Mary Haley to come all the way from Dernaheiltyahmore O'Donnell to make the cure of the worms for him. Dear, oh dear, oh dear!' She seemed as if she was going to cry as she poured out the tea.

So that's what they were doing, thought Seamus. Making the cure of the worms for him. There were no worms in his inside. There were worms under stones and in the cabbage garden, and near the egg trees where his father dug whenever he was going to fish. But how could they dare to say that there were worms like that in him? He felt shamed. He began to cry. If there were worms like that in his insides he would hear them crawling around. He didn't want to bite off AB's thumb; but when he saw Mary Haley grabbing the knife he was sure that they were going to do the same thing to him that they did to the pigs and the calves. When Mary Haley and AB got together they looked a dangerous pair indeed.

That night when he was saying his prayers, he had to tell God, in quite forthright language, that he was very sorry for having almost bitten off poor AB's thumb. He had to mention in passing that he was also very sorry for having been disobedient and for having made a disgrace of himself and of his family in front of Mary Haley from Dernaheiltyahmore O'Donnell who had come to make the cure of the worms for him. And he had to say one Our Father that AB's thumb would soon heal up and be cured, and that it would not fall off later, when the wind went to the east.

16

The monkey-puzzle

'You're a big lump of a lad now, and it's time you were going to school.' That statement of fact, coming from his father, was the first hint that Seamus received of new and unpleasant developments which could change the whole quality of his life for the worse. Other people went to school, he knew, but they were big and grown-up, and he never thought that it could happen to him. He did not want to face the fact that his days could be spent otherwise than taking jaunts in the horse cart, or riding on the ass's back while Jim Gaffney led her along and sang at the top of his voice. It would be unthinkable to spend a summer day other than looking for birds' nests, playing with Foreman and Snap or fishing for pinkeens in the mearing drain with a wriggling worm stuck on the point of a bulrush. He decided to go to the egg trees immediately and to think the matter over.

He found that he had no tobacco to chew; and, as his father was now gone to Ballinwing with the horse and cart, there was no chance of raiding his pockets and peeling off a leaf from the plug. He had acquired a white clay pipe that Tommy had brought home from a wake. So he fished it out from under the bottles and the cinders and the bolts from the railway and gripped it in his teeth. Sitting there, with his chin resting on his knees and the pipe gripped in the front of his mouth, he looked very thoughtful and profound. He could well have been a professor, who had inadvertently taken an overdose of monkey-gland essence and who was suddenly transposed from late middle-age to childhood, without having ever noticed what had happened.

He did not want to go to school. Of that he was certain. There was nothing to be gained from it. A *gossin* would be away all day from home. Of course he might avoid having to eat so much of

110

that awful stirabout if he was going to school. His mother was still talking about having his teeth 'drew'. She still didn't like the way they were growing. And his father was going on about making him a fluent speaker of Irish by sending him to Waterford. He did not want to go to school; he did not want to go to the dentist; he did not want to learn Irish.

His mind began to wander.

He wondered if Snap could be made to have fits still oftener. Say, every day. But then he recalled that Veronica mentioned that Snap should be drowned or poisoned. Perhaps it would be better for him not to let Snap have any more creamery milk for a while. His mother would probably forget about having the terrier done away with if nothing happened for a week or so. You couldn't be too careful with the 'ould wans'.

He sat there in the egg tree, all hunched up and with the clay pipe firmly gripped in his mouth as his mind coursed over all those important matters. He could hear the train coming out of the station at Ballinwing. He knew where it was on the railway by the way it puffed. It was very nice the way the train seemed to talk as it puffed along the railway: it seemed to say some of the things Nan-nan said when she was vexed. But the train seemed to say them in fun: 'I'll jump down your belly: I'll walk on your corpse! I'll jump down your belly: I'll walk on your corpse!'

The train kept on saying that as it came up the long slope from the metal bridge and until it came in view of Drumlahan halt. Then, as it got up steam and was racing for the hill that was Drumlahan bank, it began to repeat quickly, over and over again, another of Nan-nan's curses: 'May you burst wide open! May you burst wide open! May you burst wide open! May you burst wide open!'

It always said this as it rushed along at full speed with carriages and vans and a long load of wagons behind it. And the train always seemed in such good humour as it repeated Nan-nan's curses. Not at all like the way she said them. He listened for a long time as the noise of the train faded away into the distance.

It seemed extraordinary to him that anyone could possibly be as old as Nan-nan was. Old age was a mystery that held for him a

111

strange fascination. He was always asking Nan-nan how old she was.

'I'm as old as the hills,' was her stock reply.

'But Nan-nan how old are the hills?'

'Just as old as your poor ould Nancy Anne – and stop asking silly questions, ye little *craudaun* ye, will ye now?'

He took the matter up with her on another occasion.

'How old are you, Nan-nan? Why won't you tell me how old you are?' She was sitting on a chair near the fire at the time. She was laughing and joking and he persisted in his questioning.

'How old are you, Nan-nan?'

She suddenly grew silent. She gazed very sadly into the fire for some time. Her lips were pressed together and her hands grew limp on her lap.

'I'm old enough, God knows!' she said quietly, as if talking to herself. Then she added wistfully, and almost in a whisper: 'I'm sorry for being so old.'

She was silent for a long time afterwards and she continued to gaze into the fire. He never asked her that sort of question again.

The evil hour passed. Seamus didn't go to school then. His parents had other things to think about, including running the farm and keeping an eye on the politicians. Life went on as usual; and it seemed that he was all set to run wild for years, unhindered by the trammels of education, just as his father did when he was a boy in Ballinwing years before. It was the cruellest of bad luck that events turned out otherwise. It was a twist of fate, an evil chance; and its immediate cause was a small ornamental plant called a monkey-puzzle that grew in front of the house. Tommy had received it as a wedding present. For, when he married, some of his friends on the Creamery Suppliers Association gave him a young copper beech plant, a stool of ribbon grass and a monkey-puzzle. They said that this was because of his great interest in forestry.

He planted the copper beech between the Bramley Seedling apple-tree and the mearing drain. It was soon flourishing. He planted the ribbon grass beside the Cox's Orange Pippin. It too was soon flourishing, and he always referred to it as pampas grass. The monkey-puzzle he planted right in the centre of the grass patch that stretched between the house and the other apple-trees. It alone of the three plants never seemed to do well. It lived; but it remained stunted, contorted and very unhappy-looking.

Seamus heard much talk, and not a little argument, about manure and the manuring of crops and plants. He saw bags of sulphate of ammonia and super-phosphate lying in the turf-shed; and at the railway halt there were wagons of artificial manure in the little siding waiting to be carted away. He overheard his father saying that the apple-trees could do with a few handfuls of 'bag-stuff'. He added, as an afterthought, that the monkey-puzzle was looking a bit tightened-up and that they must not forget it either. Seamus decided to take matters into his own hands.

He got a large glass jar with a crack in it. Into it he poured salt, oatmeal, some dusty turf mould, flour, sugar and spring water. With a large tablespoon he stirred the ingredients to a fine paste after he had added some paraffin oil and a few drops of turpentine. Veronica had her usual large number of hens then and, among other things, she had a big tin of a powder with the trade-name of Hencall. It was supposed to cure all sorts of ailments in hens and turkeys. There was a large cardboard box of Karswood poultry spice within reach also: it was claimed that it could assist hens to lay eggs in abundance. Seamus added four heaped tablespoons of each to his jar and stirred them in vigorously. The mixture soon took on the consistency of a thick paste.

He approached the monkey-puzzle and pondered the situation. He held the glass jar in one hand and the spoon in the other. He did not like the idea that some people had of throwing or shaking manure on the ground beneath a plant. Anyone could see that manure should be supplied from the top. In that way it would soak down into the plant and cause it to grow. After all, people took in food from the top, and not from the bottom, didn't they?

With this thought in mind he tried to use the spoon to put some of the paste on the topmost branches of the monkey-puzzle. He made little headway. Then he put the spoon in his pocket, placed the jar on the ground and, taking a handful of the paste, rolled it into a sticky ball and impaled it on the topmost bud of the unhappy plant.

He stood back and looked at it. He was well satisfied with his work, and he tried to tell Veronica about it later on.

'Don't be such a little *glincín,*' was all she said as she hurried away to do something that needed her attention. She had a bucket in each hand as she vanished from view. She did not grasp the awful significance of what he was trying to tell her.

He sometimes forgot to manure the monkey-puzzle; but he only missed two or three mornings in the week, at the worst. He was always surprised that the manure which he stuck to the top bud would have vanished without trace so quickly. The monkey-puzzle must be taking in all the food, he thought. He was greatly encouraged. With renewed enthusiasm he prepared another jarful of the mixture. It had the usual ingredients; but this time he added a new commodity, tea leaves. He stopped using water and added skimmed milk instead. There was more food in it.

It went on for weeks, and several times the glass jar was filled and emptied. He tried to tell them of the task he was engaged in. He expected praise, or even reward. Yet they grew impatient and lost interest when he began to tell them the details: they would not listen. But he knew they would listen one day. Wouldn't it be great if some morning, when they all got up, the poor monkey-puzzle had grown suddenly up into the sky, just like what happened in 'Jack and the Beanstalk', a story told to him by the Martin girls so often.

It was noticed, after a time, that large numbers of wild birds were being found dead around the house, in the lane and on the road. There were finches, robins, wrens and titmice. Magpies and jackdaws became so tame and so sleepy that one could almost touch them. This tameness and sleepiness was soon to spread to the domestic fowl. Hens were found wandering around in the dark when they should have gone to roost hours earlier. Turkeys became very wobbly of gait; ducks betrayed no desire to go into the wine-dark waters of the mearing drain in the morning or to swim away as usual. Nan-nan felt that there must be someone around with an exceptionally evil eye. AB added three further Hail Marys to the rosary.

A month passed. More and more wild birds were dying. Hens

114

were laying eggs in showers: some with no yolks and some with no shells. Then they'd abstain, and there would be no eggs for a week or two from them. Turkeys refused to walk. For two awful days the ducks obstinately remained in the duck house and refused to budge. They seemed to be dozing most of the time. Jackdaws fell down the chimney and arrived on the hearth, dazed but alive, to the consternation of the household. Nan-nan sighed for the services of the ould Doctor. AB redoubled her prayers and spinkled holy water liberally.

The geese seemed unaffected by the plague. No-one knew it at the time, but this was because they did not come across the mearing drain: they remained around the ould house and the double ditch. All the family made discreet enquiries elsewhere and with the neighbours: were they experiencing any trouble with their hens and ducks? Any unusual behaviour? No? Then it must be something peculiar to the Flynn flocks themselves. Yes, of course it was a disgrace. No, it was out of the question to ask the County Poultry Instructress, Miss Burke, to call. Next thing it would be in the *Leitrim Observer,* or worse still, the *Anglo-Celt.* No, it would have to be kept a family secret, like falling into the mearing drain or the crystal ball.

It was at that stage that the hens began to die. Standing at the table and gazing out through the window, Veronica was in tears at the loss of four of her Rhode Island Reds that she had received as day-old chicks from Mr Richard Rodwell who lived 'just outside Manchester'. There indeed was all her work gone down the drain. She had wrought hard to build up her flocks. Times were bad and she had hoped to do well with the fowl, in spite of all. It was hard luck. Her hopes were dashed; her prayers unanswered. Absent-mindedly, she could see Seamus doing something at the monkey-puzzle. Tired of thinking of the plague that was ravishing her flocks, her mind seemed to find escape in watching her first-born working diligently at the ornamental plant. But what was he doing? She noted that he was growing, in spite of everything. Yes, but what was he up to at all?

Two hens, giddy Anconas of course, wobbled over dizzily and began to peck eagerly at stuff that he was taking out of a glass jar and putting on the monkey-puzzle. What in the name of God was he doing? She watched carefully. Fascinated, she saw that he took handfuls of stuff out of the jar and fixed it in a lump on the point of the bush. She immediately realised that lately she had seen him foostering around it a lot. 'And, God bless us, the monkey-puzzle is dead! Rotted to the ground. And all the leaves withered and crinkled.'

She ran out to where Seamus was standing, deeply absorbed in his jamjar.

'What's that you have there, me laddo?' She was right behind him.

'Manure,' he answered, without turning around.

'Manure? Where did you get it?'

'I made it myself.'

'How?'

Only then did he turn around to face her. With pride he told her the recipe. He knew the ingredients by heart now, and he went into great detail and was soon almost out of breath with enthusiasm. It was surely great stuff, for no matter how much of it he mixed, the poor monkey-puzzle soaked it all in as quick as anything.

As he talked she watched the two Anconas gorge themselves and then lie down on the grass and go to sleep without putting the head under the wing. The mystery was solved for her. She grabbed her son by the collar of the gansey and roughly marched him into the kitchen.

'Nan-nan! AB! Where's Tommy? Will yez look at this? Look quick at what the *glincín* is doing, will yez? For the past two months, for all we know! Look into the jar, will yez. He has the monkey-puzzle killed and half me hens poisoned.'

She grabbed the egg tree switch that she kept on top of the dresser for making him eat his stirabout and she beat him with tremendous fury on the bare legs until he was howling with pain. Worse than the wields of the switch for Seamus was the surprise and the disappointment. He did not dream that he was doing any harm: he thought they would welcome his attempts to manure the poor sick monkey-puzzle and help it to grow, even if it didn't ever reach Jack-and-the-Beanstalk proportions.

They all felt let down. Veronica mourned the ruin of her flocks of pure-bred hens. Nan-nan was let down because it turned out to be something simple instead of a bad case of the evil eye. 'He's a tory,' she said, 'an outright tory.' AB felt let down that a *glincín* of that size could do so much damage under their very noses. 'He should be transported,' she murmured. 'He should be given bread and water. The cat-o-nine-tails is far too good for him. He'll drive us all into the workhouse, if God doesn't change him.'

When Tommy came in he listened to the story in utter bewilderment. He examined the glass jar, and was about to taste some of the mixture, when all the women screamed at him not, for God's sake, to put his finger in his mouth in case he'd poison himself. As a rule he tasted everything he gave to livestock, including medicine.

'It's all right! It's all right!' he shouted at them irritably. 'I'll not fall asleep or start laying soft-boiled eggs, even if I do taste it.'

He was livid with rage. He stuck his hands deep into his pockets and strode out to the monkey-puzzle he had planted the year he got married. He could see plainly that it was withered to the ground, poisoned. He could not speak. He swayed. He looked up at the copper beech; and then at the pampas grass. Had the *glincín* got at them also? After a while he walked slowly back to the house.

'I'd bate ye within an inch of your life, the day; only yer mother has done it already.' He looked very fiercely at the sniffling Seamus.

'There's the makings of a fine quack doctor in you, me boy! Or mebbe a bloody yahoo. I'm goin' to put manners on you or, be the holy farmer, I'll die in the attempt. You prepare yourself for school. Be ready for off Monday morning.'

It was in this manner that Seamus's education got under way.

Tommy never forgot the monkey-puzzle all the days of his life. He seemed to mourn it as if it were a friend, and he often alluded to it and to the manner of its death. Characteristically, he never tried to have it replaced.

17

St Anne's

The following Monday morning, as his father had threatened, Seamus was prepared for school. He was washed and combed and his shoes were polished. A new school-bag with a pencil and a jotter were bought for him. Two slices of bread and butter and a small whiskey-bottle of milk were placed in the school-bag. When he was almost ready, Veronica had a thought. Quickly she strung a medal of St Benedict and an *agnus dei* on a piece of thin twine and roughly hung them round his neck beneath his shirt and next to his skin. Just then a knock was heard at the door. It was Philip Scollan, with blond hair and a faceful of freckles. He had come to take Seamus to school. As the two turned to go AB flung the iron tongs after them. They landed with a clatter at their heels. Neither looked back.

When they reached the railway, Philip proceeded to give Seamus some sound advice. He continued talking as they stepped from sleeper to sleeper on the narrow-gauge railway line the whole way to Ballinwing.

'If ever you forget your lunch you can go to the nuns and you can get your lunch from them. They come into the schoolyard every day with plates and plates of bread and jam. You only have to ask for as many cuts as you want. Never take your lunch into the lavatory. You could get fever that way. And you want to watch your books and pencils in case they'd be stole. Always keep the buckle of your bag closed tight.'

Soon little groups of boys and girls could be seen going on along the railway. They too were on their way to school. Philip put on a very serious face and went on to warn the new boy about certain people.

'D'ye see that tall fellow with the blue coat? Well, watch him!

Very quarrelsome. Always fighting and calling names. And if you ever play marbles or buttons with him, be careful. He'd rogue ye.'

They crossed the metal bridge that carried the railway over the canal.

'Those girls behind us,' said Philip. Seamus looked around. Philip gave his arm a sharp chuck. 'Don't look around at them, ye flamin' little eejit! They might think we were talking about them. Well, them lassies are always skinnin' from school. D'ye see that fort over there?' Philip pointed out a dense mass of whitethorns and ash at the corner of a field on the gentle slope of the hill. 'That's where they hide all day when they're skinnin' from school. Stealing apples, lighting fires, playing games, smoking fags . . . Of course no-one knows that, only a few. And you're never to tell anyone what I told you now. Never tell anyone, no matter who, about the girls skinnin' from school up there in the fort.'

They were soon on a straight stretch of railway line and going up a slight hill.

'D'ye see that fellow with the bare legs? He has an awful dirty tongue. Always cursing and using filthy language! Never say anything you hear him saying; or, be Jaysus almighty, your father and mother'll kill you.'

Philip warned his charge about the nuns also. Some of them 'couldn't be faulted'; but Sister Mary Joan was a 'walkin' bitch and no mistake'.

At length they came near to the town, and they got off the railway by climbing over an iron gate. They followed a beaten path across a rushy field with several strawberry cows grazing in it; they climbed over a stile; skirted a noisy stream, climbed over another stile and came out onto a lane with the canal basin on one side and a railway on the other. Where the lane joined the street, a crowd of bigger boys were gathered, lolling against the wall and arguing loudly. Philip led Seamus through them without a word and they were soon at the school where the new boy was handed over to Sister Benignus. She was very friendly and nice and she tried to make him talk. When this failed she took him on a walk around the noisy schoolroom. Not a word could he say: he was muzzled by shyness. She took him to the doll's house at the lower

119

end of the room. It amazed him: he had never seen anything like it before. It was two storeys high, with a slated roof and it had a kitchen and a parlour and several bedrooms with tables, chairs, pots, pans, cups and saucers.

'It's just like Uncle Peter's house at Lisagirwin,' he said to the nun, smiling. She smiled back at him and nodded.

A bell rang somewhere, and there followed a short prayer which all, except Seamus, shouted out at the top of their voices together. Afterwards there was a session in which everyone tried to make animals and birds and horse-carts out of plasticine. Then came sums, with a ball-frame; and when that was over they all went out to play in the long, narrow schoolyard with its high walls. Someone showed him the lavatory, which was so dirty and smelly that he never went into it again. From then on he began to carry his water for long periods of time; and later he became very resourceful at getting rid of it in the most surprising places whenever he was short taken. Back in the schoolroom there was catechism.

'Who made the world?' inquired Sister Benignus.

'God made the world,' shouted twenty young Catholics.

'Who is God?' persisted the nun.

'God is the creator and sovereign lord of heaven and earth and of all things,' proclaimed the infants of Ballinwing.

He knew all that long ago: it was old stuff; Veronica had dinned it into him with long-suffering patience. But to hear it shouted out on his first day at school, to hear someone else other than himself asserting it made a profound impression on him.

Matters of the soul were interrupted by a short session of drill: the pupils stood in rows between the desks while Sister Benignus, at the piano, played all sorts of gymnastic music as the young people moved their arms up and down and in all directions.

Lunch-time came. He followed the crowd into the schoolyard. When he saw others eating their lunch and drinking milk out of small bottles that they took from their satchels, he did the same. Most of the boys ate their lunch as they ran around playing tig, trains or cowboys. The girls were skipping or playing ring-a-rosie or tig.

Eeckle ackle porter bottle,
Eeckle ackle out!
Pig's snout, walk out!

All who were in the game were eliminated in this way. The last one had 'the tig'.

A nun, as Philip had said, stood there at the gate in the wall with a large pewter dish heaped with slices of bread and jam. She held it out carefully for the children, who immediately came running up and snatched a slice each.

'Any more for lunch? Anyone else for lunch?' she shouted in her high, thin voice again and again. For a long time she stood there looking searchingly up and down the yard and calling out anxiously. When eventually she was sure that no-one had gone without lunch and that her services were no longer needed, she returned through the gate and bolted it behind her, a demure lay-sister in her white apron. Her pewter dish was still heaped high with bread and jam.

A bell rang and they were ushered into a room and given slates. These slates were sheets of three-ply wood. With chalk they wrote the ABC and simple words.

A half an hour elapsed and the slates were collected, with much clattering, and put away in a cupboard. They all stood again in rows between the desks for singing. He felt shy of singing when there was anyone listening or looking; and it came as a great surprise to him that all the other children sang with such gusto and such evident delight. They sang two songs in Irish first, which he did not know nor understand, but which he considered to be hauntingly beautiful. Then they sang two cheerful songs in English.

How jolly it is on a long summer's day
To go the meadow and work at the hay,
To mow it, and toss it, and turn it to die,
And carry it homeward when red is the sky.

It was a long, slow song. Soon they got into a more mocking lyric about the crows.

The first crow couldn't fly at all,
Couldn't fly at all, couldn't fly at all,
The first crow couldn't fly at all,
Of a cold and frosty morning.

The second crow fell and broke his jaw.

The third crow couldn't fill his crop.

Sister Benignus called Seamus aside; flicked briefly through the pages of a schoolbook and gave it to him. He noted that Jack the giant-killer was there.

'Tell your Daddy and Mammy to give you sixpence for this book tomorrow. Give the sixpence to me in the morning. D'ye hear me now? This is your first day at school and you can go home early, sonny.'

She put the book in his bag and closed it. Then she called one of the bigger boys, Sean Galloghy, and told him to take Seamus down the street as far as the hall and to show him the way to go home from there. It was a hot, sunny day and Sean took him carefully by the hand and walked with him in silence as far as the hall. He then told him to walk up the town as far as Daly's Corner and to turn right there. He could then follow the road to Aughabeg bridge. He warned him above all things not to go home by the railway on his own, in case he'd be killed by a train. It was evident that Sean Galloghy had heard of the bad habits some people had of using the railway as if it were a public road.

'Stick to the road, won't you? And watch out for motor cars. Keep well in on the grass.'

Sean seemed very worried about him and shook his hand solemnly as if he might never see him again because a train or a motor car was bound to run over him soon. Then he suddenly turned around and ran back to the school, leaving Seamus to find his way home.

He went only a few steps when he suddenly stood up in amazement. Looking up the wide street of the town he could see the heavy, dark shadows of the shops and houses stretching across it. Just a few people and some dogs could be seen moving along the footpaths, with a lorry or a car parked here and there. He was used to seeing that street crowded, after Mass, or whenever Nan-nan and AB took him to the fair or the market. Now it was utterly deserted and silent and the deep black shadows contrasted so sharply with the brilliant sunlight. He felt a little afraid to walk onward and up that street with its silence, its loneliness and its heavy, dark shadows.

The road home was a long and tiring one.

All was not sunshine in the schoolyard. The town boys frequently referred to the lads from the country as 'country buffers' or 'buffmen'. The country boys caused insult and indignation by referring to all town boys as 'Ardnaboes'. This provoked violent tempers and blows: for while the country people were all alike, socially and culturally, there were many strata and substrata in the social and cultural life of Ballinwing, or so the Ballinwing people liked to think. The use of 'Ardnaboe' as a blanket term of abuse, or for name-calling purposes, was something that outraged many of the elect and that hurt everyone to the inmost marrow, including the Ardnaboe children themselves.

The terms 'buffer' and 'Ardnaboe' lost much of their cutting edge as the schoolgoers grew older. By the time one left school they were seldom heard except in tactless jest or in a confidential *sotto voce*. In adult life it would have been considered unmannerly or silly to use either term openly; but in the yard of Ballinwing Infant School (St Anne's, to the knowing) the cat came out of the bag with every claw bared and ready. Here was where the stray word, said or unsaid, was taken up and translated into naked action and a living faith by those who were being taught and moulded under the patronage of the good St Anne.

The political tensions of the great world beyond were not shrugged aside either and they manifested themselves here more sharply than anywhere else in the school system. The end wall of a wooden shed in the yard, where classes were held in the summer, was chalked all over with the political slogans of the day: UP DEV! DOWN DEV! UP IRA! DOWN ACA! These were clearly visible to all; and social unrest, accompanied by physical violence, could ensue

123

when one fanatic rubbed out his rival fanatic's slogan and chalked in one of his own instead. All this was perpetrated by people who could scarcely write or recognise the other letters of the alphabet themselves. No doubt the nightly paintings on walls, roads and bridges all over the town and country were having their effect on the clean pages that were the minds of the youth of Ballinwing in general and the denizens of St Anne's in particular. It sometimes found expression also in song as a group marched around the schoolyard when no nuns were within earshot.

Up de Valera, you're the champion of the *fight!*
We'll follow you to battle, 'neath the orange, green and *white!*
And then we'll tackle Duffy, an we'll roll him in the *shite!*
And we'll crown de Valera King of *Eye-ur-lant!*

The preoccupation with politics, as well as with playing tig and trains, tended to die out in the older age groups. Their places were taken by parish football, fishing, books, hunting with the tongue-hounds and the endeavour to hold one's own in the realms of dirty, double-meaning talk and general bad language. Many took to smoking with a dedication that was impressive in its single-mindedness.

The new curate, Fr Bradley, who had replaced Fr McFee after the bank robbery, began to do his routine school visits. He soon became a great favourite. He was a quiet, sincere, austere man; and it could be guessed that he would become very angry indeed if need be or if the occasion demanded. On his arrival in the town he founded a branch of the St Vincent de Paul Society to look after some of the needs of the very poor. He also joined the golf club, which endeared him to the rich.

His popularity among the schoolchildren sprang from the fact that he never asked the usual stock catechism question that was so hard to answer and so easy to forget for a young mind. Instead, he probed in a quiet, persistent, low-key manner in an endeavour to find out what one really knew or understood. He always tried to get one to use one's own reason and commonsense. One of his most telling probes concerned Confession, which had sorrow for the sins committed as its prerequisite.

124

'But supposing you forgot to be sorry? Would your sins be forgiven then?' he would ask.

This was a serious and a fascinating question. It was also a question that struck home deeply in the young consciousness. For it frequently came to pass that, in an endeavour to follow all the simple rules that theology required, and in an anxiety to tell the sin, the whole sin and nothing but the sin, a young desperado could, and often did, forget to excite himself to a sincere contrition for his sins and transgressions. This was a question of great moment for those who were learning the Catholic faith and also for those who were trying to teach it. One often realised, with horror, when Confession was long over, that one had indeed forgotten to be sorry.

The nuns, Sister Benignus and Sister Diane, quickly began to prepare Seamus for his First Communion. They told him and those who were in his class how to approach the altar reverently and how to receive the Host: how to let it melt on the tongue and how to swallow it. And Sister Benignus took out her little pocket watch and made the class remain silent for the length of time that she estimated would elapse until the bread was absorbed into the young blood of the First Communicant.

There were pages of catechism to be learned; but this presented no difficulty to Seamus, for Veronica had pounded it all into him at home, ably assisted, and fully approved, by Nan-nan and AB, his grandaunt-in-law and his grandaunt in blood.

On the Saturday of his First Confession, Fr Bradley seated himself at the altar rails and started his work. He did not want to overawe the newcomers by having them enter the penitential darkness of the confession box. Seamus watched the other sinners kneel beside the priest and then quickly get up and walk away after he had raised his hand over them in absolution. He felt panic-stricken.

He could not tell his sins as quickly as that. The nuns had outlined for him and the class what the sins were likely to be in both shape and form. But it only went to show how little those nuns knew about real life. He had his own ideas of what was, and what was not, a sin. All the apples stolen, all the lies, all the bad words, all the frogs blow up like balloons by putting a straw up their behinds, and the stolen tobacco for chewing in the egg trees. They had all to be remembered and told. And what about the two gramophone records broken, that no-one ever knew about? And then what about the time he broke the necks of the two prize pullets when he tried to put them to sleep? Or the section of honey he stole and gave to the Martin girls, when they were having one of their 'tea parties' in Peter Sheridan's beech wood? He had tried to get the girls to cook the pullets so that he would have got rid of the bodies. But the girls threatened to tell on him instead. The section of honey calmed them. How could a *gossin* tell all that in so short a time?

Then another thought occurred to him: all the other kids were leading good holy, Catholic lives, while he was a black sinner. It would take Fr Bradley and himself a week to work their way through the whole thing. When his turn came he walked up the aisle to his confessor like a man who was about to undergo a session of dangerous surgery that would, perhaps, kill him. In this case there seemed to lurk the added hazard of disgrace, as well as of death.

And yet, it didn't turn out like that at all. He said the opening prayers word-perfect, and then rushed bravely into a recital of his sordid past. He got only as far as blowing up the frogs when Fr Bradley stopped him in his tracks. Then, just the same as during his visits to the school, he began to ask quiet questions and to direct the penitent's attention along other paths. He impressed Seamus by taking him so seriously: just as if he were a grown man instead of being a child, or a *glincín*. The Confession was over in a few, short minutes; and he arose to his feet and walked back to his place relieved, and somehow feeling a more important person.

The First Communion next morning went off as smoothly as the Confession did. There was no trouble swallowing the Host. Everyone said he would feel happy because of the arrival of God, in the form of the Eucharist, in his soul. He did not feel one bit of difference; but he decided not to tell them so. Instead he felt that he was growing up; that he was entering the realm of man; that he would be able to go to the altar and 'receive', and no nonsense and no questions asked. This was one area where no-one could criticise him or call him a *glincín*: he was on his own in that regard, no matter what anyone else could do now. He was gaining a degree of independence.

A dark, dull Sunday followed with heavy skies and a warm wind. The nuns insisted that all who had made their First Communion should go to the convent for breakfast and that they should spend the day there playing in the grounds and on the farm. It looked good.

Towards evening they all assembled around the new statue of Christ the King to have their photographs taken. The statue was situated high at the summit of a circular rock garden. The girls climbed up daintily in their long white dresses and veils and seated themselves around Christ's feet. The boys were dragooned to seat themselves in a row lower down. Sister Diane, the convent photographer, arrived with her instrument and after much screwing and gauging was at last ready to snap her lens. She looked towards the sun many times; walked back and forth to get the correct distance again and again, and called for silence. By then the First Communicants were getting restive, and a fight was about to break out among the rock plants. Order and silence were quickly restored by Sister Benignus. And then, before anyone could notice it, the photographer had snapped the scene and the gathering broke up for ever.

Two weeks later the developed film came back. Everyone gathered around to see the First Communion group. Christ the King was very photogenic and looked extremely regal and sad. The girls, nestling in spotless white at his feet, seemed to be giggling merrily. And the boys, where were they? What happened to them? Where were they gone? They were nowhere to be seen. Was it some sort of a miracle or something? Only after a time was it noticed that there were twelve curious and rounded dark objects at the bottom of the photograph and stretching in a line from one side to the other. Closer scrutiny revealed that the twelve objects were the tops of the heads of the male half of the First Communion class. In her anxiety to get Christ the King fully into the photograph Sister Diane had forgotten about the most needy of his spiritual subjects.

127

After three years with the nuns in the Infant School the boys and the girls separated. The girls went to Our Lady of Lourdes, a tall, gaunt, two-storey building on the other side of the convent lawn and past the statue of Christ the King. It had '1928' daubed in dark red paint high up on the apex of its gable. This was the year in which it was renovated. The boys went next-door to Ballinwing Boys' National School where classes one, two and three were taught by Mrs Canning and classes four, five and six were taught by Master Creamer. Mrs Canning was eternally knitting and Master Creamer smoked incessantly.

Mrs Canning got sick with gallstones. She was away for three months; and her niece, who was not a trained teacher, took over in her absence. During that time pandemonium reigned supreme. When she returned, small, wrinkled, weak-voiced and smiling wanly, she found that her three classes had slipped into a state of anarchy. It took her a long time to restore order, to stamp out rebellion and to have classes happening in their proper sequence again. But she succeeded. Soon she was knitting as furiously as ever.

In normal times she maintained control by a mixture of threats and manual violence. 'I'll leave weals on you,' was a routine threat designed to induce compliance as she flexed her muscles and brandished the cane menacingly. Everyone knew that she wouldn't leave weals on anyone; though she could leave palms tingling and stinging when the furies really took possession of her. As a shock tactic, she occasionally slapped both cheeks of her victim at the same time. This was achieved by bringing her palms violently together as if applauding. She had to make sure, of course, that someone's head had got in their swinging path, so that violence could be administered. 'You booby! You lump!' she'd cry. 'You have a head like a hen!'

She kept a small French fiddle in her locker; and now and then she would suddenly whip it out in the middle of a class and fling it across the room to Gerry Costello, a thin, dark-haired fellow from Ardnaboe. It was incredible how he could snatch that flying musical instrument out of the air: a flick of his arm and he had it. He was an outstanding player: reels, jigs and the 'Cuckoo Waltz'.

128

He could also sing; and no-one could put the same feeling of life and death into 'The Boston Burglar' that he could put into it. Another great singer in the third class, though rather nasal and somewhat lachrymose, was Teddy Harrington, whose father was a fireman on the railway. 'Where are you going, pretty bird?' was his sad song. 'We all went down to Mick McGilligan's ball' was his jolly song. These two songs constituted the extent of his musical range and repertoire.

Mrs Canning was also responsible for teaching singing to the whole school. At very irregular intervals she assembled all the boys around the walls of her classroom and took out her tuning fork. She proceeded, with varying degrees of success, to give them a note; and as soon as she got them going, she hastily grabbed the cane and began to lead them up and down a bit of old oil-cloth that was hanging on the blackboard with the tonic sol-fa dimly engraved on it. This usually led to argument and recrimination rather than to music. She called the tattered oil-cloth a modulator.

Seamus hated it all. He couldn't follow it, in any case; he hated to sing then, but he liked listening to singing. So he complied with the requirements of the Department of Education by standing obediently in the row, but with his mouth opening and closing soundlessly, like a fish, or like one of the *libín*s that he often caught in the mearing drain and kept alive in a jamjar. He always found it dead and floating on its back, wide-eyed and open-mouthed, later on next morning.

She regularly ended her class by teaching actual singable songs: and no-one could do this better than she could. The songs she taught were all in Irish and they were significant and fundamental to the native language and culture. They were also of outstanding beauty. '*Mall Dhubh an Ghleanna*', '*Óró 'sé do bheatha abhaile*', '*Bheir mí ó*' and '*Sean Dún na nGall*'. If she was ever remembered in later life, when she was dead and gone, and the young larks scattered and soaring elsewhere, it was probably by virtue of the songs she taught them. A snatch of any one of those songs heard in any part of the world later could send thoughts back to that dim schoolroom with the cardboard pictures hanging around the walls, the little clock that was always rolling on its side and going

129

slow, and the old calendar, featuring the two Bisto kids, hanging high under the ceiling, and well out of reach.

The town lads could stop a class any time by standing up and announcing to Mrs Canning a bit of shocking news of some event in the town, or by announcing news of a simple event in a shocking way.

'Please ma'am, did ye hear that John Dolan went to hospital this morning, ma'am, in an ambulance with a-pin-des-aytus, ma'am.'

Anything like that was worth fifteen minutes of school time at least, and could put by an evil hour: spelling, tables or long division. You had to hand it to the 'Ardnaboes' at times like that.

The 'buffers' got their hours of glory too when a farmer, who was sitting happily on top of a load of hay on his horse cart, was struck by a train at a level crossing. Four of his cows were involved in the accident also.

It was possible to halt the class several times a day as the cows died, or nearly died, one by one. Grizzly details of how the vet sewed up the horse kept Mrs Canning's face permanently screwed up. She stopped knitting. Then the farmer began to hover between life and death, and the engine driver was going to have a nervous breakdown. It was all great stuff. And, by watching the clock carefully and keeping one's head, many nasty subjects, like decimals, long division, Irish spelling and reciting could be pushed aside and virtually banished from the curriculum by the great events at the level crossing and elsewhere.

The parish priest was old and feeble and unable to do any work. Every morning he could be seen from the classroom as his housekeeper helped him down the steps of the parochial house and as he set out on his slow, doddering walk down the long gravel path to the gate. After leaning across the wall for some time, he would walk back again, very slowly and quietly. His young maid, Kitty, helped him up the steps.

An occasional visitor to the classrooms was Seán McBrian, a puckish-faced, lanky man from County Galway. He was a native

130

Irish speaker, and he told jokes and sang songs in the language. The Department of Education allowed people like him to visit the schools. It was hoped that such visits would help popularise the Irish language. Sean never stayed for more than an hour but he was highly popular, although practically none of the pupils knew enough Irish to understand him fully.

The doctor visited the school every two or three years and examined and weighed everybody. His nurse tested the eyes and searched for lice. A few months later the dentist came and extracted the decaying teeth. He was most unwelcome.

A very welcome visitor was a local man who suffered periodic bouts of hilarious insanity. At the outset he always donned a heavy, dark overcoat many sizes too large for him. He then proceeded to tighten the coat around him by stuffing large quantities of old newspapers inside it. It usually took a week to complete the operation; but by then he had assumed gigantic proportions. The next stage of his derangement manifested itself in music. With the hat pulled well down on his small shaven head, he went around the town playing a French fiddle. This consisted of merely rubbing the instrument across his lips and blowing into it as he went from door to door or as he accosted someone on the street and began to play at them. There was no getting rid of him. It gave great satisfaction when he came to the school-room window, huge in his paper-stuffed overcoat, and began to play at Mrs Canning when he saw her through the glass, quietly getting on with her knitting. She didn't know what to do. It went on for nearly half an hour. Everyone was delighted at her discomfiture.

'Give him a pinny an he'll go,' shouted one of the Ardnaboe lads finally.

So she opened the window, gave him a penny and off he went.

As the insanity abated, he ceased to play his instrument. Soon after he could be expected to unstuff himself of newspapers. In a few weeks he was as right as rain and out snaring rabbits and trapping pheasants.

Jack Martin showed Seamus how to make a bird-cage out of the spokes of an old bicycle wheel and bits of wood. He also showed him how to make a bird-cradle for catching birds for the cage. Then Jack got a Diana pellet gun as a present from his aunt in Belturbet and he took Seamus with him when he went out to shoot birds, just as his father did on Sundays during the shooting season. They shot wrens, robins and thrushes. Two blackbirds were shot, one after the other, which they plucked, cleaned and boiled in an old tin after lighting a fire. There was not much flesh; but the soup was good.

Nan-nan said that in the old days men would fire with buckshot at a flock of stares in a field and that one shot could kill a dozen birds or more. You had to wring the heads off the dead birds immediately and throw them away. Every stare had a little bag of poison in the head that burst at the time of death and soaked through the whole body unless it was quickly removed.

Jack and Seamus met frequently at school and sometimes came home together, although Jack was a bigger boy, in a much higher class, and got out of school very much later. Seamus would walk slowly homewards along the railway. He placed his ear to the telegraph poles and listened wonderingly to the mysterious humming. It was like eavesdropping on another, distant, unknown world. He wandered slowly through the grass and collected roasted snail boxes, left white and hard after the fires started by the sparks from the railway engines along the slopes and cuttings. Jack usually caught up with him before long. And sometimes the hectic swapping and bargaining of the schoolyard was extended to the two now dawdling home along the railway line: snail boxes for oaten bread, pencils with rubber attached for marbles, coloured chalk for buttons, sweets for apples, butts of cigarettes for comics, rollers made from cocoa canisters for pram wheels, cigarette cards showing fire engines, race horses, aeroplanes or English footballers for catapults or transfers.

Seamus hated intensely the classroom aspects of school. He was always at a disadvantage, somehow. Except for catechism he never did homework. Tommy and Veronica never seemed to have heard of it. And as for Nan-nan and AB, when they were at school, work was done on a slate with real slate pencils, and homework could not be attempted then.

On his way to school in the mornings, even if there were others around, he would secretly say many ardent Hail Marys that Mrs Canning would have another attack of gallstones. Or it would do just as well if she were to slip and fall and break her leg on the sidewalk flags at the courthouse, where so many others had slipped and fallen and sustained broken bones. He would settle for either. He could not forget that glorious three months of anarchy when she was ill. But now she apparently enjoyed perfect health, despite all his prayers. He watched her closely for signs of approaching collapse: a cough, frequent use of her smelling salts or going to the lavatory too often. Her health seemed to hold out, however; and he began to have serious doubts about the efficacy of prayer and of what his parents told him about it.

'God will certainly give you what you pray for, if you pray sincerely and hard,' Veronica was constantly telling him.

'God is everywhere. He is always listening to your prayers,' his father assured him.

That was all a joke. It didn't matter what his parents or AB and Nan-nan said about prayer. And Fr Bradley must be wrong too. It was just the usual grown-up talk designed to keep the young ones quiet and obedient. It was clear that one did not always get what one prayed for; and the appearance of Mrs Canning, seated blandly at the head of the class, pink-cheeked and knitting, was living proof of that.

On his way to school one morning he heard that Maureen Redican had been killed the previous evening. She had been one of the girls in the next higher class to his at St Anne's. She had a narrow, tanned face, and straight, streaky, ashen hair. She was always in haste; rather silent, but always rushing around as if looking for something. She was playing on the evening of her death with some other children. They were skipping. Suddenly she broke away from the small crowd, ran towards the butcher's meat-stall that was parked in the nearby shambles, quickly climbed up on its bench, found the iron bar under the eave where the meat was hung on market days, jumped towards the bar, grasped it and began to swing from it with her hands. She had done this often before, but she did not realise that she was growing. The meat stall toppled over and killed her instantly.

133

The children screamed and ran away when they heard the thud and saw the jerking body. The doctor walked away shaken and grim-faced. The Guards shook sawdust on the pool of blood. The nuns laid out the body on a rough, bare table in a white First Communion dress, with white socks to match on the feet. The table was in an unused, draughty room, in the market gatehouse with the blue-faced clock over the door, where her parents lived.

Crowds of schoolchildren went in to see the corpse and to say a silent, respectful prayer, as the nuns had told them to do. The dead girl did not look anything like what she was in life. She was so dreadfully pale. A neat oblong of cotton wool was placed over her mouth. On his way out Seamus happened to look into the kitchen. The dead child's mother was standing over a small fire that smouldered in a grate. She was slowly stirring something white in a black saucepan. She was slouched and silent and she wore a white overall which was soiled, but which was not unlike a doctor's coat in its cut. There was no-one else in the kitchen. It seemed dim and cold. She looked stunned and crushed. Her husband, the dead child's father, was that honest man, old Willie Redican, who had found the money robbed from the bank and hidden in the rick of hay a few years earlier. His wife now looked very much alone as she stood there by the weak fire, stirring the white food in her little black saucepan.

After the third class, the pupils left Mrs Canning's room and went next door to the large room where Master Creamer taught the fourth, fifth and sixth classes. On the walls hung a number of huge maps – Ireland, Europe and a map of the two hemispheres. One immense map, which was never used, was hung very high up where no-one could reach it, with the words, *Bremen North German Line – Mercator's Projection,* in large black letters. Its inaccessible position on the wall was similar to the position of the Bisto kids in the other classroom.

Nearly all the pupils in Master Creamer's room, but especially those from the town or the 'Ardnaboes' as they were called in anger or malice, smoked heavily. Frequently during classes they asked in Irish to be allowed to go out to the lavatory.

'An bhfuil cead agam dul amach, más é do thoil é?'

'I suppose your tongue is itchy for a smoke, now?' would be the half-evasive, half-taunting answer of the evil-faced Master Creamer. Eventually, after further reluctance was displayed, he would grant permission to *dul amach*. He could not be sure if the applicant was malingering.

He smoked heavily himself, pulling on the cigarette greedily, and as if for dear life. It would be wet and discoloured halfway up its length – a soggy and unpleasant spectacle.

He was a lanky, bespectacled, brown-skinned, red-nosed man with baggy trousers and a gravelly voice. He failed his early examinations when studying medicine, because of his obsession with soccer football. It was then that he switched to the teaching profession. He was a strong supporter of de Valera. He had an anti-farmer, anti-rural attitude of mind, although he was very much of rural origins himself. 'The pen is lighter than the loy,' he often growled sarcastically at those whom he considered to be of low academic potential.

'Three things an Irishman can never trust,' was another of his pronouncements, 'a cow's horn, a horse's hoof and an Englishman's laugh.' Invariably he immediately went on to give his translation of that in Irish. 'Mary McSwiney. The greatest Irishwoman of all time,' was another favourite.' There were decent Irish people who nicknamed her 'The Sea-green Incorruptible'.

He rarely used the cane: he punched his victims between the shoulder blades instead; or hauled them to their feet by pressing his cigarette-smelling knuckles under the ears and then lifting them upwards.

'Sleep standing!' was his command, as the pupil was compelled to hoist himself higher by standing on the seat of the school desk for half an hour in expiation for his transgressions.

He now had an obsession about Gaelic football and Gaelic games in general. He drank too much and he coughed like a horse. He was at the beck and call of the clergy. While the clergy themselves could be popular indeed, anyone who was popular with them was considered slightly suspect and perhaps trembling on the fringe of voteenism. Master Creamer was the mainspring in organising the annual Corpus Christi procession which, amid singing and bunting, wended its unwieldy way successfully through the streets of the town every summer.

Seamus's hatred of school and of all it stood for increased with the years. He would willingly stay at home and joyfully do all sorts of heavy and hectic work around the farm from dawn to dusk. School seemed pointless in every way; the farm and its work he found absorbing and exciting. Algebra, dictation, interest, decimalisation, declensions and conditional moods could not compare with the excitement of getting work done and of seeing plants and animals grow and selling and buying and making ends meet.

He liked the visits of the school inspector and he always did well then. He liked to answer the questions put to him by that demure little man, with the dead, sandy hair and the gold-rimmed spectacles. He still liked school when Fr Bradley came, dressed so neat in spotless black, with his gold watch-chain and its sparkling, gold passion cross. He still asked his surprising indirect questions; he still made everything so interesting; and he was so kind and understanding in the confessional. He preached too long on Sunday, of course, for Seamus's liking, but a *gossin* didn't have to listen to him then. What he did on the golf course was a closed book, a confessional, to the farming people. But when he unchained his red setter dog and went out on the hills shooting snipe he stood naked and exposed before the rural multitudes, to the sound of fruitless gunfire. He liked shooting, it was true; but he must never have shot to kill.

'No good!' exclaimed Ned Martin in disgust and in private. 'Couldn't hit a turfstack! How could he? With four eyes. He should stick to the catapult.'

Nevertheless, his visits to the school were welcome despite his faulty marksmanship.

Most of the town boys joined the local troop of the Catholic Boy Scouts and they could be seen 'receiving' at the altar rails once a month at first Mass. No-one from the country ever joined the Boy Scouts: it was considered that there was something vaguely sissyish about it; and one knew that if one joined there would be ragging from young and old alike. Country people would think it a waste of money, a show-off and peculiarly suited to the soft mentality of the town.

Every year as winter approached the teacher collected two shillings and sixpence from every pupil for coal-money. Everyone paid without distinction, and in this way the school was kept warm.

Fr Hughes, an Irishman from the Nigerian mission, came and gave a show of lantern slides in the hall. It showed a very strange mode of life: food of palm oil, pepper and rice and miles and miles of jungle with all sorts of animals, none of which seemed to frighten or alarm Fr Hughes, according to himself. There were the graves of native Africans, with token fences around them made of canes stuck in the ground at the grave edge. Little bits of ribbons tied to the stakes called to mind the ribbons tied to the bushes around Patrick's Well on the road to Tullylakenmore by those who sought cures for bodily ailments. Fr Hughes was trying to raise money for the missions. He was also hoping that someday a few of those youngsters who were listening to him would become priests and nuns and carry on his work in Africa. He sang songs the people sang, most notable of which was a song sung by the relatives of a dead man when they periodically visited his grave. Fr Hughes sang them in an African language.

> You were a great man,
> You know that we liked you very much,
> Yet, we hope you stay where you are now,
> And not come back to us again.

There were photos, also, of the graves of Irish priests who went out to Africa and who had died – some suddenly of black fever, and some old and tired after a lifetime of work. A priest or a nun could go out there and never come home again, even on a visit. The mood engendered by the lecture was one of overwhelming sadness and loneliness, although Fr Hughes was obviously a happy and jolly man and dedicated to his vocation. He could sing the songs of Africa; and he had not forgotten the songs of Ireland

137

either; the most memorable of which was 'The Minstrel Boy', which he sang with great spirit and in a clear, musical voice.

As a result of this visit some of the town kids began to save their pennies and to adopt black babies with the funds eventually accumulated. They had the privilege of having the baby called after them; and it came to pass that there were Seans and Patricks and Sheilas and Lizzies deep in the African jungle with white counterparts in Ballinwing. For a time this activity remained very popular. Again, it was not for the country children: it was good work indeed, but, like the Boy Scouts, it was considered to be frivolous and best suited for the town cast of mind.

One could ask the teacher for permission to go out for a drink of water, as well as to go to the lavatory. When the new water-works scheme for the town was completed, a metal pressure pump was installed in an enclave beside the school gate. Master Creamer raised no objections and made no comment when any of his charges asked permission, always in English, to go out for a drink of water. It was never explained why one should go to the lavatory through the medium of Irish, but go for a drink at the pump through the medium of English. Although the master did not realise it at the time, much of the thirst was bogus, and a little of it was caused by having eaten the thick slices of soda bread and butter that most of the boys took with them in the mornings for lunch. The real reason was that it afforded an opportunity to play with the pressure pump, a new invention, so far as the youth of Ballinwing was concerned. You could spray the passers-by by placing a palm under the spout and turning on the pressure. You could direct jets into the windows of passing cars or lorries. The old, who could not give chase, or the familiar, who would not mind, could be sprinkled. You could try to hit the wall on the far side of the street with a jet. You could make a rainbow in the sunny weather.

Once, as he slaked his thirst at the pressure pump, Seamus heard the sound of singing coming from the girls' convent school. It was a song in Irish which he knew well. He was struck by the clarity of the words, the pace and the movement of the singing, which made the song seem almost new to him, as well as the purity and lightness of the voices. It was a surprise to think that these girls, most of whom he only vaguely knew, could now sing so well. It contrasted so sharply with what he and his mates could do. The nuns must indeed be as good at teaching as they were said to be.

Such was the stuff that school was made of. Seamus got little enjoyment from the teaching, except for history. He made little progress at anything else. He learned to hate the Irish language. This was because of the excess of grammar, the worst feature of which was the declensions, that they were expected to learn. At one time, he and Jack Martin rather liked Irish and, of their own volition, would try to speak it and to crack jokes in it. But that was before Master Creamer got working on them. One of their jokes concerned Jimmy Murray, who was nicknamed 'the Musk', which was an abbreviation of 'muskrat'. This was an escapee rodent at the time in Ireland; it was feared they would undermine masonry foundations and cause houses, churches and bridges to collapse in rubble.

> '*An bhfuil an* Musk above?'
> '*Ó, níl an* Musk above.'
> 'Then, *cá bhfuil an* Musk?'
> '*Ó, tá an* Musk away –'
> '*Tá sé ins an* meadow –'
> '*Ag* mow-oo hay'.

He remembered his first day at school vividly and in great detail. In later life he could never recall anything of his last day at school. He left it without regret and with a sense of relief. He felt that he took away nothing from school that was of any use to him or that was of any pleasure to him. Compared with the great world outside, school was anti-life. It was a dead, dismal episode in his existence and he tried to forget it as quickly as he could. And, of course, it might never have happened if he had had the good fortune to keep away from that stunted, contorted, unhappy-looking monkey-puzzle that his father had planted in front of the house the year he got married.

18

The gunmen

Danny Mulvey and Berney McGovern knew all about it almost as soon as it had happened – the attempt to shoot Mr de Valera. Danny wasn't at the meeting where the murder was planned to take place. He would see Dev in hell first; and that went for all the politicians so far as he was concerned. Danny did not have to be told who it was who had the necessary know-how or the recklessness to try to put an end to de Valera's career. Berney McGovern would vote for Dev and canvass for him at election time, but he would not attend a meeting if he could avoid it. He hated 'spouters'. Besides that, if he went to a meeting he'd have to take drink and buy drink. For this reason alone he couldn't have seen de Valera, shot or unshot. Tommy was in town that day buying cabbage plants and cursing under his breath the pigeons that had devoured his own plot of plants: picked to the bone, behind his back. He saw de Valera going up the town in a fast and noisy motor car. It was his one and only glimpse of the great man. He didn't feel at all deprived because he had only glimpsed Mr de Valera.

There were three men actively engaged in the shooting plan; but they depended critically on a fourth man, who would be quite a distance away from the murder scene. The plan consisted in shooting Mr de Valera as he addressed a meeting from the stage of the parish hall, just across the bridge from the stone-cut market house and its blue-faced, idle clock.

The success of the enterprise depended on Willie McAdoo who supervised and attended the dynamo at the sawmill that produced the electricity for the town's light from dusk to midnight. He was expected to cause the dynamo to stop dead, just at the right moment, when de Valera was addressing his followers in the parish hall. This would pitch the room into total darkness. The marksman would be in the crowd, in the guise of a half-drunk heckler, and not far from the stage. He would have to be quick; he would have to be alert; he would have to shoot at the spot on the darkened stage where the President was last seen alive. He was a crack shot, of course. None the less, as well as being highly dangerous for the leader of the Irish at home and abroad, it would be touch and go for those lesser Irish who were sitting near him on the stage.

The meeting started dead on time, but it took the local patriots longer to get through their opening remarks and set speeches than had been anticipated. After all, this was their greatest hour. Not one of them ever dreamed that it could also have been his very last; and that as well as standing on the stage of the parish hall, he also stood on the brink of posthumous fame and of Eternity itself. It would have been a signal honour, of course, to die by the side of the leader.

Eventually Mr de Valera got up to speak. He could scarcely get a word in edgeways: the tightly packed throng almost lifted the roof off the hall at his every utterance. In the few gaps that came in the cheering, he promised the Irish dignity in the eyes of the world, total freedom and speedy reunification of the national territory. He promised the county industries, mills, flourishing markets and a quick end to emigration. The cheering lessened when he went on to tell them about the nation's agricultural outlook; but he dazzled them with the intricacies of the economic war with Britain, its strategy and its tactics and its inevitable outcome.

During the time that de Valera's speech was in progress, Willie McAdoo settled himself as usual into a comfortable chair in a small room behind the dynamo. But this time he locked the door which opened to the street, something which he had never done before. His chin was resting on his chest: he was pretending to have fallen asleep. He noticed that the engines were running sweetly that night. He was secure in the knowledge then that no-one but himself could reach the dynamo, the machinery or the switches.

Meanwhile, one of the assassins at the hall became impatient for blood and, fearing that the speech would end sooner than was

141

expected, he jumped on his bicycle and tore off for the sawmill where the dynamo was situated. He was anxious to see what was causing the delay; he was eager to be helpful if necessary. He was in great haste, of course. There were no brake-blocks on his bicycle. Incredibly, he crashed with great force into a parked car just outside the dynamo shed. He was dazed, he was bloody and his groans were loud and piteous.

On hearing the resounding crash Willie started and sprang to his feet. He forgot completely his own private plans for Mr de Valera and he tried to get out to assist the injured, whose calls for help he could now hear. But he could not open the door: he had forgotten that he had locked himself in. It also escaped his mind that he had 'mislaid' the key. In panic he rummaged in his many pockets and in two drawers before he recalled the whereabouts of the instrument. When he reached the street he found the cyclist with his head and shoulders sticking inward through the windscreen of the parked car. His bicycle was lying in the middle of the street and he seemed to be saying something very serious about greyhounds.

Mr de Valera made a very long speech. When he finished he sat down, safe and sound, to the thunder of hysterical applause, rather than the bark of gunfire. The electric light did not fail, and after a time the meeting began to break up in a quiet and orderly way.

When the marksman saw this he stopped fingering the loaded weapon in his pocket. He shouldered his way through the crowd and escaped to the street. He hurried to the sawmill and found the cyclist sitting dazed and bloody beside the running dynamo. He was nodding vaguely towards Willie. Concluding that his comrade must have been beaten up by Willie, the marksman attacked him with his fists. He was quickly pushed by McAdoo into the small room and the key was turned briskly in the door. He was now imprisoned and helpless.

For a few minutes he ranted and raged. Then he remembered that he was armed. Promptly he began to fire at the lock in an attempt to shoot himself free. It was a big comedown in a short time from attempting to shoot a president; but life has its ups and downs, as is well known. The gunfire cleared the mind of the cyclist who shouted at the marksman to stop firing or the police would come and arrest them all. Viciously, he fired his last round into the lock. Silence followed. The door remained closed. He was still locked in.

It took Willie a long time to break open the door with a tommybar. The gunfire had jammed the lock and the key wouldn't turn. When eventually the prisoner was freed he was in a surprisingly chastened mood. He picked up his cyclist comrade, who in turn picked up his bicycle from the middle of the street. It was with relief that Willie saw the three of them moving unsteadily down the hill in the direction of Main Street. He closed and locked the street door again and looked at his pocket watch. Eleven o'clock. A hour to go. It had been an unusual night to say the least of it. Once more, he seated himself in his comfortable chair behind the humming dynamo.

Willie McAdoo, a Protestant man, had let the engines and the dynamo run normally from dusk to midnight. He did not tamper with them nor switch them off at the arranged time. He saw to it, by a simple move, that no-one else could do it either. He saved many lives by his brave inaction. He prevented Ballinwing from becoming another Bealnablath. Even had he not crashed into the parked car, the man on the bicycle could not have reached the machinery or interfered with it. McAdoo had effectively blocked him out.

Willie had known that it was to be a tit-for-tat killing, a wild act of revenge for the death of a native son. Had he refused to promise to stop the dynamo when he was first approached, he had realised that, in the end, he might be compelled to do it at gun-point. This would have ensured the full success of the scheme. The shots would have been fired; the plain-clothes men would have retaliated; a stampede would have followed towards the narrow door and the long sloping passage that led to the street. Almost certainly the assassin would have been arrested sooner or later. He would have been charged, tried and hanged, according to the due processes of the law. And Willie McAdoo could have been jailed, sacked, disgraced or shot.

But by giving the impression that he was, more or less, afraid

143

to refuse to co-operate, and then by not interfering with the electric current at the critical time, he managed to let an evil hour pass by. Afterwards, when it was all over, no-one could point a finger at him in praise or indignation.

Yes, he was bitterly opposed to de Valera, but he wasn't that bitterly opposed to him. There were free elections, weren't there? Also, it is probable that Willie never realised how safe he was in that town and at that time. He was a Protestant working man: no-one would dream of laying a finger on him. Anyone who would do such a thing, would never, never live down the disgrace of the deed. But it is highly unlikely that Willie had an inkling of that himself. In the eyes of many local people, it would have been far worse to shoot him than to shoot Mr de Valera.

Much as the Flynn household disliked de Valera, the attempt to shoot him outraged them. Veronica tightened her lips to a seam as she poked the fire in an abstracted way with the tongs. 'The notorious villain!' That was all that she would say. But she repeated it over and over again as she continued to poke the coals and to think of the marksman.

Yet, had she and her family and other similar families at that time no share in the guilt for the strife and the violence of the day? Was it not, to a considerable extent, sustained and nurtured by the immoderate tenor of their conversation about public life as they sat around the fire at night when the ceiliers came in? Although of tender years, and expected to be seen but not heard when his elders were talking, Seamus found it a complete surprise that the grown-ups of the household were against shooting Dev. His mother's indignation and her calling the marksman a 'notorious villain' was something which he had not expected. It took him unawares; it impressed him permanently. He had invented a secret game in the pines behind the beehive of 'shooting Dev'. He quickly gave it up. The adults, he noted, said one thing but did another.

Seamus always wanted to know in later years who was the man who nearly shot Dev. No-one would tell him. There was no point in pleading with his father or his mother. So he tried all his skills on Nan-nan and AB. 'Ask no questions and you'll be told no lies,' he was told sharply.

He was a grown man himself before the identity of the marksman was disclosed to him, 'the man who nearly shot Dev'. It greatly surprised him. The marksman was then a quiet, hard-working and responsible citizen with little apparent interest in politics. He was meticulous in observing his religious duties also. One wondered if he ever said a prayer for Willie McAdoo, the man who had saved him from himself on that dark evening so long ago, when the lights did not fail because the dynamo was not stopped, and life had gone on as usual and in its humdrum way.

Mr de Valera didn't like it at all when he heard later on that a few of the Ballinwing boys were thinking of shooting him. He was very offended indeed; and he threw his cap violently on the floor and then kicked it out through the open window. As was well known, he was a great man for fresh air and early morning walks. He was supposed to have shouted then at the top of his voice that Ballinwing, and indeed the whole county as well, would never get anything from him while he was in power. And from that day onward the impression grew that the town could never get any of the new industries that were going at the time. It was accepted that the whole county would remain poor and backward, for all that Dev cared, and that the roads would remain bad and the population continue to plummet. It was indeed a very heavy price to pay for not having shot Mr de Valera. Yet, the people shrugged and took it all in good part. And they then went on to vote for him overwhelmingly and with diligence and loyalty for the next thirty years, or until he retired and went to the Phoenix Park.

Willie McAdoo did not last that long in his job. He was an older man, and he retired many years earlier than Mr de Valera did. And, of course, no-one seemed to notice it when he quietly reached the age of sixty-five. Then one night he switched off the dynamo for the very last time at the sawmill; he lit his pipe and, buttoning his overcoat, cycled home unnoticed in the darkness.

19

Scollops

Mrs Martin came down the road pushing a pram. Asleep inside it was the baby whose skull Seamus had fingered to see for himself if the skulls of infants were soft at the crown. She took the baby in her arms and began talking to Veronica about chickens. Veronica sat down, took the baby and began to dance it admiringly on her lap. It was morning. She sang:

> Clip clop my little horse,
> Clip clop again.
> How many miles to Babylon?
> Three score and ten.

> Clip clop my little horse,
> Clip clop again.
> Can we get there by candle light?
> Yes! and back again.

Nan-nan was peeling a few Bramley seedlings for a cake. She was busy. Something or other must have reminded her of the rhymes recited to children when she was young. She dropped the apple and the knife. She'd show them how it used to be done in Tullylakenmore. Placing her hands on her knees she bent down towards the child. There was a very serious expression on her face:

> Did you hear the wan about Molly McGlory?
> She went to the wood and she killed a tory.

> Did you hear the wan about her brother?
> He went to the wood and he killed another.

No-one present, perhaps not even Nan-nan herself, knew it then, but she had just recited one of the oldest of Irish nursery rhymes. It

146

was recited to childen for generations, back to the seventeenth century. It made the child on Veronica's lap stop, stare and then gurgle delightedly with laughter.

After a while Mrs Martin left with her pram and her child and her talk about chickens. Veronica accompanied her to the gate at the lane where they lingered in conversation. While all this was going on, a very serious event took place in the kitchen. Nan-nan caught Seamus feeding his stirabout on a spoon to Foreman, the tongue-hound dog.

She could scarcely believe what she was seeing. Then it struck her like a blinding flash. Stirabout had almost ceased to be an issue for some time; and she had concluded that the *glincín* was coming around, growing out of his childish ways and eating what was put in front of him in a no-nonsense fashion. She thought there was a little more colour in his cheeks lately too. And now the delusion was shattered. There he was, hunched forward at the end of the table, calmly spooning his stirabout into the dirty dog's mouth when he thought that no-one was looking. And as brazen as you please.

She shouted at him. He started and looked at her in terror. And then it happened: he withdrew the spoon from the dog's mouth; stuck it noisily into the mug and began to spoon the stirabout into his own mouth frantically.

For once she was speechless. Her hands moved helplessly. She sat down. Luckily there happened to be a chair behind her. She wanted to tell that *glincín* to – stop – eating – that – stirabout. She want to tell him to – stop – putting – that – spoon – in – his – mouth. She could not find the words at first. A few silent seconds followed. Her hands and feet fidgeted nervously before she recovered the power of speech.

'Sthap! Sthap! Sthap it! – ye dirty imp of the devil yeh,' she screamed. 'Putting the spoon into your mouth after that dirty brute of a hound having it between his teeth and licking it too with his stinking tongue.' She spat into the fire in disgust. Her face was contorted, her eyes watery.

She called to the others in a faltering voice. She suddenly seemed weak and fragile; the first time Seamus had ever seen her like that. She told them what she had seen. Tommy came in later and had to be told the whole story over again. They were speechless; they were disappointed. What in the world were they going to do with him at all? Veronica, when she recovered a little, said that she supposed he was spooning stirabout in the same way into Snap's mouth – Snap, who they all knew was out of his mind with fits or rabies or whatever it was he had.

'Oh don't say that, Veronica,' pleaded Nan-nan. 'Don't say that! Don't say he's bad enough to do a thing like that.' Her voice was small.

'The cross of Christ be about us!' exclaimed AB in horror.

They half feared that if the *glincín* was spooning his stirabout to Snap they could all be infected by now with fits or rabies. They looked at the *glincín* seated at the lower end of the table as if they expected him to start barking at them any moment, or snarling or frothing at the mouth, and with his eyes gone bloodshot as well.

He could have told them, of course, that he had never given Snap spoons of stirabout. The reason for this was that Snap was too low, too small and too near the ground. You would have to bend down to get the spoon into his mouth. He had Foreman well trained for the stirabout. When Nan-nan or Veronica gave him a mug and a spoon and ordered him to start eating, he made Foreman go under the table or in between the chair and the wall. That dog could take the stirabout off a spoon just like a Christian. And he was the right height: you didn't have to bend down.

Seamus always took the first spoon of stirabout himself, just to show the humans who were in the kitchen that he was complying with their wishes. After that he spooned the food into the animal's mouth. Of course he kept moving his jaws up and down, just as he did when singing at school or when praying, and he had learned to make the most convincing swallowing sounds which seemed to have gained him a very high opinion in the household.

And now this! He knew he should have been more careful. He supposed it would be stirabout night, noon and morning from now on. He noticed then, with some surprise, that the grown-ups seemed to have forgotten about him. He had expected to receive a heavy thrashing; or worse still, to be sent to bed for the next twenty-four hours. Instead they were deep in conversation and quite oblivious to his presence. It was a domestic crisis of extreme seriousness. Tommy, who had remained silent throughout, could be heard talking decisively.

'Yez may put down as big a fire as yez can and boil as many pots of water as yez can. Then, every knife, fork and spoon, every mug, plate and porringer in the house will have to be boiled time out of mind.'

'And that Snap article will have to be done away with at once,' added Veronica sharply.

Seamus seized the opportunity presented to him and escaped unnoticed from the kitchen. Life was getting difficult. He decided to make for the egg trees where he could have a think and a quiet smoke and recover his dignity and his self-assurance. However, when he reached the old spot he found to his dismay that the egg trees were no longer there: they had vanished! It was now his turn to find himself speechless. He felt naked and unprotected as well.

For the egg trees were cut to the roots; all but a foot. And, as he stood there looking at what was once his haven and his refuge, he realised that Tommy and Jimmy Gaffney had done it. He recalled overhearing their conversation about having both their houses thatched and that they would need to point plenty of scollops. And the two men had just cut everything in sight.

He walked over to the turf-shed. Hung high under the topmost rafters he could see several neat bundles of scollops tied with hay-ropes. They were all that was left of his egg trees. The bundles would season nicely up there under the rafters in readiness for the thatching to begin.

He returned to his refuge and had a closer look. He noticed with pleasure that all the bottles and crockery were still there, as well as the bric-a-brac he had collected from the railway. They all lay untouched among the stumps of the egg trees. He knew also that in a year or two the egg trees would have grown up again and that he could come back there for solitude and renewal. He was about to walk away when he had a thought. He stooped down among the stumps and assured himself that the horns Uncle Peter had cut off the bullocks were still there. He would find another place for them soon. Then he searched further and found the Lough Neagh hone. He put it in his pocket and crossed the mearing drain by the plank. Strangely, AB hadn't missed it from the drawer in the kitchen this time.

He wandered over the fields towards the ould house, where the byre and the hayshed were. At St Anthony's Gap he climbed up on the double ditch that had a row of thick whitethorns and black sallies growing on both sides. It was where the geese sometimes nested when there were no foxes about. He came to where a tree had fallen, but had continued to grow, and was now covered with ivy. There was a nook at the side. He crawled in and seated himself. He had no smokes and no chew. So he had to content himself with his thoughts.

As he sat there among the dead leaves he considered that all the fuss about Foreman eating stirabout off a kitchen spoon was indeed very foolish. He had often opened Foreman's mouth and looked in. It was as clean as a whistle. His teeth were clean and shiny and his tongue was red and fresh. It was far cleaner than Nan-nan's tongue when she stuck it out every morning before the looking-glass to see if it was coated. Foreman's lips and the inside of his cheeks were black and shiny, just like washed coal. And he had sixty-four teeth; far more than Nan-nan, who had only a few left.

He had looked into the cat's mouth also, though it wasn't easy, and had tried to count her teeth. He saw the hairs on her tongue that she used when lapping milk. He looked into the ass's mouth and tried to count his teeth. And when he grew up he would be able to tell the age of a horse or a cow by looking at their teeth. Uncle Peter told him he would teach him how to dehorn bullocks and how to castrate yearlings. He didn't want to learn either of these skills, but he wasn't letting on. He would love to be old enough to ring pigs. Whenever Matthew McGoohan came over from Glasgow they had to let him ring a pig, even if the pig didn't need rings. This was done to oblige him. He said it made his holiday.

Just as in the egg trees, the birds came very near him in the hideout on the double ditch. He could see them breathing as they looked at him: first with one eye, then with the other. He remembered that there were puffballs growing on the double ditch at the end of the hayshed. When you tore a puffball open a lot of dark green dust came out. Nan-nan said that the dust could stop a badly bleeding wound. And if you had a cut that was festering or bleeding the dust could heal it quickly.

He was going to try again to get his father or Jim Gaffney to take him to see the moving island on Lough Ooragh. It was a small lake with plenty of good fish. They could take him on the bar of the bicycle any Sunday in the year. The small island with sallies on it floated slowly across the lake according to what sort of weather was expected. If bad weather was on the way it moved to one side of the lake; if good weather was coming it went to the opposite side. Those who knew the movements of the island could tell when frost or snow or thunder was coming. Seamus felt he wanted to see it soon. It was only four miles away in the parish of Clonmoher.

He also wanted them to take him to the cromlech at Ballydoon. He often saw it in the distance; but he wanted to be beside it and to see how it was built. Jim Gaffney said that when he was young and skinning from school he often sat on the cromlech all day in the sun. Seamus's father said it was more than four thousand years old. Just as old as the game of hurling.

After a time he returned to the house. He kept very quiet. There was a huge fire of turf and sticks burning on the hearth. Three pots, all of them full with cutlery, household utensils and crockery, were boiling with a sound that reminded him of the noise Veronica's plum puddings made when being boiled on Christmas Day. Nan-nan stood before the fire anxiously looking into the flames. She held a sod of turf in each hand. Her stance resembled the ould Doctor as he built a fire in his kitchen in that vain attempt to bring back to life the dead Julia Cafferty, whose body had vanished from her coffin in the chapel yard.

His thoughts were interrupted by a confused yelping outside. It sounded like Snap's voice. When he went to investigate he was just in time to see Tommy going out through the gate and into the lane with a sack on his back. Something inside it was moving and struggling frantically.

151

Seamus ran down the path to the gate. He could see his father walking rapidly up the lane towards the canal with the moving sack on his back. He knew that it was the end of Snap. He turned then and began to walk slowly down the lane. He raised his head and noticed that three boys, one of whom was older than himself, were standing looking at him. Suddenly they ran off. The three of them were wearing petticoats.

20

Franco

Mussolini invaded Abyssinia and everyone around Drumlahan hoped that he would be soundly beaten. Tommy said that when he was a *gossin,* the Abyssinians had cut the Italians to pieces at a place called Aduwa. He hoped they'd do the same again; sometimes he felt sure that they would. Ned Martin read the *Irish Independent* carefully in the evening after he came home from work on the railway and he referred to Mussolini as a case-hardened brute. He was going out to slaughter poor innocent black people who never did any harm to anyone. To make it worse, the Abyssinians were Christians, something Ned didn't know until lately. They weren't Communists, or other riff-raff.

'Never mind!' said Tommy. 'They did it at Aduwa, and maybe to God they'll do it again.' In what seemed like an afterthought he added, 'You know, Catholic people like the Italians should know better than to do a thing like that. It's very mean. It's a very dirty turn they are doing to decent, innocent people.'

Tommy was of the opinion that Mussolini was not half bad, if he would only keep away from war and plundering. He did succeed in draining the Pontine marshes, didn't he? Even the Popes and Julius Caesar had failed in their attempts to drain them. It was all good land now, giving crops and grazing cattle. He wished to God that Mussolini would take a walk around Drumlahan and Ballinwing and do some draining. There were plenty of Pontine marshes in the west of Ireland for the likes of the bold Mussolini. And he made the trains go on time in Italy for the first time ever. And it must never be forgotten either that he gave the Pope an independent state. It was the first time that the Pope had proper freedom since the days of Garibaldi, when that man McKeon from the mountain went out to fight for His Holiness,

153

just as plenty of others did too. And then, in Musso goes to Abyssinia taking all before him.

'It's a disgrace for a Catholic country to do a thing like that. God knows it is,' concluded Tommy heatedly.

Veronica stood outside the kitchen door silently mixing a bucket of hens' feeding. Musing to herself she was overheard to say vehemently, but almost under her breath: 'Mussolini, the reptile, the reprobate . . . to start the war like that!'

There was a larky song sung at that time by the boys who went to dances on bicycles and who played pitch-and-toss at Aughabeg crossroads:

Will ye come to Abyssinia, will ye come?
Bring yer loads of ammunition and yer gun.
Mussolini will be there,
Shooting bullets in the air,
Beyant in Abyssinia in the sun!

Soon Ned and Tommy saw the big black arrows on the south-east frontier and along the border of Italian Somaliland whence the invasion was launched. The reports in the papers were bad. It became clear to them very soon that history was not going to repeat itself, and that there would be no second Aduwa for the Italian army. They stopped reading about Abyssinia in the newspapers. It was soon all over.

Whilst almost everyone had known well in advance that it was Mussolini's intention to invade Abyssinia and that war was imminent, few were aware of the dark clouds that were gathering in Spain. In fact, the fighting there was in progress for some time before many realised what was happening. This could possibly be ascribed to the fact that the Spanish fighting was a civil war, whilst the African affair was an international conflict. Veronica, as well as the two old ladies, might have remained oblivious of what was happening for many months had not she and Tommy received an invitation from Jack and Bridie Sweeney, two distant relations of theirs who were leaving Ballinwing and going to live in Athlone.

The Sweeneys had remained very close to the Flynns over the

years. They lived in a bungalow that they had built just above Ardnaboe on their return from America. Accordingly, one wet day in August that was good for nothing else, Billy allowed himself to be backed into the trap. Faces were washed and shoes were polished and in due course they trotted over the road to Aughabeg and into Ballinwing to visit their departing relations.

The visit to Jack and Bridie at the bungalow was a great success. Before they returned Tommy had shown the Sweeneys the scars on Seamus's head, sustained by falling into the mearing drain. Veronica repeated that his wasted appearance could be traced to the fact that he would not eat stirabout; and Tommy cut in to say that if he had the money to spare he would, nevertheless, send him to Waterford where they could make a fluent Irish speaker of the *gossin* in six months. His listeners thought he was cracked of course when they heard of the Waterford plan. But Veronica was still convinced that his teeth wanted to be 'drew'. As an after-thought, Tommy rummaged in his overcoat pocket and pulled out the hair-ball that he had found in Billy's dung. Jack had heard all about it beforehand, and when Tommy handed it to him he went as if to drop it on the floor to see if it would hop like a handball. At this Tommy became indignant and snatched it back and restored it to his pocket.

It was almost dark when they returned to Drumlahan, and both of the adults could be seen only with great difficulty behind all the stuff they had in the trap as they drove up. There were garden plants of many kinds: rose-bushes, complete with roots and blooms, French-currant bushes, fuchsias, banks of carnations, dozens of sweet williams, dahlias, peonies and a basket of tulip bulbs. There was a cardboard box of records for the gramophone: reels, jigs and hornpipes as well as a record of Will Fyffe singing 'I Belong to Glasgow!' and 'I'm Ninety-four Today'. There were a few records of Jimmy O'Dea and Harry O'Donovan. There were also bundles of books, one of which was entitled *Munster Folktales* and which was to become very popular with children and grown-ups alike when Tommy read from it for the household on winter nights at the fireside. Seated on the floor of the trap and surreptitiously devouring unripe apples was Seamus. In his arms he held a mild-looking, well-groomed stuffed badger on a wooden pedestal.

When they had unloaded the horse-trap and milked the cows, Tommy, to the great annoyance of the women of the house, lost no time in getting out one of the Jimmy O'Dea records for the gramophone. He stood there now, oblivious of the bouts of female fury going on around him, with his head halfway into the gramophone horn. He shook with subdued laughter as he listened in delight to Jimmy O'Dea mimicking the 'ould wan' from the Coombe explaining herself to the world. He turned the record over; wound up the gramophone again and listened to Jimmy, who was joined by Harry O'Donovan with their skit on the newly-issued coinage of the Irish Free State:

> The new Irish coins
> They would give you the jigs;
> Now, I put the question to you, sir,
> With horses and greyhounds
> And fishes and pigs,
> Our pockets are just like the zoo, sir.

'I was never more ashamed in my life,' said Veronica decisively as they sat down for the evening meal at the table. 'There was Bridie going on about this General Franco fellow, and the Moroccans, and I didn't know one word of what it was all about. I had to sit there like a *stucaun,* open-mouthed, till you and Jack came back from the forge.'

'Aw she must have read it in the papers, I suppose,' said Tommy, unimpressed.

'Bridie never reads a newspaper. Never did in her life. We get papers here every week, as well as on Sunday, and sometimes oftener and I never heard a single word about Spain, or General Franco. Or the Bolshies either.'

'Forget about it. Bridie and the Bolshies!' said Tommy wearily. 'It's in the papers every day. I didn't mention it. I was thinking about the hay and the turf. If you women would read more and talk less, you'd soon hear all about Franco and the boys.'

'Well you could have mentioned what was going on at least.

Jack must have mentioned it to Bridie. I never felt so bad or so let down in my life. And there was Bridie, chattering on about General Franco and the priests and the nuns getting killed. She never noticed the vegetables boiling over, she was so het up about it all. I had to tell her . . .'

'For Christ's sake will you drop it. I hadn't time to tell you. Look woman! There was that yearling with red water, and Tim's meadow cut and rotting in the rain. I suppose we'll have General Franco, and the Moroccans, and Bridie's Bolshies for breakfast, dinner and tea for the next three months!'

It was in this way that the Spanish Civil War came to one household in Drumlahan. And they had it for much more than three months.

For almost three years the war was an unending source of talk, speculation, anxiety and horror. At times it seemed to go away, to die down or to be obscured by some local event. Yet, it always came back from the wings, and when it finally ended everyone was truly relieved.

All in the Flynn household and all the neighbours were supporters of General Franco to a man. Many newspapers were bought and borrowed just to see how the war was going.

Ned Martin found strength to put on his steel-rimmed spectacles for the first time in public so that he could read the newspapers urgently and study the maps. He had had the spectacles for some years, but he was ashamed to be seen using them. The Spanish Civil War changed all that. He sat there every evening after work in his low-backed armchair in front of the fire. His long, stockinged feet moved excitedly as he studied the maps and announced the distance, to the nearest mile, between the Nationalists and the Reds, or between Seville and Badajoz. The atrocities perpetrated against priests and nuns, the burning of churches and of church property, the daubing and smashing of religious statues all gave shock and drove people into unusual silence. Women exclaimed, 'God Almighty save us this night and this day!' Men took the pipe or the Woodbine from the mouth and reverently touched the rim of the hat or the peak of the cap, in the manner customary on hearing of a death.

157

There was no respect for Mussolini after what he had done in Africa; Hitler was regarded as a funny, unmannerly little brat, whom no-one could take seriously; but General Franco was a hero. Franco was fighting for God, for the Church and for civilisation against the evil of Communism. Indirectly, he was also fighting against the awful and godless Russians.

Nan-nan was indignant when she saw the photo of a butchered priest. 'It's just like Ballinamuck and the Redcoats. It's Ballinamuck all over again. And Spain such an old and Catholic country, like ourselves!'

She made the sign of the cross and shuffled across to the dresser where she muttered inaudible prayers as she prepared the evening tea. She was on the brink of tears.

The struggle in Spain took Nan-nan's mind and the minds of many others off Mr de Valera and the economic war that some people felt he was waging against them, small and helpless farmers.

No-one knew precisely what a Communist looked like, apart from the photos of scruffy-looking Reds in the newspapers. There was a young fellow of about nineteen years of age who did odd jobs for old Peter Sheridan of the post office. He milked cows, sawed firewood, carted turf home from the bog, drew an occasional bucket of water from the well and cleaned out the byre or the hen-house. His name was Teddy Mitchell and he was the centre of great wonder among the children because he had a cork leg. He walked lamely; and when he came to work every morning on a squeaking, dilapidated bicycle, he cycled lamely also. He was a fair-haired, round-faced, frightened-looking young fellow of about five feet eight inches. He was very quiet and he had whey-coloured skin. People spoke of him in awe and with a strange form of guarded respect. For, as well as having an artificial leg, he was said to be a Communist.

It would have been difficult to imagine him butchering Fr Bradley, blowing up the chapel or raping the nuns. Of course, one could never tell: deep waters often run smoothly. Having the name of being a Communist set him apart.

Yet, no-one ever harmed him or harassed him or mentioned it

to him, although feeling against Communists was high. Perhaps his cork leg saved him from the attentions of the more truculent. He worked there quietly for about two years during the Spanish Civil War. He smoked an occasional Woodbine and drank the odd bottle of stout. Then he left suddenly on his squeaking bicycle and was never heard of again in Drumlahan or Aughabeg.

The talk around the fire when the ceiliers came in the evenings had a gloomy tinge that it took from the war in Spain. Many of the usual topics, especially those of a reminiscent nature, were pushed into the background by the pressure of events.

General Eoin O'Duffy announced that he was going to take a contingent of Irishmen to Spain to fight against Communism. He was the leader of the Blueshirt movement in its heyday, and he was a highly respected man in County Monaghan in the fight against the British and the Black-and-Tans earlier on. Tommy never forgave O'Duffy for not insisting that Kevin O'Higgins should have had a permanent armed guard because he was a cabinet minister in the aftermath of Ireland's own Civil War. Had he been properly guarded, he would not have been shot dead on his way to Mass in Dublin in 1927, according to Tommy. O'Duffy, as Police Commissioner then, had a responsibility to see to that. On the day of the murder, O'Duffy was on a day-trip to the seaside at Bundoran with his old friend Mr Tummon from Clones, a businessman and a buyer who was well known to every farmer in the Ballinwing area who had pork to sell.

Mr de Valera was against O'Duffy's expedition to Spain. It was an internal Spanish problem, he said; it was a civil war and no outsiders should intervene. Nan-nan and Tommy said that every-one was interfering anyhow, including that ass Mussolini and that little brat Hitler in Germany. Dev should know all about civil wars, having started one himself in Ireland in 1922. It was rumoured that many of the more devotedly Catholic and manly young fellows in the district were going to join O'Duffy and follow him to Spain.

O'Duffy said that Ireland, a mainly Catholic country, should feel in honour bound to make a contribution towards the defeat of the Communists. He would recruit a contingent that would go to

Spain for six months, or to the end of the war, whichever was the shortest.

Berney McGovern, Danny Mulvey and Uncle Peter said that O'Duffy just wanted to find another outlet for his energies after the failure of his Blueshirt movement, the ACA.

No-one from Drumlahan or Ballinwing, or even Clonmoher, where support for O'Duffy was strong, ever went to Spain, as matters turned out.

'That's where they should be, out in Spain fighting the godless Communists instead of fighting among themselves,' thundered Nan-nan.

About six hundred from all over Ireland went with O'Duffy in the end. They departed in secrecy. The newspapers made great and exciting reading. And as Ned Martin read out the details from his armchair in the evenings, he twirled his stockinged feet about with such emphatic gestures that Mrs Martin feared he would get one of them jammed behind the back of his neck. The churches continued to be burnt. Even the parents of priests and nuns were not spared. They too were tortured and killed, and everyone in Drumlahan privately mourned them.

The Irish Brigade was on the Jarama front and in action. They could hear the Cockney accents of some of the enemy in the International Brigade carried on the wind across the stretching territory that was no-man's land. Had matters been better organised, it could well have been the Irish and the English at each other's throats again and on foreign soil, as at Cremona or Ramillies in the past. Captain Tom Hyde from the south was killed by a bullet in the neck. Others died also and their names and photographs appeared in the newspapers. There continued to be big coverage of the fighting all over Spain, and General O'Duffy, General Franco and General Mola were on everybody's lips, and in that order also, especially in the first year of the conflict.

Eventually the tide began to turn. O'Duffy and his followers came home quietly when their term of service was up. Some despised them; many were indifferent; others claimed that they had made the right gesture, that they had played a very small, but an honourable part, in a just war. Actually, they did very little fighting.

The Nationalists and General Franco began to win the war. The Reds, or the Communists, began to have the look of defeat about them. Most people knew in their bones that all was going well in Spain now: that the Reds would be routed; that Franco would win; that the churches, convents and cathedrals would be rebuilt; that priests and nuns would soon be free to walk around like anyone else. People everywhere began to lose the very intense interest in Spain which they once had. In Drumlahan it was abruptly pushed out of people's minds by two new, but very important, events. The first was a virulent plague of foxes that was cleaning the country of poultry. The second was a rumour that a new Anglo-Irish trade agreement was to be signed in the near future which would bring to an end the disastrous economic war and lift the prices of cattle.

21

The foxes

When Tommy was a young man foxes were unknown in the Ballinwing and Clonmoher areas. They were found only in the mountains, where the diet was grouse and other game, with the occasional lamb. He well remembered the first time he heard a fox bark. It was late on a dark night in early November. He was digging potatoes that day and he had not finished putting rushes on the heap until long after darkness fell. There was the milking to be done then. Afterwards he walked the railway to Ballinwing to obtain his few small groceries at Paddy McGrail's. On his way home he heard an outrageous scream as he walked up Lisagirwin lane. It was near midnight then; not a light was to be seen in any of the local houses.

He was scared stiff. He heard the scream again, and it sounded quite near. He tried to pray, but found he could not. So he took out his penknife, opened the blade, buttoned his overcoat, turned his cap back to front and prepared to sell his life dearly. He heard the scream once more, this time coming from the lime kiln on his left, and he managed a short prayer for the souls in purgatory, a community which he expected to join soon. He walked bravely on. Eventually he reached home unmolested, but breathless and shaken.

After that terrible night the fox population increased rapidly. There was plenty of shelter for them on the whin-covered hills, but they seemed to prefer the many outcrops of limestone for their earths. They were kept under control in the years that followed by shooting and trapping and by being hunted by the tongue-hounds, of which there were four in Drumlahan alone, one each in the houses of four different farmers. Sometimes the foxes, just like the pheasants and the grouse on the mountains, suddenly vanished and were not seen for a few years. Their eventual return was always inevitable.

Whether it was the economic war or the Spanish Civil War or some other unknown factor, no-one could say, but suddenly the foxes became so numerous and so daring that nothing, it seemed, could stop their raids. They snatched a goose from near the plank on the mearing drain one night, and it became one more of Seamus's increasing duties to see that the geese were shut and bolted in the car-house every evening. No more hatching of green goslings now on the double ditch behind the ould house. The foxes broke into hen-houses and massacred wantonly all the hens inside. Turkeys and ducks were not spared either; they never touched lambs, though, as they had done on the mountains in the olden days.

The foxes may have been driven in from some other area, or they may have been constrained to migrate because of a lack of food or plunder. There had been a marked diminution in the amount and vigour of hunting done since the time of the Treaty because of the necessity of attending public meetings and of looking after the affairs of the nation on Sundays after Mass. But Ned Martin reported an unexpected scarcity of game; and he wondered if the foxes had cleared it themselves, or if the game had died out suddenly because of disease and had left the foxes starving.

So how to control Reynard? How to exterminate him? Hen-houses were fortified; netting-wire runs were erected to keep in the hens and to keep out the animals. Shotguns were oiled and practice shots taken. Fox earths were sealed, snares were hung carefully and traps were set treacherously. It was all in vain. Men looked worried; wives wrung their hands, looked heavenwards and sprinkled holy water reverently. Yet the poultry population continued to be decimated. A hen or a turkey could not dare to cross the road without seriously wondering if she would ever reach the other side.

It was remarked on by shrewd men and women among the bowl-shaped, whin-covered hills that the foxes seemed to keep away from farms where there was a tongue-hound. The four houses in Drumlahan that 'kep a hound' lost little or no poultry, and they had never been subjected to a serious onslaught by the foxes. The loss of the goose from the mearing drain was an exception; it was also carelessness. A goose in such a place and at such a time was a sore temptation to any sane and able-bodied fox.

That they spared a tongue-hound house may have been because if a hound once picked up the scent and the trail he could follow a fox all over the country for hours on end. His *goldar* – or tongue – would bring out other hounds if they happened to be unchained at the time, and the fox could find himself in a situation of extreme jeopardy. He would have to run for his life, with no chance of sitting down to devour a plundered hen in peace and comfort. Perhaps it was for these reasons that the fox's cuteness kept him away from any house where a tongue-hound slept at night.

It was further observed that nothing was so good or so effective in killing foxes as the tongue-hounds were. And a combination of guns, people, terriers and assorted enthusiastic mongrels with a tongue-hound could be lethal for any fox, no matter how clever.

The reeds at Thurles always harboured a few foxes. It was a swampy area, a few acres in extent. The reeds grew six to ten feet tall in a dense green mass that became yellow in winter and swayed in the breeze. Lower down, large *purtauns*, sometimes two feet or more in diameter, grew up from the swampy soil. A fox could have safe and comfortable bedding on the summit of one of these. Many availed themselves of the opportunity thus presented.

So, every Sunday morning in winter or in early spring, the reeds were surrounded by men with guns and ashplants and crowds of bare-kneed boys with agitated and excitable terriers. The tongue-hounds were encouraged, by the use of a mysterious hunting language supposedly known only to themselves and men like Danny Mulvey, to go into the reeds. Stolidly they obeyed and disappeared. Silence usually reigned for some time, except for the inadvertent hysterics of some highly-strung terrier of unknown ancestry who lost his nerve and began to yelp. Inevitably the first *goldar* was heard from the hounds. This meant that they had picked up a true scent: the fox was at home; and the tongue-hounds knew it and were coming to get him.

Quickly the hunt would approach the edge of the reeds on one side or the other. If the fox appeared, a gunshot or two could possibly be heard, accompanied by shouts and the throwing of stones, sticks or ashplants in anger. Distraught terriers and small boys would converge on the scene of the tumult. Usually the fox retreated and sought another exit.

It was on one of these occasions, when Seamus was doing his stint on guard along a stretch of reedy territory between two black-sally bushes, that he came face to face with a fox. He heard the faint rustle and he saw the fox's face emerge through the undergrowth ten yards in front of him. He had a useful chunk of limestone in one hand and a heavy throwing-stick of blackthorn in the other. The fox halted and looked at him enquiringly. He looked at the fox with wonder and interest: he had never seen one at such close quarters before. Was it the first time the fox had ever seen a human being so clearly too? The quick seconds passed. Seamus and the fox seemed to try to read each other's thoughts. He did not now see the hunted animal as an enemy. He could not fling that chunk of fossiled limestone.

The fox turned very slowly and went back, sadly as it seemed, into the reeds. Seamus was sure he had never seen such a fine-looking animal before. He was surprised that a fox could look so beautiful. The mysterious, enquiring expression on the fox's face remained vividly in his mind. He never told anyone else about the occurrence.

Hot on the trail, the tongue-hounds came to the edge of the reeds, turned where the fox had turned and headed back in through the dense, dark undergrowth. This meant that the fox would try to get out somewhere else. He hoped that the animal would make good his escape. A shot rang out. He started. And then another shot. It would be an instant death and no tearing asunder by the hounds. There followed an outbreak of schoolboy cheering and then a brattle of frenzied barking and yelping from overwrought terriers and mongrels.

The dead animal was taken to the police next day. Its tongue was cut out so that the marksman could receive the ten shillings that was due to him under the Scheme for the Extermination of Foxes that was sponsored by the County Council. The carcase was then sold to a man from Ardnaboe. He skinned it. He threw the flesh and bones into the canal. He dressed the pelt, cured it in alum and produced a beautiful fox-fur. This he sold to the pension officer's wife, who wore it grandly around her short neck every Sunday when she went to Mass. When she laboriously climbed the stairs of the organ gallery, where all the swanks were wont to go, Seamus often stole a glance at her as she waddled her ascent. The tail of the fox always hung downwards from her left shoulder blade, and it swung from side to side slowly, like the tail of a cat that was about to fight. This continued every Sunday for years, until unexpectedly she died in her sleep.

In this way the fox menace was partly contained. Yet, there arose a great demand for tongue-hounds. Everyone wanted to have one now. Thrifty people, who at one time regarded them as greedy brutes that would eat a body out of house and home, were now clamouring for pups. This caused great heart-searching for Tommy, Danny Mulvey and Old John Hollohan, who lived on the north side of Drumlahan hill. For these three men, people could be divided into two classes: those who 'kep' a hound and were, consequently, sportsmen; and those who wouldn't look a hound straight in the face, because they were too mean to feed one, or who, worse still, kept a greyhound, and were, consequently, miserable pot-hunters.

Long and secret debates ensured to clarify just who was fit to hold a tongue-hound pup and who was not. Old John pulled his whiskers and sideboards and expressions of great pride and of great worry chased themselves across his ancient, benign countenance. He was proud to see the much-maligned tongue-hound so popular now with all classes and conditions of people; but he had serious qualms of conscience about letting a precious tongue-hound pup into the clutches of a mere pot-hunter. Weighty questions had to be answered. Would the pup be well-treated? Would he be allowed to join the hunt when the horn was sounded on a Sunday morning? Would he be used in conjunction with a greyhound for the purposes of the pot? All these were very profound questions indeed.

The ancestry of every applicant was scrutinised. Old John was an expert on this, and Tommy and Danny deferred to him on questions of genealogy and of breeding. It was well known that a badly handled tongue-hound pup could easily become a problem-dog, who would do anything from stealing hen-eggs to hunting the back-trail. In any case they could not permit every Tom, Dick or Harry to have a pup. There wouldn't be enough pups to go around. As matters stood, they would have to go to Clonmoher for them, or Cavan. Or even to County Kerry where they had beagles.

'Beagles would be no use around here,' snapped Danny. 'You'd have to carry the buggers and run after the foxes yourself. A fox would only laugh at the likes of them. Beagles are all right for pot-hunters. That's all. They can kick football in Kerry, but they know damn all about hunting.'

Danny went off on his bicycle. He contacted a few friends in County Cavan, down at Templeport and then up at Mullahorn. In a month he returned to Flynn's with two Clarendo meal bags on the handlebars of his bicycle and a cardboard box tied to the carrier. All were full of squirming pups. They were white and tan, instead of the usual black and tan, and Tommy almost threw a tantrum when he saw them. They looked more like gundogs than hounds to him. He doubted seriously the purity of their blood as well as the accuracy of their ancestry. Old John Hollohan and Danny calmed him down. Tommy was a comparatively new recruit to tongue-hounds; John and Danny were old hands. They had seen white and tan tongue-hounds before. They convinced him that he had nothing to fear.

For Tommy's zeal was, in part, the zeal of the converted. Although no-one mentioned it to him, there were greyhounds and pot-hunters in his own ancestry. For hadn't his useless Uncle Dennis often boasted of a greyhound he owned called Flash? And wasn't making hare soup one of the accomplishments he was just as proud of as he was of being a good judge of a horse? It was Old John Hollohan who had rescued Tommy from the pot, which would have been his fate, and who had confirmed him for ever as a staunch tongue-hound man after his unexpected return from Newry and the Black North in his youth.

Tommy agreed to keep all the pups for the time being and to use his house as a clearing post. He chose a large, bright, jolly pup, a real beauty, for himself and he called him Drummer. Immediately afterwards he sent out word to the pot-hunters and to the ex-pot-hunters to come to Drumlahan and to collect their dogs. It was soon accomplished. But Old John and Tommy were outraged at the unseemly and insulting questions the people asked when they came to collect their pups.

'Tell me, is a tongue-hound a good watchdog, now?'

'Could you train him to bring home the cows?'

'Are they good with the gun? For sniffing out pheasants?'

'Would they retrieve for wan? If ye shot a bird and it fell on the water?'

'Any good at rats?'

'And what about tricks? Could you train them to bring back a ball? Or to beg? Or to jump through a hoop? The wife's keen on that kind of thing so she is.'

All this was sheer blasphemy and sacrilege to Old John, Danny and Tommy. They had sleepless nights. Never had they heard such talk. That anyone should ever dream of asking a tongue-hound, the very aristocrat of dogs, to bring home the cows, to hunt rats or to jump through a hoop was far beyond their wildest nightmares. It was all just too unbearable. They realised they had made a ghastly error. They decided not to bring in any more pups; not even if the foxes were to run away with the children, never mind the hens and turkeys.

The last straw came when the pot-hunters began to name their pups 'Spot', 'Shep', 'Rex', 'Nellie' or 'Sammy'. Old John took off his hard hat and looked as if he was going to pray. He had assumed, in his innocence, that every mortal man knew in his inmost soul that tongue-hounds had to be given names that related to action, movement or temperament, such as 'Foreman', 'Sportsman', 'Rambler', 'Dancer', 'Piper', 'Trimmer' or 'Flogger'. The bitches would be 'Charmer', 'Princess', 'Comely' and so on.

168

The three had reached the end of their tether. They were resigned to having blundered, to having been misguided. They were ashamed of themselves. They were depressed. Tommy looked at the clock to see the time. He had a thought, and he jumped to his feet. From behind the pendulum he took out the hair-ball and asked Old John if he had ever seen the likes of a thing like that in his life before, the handiwork of Billy of Ballinasloe.

Yes! Old John immediately knew what it was. He had seen one before. It was taken from the stomach of a horse that was killed in an accident.

'I'm very glad to see one for the second time in my life,' he laughed. 'I don't think I'll live to see the third hair-ball.'

Billy's creation seemed to cheer them up and to take their minds off the pot-hunters. Drummer, the lively pup chosen by Tommy for himself, was then six weeks old. The pup ran towards the wheels of the cart as Tommy drove in with a load of sand. Seamus was standing at the door and tried to shout, but it was useless. The pup moved in towards the walking feet of the horse and for a second or two placed his paws on the fetlock. He lost balance and fell backwards. The iron-shod wheel crossed his stomach. He yelped; and a huge ball of blood burst out through his open mouth. Seamus went away quietly to the double ditch.

22

Bundoran

Nan-nan and AB suddenly decided to go to the seaside, or the 'say' as they called it. They were able to save much of their ten-shillings-a-week old-age pension; and the bus went from Ballin-wing to Bundoran three times a week. They were pestered with all sorts of diseases and ailments, real and imaginary. These included rheumatism, bronchitis, dizziness, toothache, neuralgia, deaf-ness, singing in the ears, cracking of the bone joints, not to forget palpitations of the heart. Apart from all the cures and remedies that certain people in the neighbourhood could give them, they had their own home medicine as well which included baking soda and buttermilk, cascara, oliways, goosegrease (goose seam), flummery, raw eggs, garlic, goat's milk, honey, onions, boiled nettles and rhubarb juice. But why not give all the medicines and cures a rest and go off to Bundoran, where the good sea air and the nutritious shellfish and dillisk would do a body a power of good?

They tried to keep their plans dark, to keep it a secret from the neighbours. They thought they had succeeded until Mary Prior, an old and laughing lady going for her old-age pension at the post office, buttonholed Seamus.

'I hear that Nan-nan and AB is going to the say?'

'Thar,' he replied.

'Whisper, sonny. Tell them two not to attempt to go next nor near Bundoran without several pairs of cod-the-*gossins*! They'll need them! Tell them that Mary Prior sed it! Here, sonny! Here's a few sweets for you. Run off now. That's the good lad!'

When Seamus delivered the message, domestic uproar fol-lowed, with Nan-nan and AB unable to contain their indignation and disgust. Mary Prior should be horse-whipped, they asserted, because of her dirty language.

170

They had decided to take Seamus with them, but they did not tell him about it until the morning of their departure. He would have annoyed their heads asking 'silly questions' had they told him earlier. Veronica just wakened him abruptly that morning. She placed a bundle of clean clothes and his Sunday suit beside the bed. She told him to dress quickly, for he was going to Bundoran with Nan-nan and AB. She left a lighted candle on the mantelpiece and she warned him not to forget to say his prayers.

So off they went. Tommy had Billy harnessed and in the trap waiting to drive them to the bus in Ballinwing. They didn't bother reading the newest additions to the UP DEV! TO HELL WITH THE IRA signs on the parapets of Aughabeg bridge. They were deep in conversation, instead, about family and local matters: someone was coming home from America to buy a farm of land; someone else was refusing to get married when, in the end, the opportunity came his way. Seamus, however, tried to read the slogans. He tried to memorise them also. They were great value for shouting out in the schoolyard. TO HELL WITH THE SPANIARD was most effective when someone shouted UP THE IRA, for example.

The bus-stop was at Quinn's grocery and bar. It was a dark, overcast morning and while they were waiting they went inside and bought two bottles of porter. Tommy was not drinking then. They encouraged Seamus to drink some of the porter. He took a mouthful. In dismay and horror he tried to spit it out.

'Swally it! Swally it! Yeh dying-looking little *raunyeen* yeh,' ordered Nan-nan.

He thought better of his urge to spit, and he did as he was told. It seeped like hot tar down his throat and into his stomach. He wanted to cough; his eyes were in tears; his stomach heaved. It was far worse than stirabout. He thought that perhaps he was going to die. How he regretted having skipped his prayers that morning.

'Thank God!' exclaimed AB piously. She had been watching the whole performance in silence.

'Thank God and His Blessed Mother!' she continued. 'He'll never become a drunkard or a boozer now. You can always know a future drunkard by the way the first drop of drink that crosses his lips affects him, even if it's only a child. We had enough drunkards and tipplers in the family already, God help us! Would you like a bottle of lemonade now, sonny? Or a mouthful of tay to settle your stomach?'

'There's not much feedin' in tay or lemonade,' said Nan-nan sullenly as she smoothed down her shiny black skirt and straightened her bonnet. As always, she was annoyed at what she regarded as Seamus's sickly appearance. She would not have minded if he took to the porter, even at that age. It would put some life into him when he wouldn't eat stirabout. After all he was her godson, wasn't he? She had a responsibility. Soon the bus came down the street, coughing and sneezing, and the three climbed in, helped by Tommy. There were two cases and a square thing made of straw, which was very heavy and which Nan-nan kept referring to as her band-box.

The road ran along a railway for miles, with no fence between. They met a train, almost head on. AB pointed out to him Lough Scur, where she said that Queen Elizabeth's hangman, John of the Heads, had his castle and his prison. He killed everyone, men, women and children, let alone priests and nuns. And to make it worse, he was an Irishman, doing what that horrible English-woman asked him to do.

'He was just as bad as King Herod, in his own way,' she claimed. She seemed very upset about it all, as she closed her eyes and gripped her chin and lapsed into silence, her head jogging about with the movements of the bus.

Nan-nan pointed out Lough Allen to him. She said that it was really the Shannon, the biggest river in Ireland, England or Scotland, and that it rose in the Shannon Pot, just behind the mountain. And she told him the name of every village and town that they passed through.

The bus stopped at a place where there was a small waterfall. A tree-trunk with a path gouged in it carried the water from the fall across a stream to the side of the road. The driver, Tom Crossan, poured water into the radiator, screwed on the lid quickly, and was off again.

'What's that?' asked Seamus, pointing to what looked like

172

heaps of grey dust which seemed to have fallen from the face of the high mountain rocks. AB told him it was scree, caused by the frost and the sun and the wind over the ages. Nan-nan had fallen asleep by then, and she remained so until the bus jerked to a halt in Bundoran, with the sea and the cliffs in full view.

'Is this Bundoran? Are we here already? Oh, for goodness sake!' She was awake and ready for action.

They quickly found lodgings in a house facing the sea, but back from the street. It was at a low elevation, and it looked sheltered. From their bedroom window upstairs they could see right across Donegal Bay, with the breakers crashing against the nearby cliffs and rocks. In the evening they could see the beacon of the Killybegs lighthouse blinking continuously and without fail. AB said that it was blinking like that so that the ships out on the Atlantic Ocean could see it and know where they were going. Ships would be sinking every day, dozens of them, but for the men who kept the light burning in the Killybegs lighthouse. He thought he would like to work in a lighthouse when he grew up. Slaving away night and day to keep all those ships from sinking.

They stayed nearly two weeks in Bundoran. They walked all over the town and along every cove and stretch of strand or cliff; and they got into conversation with so many people. Early in the morning the Mass bell tolled sombrely over the town: long, deep, solemn chimes. AB often went to early Mass. Sometimes, if he was fully awake and asking too many questions, she told Seamus to wash his face quick, dress himself and to come with her.

The tide seemed to be always out then and wide stretches of beach visible, bare and rocky. The fishermen, back from the sea, drove cartloads of fish around the streets, calling 'Fresh mackerel! Fresh mackerel!' in a low voice, almost as if talking to themselves. In the chapel several priests read Mass at the same time at different altars. This seemed very strange, and rather disrespectful, to Seamus. AB was delighted: the more Masses the merrier.

After breakfast they took their usual long, windy walk along the clifftops and in the direction of the strand. The waves thumped against the rocks below. He liked to watch a wave building up, getting darker and darker and then tumbling over with a roar. They passed the Horse Pool where only the most experienced of swimmers ventured; and further on they could see the strand, with the bathing-boxes ranged in rows and many people in multicoloured bathing-suits moving around and going into the sea. Beyond the strand, on the cliff, AB pointed out the Great Southern Hotel that had hundreds of rooms and was owned by the same people who owned the railway that ran past Drumlahan at home. And behind the hotel was a rock called Roguey where the sea was always so angry that a body could be whipped away from the top of the cliff by the waves and drowned. Away beyond that, out towards Ballyshannon, were the Fairy Bridges, where the rocks were covered with banks of delightful carrageen moss. You could find little pipes hidden in the sand by the fairies out there, if you searched for them. So AB said, in any case.

Seamus wanted to set out for Roguey and the Fairy Bridges straight away.

'Troth then ye can take your aise now, me little *piodarlán,*' said Nan-nan. 'There's enough to keep a *gossin* like you with your hands full here in Bundoran, without going out there.'

They bought him a spade and a bucket and he was quickly engrossed in making sandcastles. He thought they were marvellous. He was soon joined by other children who showed him how to make bigger and better sandcastles, and even massive fortifications and battlements. Two flaxen-haired girls, a little older than he was, were very quick at turning out sandcastles and all sorts of unusual structures. The two asked him so many questions. Where was he from? Had he a father or mother or brothers or sisters? How many rooms were in the house? What school did he go to? Was he good at his lessons? Did he get slapped at school? Did he like sweets? and trains? and boats? The girls were not really friendly: they were more like teachers and it looked as if they were trying to lord it over him.

He was dumbfounded. He wasn't used to being asked questions like that or to being asked them in that tone of voice. He couldn't think of any questions to ask them in turn.

Then they asked him what religion he was. He didn't quite

understand. They thought his hesitation very funny indeed and they stopped working at the sand and giggled at him. 'We're Protestants; and we come from County Tyrone,' they told him without being asked.

He saw them many times afterwards: but he kept as far away from them as he could.

As soon as the Angelus bell rang, the road around the top of the cliff became crowded with people who had left the beach and who were returning to their hotels and lodging-houses for their luncheons or their dinners. Nan-nan and AB never went back the long walk to their lodging-house: they preferred to eat at the stalls and small teahouses. They ate large amounts of fruit, mostly grapes; and they drank large quantities of lemonade, which was so strong and gassy that it made them cry.

Later on in the day, they liked to go to the centre of the town to see the buses coming and going. They vied with each other, almost to the verge of battle, in pointing out to Seamus the different buses, and telling him where they came from and where they were going to. 'D'ye see that bus over there? No! The wan with all the wheels. Can't ye look where I'm pointing, ye blind little *stucaun*? Aye! Well, that's the Enniskillen bus. Comes and goes to Enniskillen four times a day.'

Seamus considered the conductors to be heroes: with their peaked engine drivers' caps, their black uniforms, their silver buttons, and then two leather bags, one hung on each shoulder and forming a cross on the chest and back. He decided secretly that he was going to be a bus conductor when he grew up, instead of a lighthouse man.

'And that wan over there. Where is it from, Bee? Where's yer glasses? Aye, Clones, I think. D'ye see it now, sonny? Stand up on the sate and have a good look. That's the boy!'

They were very keen he should know all about the buses; where they came from and how often they came to Bundoran. Dungannon, Letterkenny, Omagh and Sligo could be seen on the signs. His favourite was the Enniskillen bus, because it had four wheels on each side. Its conductor had two crossed bags, of course.

175

The tide was out and only the tops of the Donegal mountains were faintly visible across the bay in the afternoon haze. They bought the usual newspapers and went walking across the flat rocks and pools of sea water that stretched from the cliffs to the small harbour at West Bundoran. There were plenty of other people scattered singly and in groups over the area. There were plenty of sea plants which Nan-nan and AB began to eat, not because they liked them, but because they were supposed to be very nutritious and could cure or help the many ailments they considered themselves prone to suffer from. AB took a hairpin from her hair and proceeded to dig out evil-looking material from some shells she had just found in a cluster. She seemed to derive great enthusiasm and strength from this, for next she grabbed Seamus's sandcastle spade and began to dislodge shells from the rocks and hungrily eat the contents. She made a weak attempt to have Seamus partake of the food, but the look on his face discouraged her, and she resumed the spade-work with surprising zest for a woman of her age.

The two old ladies took off their shoes and stockings and, daintily holding up their skirts, began to paddle in the pools of sea water. This was also supposed to be most health-giving. The pools were so pleasant, so full of little fish: quite different from those in the mearing drain at Drumlahan. There were shells and sand and plants in the bottom. The water was so clear. This, too, contrasted sharply with the wine-dark waters of the mearing drain.

The two ambled around and drank handfuls of the sea water. Seamus was urged to do the same. He took a mouthful of the water and, as he expected, it was awful. It was strange how Nan-nan and AB always wanted him to eat and drink stuff that he considered tasted like poison. Yet, he found some seaweeds in the water that were very tasty indeed. Carefully, he began to peck at them.

In the middle of it all Nan-nan pulled her skirts up to her knees and began to pass water noisily and torrentially into the pool.

AB seemed to take fright and dropped the spade. Then, after looking in amazement at Nan-nan, who had her back turned to them and was gazing out to sea, she got out of the pool fast. Seamus pretended to see nothing, of course, and continued to fish for more of the tasty plants he had just discovered.

'Come out! Come out quick, ye little *amadáun*!' hissed AB. 'Can't you see?' She pointed to Nan-nan. 'Or are you blind?' She looked around in fear in case others could see what was happening. No-one was looking.

AB seemed to have suddenly lost her new-found energy. She was drooping. She became gloomy. It was the same gloom which had descended on her, and on her sister, Maria, nearly sixty years before, when their brother, James, went up the mountain wooing and came back with the woman whom they considered to be so coarse in her ways.

In the late afternoon the three always made sure to get one of the seats that were on the side of the road on the top of the cliff. One could see a nice corner of the world from there: the passers-by, the town on the left, with New York House, squat and castle-like, the traffic and, before them, the broad bay with the distant mountaintops dimly leading out to the Atlantic Ocean. Towards evening the fishing boats would hoist their sails in the little harbour and begin to move out into the bay. One or two at first; then, as the evening wore on, many more joined them. Seamus was entranced as he watched the boats going out and out; some towards Killybegs, and some towards the open sea. There were boats with brown sails and others with white sails; the sails of one boat were almost black. Out and out they slowly went, gently rocking from side to side. Soon the tide came in and thundered against the face of the cliffs. The sun sank, red and awful, behind the sea. The sharp, searching eyes of the boy could soon discern a spot of light as it blinked across the bay. It was the Killybegs lighthouse. The fishing boats continued to sail away from the shore. They would fish all night long for the mackerel which they wanted to fill the carts next morning, as AB and Seamus went to early Mass.

At night there was the good, homely meal at the lodging-house, and afterwards all the family and the guests assembled in the parlour. There would be much polite handshaking and smiling and conversation. Nan-nan was at her best and sweetest when meeting strangers; AB usually kept herself to herself, in a quiet but friendly manner. Both of them could almost say nice things about de Valera, Mary McSwiney or the IRA if the social occasion demanded it. They didn't believe in fighting in public. They could be unbelievably deft and diplomatic, but they knew where to draw the line and they never became hypocritical.

For the first few nights the conversation was interesting, general and deferential. Then, quite unexpectedly, one of the elderly men, a very vigorous old chap with a cloth cap, an apple-pink complexion and a walrus moustache, asked Nan-nan an explosive question if ever there was one. He wanted to know, he said, if she ever heard of a man who lived somewhere in south Leitrim, not too far from Ballinwing he thought, who could make cures, or help people in trouble, especially those who got on the wrong side of the Good People. He seemed to recall that the man's name was Keaney. He lowered his voice suitably when he mentioned the Good People and the man's name.

Nan-nan looked at him sharply for a few seconds. Then a light came into her eyes and she threw up her hands in delight. Did she know him? Of course she knew him! He lived just one field away from the house where she was born and reared. 'And how did you come to know about him, Mr Keenan? And you so far away as Lisnaskea itself, all that way down in County Fermanagh?'

'Aw missus, God give ye sense! Divel a wan around our parts but knew all about Doctor Keaney. And many's the man made the trip to see him and get his advice; and it must have been forty mile of ground from Lisnaskea to where he lived.'

'Tis true! Tis true!' exclaimed Nan-nan, writhing in delight and beaming with good humour. 'Yer not telling wan word iv a lie, Mr Keenan.'

'It's a long story. My father built a new house, a grand two-storey, slated house, and it's still standing. About six months after it was built, a brother and sister of his died suddenly, one after the other. They were always in good health, but once they got bad, neither of them lasted long.

'There was a suspicion that the house was built in the wrong

178

place and that it was for that reason the two young people died. One of the neighbours advised my father to go and see Doctor Keaney, quick, in case worse would happen. So off he went to County Leitrim.

'When he came to the Doctor's door he stated his case. The Doctor took him into the upper room. He took out of a drawer a black nap belt about eighteen inches long with two brass buttons on each end.

'He asked my father several questions about the position of the house. He seemed to be trying to figure out in his mind's eye where exactly it was built. Then he took the belt and began to make measurements with it on the table. He continued at this in silence for a very long time. In the end, he stopped. He rolled up the belt. He straightened himself and looked at my father full in the face.

'"No, my good man," said the Doctor. "Your house is not built in the wrong place. It's all right. That was not the reason for the deaths of the young people. Go back home now. You and yours will be all right."

'Well that's the way it turned out. Everything went well from then on. There was no more bad luck.'

Nan-nan was delighted. She nudged AB vigorously. 'Didn't I always say he could do it! There was never the batin' of the ould Doctor, Bee, when it came to the Good People.'

She seemed to feel justified. This was living proof of the truth of all the stories she had ever told about her famous neighbour. And it had turned up and had come to light in the most unlikely place: at the seaside in Bundoran seventy to eighty years after the event. She was lording it over AB now, who in her present Roman Catholicism was sceptical of such happenings, and who would try to explain them away as the work of the devil and his imps, pure and simple.

'Well,' went on Mr Keenan. 'I asked my father years after-wards, what would he have done if, in fact, the ould Doctor had told him the house was built in the wrong place. And do you know what he said? He said he would have pulled it down, stone by stone. He said he would not have left even one stone standing on another.'

'Heroo! Heroo!' Nan-nan could not contain herself. 'That was

179

a man for you! He would indeed have tumbled that house. I'd know it by what you have tould to us. Now, Bee, what did I tell you many's the time?'

AB was not impressed, and looked the other way.

After the outburst of noisy victory Nan-nan soon became her own sweet self again with all the family and her fellow-guests, who were now full of admiration for her. She went on to recount episode after episode of the deeds and exploits of the ould Doctor. She kept the house up until the early hours of the morning with her tales.

'Did she actually know him?' Although his house was next door to her father's, and just one field away, she could remember seeing him only twice. When she was a child he came into their kitchen one day. Her mother asked him if he would pull a chair up to the fire and sit down. He replied that he was tired sitting. As a child, she thought that very odd. Another memory of him was of seeing him herding the cows in the meadow. He stood with his back to a hedge, an old, heavy, stooped man, with a cap on his head, an overcoat buttoned and belted with a rope, and a heavy blanket of red flannel pulled around his shoulders against the wind.

Just as in Drumlahan, all the people, both young and old, in the boarding-house in Bundoran came in early in the evening and sat up late at night as she held the stage with her banshees, changelings, galloping horsemen, fights and fairies. No-one went out in the evening. No-one went to the entertainments in the Hamilton Hall, where a black man was eating fire, and where an Englishman was sawing his wife in two. One couple postponed their departure from Bundoran for a few more days, so taken up were they with her talk.

As they went along the high road on the cliffs to the strand they tried to keep Seamus on the sheltered side of their two persons to protect him from the very strong sea wind. AB battled bad-temperedly with an umbrella; Nan-nan kept a corner of her warm, heavy, black cape over his shoulders. 'The poor little *raunyeen* might get his death of cauld,' she mused. 'Then we'd have to spend our time putting hot castor-oil on brown paper and pressing it to his chest.'

180

The mere thought of Nan-nan's castor-oil and brown paper nearly made him cry. He felt sure that pneumonia could not be worse than that awful cure. Her cures spelt terror for him.

The waves were chasing belligerently up the beach and against the rocks. There was rain as well as spray in the wind as they passed the Horse Pool. They decided to go to the swing-boats and the hobby-horses, where there was more shelter than on the beach or along the cliff.

On reaching the arcade Seamus wanted to get up on a hobby-horse. No, they said: he was too young. Couldn't either of them go up on the hobby-horse with him, if he was too young, he wanted to know. AB burst into a peal of laughter, which soon turned into a fit of coughing. She quickly recovered. 'You go up with him Anne. Gwan, Anne!'

'I'd look well up there; wouldn't I? Like a *gunkauny*, at my time of life,' she answered severely. 'You go up yourself, smart wan!'

'No! You go up Anne: you're the youngest, and you're his godmother as well.'

'That's right, Nan-nan,' chipped in Seamus. 'You come up with me. Just for a few minutes.'

'If you don't shut your *chlab*, ye unmannerly little *glincín*, ye'll get a *leadóg* that'll stiffen ye! Now d'ye hear me? Another word about the hobby-horses and I'll walk on the skin of your neck.'

Nan-nan waddled away towards the fortune-teller. But she couldn't be seduced by that either. The ould Doctor knew what he was doing. So did their cousin, Scotch Bridie, that's Mrs McGoohan from Glasgow who could read the cups. These town tricksters were only catch-pennies, pure and simple. AB believed in the power of the fortune-teller and in cures and curses and the like. She would not indulge in them though, because the Church condemned them and forbade them. They were the the devil's work.

There were people busy at the shooting galleries, and some were throwing wooden balls at dolls. Bowls of goldfish, as well as watches, clocks and jars of sweets, could be won by throwing rings. There were rows of brown boxes with eye-holes standing against a wall where grown-ups could put a penny in and have a look, and come away laughing and giggling. Seamus wanted to see what was to be seen also, and was whinging about it. Suddenly AB put in a penny, helped him raise himself to the eye-holes and to have a look in. He saw a man lying on his side on a low bench and four girls, with hardly any clothes on, sitting on top of him.

'Now are you satisfied, you little *aurcaun* ye?'

He wasn't. The swing-boats were in full movement. He wanted the two to take him up. The place was crowded and the hobby-horse organ was blaring out 'It's a long, long way to Tipperary'. He noticed that both of his grandaunts were singing along with the music as they moved from place to place in the fun fair. He could not hear their voices, however, with the noise. But he could see their lips moving and their heads tossing.

There were so many churches and chapels in Bundoran. Nan-nan always stopped when they came near one and read the sign-boards. There were several Methodist churches, a few Presbyterian churches, one Church of Ireland and one or two that didn't say who or what they were. On Sunday evenings the church nearest to their lodging-house rang its bell for ages and ages. Seamus sat on the grass and watched the little bell swinging up and down quickly. It had a fast, cheerful sound, just like the bell of the Protestant church in Ballinwing, and quite unlike the sad, heavy, crashing sound of the bell of the Catholic church. Also, one could see the bells in all the Protestant churches, including the one at home. The Catholic bells were always hidden in the belfry and sounded so sad and so serious.

Not far away, out in the fields, were two large buildings: the Boys' Orphanage and the Girls' Orphanage. AB explained that those poor childen had no homes of their own and no parents and that they had to live there until they were old enough to be sent out to work, just like Jim Murray.

'Will they speak like Jim Murray when they go out to work?'

'No! Of course not. Jim comes from Lancashire.'

'Will they play football like him?'

'Maybe. Maybe. I really don't know.'

'Will they sing like him? And get drunk?'

'Now that's enough! No more silly questions from you, me boyo.'

182

They were beginning to think that some day soon it would be time to catch the bus and go home to Drumlahan. Then everyone persuaded them to stay for just a few more days for the air display. There would be plenty of aeroplanes flying around, of all shapes and sizes. It would be worth seeing. They decided to stay; and AB wrote to Veronica to explain the delay and all about the expected aircraft.

So one morning punctually at eleven an autogiro came in from the west and hovered high over the field where the planes were to land. Five minutes later the planes arrived: seven small ones with two seats and one very big aeroplane with three seats and four wheels. They circled the town several times and then came to light on the field that was prepared for them. It was curtained off around the sides with lengths of canvas and tarpaulin.

The air display lasted for four days. You could get a trip over the town and out as far as Ballyshannon for nine shillings. You could also fly upside down if you wished, or loop the loop. The two old ladies thought it was great fun; but they were very afraid in case someone would fall out when the aeroplane was upside down and break a leg or an arm. Worse still, one could fall into the sea and get drowned. The noise was deafening, but everyone seemed to enjoy it. One day a plane flew up very high; and then someone jumped out. Immediately, a large yellow parachute opened and came sailing down into a field to the east of the town. Seamus saw it as he was making sandcastles. When he excitedly told Nan-nan and AB about it, they wouldn't believe him. They made enquiries, found he was telling the truth, and promptly started to blame each other for talking too much instead of keeping an eye out to see what was going on in the world around them.

As the air display neared its end they began to talk about going home again. AB wondered would it be worthwhile to go to the Hamilton Hall, for just once, to see that Englishman sawing his wife in two. And the black man eating fire. Maybe he came from St Helena and could tell her more about the sun crackling as it rose in the mornings. Nan-nan thought it would all be a catch-penny and that they would be better off to go and have another of those baths of hot salt water in the bath-house in West Bundoran. Seamus wanted to go to Roguey or the Fairy Bridges or up on the hobby-horses. And then, quite suddenly, they bought bags of dillisk, carrageen moss and salted fish and packed them. Next afternoon, complete with cases, bags and the straw band-box, they clambered into the bus and set out for Ballinwing. As the bus swung out of the town, Nan-nan looked back. 'Goodbye, Bundoran! I suppose I'll never see you again.'

AB nodded her head jerkily behind her veil and rubbed the index finger of her right hand across the palm of her left hand. They both looked very sad.

23

The Yankees

When Seamus told Jim Gaffney about the air show in Bundoran
he was delighted and asked him so many questions. He went on
then to talk about a big air race that was going to take place from
London to Australia. He had much to say, as usual, about Amy
Johnson and Jim Mollison and Lindbergh, and also indeed of Jim
Fitzmaurice and his German friends, who flew from Baldonnel to
America in 1928. He also chatted on about another Irishman,
named Scally, who was going to fly to Ceylon soon. And of course
he had a song upon the tip of his tongue to suit the occasion and
his enthusiasm for flying:

I'm an airman,
I'm a quare man,
I can fly, fly, fly, fly,
Right up into the sky,
Where the buffman he can't catch me,
And I sing bye, bye, bye, bye!

It was one of his usual inventions, one of his spur-of-the-
moment compositions. He hammered out the unusual beat as he
drove hobnails into the new soles he had just put on his heavy
boots. After that he put new leather on the soles of his light
Sunday dancing shoes, or 'me crabshells' as he called them. It
could only have been two days later that he made a tidy bundle of
his shirts, vests and working clothes. He didn't forget the newly
soled boots and shoes either. Dressed in his Sunday best he told
Mary, his mother, that he was going on a trip. He did not say
where to; but she had a pious hope that he was somehow off to
Lough Derg, and going to turn over a new leaf. She was mistaken
in this. He went out the door, jumped on his BSA bicycle and set
off for England.

Two hours later, Katie, his sister, happened to be in one of the fields near the railway. She had been looking at trains going up and down all her life, but she stopped what she was doing to look at this one also as it rumbled past. To her surprise she saw her brother Jim standing out on the carriage platform, smoking a fag. It looked as if he just wanted to be seen. She immediately knew what his intentions were. She didn't tell her mother for a day or two. Meanwhile, the mother's mind kept going back to the odd old granduncle who often went away for long walks during the night, yet who always came back in the mornings, but who eventually ran away to sea and never came back again.

When the news was finally broken to her, the neighbours crowded in during the evenings to console the two women. It was almost like a wake. The mother and sister were so hurt because of the deception, the trick they claimed he had played on them.

'Why didn't he tell us?' lamented Mary, when she heard of his destination. She ought to have known that it was not the only-begotten son's style to tell anyone where he was going, whether it was to a dance to pick up a woman, to the town to play cards, or to England to earn some money and to see the world. This time he relented and told the boys at Ballinwing railway station where he was going. He could not face boarding the train at Drumlahan, with Mrs Martin taking in every move and putting two and two together. Finally, he came to a halt in Chapel-en-le-Frith, in Derbyshire, where one of the neighbouring men had a job waiting for him in the nearby lime kilns.

People in Drumlahan did not consider it a disaster, after all. Mary had a troublesome son, it was true. But he was a great workman; that no-one could deny. And it was no crime to go off to Derbyshire, even if rather abruptly. Veronica felt that it was not all that abrupt; but she thought it better to keep her mouth shut on the subject. She knew he had been looking into the crystal ball a lot recently, and then walking away in silence. On the last occasion that she saw him, she asked him if he had seen much of interest in the ball lately. 'Enough,' was his gruff answer, as he walked away with his hands deep in his trouser pockets and the cap pulled down well over his eyes.

In a few weeks all settled down again. A letter came from Jim. And for almost a year afterward his mother was referred to privately, and discreetly, in the neighbourhood, as 'Mary, deceived without sin'.

On the Sunday morning following Jim Gaffney's departure there were two large trunks on the side of the road, just at John Stretton's gate. They were very like the pirate chests Seamus often saw in *Our Boys*, but they were bigger. Their appearance at the gate meant that the Yankees were home. Tim and Judy, brother and sister, had returned on a visit from New York to see their parents, Joe and Mary, before the old people died.

Tim was a policeman. He wore a real Yankee summer hat and he eagerly took part in all the farmwork that he had been so used to before he went to America fifteen years earlier: he cut turf in the bog; he mowed and reaped; he carted and milked. He could place his hands each side of Seamus's ears and lift him up, or swing him around without breaking his neck. He was a quiet, gentle man with little to say. He looked neat and spotless in appearance as he walked, very upright, down the road with a pitchfork on his shoulder and his Yankee hat.

His sister, Judy, was married to a German. This interested everyone, especially the children. All the young ones stared at her, but quickly looked away if she happened to look in their direction. What must it be like to be married to a German, they wondered. What was he like? What were Germans like? It must be a funny thing to be married to one of them. But, of course, Judy didn't seem to be anything the worse of it, if one went by appearances.

Judy and Veronica spent a lot of time talking together. They got together at every opportunity. They conversed very quietly and very carefully and in low tones. They went to the spring well for water together. They fed the calves together.

The brother and sister, like all Yankees, had to visit every house in the townland. There was a lot of visiting and many little parties. Before they returned to New York, they gave a big spree with eating and drinking, fiddle-playing and dancing in the barn at the back of the Stretton house.

When the dance started everyone sat as if petrified around the barn walls, while the fiddlers fiddled frenziedly in an attempt to bring them to life. No-one wanted to be first out on the floor. Then Berney McGovern came to the rescue, although he was almost an elderly man by that time. He stepped onto the vacant floor. For a minute he stood there tapping his toes and listening to the music. Then he suddenly beckoned to his third daughter, Maura, who was seated near the barn door. Dark-haired, smiling, pale-skinned and full of feigned incomprehension, she came towards her father. He unceremoniously placed her at his side; and at the turn of the music they went straight into the reel. Soon the floor was crowded and the spree was in full swing. Berney, having done his duty, bowed to Maura, and left the barn.

'Lord, isn't it a pity Jim Gaffney isn't here the night! Wouldn't ye miss him now! Lord, but he'd be in his element a night like this.' It was a snatch of conversation, heard above the music and the bustle.

Twenty yards away, in the dwelling-house, the hum of quiet conversation hit the ear. In the upper room an abundance of food was being enjoyed. In the lower room, below the kitchen, a barrel of porter was tapped and the brew was continually being distributed in frothy mugfuls to all the older men, who had congregated themselves in the spacious kitchen. Berney McGovern was among them now. The women, having eaten in the upper room, gathered around the tapped barrel in the lower room, drinking, for the most part, a staid port or a sherry. Suddenly there was a tremendous explosion followed by screams and shrieks from the women. There were sounds of panic and stampede. 'Tim! Tim! Where are you Tim? Quick! For God's sake Tim, the barrel's bursted!'

At that, something hit the lower room door. In the kitchen a man dropped his mug of porter and it smashed on the concrete floor; another nearly choked himself. A tide of rich, brown liquid surged under the door and up towards the kitchen fire on the hearth, like a monster flicking a hungry tongue. Some jumped out of the way nimbly; others remained stolidly seated; a few raised their knees chin-high as the brew passed beneath their chairs and onwards towards the kitchen fire.

Just in time Tim came in. He rushed into the room and immediately dammed the flood. He simply replaced the tap that had been forced out by the pressure of the beery gas.

The kitchen and the lower room had to be evacuated while the floors were being washed and dried. Men stood disconsolately here and there with empty mugs in their hands; the women evacuees took refuge in the flower garden and were soon deep in their usual, serious, quiet conversations and gossipings. After a time the men recovered the power of speech and they gathered in a little crowd beside a clump of French-currant bushes. A few of the guests were also, like Tim and Judy, Yankees home for a holiday to see old parents. With empty mugs in their hands, they began to question the locals about the far-reaching political developments of the day. They were soon fully informed men indeed.

'And after all that, is it true that there is a Jew in the Dáil?'

'Troth then it is. There's a Jew there all right.'

'You mean to tell me that there is a Jew in Dáil Éireann?'

'That's true. Isn't it a terror to see a thing like that? You could never believe that the like of that could ever happen here!'

'We are living in terrible times, God knows. Terrible times indeed.'

Someone called from the door to say that the floors were washed and dried and that everyone should come back in. Meanwhile the dancing in the barn went on with unabated zest and without break or interruption: the stirring music, the rumbustious dancers.

24

Death

A month after the spree AB died. As Seamus came home from school he saw Fr Bradley's grey-brown two-seater car parked near the wall of the dressed-stone bridge at the foot of the lane. It was a dusty, battered little car and he wondered what the priest could be doing in the house. It was a cold, dark day with a dry, easterly wind. When he entered the kitchen, Fr Bradley was coming out of AB's room. 'The pulse is a bit jumpy,' he was saying, 'but she'll be all right, I think. Of course, she is a big age. She has the years on her.'

After a little chitchat and some of his usual bantering with the children, he left. Tommy walked with him to his car; Veronica went into AB's room and closed the door behind her. Nan-nan prepared the children's dinner.

'It was just one of her attacks,' she explained to Seamus. 'She'll be all right, please God, as soon as the weather softens and the wind changes from the east. Fr Bradley annointed her. It was the right thing to do. And he gave her Holy Communion too. We never know. God help us this night and this day, and let the evil hour pass!'

During the dinner Veronica was in and out of the sick-room. AB was breathing heavily and could hardly speak. When the meal was over, the children were sent out of the house: an errand here and there and a trip to Strettons' for the loan of a hedging knife for fencing. The evening passed in its usual way. Darkness soon fell; and when the pigs were fed, the foddering done and the cows milked there was homework for the girls and games of draughts and reading the headlines of the *Irish Independent* and the *Anglo-Celt* for Seamus. He marvelled at the pictures of Hitler, de Valera, James Dillon, Roosevelt and crashed aeroplanes. There were so many pictures of crashed aeroplanes in the newspapers that whenever he drew an aeroplane it was always of one in a crashed position: nose buried in the earth and the tail sticking upwards at an angle. The doctor, it seemed, had seen AB earlier in the day and the improvement he promised had not come about. She was much worse and Tommy talked of going to Ballinwing to see the doctor again. The house became serious and silent.

When it was bedtime, and she became aware that the children were going to their rooms, AB enquired where Seamus was. She wanted to see him before he went to bed.

'Come down here, Seamus! AB wants to speak to you,' Tommy called from the bedroom where he was sitting with her.

Seamus went into the room. She said something which he could not understand. Her chest was very noisy and she was breathing fast.

'Go nearer to the bed, can't you!' Tommy urged.

He did so. AB said what she had to say in a broken, wheezy, gasping voice. He could not understand a word of what she said; but he pretended he did and nodded again and again. When she stopped talking to him he left the room. Veronica was sitting on a chair, silently weeping, when he bade her good night.

Tommy called Seamus next morning. 'Time to get up! It's eight o'clock.'

Then, almost as an afterthought, he added: 'You won't be going to school today. AB is dead.'

He dressed quickly and came down to the kitchen where he found his father eating breakfast and Jack Martin sitting on a stool drinking a mug of tea. Veronica, Nan-nan or the other children were nowhere to be seen. To Jack Martin's questions, Tommy said that AB died at three o'clock in the morning. When he saw she was dying, he lit the blessed wax candle and held it in her hand and began to recite the rosary. He did not waken anyone else in the house. When he saw she was dead he pulled the sheet over her face and quenched the blessed candle. He left the room then and closed the door.

During the next three days there would be no work done in Drumlahan by the neighbours, as a mark of respect for the dead.

No matter how pressing the work might be, it was avoided. Only the bare essentials, like milking cows, feeding the pigs and cleaning them out, would be seen to. This was in accordance with the custom of the countryside.

After breakfast Tommy sent Seamus to ask John Stretton if he would go with him to Ballinwing to buy the corterments. John agreed as a matter of course. A neighbour always accompanied the bereaved when going to buy the goods for the wake and for the funeral.

Soon after they drove away in the horse and cart, John's mother, Mary, and Mrs Berney McGovern came to stretch the corpse. This entailed taking it out of the bed, washing it, combing and fixing the hair and then dressing it in the dark-brown habit. The corpse was placed between white sheets on the bed, with a high pillow and a white bedspread. AB's heavy rosary beads were entwined in her fingers; the steel crucifix, with the black centre for a happy death, was propped up by the dead thumbs. The old bog oak Penal Mass cross engraved with the date 1723, which she cherished all her life, was placed unobtrusively on her breast. A small bouquet of early daffodils rested on the white bedspread.

On the nearby cross-legged dressing table stood three polished brass candlesticks with candles burning in all of them. Also on the table was a dinner-plate with a small portion of cut and partly-teased tobacco, a box of matches and two new clay pipes that Mrs McGovern brought with her.

AB seemed so different: saintly, very austere, yet not severe, but dignified. Her under-lip pouted a little in a way it had never done during her life, at least not during her old age. Seamus wondered secretly at times during the day if it was all true and if AB was really dead. Could it be a mistake? Could she never come back again?

Their task accomplished, the two women were sipping tea in the kitchen when Tommy and John Stretton arrived back from the town in the horse-and-cart. Billy seemed to know that something unusual was afoot and he trotted like an amiable hunter in and out the road to the town. In the cart they had a large supply of clay pipes and of tobacco as well as tea, sugar, loaves, currant cakes

192

and a few bottles of port and sherry. All this would be needed to treat decently the many callers and sympathisers who would come to the house to pay their respects to the dead.

The old people came during the day, in ones and in twos. Some were smart and spry: others hobbled, some with the aid of sticks. One old man came riding an ass. 'I knew Bee well when she was a young girl, more than sixty years ago. And a fine sweet girl she was in them days. She had bad luck, the poor little devil. She must be over the eighty mark now, I suppose.'

They came up the lane and falteringly came to the door. The men bared their heads, made the sign of the cross very off-handedly, and were taken to view the corpse. The old women came in directly and with less hesitation. And there were the usual few children on their way home from school. They came in wide-eyed and whispering. Few of them had ever seen a dead person before. This was their chance. Some remembered to say a prayer.

The cows were milked, the calves fed, the pigsty cleaned out and fresh straw thrown in for the pigs to root through and tease; the hens and turkeys went to roost and the drake and the line of ducks came quietly up the bank from the mearing drain. A touch of March frost hardened the evening sky; and people, mostly men, began to come to the wake. At the door, all bared their heads, made the sign of the cross quickly, said a brief, silent prayer and were each handed a new, white, clay pipe primed with roughly cut plug tobacco. They shook hands with Veronica and Nan-nan and took a seat with those already within. So many came that it was, as was usual at such events, necessary to borrow stools, chairs and forms from the neighbours, the Martins, the Strettons and the Galloghys. A dense fog of tobacco smoke hung in the kitchen.

Seamus began counting the mourners. Veronica gave him a light slap on the cheek, and in a very severe manner told him never, never to dare again to count the people at a wake. It was wrong; it was bad manners; and, moreover, it was unlucky. The men talked in low tones about everything imaginable: the likelihood of another war, the price of cattle and pigs, the price of feeding-stuffs, Indian meal in particular. They went over who got married and who was likely to get married; who won the recent football matches; and the plague of foxes that was cleaning the county of hens. In threes and fours they were taken quietly into the next room for tea.

It was surprising all the people who turned up for the wake. How quickly the news of a humble death had spread! People who were never in the house before and who knew the family, but who could scarcely have known AB personally, arrived. Distant relations turned up. And people who were not known to be relations, until the matter was later considered in full, all knocked quietly and respectfully at the door, crossed themselves, said a prayer, shook hands, smoked a pipe, chatted for a while and then left.

By eleven o'clock many began to leave, after enquiring if any help was needed to dig the grave in Ballydoon next day. The children were sent to bed. By midnight, ten or twelve were left: they were the close neighbours and cousins who would sit up and keep vigil all night. As usual, many others volunteered to sit up; and, as usual, it was respectfully and thankfully declined. Those who were sitting up urged the household, Nan-nan, Tommy and Veronica, to go to bed, saying that they would look after everything for them and that they needed to sleep. The household gladly agreed.

Veronica seemed very downcast. Tommy seemed a bit dazed and wistful. Seamus, listening to all the talk from his own bed, was still secretly asking himself if it was really true and would AB never go out walking again. Nan-nan shuffled off to bed in canvas slippers, outwardly quite jolly, but very surprised all the same, and a little shocked, that poor Bee went off so footy after all.

He awoke at dawn to hear the rattle of teacups and saucers and some of the mourners leaving, opening the door and loudly bidding one another goodbye. It surprised him that they should talk so loudly and someone dead in the house. Those who talked loudest were the town cousins, who could not know better. It was a new day and the usual work would have to be done no matter who was dead: milking, foddering, feeding pigs and calves. He would have to give a helping hand at every job as usual.

During the afternoon a few more of the neighbours, who could not come the night before, dropped in. And a few more distant relations, from God only knew where, came in for a brief call. There was the quiet handshake, the short, matter-of-fact prayer, the bit of chitchat about the price of eggs, cattle or the latest doings of de Valera.

Everyone in the house seemed less withdrawn than they had been the day before. Nan-nan was in great spirits and talked politely to everyone who came; Veronica wept openly and constantly, and muttered over and over, 'We are alone now. We are completely alone, now.' She and AB had been very close together from her early youth. They had shared secrets and confidences from the time that AB ran away when Veronica was a child. Veronica's mother, the eloping Maria, had died when she was very young, and AB, in a way, took her place. And perhaps AB regarded Veronica as the child she might have had, if Uncle James had not talked her into postponing marriage so that he could buy the land and useless cows with the money which was rightfully hers so many years ago.

The room where the corpse lay was now deserted, and Seamus went into it and began to tease the hard, plug tobacco that smelt so richly on the dinner-plate on the table beside the brass candlesticks. The tobacco reminded him of his egg tree days, as he leaned against the table adventurously teasing it in the manner he saw his father and all the pipe-smoking men tease their tobacco before they had a smoke.

There was no-one in the room but himself and the corpse. He found that, after a while, the corpse seemed to attract his attention more than the tobacco; and he gradually ceased teasing, and began gazing at the face in the bed. It was so difficult to believe that it was really AB. And yet, the corpse was so real and so impressive that it was difficult to remember AB as she was in life. The corpse seemed to obliterate the past. He resumed teasing the tobacco. Then, abruptly, he stopped and, walking towards the bed, touched the corpse lightly and gently on the bridge of the nose with the thumb and the index finger. It was so cold! He jerked his hand away. He resumed teasing the tobacco. Someone called him and he left the room.

It was arranged that the removal would be at five o'clock. Well before that time people, all of whom were men, began to gather at the foot of the lane, along the road and on the dressed-stone bridge. Most were wearing caps at jaunty angles and blue serge suits. The older men smoked pipes; many of the young men smoked Woodbines. They were all well groomed and they chatted in subdued tones about everything near to them: prices, wages, the weather, ploughing, setting potatoes and general gossip, not forgetting football.

'Here's the hearse.' And, sure enough, the driver's head, topped by a tall black hat with a white band around it, could be seen rising behind the crest of the hill on the road surface. Next, his body appeared, dressed in black with a snow-white sash across the right shoulder and knotted at the left hip. He was seated high over the cabinet of the hearse and the two plumed heads of the black horses nodded on each side of him as they advanced. Quickly they crested the hill and came briskly down the stony, sandy road and halted at the bridge. The driver jumped down and opened the hearse door. Two men took out the empty coffin and carried it to the house, shoulder high, one at each end. They were John Stretton and Francie Heaney. Carefully they took it into the room where AB lay stretched.

The house was crowded. Some prayers were said and all those present took a final look at the corpse. John Stretton opened the coffin. It was half-full of wood-shavings. He flattened them out with his hand. Then he sprinkled them heavily with holy water from a bottle that he had quickly pulled from his pocket and which he had brought with him to the corpse-house for that purpose. He looked haggard and weary: he was silent and withdrawn. The two women present, Mrs McGovern and John Stretton's mother, Mary, took the Penal Mass cross and laid it on the table. It had served at, and had witnessed, such events for generations since 1723. They lifted the daffodils and pulled down the bedspread. John and Francie wrapped the undersheet carefully around AB. She was fully and completely in white now and not a bit of the dark-brown habit could be seen. Her head was partly hooded by the spotless linen.

196

Then, very quickly, and with complete understanding of what each should do, they lifted the stiff body and placed it in the coffin. All the household went into the room to view the corpse in silence. Veronica was weeping bitterly. AB looked very pale and very frail, very austere, yet very gentle. Her underlip seemed to protrude a little further. But the men quickly put the lid on the coffin and screwed it down firmly.

With difficulty they got the coffin out of the small room and through the kitchen. They went through the door, helped now by the other two who would carry the coffin at various times until it reached the grave, Tommy and his nephew, Hugh. Outside the house, they placed it resting on two chairs. There was the usual pause to give everyone time to come out of the house into the open. It was at this stage, in the old days, that Mass-offerings were placed on the coffin lid after a two-night wake. During the pause, Nan-nan, sitting silently by the fire and gazing into the *griseach,* was heard to say: 'Well, I suppose it won't be long now till I'm going meself too.' Her voice was sad and small and beaten.

The four men carefully hoisted the coffin onto their shoulders. Very deftly, Francie Heaney knocked the chairs on which the coffin had rested, so that their seats faced the ground. This was as custom required. They lay there until the coffin was slowly carried down the lane and placed in the hearse.

Then the black horses moved up the road at a sharp walk. Most of the men walked behind the hearse for the two miles to the parish chapel at Ballinwing, but there were a few horses-and-traps, and plenty of bicycles. Odey, Nan-nan's brother, arrived on his noisy, iron-shod sidecar, late and wheezing, and joined the mourners.

The funeral moved on to the crossroads at Aughabeg and then over the bridge, where a new display of political slogans had just been painted. Road users were asked to RELEASE THE PRISONERS and were warned to BEWARE — ALTACULLION HALL IS STILL BOYCOTTED. AB's funeral, or her 'birril', as she would have called it, calmly followed the road she knew best during her life. It went along the wood, beside the canal, passed the Mile Tree, up the hill, passed the waterfall and the chestnut trees; it skirted the old orchard, passed the limestone quarry where the stone-crusher was working that day, down the hill, over the railway, and into the town.

Mrs Tubman began to toll the bell as the four men took the coffin from the hearse and carried it up the gravel stretch to the chapel door with the blue, worn, stone step. The coffin was placed on the top of the seats on the men's side of the aisle. The rosary was said. It had a dignified sombreness.

They returned home to Drumlahan in darkness. It was frosty, and a three-quarter moon hung high in the sky behind a gauze of distant haze. The neighbours helped to feed the calves and pigs and to do the milking and the foddering. As he gave a hand at these chores, Seamus felt that there was something hard and bitter in the night. He could not cease thinking of AB closely wrapped in that ghostly white sheet and lying there all alone in the stark, dark, cold chapel before the vast high altar, with the roof so very far above her and the faint red light of the sanctuary lamp flickering through the darkness, the cold and the awful silence.

The funeral was arranged for two o'clock next day and neither Nan-nan nor Veronica attended it. Tommy, Seamus and Uncle Peter and some of the cousins set out early. They were joined by John Stretton. When they reached the chapel they were astounded to see two coffins resting in front of the high altar, instead of one. There was a big crowd in the nave of the chapel. Everyone was wondering whose funeral would be first. Fr Bradley came out in his surplice and stole to the altar rails.

'I'll take Miss McCartin's funeral first,' he said in a matter-of-fact tone of voice and went on with the liturgy. When he had finished the prayers he walked down the aisle to the coffin and sprinkled it with holy water, and Tommy, Uncle Peter, John Stretton and Francie Heaney went behind the altar rails where a table was standing. They placed their money-offering on it. And then, hesitatingly at first, those in the seats came up, walked past the table, placed there a shilling, or at most half-a-crown, and proceeded to the left transept, where they seated themselves. The money was counted afterwards. Tommy told Fr Bradley what the total of the offerings amounted to. When they had taken their seats again in the nave, the priest began to speak.

He thanked them for the offerings which amounted to eleven pounds, and, as was customary, went on to say a few kind words for the dead. He praised AB for her holiness, her goodness and for her devotion to the Church and to God. She was a God-fearing person; she suffered much, but bore it with patience. He offered sympathy. He asked everyone to kneel once more and join him in saying one Our Father, one Hail Mary and one Gloria for the repose of her soul. Fr Bradley always prayed a lot for the faithful departed.

The four men quickly shouldered the coffin. The bell tolled sorrowfully and the coffin was carried slowly down the aisle, out through the porch and down the chapel yard. Gusts of March wind plucked at Fr Bradley's white, starched surplice as he walked slowly before the coffin reading the sonorous Latin liturgy audibly from his breviary. At the gate the hearse was waiting. The bell ceased to toll and the sound of the coffin going into the hearse was a slow, ominous growl.

The funeral moved slowly down into Main Street on its way to the graveyard. There were three traps, one sidecar, dozens of bicycles and one motor car. As the hearse went down the street men paused, as was customary, doffed their caps and made the sign of the cross. Children, well-trained by the nuns, crossed themselves, but added 'Compassionate Lord Jesus grant them Eternal Rest,' and raced on. It was the most important event and the most striking honour AB had ever received. There had been nothing in her life to equal it.

She was buried among all the Aughabeg McCartins in the middle of the old and overcrowded graveyard where all the graves faced to the rising sun. The ancient walls of the thirteenth-century Cistercian abbey sheltered the grave from the cold east winds that she feared so much during life. There were nine brown skulls and a heap of bones resting beside the huge mound of mouldy earth along the open grave.

Fr Bradley continued the Latin prayers. He said the Our Father and everyone answered him. He sprinkled the coffin in the bottom of the grave, very skilfully, holding the bottle with one finger stuck into the neck. The blobs of holy water fell heavily on the timber and the breastplate. He then took a shovel and threw three small shovelfuls of the heaped mould on the coffin: Father, Son and Holy Ghost. When he had finished, Francie Heaney took the skulls and bones and dropped them into the grave slowly and carefully at the side of the coffin. They looked more like old mahogany timber than anything else. A few of the neighbours grabbed shovels and the filling of the grave quickly began. It was terrible to hear the thud that every shovelful of soil made on the coffin and on AB.

Seamus watched the coffin gradually disappear from view. Finally, there was only a little bit at the foot that remained visible. He watched it closely. It remained visible for a long time. Then there was a little shift in the soil, a little slide of the mould, and it was hidden from view. It was the last of AB.

Tommy stood at the foot of the grave in a brown, belted tweed overcoat. For once in his life, his hair was properly combed and parted. He held his hat in his hands. Somehow, he seemed apart from the rest of the crowd. He looked very thoughtful and sad and resigned.

When the grave was filled, those who took part in the work clapped the mound into a neat shape with the back of the implements. Then all the implements, including a loy, were laid across the grave in the form of a cross; and those present, with one accord, promptly dropped to their knees for a last, private, silent prayer for the deceased. The silence was deadly and complete. It was the final goodbye at the end of a life.

The neighbours who dug the grave were taken to one of the public houses in Ballydoon village for a quick drink, as was the custom. It would be whiskey in the case of a funeral. Tommy did his duty.

Nan-nan was pleased that AB's funeral was taken before the other one, that of an asthmatic, gentle little lady named Judy O'Hara. She believed in the old superstition which said that when two funerals took place from the one church on the same day the soul of the second would have to carry water to ease the fires of purgatory for the soul of the first. The second deceased could not get into heaven before the first one either. This belief could outrage the Church and earn its condemnation, for all Nan-nan cared. She knew her own mind in matters of that sort.

During the meal that followed the burial, Nan-nan kept coming back to AB's funeral, and how she got in first. A few of the distant and long-lost cousins were there also, and soon the conversation was back to normal. One of the cousins, Patrick Creamer from Aughawillan, happened to look out the window.

'There's Eddie, the soldier,' he almost shouted. The nephew, for whom AB had washed and darned and knitted when he was on the run from the Black-and-Tans, walked in through the door. How proud she would have been to have had him at her 'birril'. But he was too late. He had come as fast as he could in his Baby Austin from Cork, where he was an officer in the Irish army. He went to the graveyard and found her freshly made grave. He knelt, said a prayer and continued on his journey to Drumlahan. His brother, Georgie, AB's other nephew, was, of course, not present. His name was not mentioned and his grave was unknown. And no-one was ever to go to look for it or to say a prayer by its side where the British army left him, not far from Salonika in distant Greece nearly twenty years before.

25

New engines

The trains continued their daily ups and downs. New sleepers had been put in for miles and miles and in the summer heat they oozed warm tar, which Seamus and Jack Martin and many of the other schoolboys and girls loved to walk in, in their bare feet. Then, when the feet had collected sufficient tar they walked in the dry, dead grass, or in the sand and pebbles. Soon they had sand or pebble sandals. It was great fun. And it sometimes took the whole evening to get rid of the conglomeration.

The trains came along punctually at times the people knew about; but the milesmen could come along at any time, walking or on a bogie. They always gave the schoolgoers a jaunt on the bogie. Now and then the Permanent Way Inspector could come, pedalling along on his four-wheeled trolley, and mark with yellow chalk any rail, sleeper, fishplate, gate or fence that he considered required immediate attention or repair. The milesmen were always around promptly after him to do the necessary work.

A considerable degree of confusion arose when Seamus and Jack Martin obtained some yellow chalk at school which was of the same colour and shade as that used by the Permanent Way Inspector. They then went on to mark clearly everything that they considered needed immediate attention. This included several rail joints, two gates, half a dozen sleepers and a few dog-spikes. All were scattered along the two-mile stretch of line which ran from Drumlahan to Ballinwing. Lastly, they marked in three or four places the metal bridge that carried the railway across the canal.

It had all the makings of a serious incident, of a dire emergency. Milesmen came, in haste and in sweat, to the bridge; a policeman hurried across the fields from the town road; a train hesitated for half an hour at the station in fear and in doubt. No risks could be taken: orders were orders and regulations were, indeed, regulations. Finally, a few frantic telephone calls convinced everyone that the Permanent Way Inspector had not chalked the metal bridge at all. And then, when still more chalk marks were spotted in unconvincing positions, such as on dog-spikes and gates which could not possibly need attention, traffic began to flow with more confidence and less nervousness.

Immediately afterwards, four inspectors came to look at the bridge. It was pronounced fit and well; and the milesmen were reminded that it was their responsibility to see that trespassers were prosecuted and kept off the line. The milesmen in turn warned the parents; for they knew soon enough that it was not sabotage, but merely schoolboys' doodling. The parents threatened all the children; for no-one had any idea who the chalkers were.

'Would you all like to have to walk the extra mile to and from school every day, winter and summer? No? Well then there had better be no more chalk marks on the railway line. Have your choice.'

The milesmen and the station master could have stopped the children had they pressed the matter, and they would have had the full support of the Guards. However, they did not want to quarrel with the parents, who were their neighbours, and the matter soon died down.

From time to time in later years, some unauthorised markings in yellow chalk did occur. By then the milesmen were able to know immediately if they were fakes; and they never confused them with the genuine article of the Permanent Way Inspector.

Rakes of coal were going up to the wide-gauge railway at Dromod. They amounted to two additional special trains almost every day. Coal also went up with the ordinary passenger trains. All this was because of Mr de Valera's intensified self-sufficiency policy. It gave plenty of work to the railway itself, and it also gave employment in the coalmines.

'The crooked ould villain!' spluttered Tommy, referring to de Valera and economic self-sufficiency. 'When Cosgrave's government started the sugar-beet factories, de Valera jibed that the sugar could be imported into Ireland cheaper. And when Cosgrave started the Shannon Scheme, to make cheap electricity for the country, de Valera shouted that it was a white elephant. Now the ould scoundrel is boasting that it was all his own idea.'

Another form of traffic that Mr de Valera brought to the railway that went through Drumlahan was the old-cow special. The cattle trade was depressed because of the economic war with Britain. A canning factory was established at Roscrea, County Tipperary. If it was difficult to sell young cattle in those days, it was impossible to sell old or derelict animals, especially old cows. Accordingly Mr de Valera initiated a scheme whereby unsaleable cows could be exchanged for fifty shillings and sent to Roscrea. From then on many special trains went up the line from time to time full of old and weary cows on their last trip.

'Send him to Roscrea!' was a jibe often shouted at football matches if some unlucky player was having an off-day or moving slowly.

When a narrow-gauge railway in Cork closed down in the early 1930s four of its locomotives were sent three years later to run on the Leitrim, Cavan and Roscommon railway. Tommy said that the new engines came from the Cork, Bandon and Passage line. They were relocated because of the flourishing coal trade; and their arrival caused a great stir among the young people, and, indeed, also among the grown-ups.

The new engines were much different from the old ones that had been puffing up and down past Drumlahan since 1887 when small farmers like Uncle James and big landlords like the Hon. James Burroughs, in an unprecedented outbreak of goodwill and co-operation, had worked closely together to get the first trains running.

All the new engines had a large number in front and on the rear, 10, 11, 12 or 13. The old engines had unobtrusive numbers on their sides, 2, 4, 5, 6, 7 or 8, but also a name in prominent lettering, such as Kathleen, Isabel, Edith or Elizabeth. The new engines were bigger, longer and higher over their wheels than the old ones. They had large tenders in the rear for coal; and they had sharp whistles, almost like a stone-crusher or a steamroller.

Strangest of all, they had no cow-catchers. This excited everyone's curiosity and disapproval. Every engine should have a decent cow-catcher in front, was the general belief. To be without one was like a man running around with his trousers off, or at least with his fly open.

If you watched the old engines closely when they were pulling a long load or going up a steep hill, you could see that with every puff they lifted their front wheels and noses, just a little. The new engines, with red paint in front and red paint behind, were so long that they never budged, no matter what the speed or what the load.

Number 13 was the first of the new engines to come, and whenever its whistle sounded it caused immediate loss of attention among the boys, and among not a few of the girls also, in the schoolrooms around Ballinwing. Concentration flagged; multiplication tables lost their inherent logic; false notes were sung when Mrs Canning banged the tuning-fork three blessed times and couldn't get her pupils to take the right note. Too many of them were inclined to give her back a note nearer to the whistle of engine number 13 from the Cork, Bandon and Passage line. She lost her temper with them once more and called them boobies and crows. When the younger ones played trains in the schoolyard, even they had altered their style of shunting, pulling and puffing, to conform with the movements and the sounds of the new age of steam.

No-one could say exactly when it started, but a rumour began to go around that number 13 was a flop, a washout, a lame duck. This soon became a cruel disappointment to the kids and a source of derision for everyone else. It leaked out slowly that number 13 could not get across Drumlahan bank without backing down the line, spitting on its hands, as it were, and then taking a desperate run at the hill. At school Seamus was pressed to confirm the truth or the falsity of the rumour, seeing that he was well acquainted with that part of the railway. He had seen it all with his own eyes, of course, but he became evasive. He said that when number 13 went by he was doing his homework – this from someone who never did homework – and he told plenty of lies of every sort in order to cover up as well as he could for the unhappy locomotive.

Ned Martin never heard the beating of it. As everyone knew, every train that ever stopped at the station just restarted when the guard blew his whistle and labouringly but successfully surmounted the bank, which was nearly a mile long. Number 13, however, could not do this after restarting; and when it would have almost reached the top it would stop dead. The driver then reversed down the hill with much clanking and whistle-blowing, and Mrs Martin came rushing out, hustling the children indoors, counting them to make sure they were all there and then dashing out and opening the gates just in time for the wagons, vans, carriages and number 13 itself to trundle by in reverse.

About half a mile further down the line it would halt. A long pause always ensued while steam was raised almost to bursting point. Then came a blast on the sharp, stone-crusher whistle, a few snorts and stutters caused by wheels that would not grip without more sand, and number 13 was away for the hill. It usually got over on the first go; but those who lived in the vicinity of the railway knew well that it had often made two and sometimes three attempts before the journey could be completed. Seamus tried to keep that dark at school also; but of course it leaked out in the end.

All this evoked much derisory laughter among the adult population. The likes of it was never seen or heard of before – an engine that couldn't cross 'the bank'. They shook their heads and tightened their lips at the daftness of the new and the newfangled. They saw it as a case of arrogant pride having taken a fall.

But it caused deep disappointment in the children. Number 13 was something new and exciting. It was stylish-looking, exotic, big and colourful, and it came from faraway West Cork. It was a pop star, an adored one. Yet it was found to unable to deliver the goods, and it had let everyone down.

When morale was at its lowest and minds and hearts were beginning to turn away from the railway, another new engine suddenly arrived, number 11. It was the same make and design as the first one, and it came from the same place. But this one was no lame duck of a locomotive: it could travel very fast; it could pull any load that was hooked to it; it had the same sharp whistle as number 13; and it could cross Drumlahan bank without a stumble. It became popular; and there were many devotees in Mrs Canning's classes who claimed that they could easily distinguish between the whistle and puff of number 11 on the one hand, and the whistle and puff of number 13 on the other, even if both were heard from miles away in the distance.

Seamus did not join in the general enthusiasm for number 11. He did not know why, really. He felt a little sorry for number 13. In any case he did not like the number eleven itself. Was this because Joe Cafferty, who was a bully, was said to be eleven years old? Or was it because he himself was eleventh in the class when it came to the hated spelling?

The new engine ran up and down in great spirits, pulling passenger trains regularly; but also doing odd jobs such as coal specials, cattle fairs and rakes of ballast for the permanent way. Then, after a while, number 13 began to perform a little better also; and it was the cause of much heated debate. Many knowledgeable people were saying that the difficulties number 13 had encountered at first were nothing more than those brought about by the drivers and firemen not knowing how to handle a locomotive which was new to them. The crew of number 13 rejected such a suggestion. They could make anything with wheels go over Drumlahan bank, they asserted. They were adamant in saying that she was an old crock, a heap of junk and that she should be shunted down a siding and left there to rust herself peacefully to death.

Nan-nan said that she wouldn't, for the life of her, travel on the train from Drumlahan to Ballinwing if either of the two new engines was pulling the carriages. They didn't look safe to her. The sound of the sharp whistle would split one's ears and deafen one. And then look at the set of them! Too many wheels and no cow-catcher. No! She didn't like these newfangled engines at all. She'd rather walk or go in the ass-cart.

And then one evening, and quite without warning, news went out that two more engines had arrived from Cork. They were carried on the wide-gauge to Dromod and then lifted by crane and placed on the rails of the narrow-gauge line, according to account. Steam was got up, and they came down the line to Ballinwing, hooked together, whistling, hissing and clanking. Seamus was on a trip to Tullylakenmore then and he felt deprived not to have seen the arrival of the two. However, his acquaintances at school gave him all the details.

He opted immediately for number 12. Many in the school chose number 10; but support for all of the four engines was almost evenly divided. Even number 13 got back a considerable amount of support when the rumour that its early problems could be attributed to bad driving took effect. It was running around like a race-horse now. And it was beginning to be said that the new engines were not built in the first instance for a hilly country like Leitrim. Neither were they fitted for a railtrack with such sharp turns as those they had to contend with now. Nevertheless, they all continued to move briskly.

However, partisanship was fierce; and children clung to railway gates and hung across wire fences above the cuttings or looked up from the bottom of embankments to see how their favourites were behaving and which was really the fastest. Seamus knew that number 12 could get over the Drumlahan bank easily; but every time it passed on its way to the hill he said a fervent Hail Mary, just in case. It would be so humiliating to have to face the whole school next day and give a puff-by-puff account of how number 12 faltered, halted, and then came trundling backwards down the hill to have another try. He said a whole rosary, the five glorious mysteries, in petition to God that it would never come to pass that number 12 should fail to get safely across Drumlahan bank. And he promised God also that there would be another rosary there for the asking, if it were ever needed. He wondered if engine-drivers and railwaymen and railways themselves had patron saints, just as fishermen and missionaries had? It would simplify matters considerably if they had.

None the less, as the weeks and the months went by, he had to admit to himself that number 12 was not just quite as fast as the others, and certainly not as fast as number 11. He viewed number 12 from the top of the cuttings and across the meadows and fields;

and the cold conviction began to lurk somewhere inside him that he had backed a loser again. It didn't come down Kiltymooden hill and over the metal bridge with the same freedom and the same abandon that number 11 did. Of course he never dared admit all that to anyone else.

He asked Ned Martin, a ganger now, and a man who could talk trains all night, which of all the new engines was the fastest. Ned assured him that it was number 11. Of course if number 10 had a new fire-box and a few new valves, there wasn't one of them could touch her. A regular Flying Scotsman and no mistake. Seamus was pleased that he had the foresight to question Ned when no-one else was listening. It would be spread far and wide. The shame, the scandal, would be out.

He needed time to think. So he retreated to his hideaway on the double ditch. He could hear the trains leaving the station in Ballinwing when the air was clear, and he could see the plume of smoke long before they reached the metal bridge. If the smoke lingered in a long plume after it was puffed out through the funnel, people said it meant that the weather would be bad and rainy. If the smoke vanished soon, or fairly soon, after leaving the funnel, good weather could be expected. The new engines puffed to a different rhythm, level, fast and light. The old engines continued with their old rhythm. 'I'll jump down your belly: I'll walk on your corpse. I'll jump down your belly: I'll walk on your corpse.'

He sat there all hunched up on the double ditch listening to the noise of the train dying away in the distance. And as he worried about the performance of number 12 he got colder and more lethargic and depressed and he didn't want to move.

He knew that others at school were saying prayers for their favourites: 'Sacred Heart of Jesus I place my trust in thee that number 10 will go faster than number 11.' There would be the odd Hail Mary, the occasional brief visit to the chapel. Many the little white votive candle was lit in the candelabra in front of the high altar to speed up a favourite locomotive. Competition was tough. He half regretted he had opted for number 12. But he could not back out now.

He promised God a Holy Communion if number 12 could be speeded up a bit, just a little, a few feet only. And he promised moreover that he would say his morning and evening prayers more carefully and that he would stop taking short-cuts from halfway through the Our Father to the beginning of the Act of Contrition. He knew that God would like that.

And then he had a brainwave. Bad language and cursing! He would stop using all forms of bad language right away; that very minute. That should certainly put number 12 well out in front. He felt confident that the idea was a winner, a masterstroke. And he was pleased to note that, although they continued to pray and to light the occasional candle, none of the other lads at school had stopped using bad language. It delighted him to hear them using it now. He knew he had stolen a march on them and that number 12 would soon improve and begin to inch forward. He gloated over the blindness of the others. He did not forget that he had once lost faith in prayer, when Mrs Canning didn't get another attack of gallstones. Well, let bygones be bygones! With a renewed faith he prayed for number 12 and smiled when he heard the sweet sound of bad language all around him.

There was no end to the splendid spiritual uplift that the four new engines from Cork wrought in the hearts and souls of the youth of Ballinwing and the surrounding districts. It was far more useful than a mission could ever be, with its thundering Redemptorists or its Franciscans calling down the wrath of God on little heads. It even outshone the most diligent efforts of Fr Bradley, for a time. And as those four engines puffed and rattled their way under slanting plumes of smoke between the hills, along the lakes and across the meadows, they had a lot to answer for, and a lot to be proud of too.

Everyone in the house noticed the change in Seamus. He had suddenly become obedient; he would eat whatever was put before him, even the hated stirabout. He would go wherever he was asked on a message, quickly and without argument. He had not to be called several times in the morning: he was up like a lark.

Veronica had always told him that he should pray for the dead at every opportunity, just a short prayer, and that he must never

210

forget AB, who had thought so much of him. It was Christian charity, she said, to pray for those who were gone. He complied indeed whenever he remembered it. But times had changed; and as things stood now on the railway the poor suffering souls in purgatory would have to look after themselves for the time being. There were very pressing matters on hand now, and the dead would have to have patience.

The months and then the years passed on and the four engines remained about the same. Number 13 continued to cross the hills in a manner which did her credit. Number 12 never could get up that little extra spurt of speed that would have looked like an answer to a prayer; but no-one seemed to notice this, except Seamus, and he kept it all to himself. In time the four engines became accepted by everyone, and they puffed and clanked up and down the railway just as if they had been there for ever. And so it continued for many years. A few other engines arrived also. They were hardly noticed.

It seemed that matters would continue like that indefinitely, with the buzzard clock blowing every morning to tell the town and the country that another day had begun, and the trains and the coal specials passing up and down to tell the time and to divide the farmwork.

But all things must end; and so also one day did the railway, and the engines and rolling-stock that were so much a part of it.

The lorries and the buses took the railway's trade away. Stunned and bewildered by the shock, it became doddery and inefficient. Goods for delivery at Ballinwing could go up and down the railway for days in the same wagon or the same van because no-one remembered to take them off or leave them on the platform for delivery at the correct station.

When the final blow came everyone was ready for the dismemberment. And the last train had scarcely braked when men were at work digging up sleepers, unbolting rails, carrying away machinery and wagons.

'Couldn't we keep an engine, a carriage and a few wagons, and mebbe a few miles of the railway itself, for ould time's sake,' a weak voice was heard to plead. 'Sure, it would be good for the

211

tourists,' the voice went on, trying to sound practical and man-of-the-world.

'Fuck the tourists!' he was told, as the boys who once lit candles before the high altar for the success of their favourite engine, now, as men, pulled the railway apart and carried it away on the cheap.

It was unique. There was nothing like it elsewhere in the world; with its carriages that were once destined for India, with its mixture of quaint locomotives and its railtrack that ran for miles along the public road and then on the banks of the sombre canal. There was no-one now who could say a prayer that number 12 would go just that little bit faster and, perhaps, escape the clutches of Mammon and the internal combustion engine of the roads. And there would be no talk of a ghost train in the years to come either, for no-one would be able to see it: Ballinwing had long ago ceased to believe in such useless things.

26

The hayshed

The hayshed that Tommy built when he married into the place was situated conveniently between the ould house and the road. The byre and the stable were built of railway sleepers in the form of a lean-to against the hayshed. All the horse's harness as well as swingle trees and traces were hung in the hayshed in a dry but well-ventilated position on the lean-to wall.

In spring and early summer, when the hay was nearly all used up and there was little in the hayshed except the horse-cart, the ass-cart and the plough, the swallows came and built their nests high on the rafters and beams. Sometimes the gander with two geese and the growing goslings came into the hayshed, forsaking the double ditch where they had nested, for reasons best known to themselves.

Throughout the year, the hayshed always had plenty of visitors. The two dogs, Foreman and the new sheepdog Carlo, occasionally came in, seemingly on impulse, and each would burrow a hole for himself between the bays of hay. On cold mornings the cat could sometimes be seen asleep on the hay; but generally she crouched comfortably on a beam over the cows' heads in the byre.

The fragrance of the hay and the rich smell of the cows' breath were both very noticeable. One could sometimes get the good smell of fresh milk from a cow's breath if she belched gently when chewing the cud. This was particularly evident soon after calving, or when the cows were out on grass.

Because it was far removed from the dwelling-house and near to the road, the hayshed became a convenient place for others to go also. The occasional tramp or wanderer was often surprised there at the dawn of a frosty morning when foddering was in progress. Large numbers of animal bones, clean and polished, could sometimes be found there. They were brought in by Foreman or Carlo, or indeed by the neighbouring dogs, so that they could have a quiet gnaw in comfortable surroundings.

To courting couples, Tommy's new hayshed was a godsend, and they came from far and near to avail themselves of the comforts it afforded for their nocturnal exertions. It was private. Neither would a dog bark, as in the case of less well-situated haysheds. Tommy's dogs would normally raise the roof and give the impression of being ready to eat alive any stranger whom they encountered. Yet, they became cuddly and welcoming and kept the secret whenever young wooers entered the hayshed. The goings-on that they witnessed in the hay must have changed their canine characters. And even the geese, who from the time of St Paul were wont to give the alarm, also seemed to enter into the spirit of things and remained silent. All the wooers had to do was to hide their bicycles along the road and walk in.

At first Seamus and the other local children could not quite understand why people were so eager to go into the hayshed in the darkness of the night. To steal hay? To steal milk from the cows? Or perhaps a sucking pig from the sty, for a secret feast? Of course nothing was ever stolen or rustled. The visitors had more pressing business in mind than mere theft.

And you could find the most interesting things in the hayshed any morning of the year, even in summer when there was little or no hay left from the winter: packets of cigarettes, some of them full, money, bracelets, gloves, delightful brooches, a woman's silk stocking, a man's cap, a dandy little electric torch, handkerchiefs, a prayer book, sweets and chocolate, half a packet of biscuits, a cigarette-holder, a pipe, a bicycle pump, rosary beads.

Generally the hay was not disturbed; sometimes there were signs of dire struggle. Once, a whole bench of hay, complete with hay-knife and a stump of a scythe-stone, came tumbling down and buried the two dogs completely. When Tommy came to fodder the cows next morning he proceeded to pitch back the fallen hay. He was surprised when the two dogs bounded out in great trim, smiling and snorting and full of life. They were having

214

great fun. The unseemly demeanor of the two animals infuriated him, and he made a vicious swipe at them with the pitchfork. 'If yez were any good, this wouldn't happen.' He knew that tongue-hounds were good for nothing but hunting. Yet, this *stucaun*, Foreman, could at least have managed a bark. But no.

All these events caused Tommy great worry. He really did not mind if the wooers used his property for their needs and requirements; but he feared that the hay would be accidently put on fire and all his stock and housing be destroyed. He feared that some article lost in the hay could be swallowed by a beast and result in death or loss: pins, hairslides, little religious badges, lengths of elastic, or buttons. Morover, he was the object of much fun-poking, which he did not relish. 'What kind of a rough house is that I hear you're keeping, Tommy, *a mhic*? 'Twas daycent of a man to built a hayshed in such a private spot. Aren't you the nice *róúil* fella to let them go for a tumble in your hay!'

This he did not like; but he could put up with it. He feared most the loss of a beast. A horse had only one stomach and could handle most things and pass it out in the form of a hair-ball, if necessary. A cow had four stomachs, but could handle little except pure food.

So he bought an expensive padlock and he bolted and secured the gate with thoroughness and care. The wooers crept in through the close-set iron bars. He added more bars and he reinforced them with barbed wire. The visitors simply scaled the gate. He heightened the gate with a timber frame and he added barbed wire entanglements. They made holes in the hedge and crawled through on all fours.

When, very soon afterwards, business increased at the new galvanised iron hall at Aughabeg crossroads, life for Tommy became almost impossible. The new hall brought crowds of dancing young men on their humming bicycles from places as far apart as Corriga, Altacullion or Drumbrick under cover of darkness. The girls of Aughabeg and Drumlahan were determined to cash in on this windfall of muscular manhood while the going was good. Traffic around Tommy's hayshed became heavy, almost congested.

Ned Martin, who considered himself to be an expert on dogs and their thinking habits, advised Tommy to tie the two dogs in the shed during the week, but to starve them. So he tied both of them with a plough trace to each of the two end pillars, and he starved them. This should arouse their watchdog instincts, it was thought. When Sunday night came they raised such a hullaballoo when anyone passed by on the road, never mind entering the hayshed, that every other dog in the neighbourhood went mad barking. The noise continued to midnight. Foreman sat on his haunches and bayed piteously. Carlo lost his usual enquiring bark, and a hysterical yelp came into his voice. He seemed on the verge of having the fits.

Tommy knew that he could not deny the countryside its sleep, even if his cattle and his hay went up in flames. He disappeared out the door with his hat pulled down well over his ears and a bucket in his hand with food for those who were in chains. In a few minutes there wasn't a sound to be heard. The watchdogs had dined, had curled up for the night and were fast asleep.

From then on he began to feed them a little more food, but he never exceeded two collations daily. He tried to achieve a brinkmanship that would deter the wooers, but that would not lead to open conflict with his neighbours. Towards the weekend the dogs received one collation only. The animals acquired a lean and hungry look. For the following two weeks they put up a stiff resistance; though there was some evidence that efforts had been made to seduce them with tit-bits from the pocket and the handbag. However, from the third week onwards matters went completely wrong.

The two dogs suddenly became drowsy. Also, they became very broadminded once more. A whole regiment of wooers could go in and out past them for all they cared. Tommy was puzzled and he toyed with the notion of a return to stark starvation again. Ned Martin felt that he had lost face; the dogs were not behaving according to his experience of how dogs should behave. Tommy felt his dogs were betraying him. 'It feels just like being let down by your own flesh and blood,' he mused bitterly. Then he corrected himself, 'Almost like one's own flesh and blood.'

216

The cause of the trouble was Louise Martin, Ned's youngest daughter. In her way, she knew far more about dogs than her father did. Moreover, she was always on cuddling terms with Foreman and Carlo. But she had some long-term plans in her mind also that she wanted to bring to fruition.

She was far too shy and too modest to cash in vulgarly on the current man-hunting and man-eating activities of the rest of the girls. Yet she did want a slice of the cake; but on her own terms, of course. Accordingly, she let it be known, in an indirect and quiet way, that if someone would fix her up with that red-haired Mulloghan fellow from Carrigallen who rode the three-speed Raleigh, she would render the two watchdogs at Tommy Flynn's hayshed harmless. She left the matter at that for those who were interested to think it over. She then put on her coat, fixed the beret on the side of her head, picked up her prayer book and rosary and walked quietly along the railway line to the Sunday evening Benediction. She was in good time: she was just at the creamery when Mrs Tubman began to ring the chapel bell. Louise was a planner.

There was no further use in the two dogs. They just welcomed the wooers with wagging tails and whimpers of delight. Ned couldn't understand it. Tommy looked up at the single-barrelled shotgun hanging on the chimney breast, high under the ceiling. Veronica followed his gaze.

'Now don't be thinking of that. Put that out of your mind entirely,' she ordered.

'A few blasts in the air over their heads could do the trick,' he said morosely.

'It could indeed. And it could land you in jail too. That would be a nice kettle of fish, wouldn't it?'

He replied that he supposed she was right. Sooner or later he was going to suffer loss. Of that he was sure; a cow, a calf, or maybe the whole thing would go up in smoke. An air of defeat and despondency settled on the household and on Ned Martin, who considered himself involved in the events also. He was far more involved than he could ever have imagined. It was then that he had one of his many bright ideas. 'A mantrap! A mantrap! The very

217

thing! That's what you want for your hayshed, Tommy! A good mantrap!'

Ned explained himself then. He saw plenty of mantraps at Crom Castle in County Fermanagh when he used to go there to cut trees in the demesne and then to snig them out to the road. The gamekeeper had several mantraps and he used them to trap poachers. He showed Ned how to set one and how to lay it in the grass or leaves. It snapped and gripped the poacher around the ankle. It would hold him fast until he was released. It always took two men to release a trapped poacher: the spring of the mantrap was so strong.

'I don't know why I didn't think of it before now, Tommy,' he went on enthusiastically. 'You get a shoeing of a cartwheel and I'll get a few old wagon springs at the station. There'll be no trouble getting it welded. I'll have a good mantrap for you in no time.'

He was very pleased with himself. He was also pleased because it was an opportunity to attempt to make something that he never had made before, like his boat and his beehive and his grinding stone.

'If you caught one or two of them in the hayshed with the mantrap they'd all go away, Tommy, and never come back. If you caught a few of the lassies that would crown it.'

It never occurred to him that the very first victim of the mantrap might well be one of his own daughters, as the teeth snapped on a shapely leg.

Nan-nan had a bad wheezing on her chest, and moreover she did not know what the country was coming to at all. She always knew, at the back of her mind, that haysheds were bad for man and beast: hay heated in them; there was far too much dust; hay came in in dribs and drabs compared with one good day's work making a rick when she was a girl. All the fun of hay-gathering went out when the hayshed came in.

'You're wrong there, ma'am,' said Ned, in an outburst of hoarse laughter. 'There's far too much fun connected with some haysheds that I know of these days.'

And bicycles! She never liked bicycles. Bringing blackguards and *ramscagh* to that hall at Aughabeg and leading the daycent little girls of the neighbourhood astray. Bad and all as the hayshed was, there would never be any trouble with it but for the bicycles and the tin hall. She felt that Tommy was no man if he didn't take down that gun and make a cabbage-strainer of someone's arse as they climbed over the gate.

'No, no!' said Veronica emphatically. 'That would be going too far.'

'Why don't you tell the Guards?' asked Nan-nan.

'No! After all, most of them must be neighbours' childer. And they don't mean any harm anyway,' said Veronica.

'If the shed and the hay and the cows go up in flames and smoke, you'll not get much thanks from the neighbours for your softness. I'm telling you Veronica, you and Tommy are far too gutless.' She became very incensed. 'If yez two don't do something soon, when I get rid of this wheezing that I have on my chest, I'll get a pitchfork and walk up and down that road every night. And God help any coorters that come near me!'

'No! Take care of yourself for the present,' said Veronica in a placatory tone. 'Things aren't that bad yet.'

'Why don't you go to Fr Bradley and get him to read it out on the altar at Mass?' Nan-nan urged.

'For God's sake will you whisht woman!' said Tommy sharply. 'I'd look well going to Fr Bradley with a yarn like that. He'd burst his sides laughing at me, so he would! And I'm sure Fr Bradley knows all about that hayshed and its troubles already. There's nothing that misses him. He knows every stir. And if he was daft enough to announce it on the altar, I'd be the laughing-stock of the country. What would happen if that hayshed got into the *Leitrim Observer* or the *Anglo-Celt?*'

The mantrap did not appeal to him either. He felt sure there would be a legal snag in it somewhere. In any case, Ned found that it would take a couple of weeks more before he could get one together and fully tested. In the meantime Tommy decided to go to the hayshed every night that visitors could be expected and to sit there on the hay with an electric torch. He'd order the wooers out as soon as they'd come in. When the time came, he took a pitchfork with him in case they became violent and he had to defend himself.

On his first encounter he told the couple that they would have to leave. He was sorry, he said, but he was afraid his property and his stock would be reduced to ashes. They said they understood; they would go; they asked him to turn off the torch so that they would not be recognised. He heard their bicycles rattling away into the darkness over the road.

This went on for a few weeks: he apologising for the inconvenience caused; they hiding their faces; saying they understood and then departing in a cloud of scented soap, brilliantine and politeness.

One night he dropped off to sleep in the hay, for the routine was killing him. Two visitors came in unheard and settled down for their session. Progress was normal, but when matters were getting interesting, a loud and unseemly snoring suddenly started up nearby. They were frightened at first; but they quickly recovered. They concluded that it was a tramp or a wanderer who had come in while they were distracted.

The young man shouted, 'Who's there?' The owner of the hayshed awoke with a shout and a snarling snore. He gripped his pitchfork; and when his mind cleared and he found his torch, he also called out, 'Who's there?'

'Never mind who's here,' ordered the wooer. 'This is no place at all for tramps and strangers. I'm warning you never to smoke or to crack a match here and burn down this daycent man's hay and cattle. And I can tell you that if this shed is ever burnt or if anything goes wrong in it, a few of us fellows will folly you on bikes and you'll never forget it. You could find yourself in the canal with a hundredweight of cement around your neck. D'ye hear that now?'

'I hear yeh,' replied Tommy.

Well, there was no answer to that. He pocketed his torch; left the visitors to it, and quickly went home to bed. The hayshed that he had built at such cost and such labour was in good hands, he had to admit.

And so a tacit compromise was reached. They kept the story from Nan-nan; and she soon lost interest in it, in any case. The coming of the bicycle, the arrival of jazz and the galvanised iron halls changed people's social habits; and Tommy's hayshed, that was catering for a new form of farming, was put to additional uses that he could never have envisaged when he built it.

The cat continued to crouch sleepily on the beams over the cows' heads; the dogs continued to take in their bones and to gnaw them in peace; and Seamus continued to collect the bric-a-brac on the mornings after the nights before. Some he merely threw away; but anything that possessed an enduring value, or a strangeness, he added to his hoard in the nook on the double ditch with the railway cinders, the bullocks' horns and the Lough Neagh hone. His most spectacular find was a pair of ladies' high-heeled shoes of high quality, very ornate and of American make. It was evident that some girl or other had had to find her way home on a frosty night in stockinged feet. He didn't know what to do with the shoes for a time. Finally, he dumped them secretly in Peter Sheridan's beech wood where the young Martin girls had boxes and shelves for their games of make-believe house and shop.

And Louise Martin? She got her man, decided he was far too wild for her taste, but resolved to hold on to him as a face-saving device. She was too shy and restrained to compete in the rumbustious market in human flesh that was going on all around her at that time. Finally, she concluded that she liked dogs better than men – or at least the men that were available to her – and she got a job in kennels near Dublin. She subsequently upped and went off to California. She was never heard of again. To her dying day, Mrs Martin never failed to weep copiously for her missing daughter, especially at certain times of the year, such as her birthday, her First Communion day, her Confirmation day and the anniversary of her first day at work.

27

Confirmation

The old, old bishop came and gave Confirmation to two hundred and fifty-seven children in the chapel at Ballinwing. It was packed to capacity with the children, their parents and the general public. Everyone wanted to see the bishop, who was so old and so feeble that he seldom came around now. Jack Martin said his father told him that the bishop came this time only because he was afraid there would soon be war, and that he wanted to have as many confirmed as possible before the Germans came.

All the girls were made to take the Confirmation name of Teresa by the nuns, because it was the third of October, the feast day of St Teresa herself. The boys had names suggested to them by their parents, and they chose widely. Seamus was very hurt because everyone in his class had a Confirmation name and he had none. His father and mother, always forgetful and preoccupied, never thought of it. He hoped to the very last minute at the altar rails that someone would think of it, or in fact ask him if he had one. No-one asked him. He tried to draw the talk around so that someone would come to his rescue. No-one came.

The old, old bishop paused when he saw that there was no Confirmation name on the card. But Fr Bradley, who was helping the bishop, got over the difficulty by immediately suggesting that the first name be used instead. The bishop quickly recovered, made the sign of the cross on the boy's forehead with chrism, said the short prayer in Latin, tipped him lightly on the cheek to remind him that he would have to suffer for Christ, and then passed on to the next kneeling child. That night Seamus remained awake late into the darkness worrying because he had no Confirmation name. It seemed to him that something irrevocable had happened, something lost that could never be recovered.

222

On the day after Confirmation he suddenly noticed that he felt no change in his make-up or in his mind. He went over the seven gifts of the Holy Ghost which he was supposed to have received: Wisdom, Understanding, Counsel, Fortitude, Knowledge, Piety and the Fear of the Lord. No, there was no change at all. He felt no wiser: he understood nothing more; he had no more knowledge than he had before the bishop came. As for Piety? Well, the less said the better about that. And he wasn't exactly shivering in his hobnailed boots with Fear of the Lord either.

He was convinced that there must be something wrong. The Confirmation name – could that be it? Could it be that because he had no Confirmation name he hadn't received the sacrament correctly? That could be a difficult problem; and there was no-one with whom he could discuss it, except Jim Gaffney, and he was in England. There was nothing for it now but to find out from others who were confirmed with him whether they felt OK. A considerable amount of desultory and hooded questioning followed; and in the end he concluded that none of those he spoke to felt charged with holy zeal either. They were just the same as himself. His mind was soon at rest.

First Communion was a great spiritual event; but Confirmation was something you accepted as it came; and you let the bishop and the grown-ups sort out the details. Yet, he was relieved that it was all over. He was a man now, just the same as every other man in the parish, so far as religion was concerned. There would be no more examinations, no more worry; he had something that no-one could take from him. Also, from now on it was himself and God and the devil; and he felt he could handle both of them. His parents and Nan-nan were a different matter, of course. They remained a deep and complex problem for him, and he had little hope of improvement in their behaviour and attitude. Apart from all that, one of the things he rejoiced in, in later life, was that he hadn't a Confirmation name. It would have been a profound embarrassment to him all his days.

Imperceptibly he began to notice that Confirmation had been a watershed in his life to a far greater extent than he could have ever imagined. Life was never the same again for him. It may have been true indeed that the sacrament which he had just received had little effect on him personally, or spiritually either. Yet it had a profound effect on his parents and on Nan-nan. Their attitude to him underwent an enormous change.

They began to give him more freedom, far more than he had ever expected or ever wanted at that stage of his existence. They came to realise, it would seem, that he was growing up and that a change was called for in their attitude towards him. This may have been the work of the Holy Ghost; it may also have been the local tradition of rearing children now asserting itself.

At all events, the first significant measure of emancipation which he experienced was in being frequently allowed to go up to Martins' to listen to the new wireless and to remain there until after the ten o'clock news. The one proviso to this was that he had to be able to tell everyone at home the headlines of the news as well as full details of the weather forecast on his return.

Ned Martin had just bought himself the wireless, which was the first of its kind in the neighbourhood. He was very anxious about the danger of war, and he was convinced that the newspapers were too slow with the news. He had an intense dislike of Hitler: he didn't like the way he looked or the way he sounded. Although rabidly Irish in sentiment, he had great faith in the British when it came to matters of world peace and stability. He was also deeply concerned about his three sons-in-law in Birmingham who were of military service age.

Everyone else was concerned about the likelihood of war also, but it seldom occurred to them that the country could ever become involved in war now. Ireland had gained freedom. To them the basic feature of an independent Irish state was that it could stand on its own feet. It was free to say no, and to be listened to. De Valera had said that Ireland would be neutral should war break out. All the local people who gathered into Martins' in the evening to listen to the news were in full agreement with Dev in that respect.

The news from the BBC Home Service came on at nine o'clock at night. Everyone listened in utter silence. They had to. Ned wouldn't tolerate a whisper while Frank Phillips, Alvar Liddell or

Bruce Belfradge was talking. The craggy, pipe-smoking men, tidied up in haste after a day in the fields, hung on their every word. It was a new sort of ceiliing: ould Doctor Keaney had passed away in more senses than one.

The clock on the mantelpiece chimed in concert with Big Ben. But Ned always checked Big Ben against his own heavy Ingersoll pocket-watch. All the world was well if Ned's watch, Ned's clock and Big Ben were stepping together through the vastness of time, tick by tick. At ten o'clock Radio Éireann's news came on and it was compared closely with the earlier BBC. It gave a wide coverage of national news, of course, but on foreign affairs it sometimes gave more detail and background than the BBC. This was because it came out later in the night. The neutrality policy was coming over loud and clear also.

It could have been only a month after Seamus was first let go to Martins' to listen to the wireless at night that Tommy told him in cold blood that he could go with the boys on the following Sunday to the hunt in Clonmoher. He was so astounded that he didn't know what to say. But off he went, leading Foreman on a brand new dog chain. A lunch of sliced soda bread and butter was stuffed into his overcoat pocket. They started a fox and had a good hunt, moving over the fields and across the hills to the cry of the hounds. It was a day to remember.

Just as unexpectedly, Veronica informed him that he could go with Philip Scollan and the Galloghy boys some night to see the travelling cinema show in Ballydoon hall. He saw Charlie Chaplin for the first time, and laughed himself to tears. He saw Victor McLaglen in *The Informer,* a film about the Black-and-Tan times in Dublin, and he was scared stiff. He could not speak. Never before had he seen a door being broken in with rifle butts. He had never seen a man being shot to death either.

It may have been that Confirmation, or the Holy Ghost, had suggested to those around him that they had not been giving him enough freedom for one of his age. It may have been that they came to the conclusion they had been mistakenly coddling him because of his supposed infant fragility of health. The fact that he had survived long enough to be confirmed may have surprised them or may have caused them to feel suddenly that they had been blind to what was happening. It now appeared that they were engaged in pushing him out of the nest.

Many unexpected examples of emancipation followed for Seamus, the most important of which was when Nan-nan confided in him that he was to be allowed to go alone to the circus in Ballinwing. This also may have been caused by the Holy Ghost working on his elders, but he was disappointed nevertheless. For if he went to the circus alone, he would have to go to the afternoon performance. At school there was more prestige to be gained by having attended the night show. He managed, after some hard thinking, to outwit the Holy Ghost and succeeded in going to the night performance with his father and John Stretton, as of old.

Tommy was convinced that this could well be the last circus they would see for some time. For if the war started, all the artistes – the Germans, Spaniards, English and Hungarians – would have to go back to their own countries and become soldiers. Uncle Eddie said that in 1914 all the Germans in New York had to return and join the German army when World War One broke out.

At the circus entrance the crowds poured in. A blond-haired, red-faced man at a caravan window droned out the prices over and over again: 'One and three, two and six or three shillings'. Tommy said the man was drunk and slurring his words.

The big brass band played with gusto and it had a fine repertoire of tunes and of marches, especially for the horses going around the ring in the sawdust. Tommy seemed to know all the tunes, including the Spanish marches and 'The Whistler and His Dog'. Seamus wondered why he hissed them through his teeth only when the circuses came to town.

Of burning interest to Seamus were the nationalities of the artistes. He was far more interested in the fact that they were Germans, Chinese, Hungarians, English or Swiss than he was in what they could do. And they swung and dived from the trapeze, jumped from springboards, changed water into wine, danced on the backs of running horses, conversed by signs with thinking ponies, caught in their teeth bullets that were just shot from revolvers, put their heads in lions' mouths, made elephants sit down and beg. And the individual who droned 'One and three, two and six or three shillings' at the gate turned out to be a quiet, sober strongman who bent nails with his finger and thumb, large bars with his arms, and who juggled very skilfully with four cannon balls. Seamus did not like the clowns. He knew that for months afterwards he would dream in terror of their faces and grimaces, just as he sometimes dreamed of the faces of the mummers who went around on St Stephen's Day from house to house, singing, dancing, playing music and collecting pennies.

'Did yeh notice that every Protestant in the three baronies is here the night?' said Tommy to a crony who was sitting behind Seamus at the ringside.

'Indeed I did! Indeed I did! They never miss a circus. Isn't it a holy terror, when you come to think of it?'

This was meant as a good-natured dig at the local Protestant community, who, as a group, never failed to turn up in force whenever a circus came to town. They might or might not go to church on Sunday when their jolly, tinkling bells summoned them. But if a circus came to Ballinwing every mother's son of them, except the bedridden, turned out in force. Hard-working, thrifty people as they were, who wouldn't let a straw go astray in the field or the haggard, the sound of a circus band or the sight of a circus poster waving in the breeze seemed to have a mesmeric effect on them. They seldom danced; they never kicked football and they didn't seem to like concerts or the drama. But they made up for all that when they downed tools, dressed themselves in their Sunday best, as only Protestants could do it, and hurried off, serious-faced and highly spruced, when the circus came to town.

In the months that followed, Seamus often found himself thinking about AB and about death itself. Some time after she died, he realised that he could not remember her features or what her face looked like. He was dismayed by this. By chance he came across a small photograph of her in the bottom of a drawer. He was so pleased. Afterwards, he could remember her features vividly and what she looked like in life. Yet it seemed incredible that he would never, never see her again. Why was that? Why had it to be so? It did not seem right. It did not seem to be the reality. Was it all just a dream? Praying for the repose of her soul was of little consolation for him. He wanted to see her.

Now that it appeared to be accepted that he was growing up, it occurred to him to ask Veronica if he could gaze into the crystal ball. He was immensely curious about it. At the back of his mind he wanted to see also what life had in store for him now. Recently he was sometimes very curious about the future.

His mother began to weep when he mentioned the crystal ball. She told him that he could never use it.

'Why not?' he demanded. 'I'm big enough now.'

'The crystal ball is broken, destroyed.'

'Broken! How did that happen?' He felt outraged, cheated.

'I broke it . . . I broke it myself,' she said in a low voice. He gazed at her speechless. Then she continued:

'I made a promise that if AB was spared and got well, I would break the crystal ball. I didn't wait for her to improve. I broke it first. But she died. Poor AB! She was all that I ever had.'

She continued to weep bitterly.

He went to bed that night and he lay awake and on his back for a long time. He could now see the awful finality of death. He could faintly hear Nan-nan getting slowly into bed in her own room and talking to herself. He recalled what she was heard to say as AB's coffin was leaving the house for the chapel: 'I suppose it won't be long now till I'm going meself too.' He remembered how hopeless and sad she looked then as she gazed into the kitchen fire. And in a flash of insight he could see that one day everyone in that house would be dead and gone away. Nan-nan would die. His father, smoking his pipe and rustling the *Anglo-Celt* by the turf fire in the kitchen, would one day die. His mother's footstep, which he could hear on the linoleum in the upper room, would cease and be gone for ever and would become but an echo from the past. And Jim Gaffney would become an English soldier and be killed in the coming war. It all seemed so inevitable.

228

He would be alone then in a strange world. He imagined himself as he was now – vulnerable, still going to school, still hating it. He did not attempt to visualise himself as grown-up or in the state of manhood. He was fearful of that. But he did not then grasp that the forces which were within him, as well as those which were around him, were irresistible. They would take him in spite of himself and they would mould him in a manner which he could never have foreseen. They would persist when all those who in kindness and solicitude had attempted to make him in their own image had passed away and were gone. And the power of these forces could not be escaped.

A faint beam from the full moon which was rising behind the distant pinewood came in through the window and rested high on the wall of his bedroom. The laurel bushes by the mearing drain suddenly shuffled their leaves; and somewhere up on Drumlahan hill the foxes barked disconsolately and persistently as the night wore on. He began to feel drowsy. He was soon asleep.

Erreur
d'impression

Conception - couverture et endos

dANIEL bÉLANGER
pATRICE dUCHESNE

Direction de production

pATRICE dUCHESNE

Collaboration spéciale

yVAN bÉLISLE
rICHARD pELLETIER

Réalisation graphique

hb & cIE
mARTIN lAROUCHE

Révision des textes

aNDRÉ j. bOURBONNIÈRE
vINCENT gRÉGOIRE

Merci à pIERRE r & mICHEL b

© 2000 coronet liv
355 ste-catherine ouest, bureau 600
montréal (québec)
H3B 1A5
info@coronetliv.com

Dépot légal : 2ᵉ trimestre 2000
Bibliothèque nationale du Québec
Bibliothèque nationale du Canada

ISBN : 2-9806833-0-2

Daniel **Bélanger**

Erreur
d'impression

coronet

liv

À toi, joli chaos...

Avec sa bouche à bout portant, elle dit des mots pour cors et violons. Elle fait des gestes dont les scrupules nous rappellent qu'ils sont absents. Chaque jour, elle parle à ses fleurs pour les animer.

Elle frise la cinquantaine depuis bientôt deux décennies.

Elle frise aussi par temps humides et ne porte pas en son cœur les canicules.

Cette capsule vous a été présentée par les shampooings de la vie.

1er octobre 1996

Vous constatez par vous-même qu'un trouble grandit en vous, une émotion qui, jusqu'ici, vous laissait de glace. Vous détestiez vous attendrir en dehors de tout massage, et si une larme coulait de votre œil, vous blâmiez oignons et compagnie. Un nœud dans la gorge ne pouvait être alors qu'un chewing-gum perdu-retrouvé. Mais aujourd'hui il n'en est plus ainsi : un rien vous taillade le cœur, les feuilletons vous traînent dans la dépression. Les journaux, télé ou papier vous rendent sympathique la suppression de soi par le suicide.

Ça vous inquiète et, franchement, je peux comprendre.

1er octobre 1996

Savez-vous réellement ce que ressent un soulier une fois qu'on l'a enlevé? On connaît plus facilement un pied libéré de son corset, on en reconnaît vite les bienfaits tout en agitant les orteils pour les délier, mais un soulier... n'apprécierait-il pas qu'on le délace? Qu'on le délace complètement chaque soir? Il y a un bon Dieu pour les Hommes, pas pour les choses.

1er octobre 1996

Parfois sur des draps il y a des lignes, aussi perçoit-on d'un glas une espèce de «déling». C'est le hasard des choses. On peut voir aussi des pois dans un frigo ordinaire soulever des poids et les voir souhaiter des abdominaux de fer. C'est le rêve de certains. On ne voit plus la vie. Diriger un pas devant l'autre est d'une mathématique précise pour les uns, récalcitrante pour les autres ; tout à fait exquis. C'est la diversité des goûts, la complexité des humeurs. Puis la simplicité de vivre devient alors floue et secondaire. On devrait pouvoir se laisser bercer, l'accepter et s'endormir, sans paranoïa sous un lilas, un jour, de soleil. Je me relis et ne comprends rien.

1er octobre 1996

Décharger son revolver, en sortir les cartouches, ouvrir ces dernières, en inhaler la poudre, puis, éviter à tout prix la foudre. Ou alors prendre son téléviseur, le soulever à bout de bras, bien le sentir, vraiment bien le sentir et le laisser tomber par terre. Tenter de le rassembler en moins d'une heure, quatre minutes, trente-sept secondes et quatre-vingt-deux centièmes de seconde. Bonne chance.

1er octobre 1996

Il faut alphabétiser les tapis, les cendriers, les napperons et tout ce qui a le droit logiquement à cet alphabet. Nourrir les pantalons, les voitures et pas seulement celles de l'année.

Héberger les gaufres, les forêts, les pneus, les tissus et certaines couleurs de cheveux. Privatiser les douanes, l'armée. Ouvrir des portes, fermer des fenêtres.

Oui, chers électeurs, nous nous reposerons demain.

11 octobre 1996

J'écoutais les airs pour corps et
caleçons et j'en étais charmé. Aussi
le vioignon, le varicelle et le boisson
formaient-ils un beau trio. Que dire de
la plute et de la trottinette ou
encore de la trempette!

Une soirée comme ça, c'est rare...

11 octobre 1996

Le couper en un ne fut jamais difficile. Il suffisait d'y penser et puis hop, c'en était fait.

Le couper en deux l'était moins. S'informer ici et là, y aller de prudence, aussi, ne pouvait pas nuire. Un peu de concentration et hop, c'en était fait.

Le couper en trois exigeait plus de dextérité, de calme aussi. Il n'était pas de tout repos que de se soumettre à cette opération. Ce n'était pas un réel plaisir non plus, mais hop, c'en était fait.

En un, en deux, en trois mais en quatre, alors là, le couper en quatre était carrément irréalisable.

11 octobre 1996

Il est sûr qu'on peut parler pour parler... écrire pour noircir une page blanche ou verte. On peut dessiner des mots en forme d'idées, des lettres en forme de mensonges, des phrases en forme d'amour, l'amour qu'on a pour l'encre, la fascination du papier, le plaisir du seul plaisir d'écrire. Parler pour parler, combler le silence en forme de paix, meubler cette paix de sons en forme de bonheur, de souvenirs heureux. Il est certain que l'on peut faire tout cela, mais peut-être pas non plus.

11 octobre 1996

Imaginons une porte. Sur cette porte, une poignée. Imaginez que cette porte soit votre visage, que cette poignée soit votre nez. Ça vous change une perspective.

11 octobre 1996

Croisons un mot avec un cheveu, on obtient un motif. Croisons une muse avec son départ, ça fait une musique. Croisons ton motif avec ton départ, ça fait mon chagrin d'amour.

Paris, 11 octobre 1996

Là-bas dans un coin, immobile et figé, un objet inanimé rêve de cadence. Un peu plus à gauche et un peu plus haut aussi, une colombe espère un jour rencontrer le corbeau de sa vie.

Un plancher envie le plafond, une tapisserie jalouse une laque parfaite. Un baril s'imagine être un carafon, le regret, lui, un espoir. Bonjour, bonsoir.

Paris, 14 octobre 1996

Une spirale spire, une main manie,
Sans mot ne vient mot dire et Tarzan
Tanzanie. Une pirogue pire, un zizi
zizanie, un désir dèse, l'hémisphère
hémie, une patate pate, une tomate
tome, une sandale savate, un home
sweet home. Ainsi va la vie qui vit.

Paris, 14 & 15 octobre 1996

Je me souviens tout à coup de ce que m'avait dit la lettre M : « Combien j'aimerais être la suivante de N. » Les jours ont passé. Les mots, les mois aussi. Des phrases se sont dites. Des conversations, des discours, des chansons, des poèmes. Aux dernières nouvelles, elle précède toujours et encore la lettre N.

Paris, 16 octobre 1996

Un soir je suis sorti. Une cantatrice voluptueuse, avec de gros seins talentueux, chantait à gorge déployée des airs qu'aucun drame nippon ne pouvait égaler. Elle chantait et chantait de sa voix forte et sûre, de son âge muet, hélas mûr, la tragédie d'un seul cœur comme s'il s'agissait du sien. Le mien faiblissait à la seule pensée qu'il pouvait être le sujet de son chagrin, plus lourd que le poids lourd du plus balourd des camionneurs. Je l'écoutais, ému. Elle s'offrait à moi, presque nue, avec sa peau à demi-peinte de poudre de riz.

Je mens.

Ce soir là, je suis resté chez moi.

Paris, 17 octobre 1996

Ma mémoire se brise sur du papier
de plâtre. Mon âge séduit une seconde
rouge et une troisième verte. Je reste
calme. Un pamplemousse de souvenirs
vient s'échouer sur la trotteuse d'une
montre qui nage justement le cent
mètres haie masculin. Je garde toujours mon calme. Un foie décoratif
chante des hymnes himalayens juché
au bas d'une rampe. Tout va bien. Je
suis calme. Des lettres piétinent la
pelouse bétonnée de mon meilleur
voisin. Ça va. Mais quand tu me dis
que tu m'aimes, que tu m'aimes
d'amour, je n'y comprends r-i-e-n,
rien.

Paris, 19 octobre 1996

Nous étions les seuls à savoir que le feu dans la cheminée ne brûlait pas la peau quand on y mettait la main.

Seuls à savoir que l'alcool sur la table ne saoulait pas et que l'électricité dans les prises n'électrocutait pas quand on y enfouissait un objet conducteur.

Seuls à savoir que Paris, Rome et Londres n'existent pas. Que la lune, le soleil, les étoiles, les métaux et l'eau n'étaient rien en réalité. Nous étions assis à cette table parmi les invités et nous mangions tranquillement notre fradipolin bien frais et juste à point.

Paris, 19 octobre 1996

Dans les hôtels cossus de Paris, le jet-set international va et vient. Il regarde tout le monde au cas où il serait quelqu'un.

Paris, 19 octobre 1996

Si vous croyez que c'est facile d'exercer ce métier, métier sans horaire fixe, sans sécurité, faciles ces meetings jusqu'aux petites heures, ces concerts dans la fumée de cigarette, ces chansons qui ne sont pas encore écrites. Si vous croyez qu'il est facile de toujours être en voix, de prendre soin de sa santé lors des tournées interminables, les dîners de politesse et le reste et le reste. Si vous le croyez, ne vous détrompez pas, vous avez parfaitement raison.

Paris, 19 octobre 1996

Une fois qu'on a assumé qu'en été
il fait chaud, qu'en hiver, plein froid,
qu'en amour il y a aussi la solitude,
qu'en amitié on est parfois déçu, qu'il
y a des jours d'abondance, d'autres de
dépouillement, que le temps passe et
qu'on vieillit, assumé qu'à la fin la
mort survient, mais qu'au début on
peut aussi allumer une vie. Assumé les
départs, les adieux, mais aussi les fêtes
et les fous rires.

Une fois le tout assumé, on dirait que
le reste marche tout seul.

20 octobre 1996

Quel doigt préfèrerais-je qu'on m'ampute? Quelle oreille on me coupe? Par quel cancer, quelle fin atroce, quel froid sibérien voudrais-je être emporté? Quand souhaiterais-je tes adieux, toi mon seul et vrai amour? Quel gaz pour me gazer? Combien de temps me faudrait-il pour atteindre le sol, chutant du haut de trente étages, sans vent, sans nuit, par temps chaud et le ventre vide? Combien de questions encore avant que je ne meure d'angoisse?

5 novembre 1996

Ce n'était pas un homme de demi-mesures. Il ne buvait pas, mais si l'envie lui en prenait, il vidait comme ça de trois à cinq bouteilles de quarante onces en sept minutes. Sept minutes qui, à sa décharge, étaient quand même étalées sur un après-midi. Il ne fumait pas non plus, mais si l'envie lui en prenait, griller une cartouche de cigarettes en trois heures ne l'effrayait pas une miette. Maigre comme un chicot, la bouffe ne l'avait jamais attiré sauf cette fois d'une fringale subite : il s'était tapé deux bœufs en rut, une douzaine de poulets, quelques veaux, cinq agneaux, les fruits d'un pommier et deux ou trois champs de citrouilles. ——————→

Pour dessert, il avait demandé à ce qu'on coule sur le flanc d'un mont skiable (la pente pour expert) un ou deux lacs de sauce au chocolat. Au fond, c'était un homme simple et inoffensif. N'empêche, je ne voudrais quand même pas être le cactus géant qui se trouvera à ses côtés quand le cul va lui gratter.

2 décembre 1996

Je t'aime tellement tu sais, je serais capable de n'importe quoi. M'arracher les ongles d'orteil un à un pour que tu m'aimes, boire de l'essence super sans plomb et me flamber l'estomac. Me lancer devant un rouleau compresseur, me souffler de l'air dans le cul jusqu'à ce que j'explose pour que tu m'aimes, parce que l'amour, tu sais, c'est magnifique.

13 janvier 1997

Il ne faut pas s'attrister de sa condition. Moi, par exemple, j'ai perdu ma mère je n'étais même pas né et je suis mort avant même la fin de ma deuxième du secondaire. C'est pour dire...

13 janvier 1997

F red Blanchet. Si mon nom ne vous dit rien, c'est moi le ramoneur qui ai trouvé le cadavre du père Noël.

13 janvier 1997

Masturber.

On dirait que même le mot le fait.

28 février 1997

Je pourrais pleurer des larmes de poudre tant ta réponse négative me fut sèche et rugueuse. Répandre des bulles de sable sur mes joues irritées, des larmes de lave sur les villages de ma bouche. Dévastation complète d'un visage par le chagrin.

Imagine seulement, imagine si tu m'avais dit oui.

5 mars 1997

Mon amour, ma chérie, notre lit est un hot-dog à deux saucisses. Ta chaleur pour la moutarde, tes cheveux pour la relish et nous dormons dans la belle province comme meurent les étoiles.

5 mars 1997

Les Clackers, le Silly Putty, la Super
Balle, les Adidas pour les riches, les
North Stars pour les pauvres, les jeans
Lee, les parkas de l'armée, les souliers
plus bas en arrière qu'en avant, les
stylos à quatre billes, les cigarettes «La
Québécoise», ne pas porter de bottes
en hiver, le Crazy Carpet, le mont
Laval, l'auberge Yvan Coutu, Pour
vous mesdames, Femmes d'aujour-
d'hui, la folie des congélateurs, des
perruques, les hot pants, le soulier
Patof, les manteaux maxi, Brossard,
Acapulco, Sur le gazon sous les
étoiles, Brault et Fréchette, les Pirates
de Pierrefonds, les Dupuis, les
Ouellette, les Ducas, la plage Théoret,
le camping Martin, le pain de sucre, la
pancarte de Seven Up, Mademoiselle
Charron devenue Madame Désautels,
sœur Marguerite, sœur Yolande, sœur
défroquée Raymonde, Monsieur
Ménez, ⟶

André Charlebois, Madame Côté, Irène,
classe de neige, ti-père Dufresne,
l'école St-Raphaël, l'école Ste-Thérèse,
l'école St-Georges, Mesdames Besner
et Chandonnet, Mademoiselle Théoret
devenue Madame Charron, Marcelle
Beaulieu, Madame bleachée Paquin,
Madame Coutu, Jean-Claude «A RAM
SAM SAM, A RAM SAM SAM, GOULI
GOULI GOULI GOULI GOULI RAM
SAM SAM» Tremblay, Madame
Bouffard, les skidoos, la tempête du
siècle, Conrad Boucher, le major Matt
Mason, les hot-wheels, les skiroules,
Motoski, ArticCat, Arien, Huski,
Polaris, Panthère, Daniel Paquin,
Martine Paquin, Daniel Prévost,
Forget, Proulx, le GTO, la Austin, le
Grand Prix, la Dodge Monaco, la
Parisienne, la Duster bleu poudre.

Je tiens tout ça pour quelques
souvenirs.

4 & 5 mars 1997

J'ai dû attendre le train au moins quatre heures et puis je me suis dit : «Bon Dieu ! je suis dans un supermarché.»

5 mars 1997

La Lune suit la Terre comme un petit chien de poche et la Terre demande perpétuellement vingt-cinq cents au Soleil. Un jour, ça va péter. C'est sûr.

5 mars 1997

Un nuage s'occupait d'un jardin en pleuvant dessus et lui promettait du soleil pour le lendemain. Pas fou, le jardin but ce qu'il put, faisant semblant de souffrir à la hauteur des tomates et des carottes et d'éprouver une certaine faiblesse dans les concombres.

Je pourrais continuer, mais c'est une histoire tellement banale.

5 mars 1997

J'ai trouvé un bon moyen de parler aux oiseaux sans les effrayer : un cerf-volant avec une boîte de conserve au bout du fil.

6 mars 1997

Je sais bien que des femmes et des hommes ont inventé la lumière dirigée. D'autres, des avions à réaction, la fibre optique, le morse ou la boîte de conserve. Je suis heureux qu'ils y aient pensé à ma place parce que je n'ai aucune inventivité. Moi, au contraire, je désinvente. Jusqu'à présent j'ai tué deux chats, un chien, sept grenouilles, un lapin, deux ratons laveurs (faut voir mes chapeaux), achevé un cheval et égorgé deux cochons, un troisième la semaine prochaine. J'ai mis le feu à deux maisons, un champ de maïs et une pinède toute entière. J'ai aussi mis un terme à quatre relations amoureuses avant qu'elles ne deviennent trop sérieuses, interrompu prématurément la cuisson de cinq jambons à l'ananas et saboté sept moteurs de voiture et ce n'est pas fini, j'aurai huit ans la semaine prochaine.

7 mars 1997

Ta bouche en bonbon, ta langue au sucre, tes lèvres au chocolat, tes joues à la crème, tes cheveux au caramel, tes yeux en meringue, ton nez en nougat, ton menton de crème pâtissière, ton cou au fudge, tes épaules aux truffes, tes seins framboises au vin, ton nombril profiterole, ton sexe au miel, enfin bref, que des choses interdites par mon médecin.

8 mars 1997

Je me suis brisé sur un mur en forme d'épuisement, en rêvant que je perds mes dents. Je me retrouve au matin, blotti sur une merveille du monde. Ta peau, ton dos, ce corps qui prend l'air puis le libère. Tu dors si paisiblement. Je pourrais, pour rien en échange, tomber dans l'entonnoir qui me déverserait dans ton âme. Le matin en forme d'oiseau, le soleil en forme d'orange, ton amour en forme de paix tout au fond de ma tête. Nous soupirons, car le jour nous force à briser l'horizon.

Air France, 30 mars 1997

Mis à part le danger de crisser le camp en bas, une traversée en Bœing sur un océan bleu me donne la grâce que l'on réserve aux anges. Les nuages, tour à tour, dessinent du feutre, de la laine et des pâtés chinois hors d'atteinte. « You've changed » plays Dexter. Please Mister Gordon, don't stop. Words become notes and love turns into an exploding bomb discharging a load of anxiety in my entire body. There is Paris on A side. New-York on B side and Montreal is a dry monster dreaming of seaside.

Air France, 30 Mars 1997

I belong to a whale colony. Whales that speak French when they speak in English. We sometimes find some of them dying on the shores of their nowhere country. They were looking for a beach at the end of which there would be nothing but a jazzy, dirty, unsandy fucking street.

Air France, 30 mars 1997

Je me sentais stable et imbécile au beau milieu de la baie. Je flottais dans le trou d'un beigne au chocolat et la lune éclairait ma déveine. Je cherchais la comète. Je l'ai finalement trouvée. C'est comme un avion qui vous vole au-dessus sans jamais, justement, vous passer dessus. Une queue de poussière de glace la suit comme des dauphins escortent une goélette. C'est étonnant. J'étais en tenue correcte et plus même. Quand on vient rencontrer la sirène du glucose, on s'habille. J'avais pour elle un sac de friandises : du caramel maison et des bonbons aux patates. Elle était absente. Je flottais dans la baie, tout blanc de tristesse, ratatiné et frissonnant. On m'a retrouvé au matin, à marée basse, inanimé dans un désert de récifs. D'en parler, déjà me fait du bien.

12 avril 1997

Des poils vous poussent sur les testicules, une acné aléatoire et temporaire tapisse le gros du peu de personnalité que vous possédez, vous malodorez subitement des aisselles et les filles de votre âge falsifié ne s'intéressent plus à vous que pour votre père. À votre place, j'aurais les mêmes humeurs.

New-Richmond, 12 avril 1997

Fast. I don't wanna live fast. Deep. OK for deep.

I want: Stars deep in my lungs, rain deep in my brain, desire deep in my balls and love deep in my soul.

Slow could be right too.

I want: The sky slow in my eyes, the moon slow in my history, my past slow in my future

and you, I want you everywhere, on, in me.

Chandler, 13 avril 1997.

Elle voulait me quitter à cause d'un cheveu brun échoué sur mon épaule. Je m'explique : elle m'embrassait tendrement quand soudainement elle aperçut ce cheveu qui lambinait sur mon pull orange. Quelle crise me fit-elle! Quelle scène! Je suis blonde, dit-elle, que fait là cet abject cheveu vulgairement brunâtre? Allez ma chérie, lui dis-je, avale ce cachet et, de grâce, n'oublie plus jamais ta médication, surtout pas après ta teinture mensuelle.

6 juin 1997

Je suis incroyablement menteur. Hier, j'ai dit à mon boucher de ne plus jamais adresser la parole au végétarien que je suis devenu (foutaise). Avant-hier encore, j'ai prié le bon Dieu au corps d'un inconnu, pleurant sur cet oncle mon affection à l'étonnement de la famille éprouvée (les nuls). La semaine dernière, j'ai vendu une pierre philosophale à un arthritique (le plouc). J'ai aussi vendu un parachute défectueux à un sauteur débutant (boum). Le mensonge m'amuse. L'histoire du premier homme à marcher sur la lune, c'était moi. Hiroshima aussi et moi, c'est moi aussi.

6 juin 1997

Par la seule présence d'un facteur inhérent au haut degré d'ingérence dû au terme insuffisant des parties symboliquement impliquées, les protagonistes n'ont d'autre choix que de limiter l'immobilisation effrénée des dernières années à savoir : stopper le conflit opposant la totalité des actifs tout en proposant une issue faisant l'unanimité interrelationnelle parmi les équipes ainsi dynamisées par l'énergie non fragmentée des droits communs et ce, semestre par semestre. ⟶

En conséquence, il est impératif d'identifier coûte que coûte les agents pervers pour ensuite protéger l'infrastructure nationale du stage créatif et corporatif, les soumettant hors d'atteinte pour enfin pulvériser les chiffres et le mandat tant visé par l'industrie. Il est donc bel et bien clair qu'une remise en question s'impose et n'hésitez pas à demander toute information susceptible de combler votre insécurité qui pourrait être en ces circonstances entièrement justifiée.

Merci.

7 juin 1997

Mon amour,

En premier lieu, je voudrais t'assurer de mes sentiments les plus tendres à ton égard, tu sais combien je suis redevable à la vie de t'avoir rencontrée et pour rien au monde je ne voudrais te voir me quitter. Après avoir mûrement réfléchi, j'aimerais t'avoir pour épouse, enfin, demander dès cette fin de semaine ta main à ton père, lui qui nous a pourtant fait tellement souffrir. Il n'est pas faux de croire que nous deux, à la fin, pourrions vivre ensemble, forts de nos fréquentations qui durent depuis maintenant quarante ans, sept semaines, trois jours et cinq heures. Je te remercie et sache que je ne pourrai être au bingo de vendredi prochain pour cause de visite chez le médecin. Je te dis merci encore et te donne rendez-vous comme d'habitude au prochain premier vendredi du mois.

7 juin 1997

Je me tiens à l'arrêt-court, c'est un à un en neuvième manche, il y a deux retraits, les sentiers sont remplis et le frappeur en est à trois balles et deux prises. Le lanceur se prépare à lui lancer la balle. Le frappeur s'élance et je la reçois en pleine gueule. Je vais à l'hôpital car mon état est lamentable. À cet hôpital, on me fait une chirurgie sous anesthésie locale. Ça tourne mal. Le lendemain, je paralyse complètement du visage. J'engueule le chirurgien comme je peux en le tenant pour seul responsable de mon faciès de bois. Ça tourne mal. Il m'en donne toute une du revers de la main. Ça tourne mal. Mon épouse s'en mêle en m'avouant que ce chirurgien de mes deux est son amant depuis huit ans, qu'elle me quitte et réclame mon chalet en montagne. Je le lui cède, mais ça tourne mal.

Est-ce que je continue?

8 juin 1997

Il me faudrait des injections de chevaux sauvages, des implants de statues et des greffes d'algues marines. À quoi penses-tu dans l'aquatique, quand le sable froid se faufile entre tes orteils? C'est une question de sirène qui n'a jamais eu de pieds et je n'ai jamais vu de sirène. L'été est chaud en ville. C'est un four à cuire poteries et porcelaines, nous y vivons. L'argent fait mal quand c'est un verre d'eau empli à ras bord qu'on ne boit pas. Je suis immobilisé par un ennemi qui ne se montre pas.

10 juin 1997

J'ai trouvé au fond d'un arbre la dernière dent de l'Univers. En frappant un putois avec ma vieille Century verte, une dame de pique lui est sortie du cul. Mon arrière-grand-père a eu un fils qui a, lui-même, eu un fils qui a, lui aussi, eu un fils qui lui, est moi. Dans ma famille, nous mourons de père en fils.

18 juin 1997

J'aime conduire ma vieille Newport rouge, vêtu de ma seule nudité avec, sur la tête, un casque de bain fleuri de marguerites de caoutchouc. J'aime le faire en hiver, en été, en automne et au printemps. Je me retrouve au quartier général trois saisons sur quatre, mais le café y est bon. On parle sports, femmes et substances hallucinogènes que je cache peut-être dans mes fesses. Je retrouve mon ami le constable Lavigueur et le non moins sympathique caporal Tranche-montagne. Je me fais tabasser à grands coups de dictionnaire sur le crâne et ça me refait effectivement la diction. Des gifles, des baffes, des beignes jusqu'à ce que j'aie inventé quelques aveux. Plus que des amis, des frères. Après, on me laisse partir nu, dans ma vieille Newport rouge.

25 juin 1997

Une linotte à auge s'escrimait à l'ouvrage quand, d'un seul coup d'épée venant de je ne sais où, on lui trancha la gorge à l'intérieur de la ferme intention de soustraire la tête à son corps. « J'ai vu un éclair », témoigna la gélinotte à trois temps. « J'ai été distrait par un camelot, je n'ai rien vu », maugréa le ver à soie automatique.

Trois longues années auront passé avant qu'on ne sache ce qui s'était réellement produit mais, aujourd'hui, on est finalement content.

25 juin 1997

Je suis au salon, il fait nuit, je suis calme et n'attends personne. Tout de même, on sonne à la porte. Je me lève, il est tard, qui est-ce donc?

—Bonjour monsieur, je suis l'heure, votre heure et vous êtes l'homme dont l'heure est arrivée.
—Je veux bien l'amie, répondis-je, mais quelle heure est-il donc?
—Je l'ignore, je ne suis pas l'heure en général mais bien VOTRE heure.
—Bien. Qu'attendez-vous de moi?
—Rien, sinon attendre avec moi votre malchance.
—Et quand l'attendez-vous?
—À l'instant monsieur, à l'instant. Elle devrait être déjà là. Vous savez, l'heure de pointe se trompe parfois dans les horaires. ————————————————>

— Vous la connaissez cette heure de
pointe ?
— Non. Et après la malchance, que
fait-on ?
— Ça dépend, vous pourriez être
chanceux dans votre malchance.
— Et le cas échéant ?
— Faudrait voir avec votre Providence.
— Je n'attendais personne ce soir,
encore moins ma Providence...
— On ne sait jamais.
— Vous avez sans doute raison, on ne
sait jamais.

Aujourd'hui, je sais mon heure venue,
mais toujours j'attends cette malchance qui se fait attendre. Onze
années me séparent de cette étrange
soirée. Depuis, sur le seuil de ma porte,
j'attends cette mystérieuse malchance.

25 juin 1997

Un coucher de soleil comme on en peint dans ses rêves. C'était magnifique. Je m'étais arrêté sur un pont reliant une falaise à une autre. Je n'étais pas seul, d'autres promeneurs du dimanche s'y attardaient. Puis on a éternué, le pont s'est effondré. Par chance, j'ai pu, dans ma chute, agripper la branche d'un vieil arbre enraciné solidement sur la paroi de la falaise. J'y vis depuis maintenant cinq ans. Me nourrissant du fruit de l'arbre, des œufs d'oiseaux de proie tout en buvant l'eau des pluies fréquentes, j'en ai maintenant assez. SVP, aidez-moi.

26 juin 1997

Je t'aimerai tellement que tu friseras comme tu n'as jamais frisé, la lune te donnera ce qu'elle ne donne à personne : un bronzage uniforme et puis tu seras riche et balourde de mes sentiments débordants qui n'avaient, jusqu'ici, débordé que pour le petit hamster de mon enfance, mort injustement dans la souffleuse à neige (propulsé si loin tu sais...).

Tu ne diras pas non, j'ai confiance.

28 juillet 1997

Un jour sans pluie comme on en voit souvent quand il n'y a pas de nuages, un jour sans pluie comme on en voit souvent durant sa courte vie quand, soudain, le ciel se couvre d'un épais poumon d'où sortent des clous en forme d'eau, d'où souffle un vent à l'emporte-chapeau, le mien kidnappé par la brise distendue, je le regarde me quitter sans broncher, sans même une contraction de la lèvre inférieure, sans même le spasme de la paupière droite si gauche à exprimer mon anxiété. En résumé, ce chapeau je viens de le perdre.

28 juillet 1997

Tu m'écris : Je mange des bougies
d'allumage, des courroies de venti-
lation, des boulons et des filtres à air.
Je bois aussi de l'huile à moteur.

Je t'écris : Tu ne réussiras jamais à
séduire un avaleur de feu qu'avec un
simple et grand verre d'eau.

28 juillet 1997

Je ne sais plus qui a composé une symphonie en do majeur. Non plus qui a développé une nymphomanie endommagée. À vrai dire, je ne sais plus rien de beaucoup et ce, depuis peu. J'ai reçu une nectarine tout près de l'hypophyse et j'englobe, depuis, plusieurs sujets dans le même oubli.

C'est scandaleux. Perdre la tête fait réfléchir.

6 août 1997

J'écoute de la musique de chanvre en buvant du Verlaine à plein poumon de manière à subir des lacérations massives sur ma géographie et ma biologie.

J'écourte novembre en tétant un bas de laine à vingt boutons de Bavière et les subites pressions subséquentes agissant sur moi ne me gratifient en rien ni ne me pataphysent.

En bref, écartez-moi quelqu'un de ce sac de chips.

6 août 1997

J'ai vu l'éclipse totale d'une orange qu'on a retrouvée par la suite à demi-nue dans du mercure. J'ai aussi vu des corps immortels se liquéfier sur la place publique en apprenant la nouvelle de leur propre mort. J'ai aperçu au loin des volcans cracher de la moutarde. J'ai vu des parachutistes faire collision avec des oiseaux déréglés. J'ai vu bien des choses mais franchement non, je ne les ai pas vues, tes lunettes.

6 août 1997

L'âge finira par me tuer.

16 septembre 1997

Et ce homard qui veut être champion de nage synchronisée, cet éléphant coincé dans le piège à souris, ce fumier sentant si bon et pour comble, la chaîne trois qui se déplace sur la sept. Dis-moi que tu me quittes pendant qu'on y est.

16 septembre 1997

Toi que nul n'aime sinon que moi,
que nul n'oit qu'en présence de son
ananas, l'ai-je joui ou dus-je le jouer,
l'eus-je appris que je ne l'eusse su
vraiment? Sacrement de Tabernacle.

16 septembre 1997

La marguerite poussant sur ton nez est charmante. Tu n'as plus de cheveux (soi-disant qu'il en faut), mais en revanche ton crâne rutilant d'où jaillissent des rubis te va à merveille et, sans vouloir chuter dans le snobisme, il s'insère parfaitement dans le genre «surprise!». Au fond, c'est ton caractère unique qui t'octroie ce charisme. Tu es magnifique, mieux, ex-tra-or-di-nai-re. Je te quitte et tu t'en fais pour rien. Tu te feras bien un autre amoureux.

16 septembre 1997

Cinq jours qu'on ne nous a pas
nourris ni changés d'eau. Albert me
regarde avec appétit. Poisson rouge !
Poisson rouge ! May day ! May day !
Trop tard. Crounch !

16 septembre 1997

Dis à ta mère que j'aime sa fille pour ta sœur, sans sous-entendre à ton père que, pour son frère, j'ai séduit sa femme, pas plus que pour ta tante, j'ai méprisé ton oncle follement épris de ta cousine qui m'aima pour mon frère.

Fais vite avant que je confonde tout le monde.

16 septembre 1997

Un gros grillon bien gras était
heureux de sa performance : on l'avait
engagé aux studios de la T. N. G. BROS.
comme figurant au terme de ce qui
sera la plus grande saga des insectes
dégoûtants. Il en était rudement
content. Sa scène se résumait, à peu de
choses près, à effrayer une pauvre
enfant devant laquelle il déployait ses
ailes sèches, le tout à quelques
centimètres de son nez. Ils ont refait
trois fois par pure prudence car, dès la
première prise, toute la magie y était.
Ce gros grillon bien gras, donc, buvait
son verre et profitait tranquillement du
soleil automnal. « Ça vaut mieux que
de finir dans un pare-brise », pensa-t-il
sagement.

17 septembre 1997

Je n'en peux plus. Je n'ai plus la force de continuer. Cultiver de la saucisse est un art exigeant et épuisant. Par contre, cultiver l'idée de vendre ma terre à saucisses me plaît. Je pourrais m'acheter des arbres à jambons, mais bon, je n'y connais que bien peu de choses. Un gisement de lait ? Des plants de spaghetti ? Pourquoi ne pas aller à la ville me trouver un emploi dans une usine d'us et coutumes ou peut-être une manufacture de bonjours et d'adieux ? J'ai le temps, je verrai.

17 septembre 1997

Poncho Penetas jouait avec son revolver, un Puink's 31 à culasse limée, en le faisant virevolter au bout de son moignon droit. Sa moustache attirait les mouches, mais la sueur dégoulinant de son front jusqu'à elles les faisait fuir. Mexico en mille huit cent quatre-vingt-quatre était comme ça. Parfois comme ci, mais très rarement. La veille, Poncho Penetas venait tout juste d'inventer le taco au fromage de pétrole. Il était comme ça ce bon vieux Poncho : imprévisible. Il est si impressionnant ce Poncho Penetas.

Poncho Penetas, retenez bien ce nom。

17 septembre 1997

Je te hais et tu le sais. Non, je t'aime
voilà pourquoi je te hais. Tu es un
animal blessé, c'est peut-être pour ça
que je t'aime. D'accord tu m'envoies
paître et je te hais pour ça, mais tu
t'excuses comme un chien qui a
déféqué sur un tapis de Turquie rare et
coûteux ; ça me remue et me fait
t'aimer encore plus. Tu te souviens de
cette robe offerte pour mes vingt-sept
ans ? Je l'ai enfilée et, pour une raison
que j'ignore encore, tu as craché
dessus en y vidant ton verre de
mauvais vin d'une main et, de l'autre,
brûlé de ton cigare sucré plusieurs des
roses imprimées. Je t'ai détesté. Le
temps a passé et, il faut bien
l'admettre, la rage aussi, je t'ai réaimé
mais c'en est maintenant assez. ⟶

Le seau d'eau au-dessus de notre porte de chambre à coucher, le poil à gratter dans ma chemise de nuit, le sac de merde enflammé sur le paillasson, le fromage du Diable dans la doublure de ma veste, les couleuvres mortes dans mes souliers, me doubler sur l'auto-route et lancer par le toit ouvrant de ma voiture une poule affolée, la punaise sur le siège de toilette, mes pneus dégonflés, franchement, j'en ai assez.

Si tu continues comme ça, je pense réellement à m'en formaliser pour de bon.

17 septembre 1997

Un jour, pêchant avec un ami, j'ai perdu cet ami dans les abîmes de l'eau froide sur laquelle nous flottions à bord d'une barque sécuritaire. Mon cœur désormais entaillé ne cicatrisera plus qu'avec des larmes et de la salive. Il est tombé avec mes trois mille dollars, trois mille perdus aux cartes à son avantage. Trois mille consentis nous sachant tous deux gagnants du loto (trois millions et des crottes). Il est parti, le billet chanceux dans la poche. Je ne devrais plus en parler comme on parle normalement d'un ami.

18 septembre 1997

Un jour, pêchant avec un triple idiot, j'ai perdu le triple million et trois mille crottes qui se trouvaient au creux de sa poche parce que Monsieur est passé par-dessus bord, se noyant avec le billet gagnant du loto duquel nous avions, kif-kif, revenus et avantages. Vive les sangsues, régalez-vous.

18 septembre 1997

Je sui presque pu aphalnébète et voaci ma première lète. Beaujour agate. Jespère que tu va bien. moa aussi. di beaujour a toute ta famile et moa aussi. je sui eureu de pouvoir enfin exprimé mon idé sur des chose et des autre. . réécri moa pour savoir tes chose a toa je les atten bocou comme qu'on di. je técri en brallan comme un vo parce que je sui plus fier que ca tu meur. tou le monde disai ché moa que je seré jamai capabe. je sui conten dètre ostineu car aujourdui tu me li ma lète. lache pas toa non plus et continu de faire mentir toute le monde. envoa moa vite ta lète a toa, jai ate de la lire. a biento et fais ca vite. téo。

18 septembre 1997

Ben avait trois projets.

I - Gravir la plus haute tour.

II - Faire pieds nus le tour de la Terre.

III - Amaigrir l'homme ou la femme possédant le plus gros tour de taille du monde.

Il a réussi avec brio les deux premiers mais, pour le troisième, Ben s'est fait dévorer par le recordman de l'obésité qui est, de surcroît, le dernier cannibale recensé.

19 septembre 1997

Une rose, instruite de ses droits,
renonce au gai partage de ses
splendeurs. L'instant d'après, elle
meurt dans un pot mal informé des
rigueurs horticoles.

21 septembre 1997

Raymond le Chinois est amoureux.
Amoureux d'Ingrid, la Thaïlandaise,
qui elle est éprise de Fafard le Danois.
Pouliot, lui, de son Pérou natal s'est
entiché de Titine, l'Autrichienne.
Duchesse, la chihuahua, est follement
folle de Princesse, la hush puppy, et
Kitty la chatte pleure encore Ti-Mine
le siamois en allé. Moi, j'attends le
retour de la petite Caron, mon amour
de Tonkiki de Tonkiki de Tonkinoise.

25 septembre 1997

Je suis une tuile de porcelaine. Collée au vingt-quatrième rang partant de la gauche du plafond de la chapelle, je songe sérieusement à tomber et ce, très bientôt. Ma colle n'est plus ce qu'elle était et la clientèle de l'établissement est de moins en moins fidèle à la prière du dimanche. Marie s'empoussière, Anne ternit. Faudrait rénover Jésus qui ne voit plus que d'un œil et ne tient plus que d'une main. Cet endroit chaleureux de jadis n'est plus qu'une froide relique parmi les reliques. Je n'ai plus la force de continuer. Je ne suis pas la seule; les seizième et quarantième se font aussi de plus en plus lasses. C'est triste, mais il vaut mieux savoir quand se retirer. Je me retire.

26 septembre 1997

Zé mé présente : Olivia dé Martini. Coquetail à longueur d'année, zé fait la fête touzours. Zé mé rétrouve plou souvent qu'autrement transpercée d'oune coure-dent mais, zé fait la fête pareil. Z'entends parler dé tous lé souzets à la mode, dou sexe à la maladie, les fêtards sont sans scroupoule quant à lère vie intime. Ça mé plé beaucoup, mé c'est oune vie doure. Enfin, zé mé plains pas, zé connais des oranges et des cerises parmi mes amies qui sont sans travail et sé tournent les noyaux touté la zournée. Enfin, c'est la vie. Allez, zé dois te laisser, d'autres convives arrivent à l'instant. Ciao.

26 zeptembré 1997

Bonjour, je me nomme spirale, j'ai deux anus, quatre estomacs, neuf kilomètres d'intestin grêle, trois foies, cinq vésicules biliaires, trente et un pancréas. Croyez-moi, quand je ne digère pas quelque chose, je ne digère pas quelque chose.

26 septembre 1997

Dans le sens de l'aiguille d'une
seringue, un docteur tourne en rond.
Son patient anesthésié se lève par lui-
même, laissant pantois anesthésistes et
inhalothérapeutes. Le cardiogramme
fait comme suit : « bibop, bibop,
bibop ». Un homme sandwich entre
dans la salle d'opération criant « guerre
aux gourmands !!! » quand un officier
de la G. W. M. M. FORCES inc. le
prend en chasse. À la radio, on
annonce la mort de la médecine
moderne. Toute l'équipe s'écroule. Il y
a de ces vendredis !

26 septembre 1997

Dans un caillou pirnapède embluté, j'ai cabastré un bloutoir afin d'enciver la trinète catyrudale à sa fénaze. Alors, en un crudinois flédit, le paratoire impégident s'est automagé en une pruquedue incédite. «Aïe! dit le clotéron, ça boit le crout par mit.»

Il s'en catipège, le flinde mât, quand il préducédit le trôme à houlette. ⟶

«Blablabla», engluna sa jutre
confensée. Fraticonsée, la bédoisse ne
mit que trasoudière et palournise à sa
crège lunence. Bien flait me flougne,
que cela s'en dédigne et vite !!!

26 septembre 1997

Odette Cinquantaine trouvait que son retraité de mari la quittait trop souvent pour le golf, la faisant ainsi la veuve qu'elle ne voulait plus être. Pour un peu l'attirer, elle appliqua sur ses poils pubiens une teinture dont le vert éclatant évoquait les plus beaux départs et les plus belles allées des plus somptueux dix-huit trous du monde. Le soir venu, elle s'allongea nue sur la couche nuptiale, fraîche comme la rosée du matin sur les pelouses paisibles, attendant son champion d'époux. À son arrivée, il entra dans la chambre sans trop l'apercevoir, en lui faisant le salut habituel et négligé de la confrérie des vieux compagnons. Il se dévêtit, puis se coucha. Il était fatigué, elle, folle furieuse. Il abandonna tout de même le golf pour le curling.

30 septembre 1997

Lundi pour la Lune

mardi pour Mars

mercredi pour Mercure

jeudi pour Jupiter

vendredi pour Vénus

samedi pour Saturne

dimanche pour Je t'Aime.

30 septembre 1997

Une gerboise dans le cul d'un
cochon y fait son port d'attache.

ou

Une framboise dans le jus de citron
fait du tort et des taches.

ou

Dis Françoise, tu as lu «Les poltrons
sont des lâches»?

ou

Une ardoise dans le but qu'un soûlon
hors de lui nul ne sache.

Tout ça est affaire de goût.

30 septembre 1997

Il chante : « Je fais du salami, aux portes de minuit, j'irai voir ma mie que je l'aime, oh oui ! Je fais du foie gras avec celui d'Amanda et j'irai voir Rémi son ex-candidat. Je fais du pâté avec l'empâté de René, René le tout gras. Je termine la terrine avec les abats d'Amandine puis j'irai voir ma mie que je cuisinerai aussi. »

Les autorités sont toujours à la recherche de ce tueur en série.

30 septembre 1997

« Taxi!!! » s'époumona le touriste. «Pas si fort, j'suis juste à côté», maugréa le chauffard de taxi. Ils se sont ensuite entendus sur le prix de la course et tout est rentré dans l'ordre.

30 septembre 1997

Il a perdu son porte-monnaie dans lequel il rangeait sa tête, son sang-froid et son sens de l'humour. Une lourde perte.

30 septembre 1997

En mille neuf cent quatorze, Pedro vit au loin Carlos : - «Hé Carlos !!!» cria Pedro. Mais Carlos fit mine de rien. En mille neuf cent vingt-sept, Pedro vit encore Carlos au loin :
- «Hé Carlos !!!» Mais Carlos fit, une fois de plus, mine de rien. En mille neuf cent trente-neuf Pedro vit au loin Carlos : - «Hé Carlos !!!». Carlos ne réagit point. C'est arrivé en quarante-huit, en cinquante-sept, en soixante-six, en soixante et onze et en quatre-vingt-quatre. Puis, en quatre-vingt-douze, Pedro vit au loin Carlos :
- «Hé Carlos, Carlos !!!». Impatient, «Zé né souis pas Carlos», dit l'homme. «Dépouis mille néf cent quatorzé qué tou mé interpelle, qué lui vo tou à cé Carlos ?» - «Rien, répliqua Pedro, zé fézais ça pour lé fun.»

12 octobre 1997

Un hobe de peu d'éducation entrit
dans une pièce glacée. Il badigeodit de
berde et de toutes sortes de saletés le
tabis d'entrée de l'occubant incodu
d'ude baison idoccupée. Il ressortissà
aussitôt sans que dul de d'en soucisse
en bandant ses jambes à son cou. On
de le revoyou jabais.

12 octobe 1997

— Vous savez, une tondeuse à gazon peut vous faire plus de soucis qu'un enfant des bêtises. Je vous fait l'exemple : pas plus tard que ce matin, j'ai...

— Ne soyez pas si nerveux M. Labrie, un touché rectal n'est l'affaire que de quelques secondes.

15 octobre 1997

Insérez le taquet dans le goupille plate des côtés suggérés sur plan instruction. Enfilez module un et deux dans insertion enfilade. Coulez colle assemble avec aide de marteau les clous descendre. Vernissez tout en léchant chessé vingt-quatre heures. Réduisez température quand chaud. Servir froid avec bouton pression tablette. Si dans les yeux tombé ou avalé quand pas cuit, avertir médecin de docteur. Lire instructions de lui. C'était recette de raté-chinois, bon attépit !!!

15 octobre 1997

On recherche la personne qui a assommé la Fée des étoiles.

Récompense.

15 octobre 1997

Alors que Madame est couchée,
Monsieur se lève en pleine nuit, car il a
soif d'une soif étrange et inhabituelle.
Jamais en trente ans, il n'avait quitté
son épouse dans la partie noire du
jour pour le pipi ou le popot. Il est
troublé. Il décide, à rebrousse-poil,
d'en informer sa femme. Il la réveille.
Ce n'est plus sa femme mais une
jeune, très jeune inconnue. Il a peur, il
allume. Il n'est pas chez lui. Il crie. Ce
n'est pas sa voix. Il crie encore, sa
voix revient. «Tu rêves, mon amour»,
lui dit tendrement son amant, le
serrant très fort dans ses bras.

Trois-Rivières, 25 octobre 1997

Une maman oie et un grand gnou se racontaient les péripéties d'un ai traversant un ru sec. Ils rigolaient à pleine gueule, laissant bégueules les habitants de l'Île de Ré chez qui ils habitaient. «Dites-moi l'oie, ce ru sec de l'ai dont le gnou se moquait, est-il à l'Île de Ré?» demanda le chèvre chaud. «Oui» dit l'oie. «Non» argua le gnou. «Mais oui, insista l'oie. J'ai ouï, dit l'oie, que l'ai l'a vu et s'y noya.» «Chouette!» dit le chèvre chaud.

«Vous êtes trop bête, riposta l'oie, oui, trop bête.»

Trois-Rivières, 25 octobre 1997

Vous empestez la morue. Vos pieds
sentent l'ail et votre haleine est fétide.
Votre transpiration sent la transpiration et vous travaillez chez «Frites et
Moules». Votre épouse vous ressemble :
sous l'épaisse couche de parfum, elle
dissimule mal ce que vous ne
dissimulez point. Néanmoins, vous
aimez la vie et la vie vous aime.

C'est quoi le problème?

27 octobre 1997

— Précisez votre position, demande la tour de contrôle, précisez votre position. À VOUS...

— Je suis au–dessus de la montagne, la seule émergeant de la ville. À VOUS, répond le pilote de l'étoile de Bethléem.

— D'accord, nous vous voyons maintenant, vous vous poserez dans quatre minutes quarante secondes. À VOUS...

— Vous êtes fous, s'indigne le pilote, une étoile ne se pose jamais, surtout pas celle de Bethléem. À VOUS...

— La loi c'est la loi, aucune étoile, pas même celle de Bethléem, n'est autorisée à circuler dans ce secteur, encore moins en pleine période de la Noël. TERMINÉ....

27 octobre 1997

Un trophée de basket féminin forniquait avec celui du rugby universitaire quand l'étagère sur laquelle ils s'émancipaient s'effondra sous le poids de leur passion.

On m'a dit de vous le dire.

27 octobre 1997

Je suis un ballon de foot à l'issue d'un match éliminatoire de fin de saison. Pas de photo SVP.

27 octobre 1997

En mille neuf cent soixante et un,
à Montréal, un enfant échappe ses
ballons gonflés d'hélium au-dessus
de la ville. Depuis, l'enfant, du haut
de la Place Ville-Marie, les recherche
jour et nuit.

27 octobre 1997

Je vis en boîte. Je vis dans une boîte appartement au square St-Sulpice. Je mange du maïs en boîte, des haricots en boîte, du jambon en boîte, de tout en boîte. Mon métier de déménageur me fait transporter des boîtes. Je suis un homme de et en boîtes. Je danse aussi dans les boîtes. J'y cherche l'amour et ça me déboîte mais, quand même, vive les boîtes ! Vive les boîtes !

31 octobre 1997

C'est grave, Docteur ?

— Non, répond le jardinier. Quand on vous aura enlevé les pépins, les tiges, les feuilles et tout le reste, vous serez comme un légume neuf.

— Tant mieux, dit le concombre passé dû. Et ma qualité de vie ? renchérit le passé date.

— Votre qualité de vie ? Inaltérée !!! répond l'homme au pouce vert. Vous vivrez dans un implacable état végétatif.

— De mieux en mieux, répond le vieux verdâtre, de mieux en mieux docteur, soulagé qu'il est.

31 octobre 1997

— «Je vous prédis un avenir plus ou moins rapproché à plus ou moins long terme. Vous avez d'autres questions?»

— «Non merci», répond à la cartomancienne le condamné à mort en appel de la décision du jury.

31 octobre 1997

L'homme invente un jour la machine à caleçon (la caleçonneuse), le bois en poudre (du Poudrex), le feu liquide (de l'aquatincelle). Plus tard, les bonbons nucléaires (les Adieucaries), les ongles à rabat-fermoirs (?) et les sourires à combustion rapide. À quand la machine à café?

3 novembre 1997

Confortablement installé dans un fauteuil bleu et mœlleux de la TCHIBAGOO AIRLINES COMPANY, le passager que je suis regarde par le hublot. Étonnement. J'interroge ma voisine :

— Moidemaselle, SVP promptement-je, n'y a-t-il pas là, dehors, un brin d'irrégularité quant aux endroits que devraient camper le ciel et la Terre dans leurs rôles respectifs, à savoir : le ciel en haut, la terre en bas ? simplement-je. J'y vois, bien au contraire, le contraire renchéris-je. Pas vous ? moi-je.

— Vous avez tout à fait raison Missieu, qu'elle dit en constatant *de visu*. C'est vrai, je confirme, il y a irrégularité dit-elle-me avec ses cheveux par en haut, ses lèvres par en haut, ses joues par en haut, ses seins par en haut et son collier dans la figure. Accord commun. ➤

Nous appelons la serveuse de l'espace. Elle s'amène, rampant au plafond avec le sourire de la corporation qui fait faillite :

— Je peux vous aider ? Ha oui ! nous-je tous les deux ensemble. Que se passe-t-il ? Vous nous voyez inquiets.

— Ne vous inquiétez, nous-t-elle, simplement qu'on va s'écraser, vous voyez ce n'est pas sorcier, dit-elle-nous.

— Ha bon !!! bon-je, quand on sait, on sait !!! stress-je.

Mes papiers sont réglés et de toute façon, je n'ai ni famille ni ami. Cela n'avait pas que de mauvais côtés, agonie-je à la blague avant de m'aplatir.

Vancouver-Montréal, 4 novembre 1997

Un nez. Ça vous gâche un visage, ce visage, un rêve et ce rêve, une vie. Cette pénible vie gaspille votre mort. Cette vilaine mort vous empoisonne l'éternité, et cette éternité salit votre salut. Voulez-vous que je vous parle de votre menton ?

17 novembre 1997

Je fais du ski, enfin, sur deux planches de bois taillées à même le boulot de mon voisin. Les cèdres de mon autre voisin m'ont été utiles aussi pour me sculpter des bâtons, et puis mon père est plus fort que le tien. Je suis fatigué, je vais me coucher.

17 novembre 1997

Faites-moi penser, un jour, de vous raconter le silence du lac gelé sur lequel je m'étendais, adolescent, perdu dans la dix-huitième heure du jour, après l'école, avant le tourment des grands, à regarder le ciel dans son mystère. Faites-le-moi penser.

2 décembre 1997

Dieu, égoïste, invente le désespoir
dans le but qu'on s'en remette
éternellement à lui. Un dimanche,
complètement débordé, il part inventer
le huitième jour, les sept premiers le
laissant pour nul de fatigue à
inventorier les barils avec le monde,
son monde désespérément calé au
fond. On ne l'a jamais revu. C'est bête.

2 décembre 1997

Un homme échappe son seul testicule au fond de son soulier. En criant d'effroi, il crache sa langue à deux mètres de lui. Il se presse, se penche et la récupère. Sous la pression, son pantalon se découd, découvrant son anus. À la seconde près, un projectile (un mégot de cigarette) y pénètre à une vitesse folle, le laissant pour mort. Le tabac continue de faire des victimes.

2 décembre 1997

Un spaghetti trop cuit rêve qu'il
sèche au soleil. C'est fort.

2 décembre 1997

Ça fait des orteils qu'on ne s'est vus, agrûme-je, au fait combien? Une vingtaine, floralie-t-elle en pouffant de rire dans son ananas. Qu'es-tu devenu depuis notre dernière rencontre, me poignée-de-porte-t-elle, en me fixant du regard de son plus bleu. Oh! je vaque à des occupations personnelles et ennuyeuses, nappe-je confondu. Ah bon! qu'elle me disquette, un peu indifférente. Je l'aurais deviné, tu n'as pas changé, toujours aussi déprimant. En moi (j'aurais mieux fait de ne pas la reconnaître).

2 décembre 1997

Une gerboise vivant dans son... ha et
puis merde.

1ᵉʳ juin 1998

Vous proférez des énormités à mon sujet alors que vous n'étiez même pas présent lors des séances de torture perpétrées sur mes sujets.

1er juin 1998

26 décembre 1961.

1ᵉʳ juin 1998

Ami, laisse-moi te conduire à ta chambre, donne-moi ce sac et repose-toi dans la chaleur de ma chaumière. Ne pense plus à ces tracas dont tu subis les outrances et laisse-toi guider dans la simplicité de ma maison. La ville est un cancer, tu n'as plus à le nourrir. Ta tête et ton corps qui n'en peuvent plus, trouveront fraîcheur et réparation sur ce lit. Au fait, pendant que j'y pense, tu avais mis un dépôt de trois cent vingt-cinq dollars, il ne te reste plus qu'à verser les trente-trois mille restant demain. C'est qu'il y a eu une erreur et, selon le contrat, tu n'étais pas dans l'obligation de verser 16,3 % de la somme due avant ton arrivée. N'est-ce pas là une bonne nouvelle l'ami ? Allez, bonne semaine.

1er juin 1998

P longer dans une piscine vide est le contraire d'éjaculer dans un condom.

1er juin 1998

Un mauvais rêve est comme sodomiser une serrure.

1er juin 1998

Les fèves au lard donnent des gaz.

1er juin 1998

Je sais ce que c'est que d'être ignorant.

1ᵉʳ juin 1998

Je voyage dans le cul d'une fée en
lisant des insanités sur l'hygiène
buccale. Mon but est d'aller retrouver
The whore of Babylon, dont j'entends
parler depuis que je me passionne
pour la peinture abstraite. Impatient de
la rencontrer, je lis pour colmater mon
anxiété.

15 juillet 1998

Je me traîne comme un lombric sur du satin. Dans la rue, les églises me rappellent à mon impiété, les vélos à mon inertie et les femmes aux organes génitaux. Puis, passant devant «La Petite Maison des Pauvres», j'ai faim et j'entre dans un restaurant.

15 juillet 1998

Il y a trois ans et deux mois, nous
fêtions les sept ans et trois semaines et
quatre jours de notre amour ponctuel.
À chaque heure, mon sentiment
augmente de ,004 %. C'est bon.

15 juillet 1998

Exhibitionniste et raciste : Montrer son zizi à une esquimaude avant qu'elle ne fonde au soleil.

7 décembre 1998

À l'heure de pointe, j'ai soulevé et inversé de 180 degrés le pont traversant le fleuve.

Le personnel de jour est retourné au bureau et celui de soir à la maison.

Magie. On n'a rien vu, rien remarqué.

7 décembre 1998

Je me suis acheté le coffret de seize disques compacts enfin, l'œuvre complète de Bill Massachusetts-Guindon. Célèbre conteur du début du siècle, je l'avais choisi pour un travail important d'université sur les conteurs d'histoires populaires. En cinq mois et, à douze heures par jour en moyenne, j'ai tout écouté, décortiqué, analysé de Bill puis je me suis rendu compte d'une bourde affreuse : Bill Massa-chusetts-Guindon ne figurait pas sur la liste des conteurs à étudier.

7 décembre 1998

Je n'ai pas eu le temps de te télé-
phoner. Normal, on a pas eu de saison.
Un temps sans saison est un temps
orphelin.

7 décembre 1998

«En général» veut dire un ciel nuageux. «En particulier» veut dire un nuage qu'on regarde passer et «généralement particulier» veut dire que je ne suis pas moins fou que les autres jours.

7 décembre 1998

J'ai mangé de la cervelle au beurre noir. Un peu comme Jacky Kennedy.

7 décembre 1998

La maman ronfle. Le papa pète. Le chien jappe. Le bébé pleure. L'adolescent rouspète. Les déchets puent. La mémoire se souvient. Le temps passe. La maman meurt. Le papa craque. Le chien est gazé. Le bébé divorce. L'adolescent est vieux. Le temps passe puis la mémoire oublie.

7 décembre 1998

«PLÉNADE» veut dire «FÉNEX» en cherokee. «PROUIT» voudrait dire alors «FLÉMITHRE» en saingérôme et «ALPHADOUDA» signifie «GRINGUE» en sudanois. Les langues sont si fadiles à apprenze.

9 décembre 1998

Un coup dans les testicules   i
fait mal en
                    e   t
                          s

9 décembre 1998

Et puis un jour, on découvre dans la froideur des temps modernes que les banques ne prêtent pas d'argent et que l'État veut notre bien mais pas celui qu'on pense. On découvre aussi que Big Brother n'est pas qu'un méchant héros de livre de poche. C'est aussi celui qui vous incite à le lire.

12 décembre 1998

Je suis en vélo. Une voiture vient bien près de me frapper. Elle s'arrête. J'engueule le conducteur qui se fond en excuses. Je continue, le vilipende. Il s'excuse de plus belle avec de chaleureuses formules. Je continue, le fustige et ne vois plus clair. Il est très sympathique. Très poli aussi. Il m'offre d'aller me reconduire chez moi. Il est très, très gentil. Je quitte les lieux en furie et l'envoie promener. Je n'ai jamais eu l'air aussi ridicule.

12 décembre 1998

Je suis beau. Je me regarde et je suis beau. Seul devant un miroir, je me dandine, je pose. Quelle sveltesse, pas une once en trop. Pas une ride, tous mes cheveux. Pas de corne au bout des doigts. Pas de corne sur les talons. Des poumons clairs. Mon seul problème : j'aime les femmes d'âge mure et aucune d'entre elles ne s'intéresse aux garçons de onze ans.

12 décembre 1998

Un jour, on t'inventait. Pour la seule raison que tu n'existais pas déjà.

12 décembre 1998

Monsieur Groulx prend sa retraite.
On lui fait une fête. Gardien de prison
pendant vingt-neuf ans dans la section
à sécurité maximum, ça se fête. Dans
le discours lui rendant hommage, on
souligna en rigolant qu'il avait fait
plus de détention que la moyenne de
nos grands criminels. Monsieur Groulx
fondit en larmes. «À la différence qu'il
allait coucher à la maison», nota un
jeune et ambitieux stagiaire.

12 décembre 1998

Quand j'ai croisé cet homme qui fut vingt ans plus tôt mon professeur de géographie, je fis demi-tour et le giflai comme je l'avais souhaité autrefois, alors qu'il m'avait fait un triste portrait de ce que deviennent les cancres de mon espèce : des voyous.

12 décembre 1998

Sur les deux mille étudiants des sessions 1979 - 1980 de mon école, combien sont encore vivants aujourd'hui? Combien de travestis? Combien de malades chroniques? Combien de bandits? Combien d'enfants ont-ils engendrés à eux tous? Combien de suicides?

12 décembre 1998

Les Woolworth's, les chanteuses
Karo, Dany Aubé et Mimi Hétu, les
Dairy Queen ambulants, les boissons
gazeuses Lucky One, les barils de
chips en métal Humpty Dumpty,
les motoneiges Élan.

D'autres souvenirs.

12 décembre 1998

Quand un trophée est plus facile à gagner qu'à soulever, il y a problème.

12 décembre 1998

J'étais heureux, désinvolte. Roulant
sur la piste cyclable, je me sentais
libre, cheveux au vent et exalté.
Totalement libre alors qu'au fond,
l'État contrôlait mon itinéraire.

12 décembre 1998

Je ne dis jamais rien. Même quand on me dérange, quand on m'agresse, quand je suis noyé malgré moi dans l'idiotie des autres. Je ne dis jamais rien et en plus, on me le reproche.

13 décembre 1998

Il y a celle-là qui me raconte les pitreries de son tortionnaire d'époux.

Il y a aussi celle-ci qui m'embête avec son manque à gagner.

Lui qui me confie le poids de ses tourments.

Elle qui...

J'en suis à rêver de ma crucifixion.

13 décembre 1998

Le soir, j'entends des voix. Je parle, je réfléchis et j'entends aussi des musiques à travers l'action. Sur les accords en perpétuel changement, j'appose des mots tout en continuant de répondre au monde qui me sollicite. L'abstrait et le concret se mélangent et me mélangent. C'est la juxtaposition des dimensions dans lesquelles je ne fais plus qu'un.

Je me couche totalement exténué.

13 décembre 1998

Une sentence à vie... Les premiers jours, les premiers mois faisaient partie de la sentence à vie, les jours, les mois, les années. Après dix ans, c'est toujours la même vie. Ça devient péniblement long. Les secondes devenant des jours, les minutes des mois et les heures des ans, la mort se transforme en une cime haute et inatteignable. Plus on s'en approche, plus il y a fatigue et lenteur. La perpétuité est encore plus longue que l'éternité car on en connaît la naissance. Nous ne nous concentrons que vers la fin qui n'arrive jamais.

13 décembre 1998

Nous faisions, mon épouse et moi, l'amour devant un magnifique feu de foyer quand, dans la raie des fesses, je reçus un minuscule tison de charbon ardent. Jamais ma femme ne fut aussi satisfaite.

22 décembre 1998

Un jour que j'étais à table, m'apprêtant à piquer de ma fourchette une amourette de mouton, j'entendis au même instant crier M. Lebœuf, mon voisin du dessus. Ça porte à réfléchir.

22 décembre 1998

Pour un homme, il est certain que de se faire prendre dans les toilettes publiques totalement nu avec le robinet d'eau froide giclant dans les parties génitales avec dans la bouche des feuilles déchirées d'un best-seller de recettes de gâteaux au caroube en criant : « Niagara tu me chagrines ! » peut effectivement être humiliant.

Ça impressionne. Surtout le vieux monsieur qui tombe sur vous voulant faire bien tranquillement son pipi dans la toilette des dames.

22 décembre 1998

La question, votre honneur, n'est pas de s'interroger sur la motivation même de mon client mais bien de comprendre comment il a fait, à moins trente degrés Celsius, pour évacuer par le nez une 60 watts allumée.

22 décembre 1998

Je suis l'aiguille des minutes de l'horloge d'une ville. Je tourne en enviant celle des heures qui, pour un même salaire, s'étourdit bien moins vite à l'ouvrage.

29 décembre 1998

La solitude. La, solitude. La. Solitude.

L, a. S, o, l, it, ude. L   a

         s   o l   i   tu

d   e. L   a

             s   o   l

                 i

t   u

         d

                                    e.

29 décembre 1998

La vérité dépose des fleurs là où le mensonge, invariablement, les tue.

29 décembre 1998

Sembrerait qure je roulre mes R prus
quer la normerale. Sre serait prus qure
dres « on dit ». Sembrerait qure ça
serait vrai.

29 décrembre 1998

D'abord, cette mère que j'habitais et qui obéissait à des règles strictes de la nature me fit sortir de son corps parce que ça ne pouvait durer. Après, ce sein que je tétais avec bonheur fut remplacé par une froide bouteille. À cinq ans, ce père Noël en qui je croyais était en réalité mon oncle. À six ans, j'étais enrégimenté. À douze, les institutrices et les instituteurs ne me faisaient plus peur. À quinze, la mort m'attirait, surtout dans le métro. À dix-sept ans, l'amour me tuait pour la première fois. À vingt-cinq ans, Dieu n'existait définitivement pas. Irréversiblement. À vingt-cinq ans et un jour, j'étais sans paradis, sans enfer mais surtout, sans éternité. ————▶

À trente et un ans, alors qu'applaudi et adulé, l'amour me tuait pour la deuxième fois. Ça a continué comme ça pendant des années et des années. La vie est faite de ce qu'on reçoit et puis de ce qu'on nous enlève. Aujourd'hui, à soixante-dix-huit ans, on me donnait un mois à vivre. Voilà qu'on m'enlève même cette date probable de ma mort: ça fait plus de trois mois que je me porte le mieux du monde.

31 décembre 1998

Noël est plate dans une soucoupe volante.

31 décembre 1998

À rebrousse-poil, elle est
impitoyable. Négligée, elle est d'une
démangeaison cruelle. À quoi bon une
vie de périnée, oisive et linéaire,
presque sans nom dans une vie
dénudée de sens.

31 décembre 1998

La menace de l'obésité pèse.

3 janvier 1999

Mon frère dit que c'est mieux en ville. Il y gagne sa vie sans trop peiner. Il faudrait que je fasse mes valises et celles de ma famille. Ma femme n'y connaît personne, nous n'y avons aucune autre parenté. Mes enfants ont leur vie et leurs amis ici. Je suis sans travail depuis des lunes. Je meurs de faim. En ville, je vais mourir tout court.

8 janvier 1999

Dans le cœur d'un chien, un parasite fait son nid. À grands coups de marteau, il cloue ce qui deviendra les murs, le toit et puis le reste. Ni le temps ni la fatigue ne le découragent. Il est têtu. Entre le jour de sa décision et la nuit de son premier repos sont passés les labeurs comme les inquiétudes. La vie saura lui dire s'il avait raison ou tort. «Bon chien», pense-t-il à la remorque du moteur canin. En quelque temps, ce parasite sait trouver le confort. La bête, insouciante, ne se doute de rien et mange les restes d'un maître bedonnant. ⟶

À vrai dire, le locataire, lui, commence
à souffrir d'une famine chronique.
«Non que non», à la seule idée de
dévorer ce cœur qui sait si bien le
loger. Gris et vert, son visage prenait
les couleurs de la misère tant il ne
s'alimentait que de son remords. Enfin,
il céda. Rien du pauvre cœur du chien
ne fut épargné, rien du parasite
aujourd'hui ne reste.

23 janvier 1999

Table des matières

...

Index général

Index thématique

Aliments

Animaux

Astronomie

Sentiments

192

Achevé d'imprimer

en juin deux mille

sur les presses

d'Imprimeries Quebecor

à Saint-Jean-sur-Richelieu Québec